The
Creation
Myths

The Creation Myths

Clare Brown

BLOOMSBURY

The author and publishers gratefully acknowledge permission to quote from the following: 'Disco 2000', words by Jarvis Cocker, music by Pulp © Copyright 1995 Island Music Limited. All rights reserved. International copyright secured. 'The Certainty of Chance', words and music by Neil Hannon and Joby Talbot © Copyright 1998 BMG Music Publishing Limited (80%) / Chester Music Limited (20%). All rights reserved. International copyright secured. 'This Guitar Says Sorry', words and music by Billy Bragg © Copyright 1987 BMG Music Publishing Limited. All rights reserved. International copyright secured. 'Hallelujah', words and music by Leonard Cohen © Copyright 1996 Novello & Company Limited. All rights reserved. International copyright secured. 'Four Flights Up', words and music by Lloyd Cole and the Commotions. All attempts to trace the copyright holder were unsuccessful.

First published in Great Britain 2005
This paperback edition published 2006

Bloomsbury Publishing Plc, 36 Soho Square, London W1D 3QY

A CIP catalogue record for this book
is available from the British Library

ISBN 0 7475 7176 7
9780747571766

10 9 8 7 6 5 4 3 2 1

All papers used by Bloomsbury Publishing are natural,
recyclable products made from wood grown in well-managed
forests. The manufacturing processes conform to the
environmental regulations of the country of origin.

Typeset by Hewer Text UK Limited, Edinburgh
Printed in Great Britain by Clays Ltd, St Ives plc

www.bloomsbury.com/clarebrown

For Mum and Dad

ACKNOWLEDGEMENTS

I'd like to thank readers of early drafts of this book
for their advice, encouragement and support: Mary Brown,
Daniel Buckroyd, Rosemary Davidson, Helen Dunmore,
Victoria Hobbs, Gordon Kerr, Don Paterson
and Honor Wilson-Fletcher.

BOOK ONE: The Big Bang

The time that it takes to make a baby
Can be the time it takes to make a cup of tea.
The love that we have is so important.

from 'This Guitar Says Sorry', Billy Bragg

In the Beginning

Cressida Nelson had crossed the thin blue line. Proof positive. Despite having been convinced of the result before testing, she noticed her hand trembling as she dropped the test stick in the disposal unit. She also noticed herself noticing – the first in what would be a short-lived but intense series of out-of-body experiences, after which she would remain, inescapably and indefinitely, bound up in the flesh and blood, the viscera, of her existence. She saw the cubicle wall through a veil of tears but did not allow them to flow: this was probably a good time to put a stop to her recent glut of self-indulgence, she decided, as she rejoined Tom in the restaurant. She passed on dessert.

An hour later, her new-found sense of objectivity was amazing to her, particularly as Tom seemed blissfully unaware of it. Reaching orgasm, she was aware of its precise physiological effect upon every part of her body even as it suffused her with a pleasure sinfully undiminished by her recent discovery. Tom drew her knees up to her breasts and they gazed mistily at one another, just as they had done every few weeks for the past year and a half. Why didn't her eyes betray her? Perhaps – and this had occurred to Cressida before but she had always dismissed it as being simply too sad to contemplate – the eyes are more of a mirror than a window to anything much at all. That would certainly explain a great deal. It's a shame, Cressida caught herself thinking, such a shame that all this delightful, heartstopping, athletic joining together might have to end so abruptly and painfully.

'Do you want the good news or the bad news first?' Propped up on one elbow she had a clear view of Tom's waiting face, his reaction couldn't escape her. 'OK, bad news first. I'm pregnant.' Nothing much, except for a general tensing of the jawline and his eyebrows beginning to raise in question. It wasn't as if he hadn't been expecting to hear it sooner or later; that had, after all, been the plan. But the next bit would be more surprising. Attempting to inject a little light-heartedness into proceedings as a means of covering her nervousness, she smiled whimsically and said, 'But don't worry – the good news is: it's yours.' Nothing at all now. Glazed over. Lost for words. There had been the tiny reflex flinch which that classic form of words always elicits from even the best of men – the 'it's not mine, guv' backing away from the looming future – but Tom had regained his bland expression rapidly. Suddenly, Cressida was overwhelmed by a cool and inappropriately intellectual interest in what he was about to say, which far exceeded her current feelings of love for him. This was probably fortunate, because the range of responses available to Tom at this moment was pretty varied, but none of them were likely to make Cressida – or indeed her husband, Tom's girlfriend, or any of their children – very happy.

Having turned pair upon pair of blind eyes to the dangerous nature of their liaison, Cressida and Tom were about to emerge from their moral trance with a bang. But, though they might quickly learn their own bitter truths, they couldn't possibly foresee the complex series of couplings and conceptions about to converge upon their world, of which they were, in a sense, the begetters. The magic ring they had inhabited, their charmed circle, was already overlapping with alien cells; strangers, intruders, people from whom a mere six degrees of separation could never suffice. The bubble surrounding the tiny, sparkling Cressida and Tom world-in-miniature looked likely to explode on its ascent to the surface. But seven even tinier bubbles were about to burst into the *aqua vita*; seven uninvited guests who, although innocent of even the least original sins, would manage to combine both the tenacity and the social skills of seasoned gatecrashers. Seven babies.

1

'Are you absolutely sure you don't want to discuss this with your husband first?' Dr Fisher was an efficient and conscientious senior partner in a busy general practice based in Queen's Park – an area of North London where pregnant women apologised for not having taken the recommended daily dose of folic acid and the diseases of her patients were mainly, mercifully, hidden from public view. For several years previously, the doctor had worked in a dirt-poor East London medical centre where mental illness and alcoholism were rife. But depression and addiction manifested themselves so differently amongst the middle classes, where adequate housing and uncut drugs absorbed much of the shock. Vodka, difficult to distinguish on the breath, was prevalent, and it was almost always pure and Polish. However, unplanned pregnancies know no class distinction that Dr Fisher had ever been able to define and she was already fairly certain of Cressida's response, which was delivered in a deadpan tone with a barely detectable wobble.

'I am absolutely sure that this is not my husband's child. It is the child of my lover. He already has a child; I have two. I am absolutely sure that I have no choice other than to make sure it isn't born, and that nobody knows about it other than is absolutely necessary.'

'Whoever the father is, it is your child.'

'I am very well aware of that. And take full responsibility for what I plan to do.'

Cressida was still feeling that events were running their course some small distance away from her, but the grimness of this exchange took place in close-up and it was all she could do to stop crying. Tom's horror had not surprised her but the speed with which he had placed the blame firmly upon her head had resulted in an anger that she was now finding useful in controlling her inner turmoil. Every time she felt vaguely confused, the clear memory of Tom's litany of disclaimers popped obligingly back into her mind and reactivated her wrath. 'But you told me it was safe. You *assured* me. You can't accuse me of being careless about that stuff; I *always* offered to use something.'

'Accuse you? Of what, exactly? Making accusations seems like the most pointless possible activity at this moment, I'm telling you what's happened so that we can decide what to do.'

'Now hold on a minute. This has worked so well for so long because neither of us is prepared to shake the status quo. For the children, remember? Equality. Parity. All that. What is there to decide?'

'You're jumping to conclusions. What I mean is that we are supposed to be two people who love each other. Who have talked about wanting to make a child together. Who have discounted that possibility for all the best reasons – and yes, you're right of course, it's the worst possible thing that could happen – but *it has bloody happened*! We're in it together! Would you prefer me to just get rid of it without talking to you about it? Would you rather I'd lied and not told you and gone through an abortion *completely alone*?'

'No, of course not, I'm sorry, of course we should talk. And I'll – be here, and – help you, however I can. Calm down now. Please, there's no need to shout at me like I've done something wrong, I know how upset you must be but don't take it out on me, pet.'

Her anger terrified him but it also suited him. Although Tom knew that Cressida was far from irrational, it was always a relief when she flipped because in doing so she created a convenient stick with which he could beat her. Most of their quarrels ended in her apologising for the tongue-lashing she had inflicted on him, though afterwards it often dawned on her that he had ducked out of the argument completely by appearing to be mortally wounded by her passionate behaviour. As a result, they had rarely reached agreement on anything except their constantly burning mutual desire and a shared taste for the most mawkishly sentimental country music. Cressida, who from an early age had wanted to understand everything and make herself universally understood, couldn't fathom how anyone could live with a lesser thirst for information and the truths behind it. It drove her wild with anger, and Tom's resorting to the defence position left her quietly seething.

As for Tom, he had concluded at a similarly early stage of his development that it didn't pay to look too closely at events, especially those which were completely out of his control, which in his mind included anything to do with sex. Although of average height and build and physically unremarkable except for his bright green eyes, he had always been attractive to women, largely by dint of being permanently on the lookout for them and, having drifted energetically from one doomed relationship to the next, he had finally been caught out, as he put it, by a doting divorcee with two kids who had made a play for him during a publicity tour for his latest novel. Five years his senior and not terribly bright, Nita was a pretty, sensual and lonely woman who could scarcely believe her luck when, having confessed to Tom that her chaotic attempts at birth control had failed, he decided to stand by her. He had bailed her out of her loans, told her reportedly good-for-nothing ex either to visit his daughters every week religiously or not at all (the ex had taken this rather literally and moved to New Zealand) and worshipped their baby daughter with the truest and strongest love he had ever experienced. However, his decent streak knew some bounds and well before the birth he had begun to call up a few old flames and was, at the time he and Cressida got together, regularly sleeping with up to five other women at any one time (not actually all together; Tom had standards). Part of the deal with Cressida was that this should stop at once and he had been at least as surprised as she was that it actually did.

Back at the surgery, Cressida reiterated her position. 'Obviously, I'm keen that it's done as soon as possible, and am happy – well, am prepared, of course – to pay for a private operation.' Quite how a substantial withdrawal from the joint account could be explained away she wasn't yet sure. She still hadn't dismissed the idea of Tom coming up with the cash, and was in fact surprised he hadn't suggested it. Dr Fisher nodded sympathetically as she considered the situation. She inhaled slowly and then, with an earnest look into Cressida's eyes, said in a tone which verged on pleading, 'It's very early days indeed. The foetus is not yet three weeks old. You do have some time on your side. Time to work out whether there is some possibility that this child is your husband's. And that, even if it isn't, a termination isn't the only option available to you . . .' Cressida's mouth began to open in astonishment and the doctor hurriedly continued, '. . . although of course I realise that you don't wish to threaten your marriage or upset – um – the applecart, as it were.' She was getting flustered now. She glanced at her notes. 'Tell me, how is Jemima? Any recurrence of that little ear infection? And what about Ben? He'll be starting school soon, I expect?'

'Fine. They're both fine, thank you. Now, what do I need to do to arrange a termination?'

There was an instant, unwelcome juxtaposition in Cressida's mind; her beloved three-year-old daughter and four-year-old son, each bathed in a golden glow of health and adoration on the one hand, and this unformed and unknown embryo inside her soon to be untimely ripped etc., etc., on the other. It was inconceivable that she had got herself into this mess and even as the doctor completed some notes and handed her a telephone number with a name beneath it, it still seemed unreal to her.

'I think you should talk to a third party all the same. Another day or two won't make any difference, and I really do advise my patients to have just one conversation with an expert before I make referrals to hospital or whatever. A counsellor, you could say. Call this number between three and five p.m. It will be answered by Sister Mary,' she instructed.

'Sounds like a nun,' said Cressida, whose secondary education had been dominated by a veritable army of menopausal women all of whom seemed to be called Sister Mary-something-or-other. 'You're not sending me to a convent, are you?' she asked with a weak smile.

Dr Fisher could only smile nervously in return and say reassuringly, 'Sister Mary is an excellent nurse, very experienced in these matters. She will offer advice but not force it upon you, and she will support and help you with the decision you make. You will be in good hands. Will you see her? I think you won't regret it.'

Cressida hesitated, then nodded. As she left the room with the paper in her coat pocket, her doctor reached for the telephone with gently trembling hands.

For the rest of the day Cressida felt strangely unperturbed. She even forgot the paper in her pocket for several hours at a time. She managed the rights department in a large publishing house; it was a busy time in the office, with dozens of negotiations and contracts to complete, and the usual adrenaline rush got her through. Preparations for a European book fair in a few weeks' time were in full flow and she was already calculating how to cut short her attendance in order to fit in the termination without raising Harry's suspicions. While her Catholic upbringing meant that her sense of guilt was much more highly developed than Tom's, it was nonetheless she who always made the plans, booked the hotels, got the stories straight. He would rather be unconscious of it, allow himself to believe in the myth of falling. And although he had never had any qualms before about visiting his married lovers at home in the absence of their husbands, for some reason he was as adamant as Cressida that he would never come to her house. So, Cressida got practical when she had to be, an uncomfortable but effective pragmatism drove her onwards. But right now she was taking a leaf out of Tom's book and refusing to think too deeply about her plans. Don't look down now, said the voice inside her head, it would be ever so easy to fall.

'Hello, darling. Good day at work? Here, have this.' Harry removed her coat with one hand and passed her a large glass of Rioja with the other, planting a kiss on her mouth in the meantime. 'No lectures this afternoon, so I picked Ben and Jemmy up early from nursery and took them to that indoor bouncy place. We had a great time.' Cressida was frequently stunned by her husband's eternally sunny nature and had never worked out why she had fallen so fatally for Tom's far less obvious charms. As well as being of a happy disposition, Harry was tall, dark, athletic, charmingly tousled and beautifully proportioned. She was continuously ashamed as well; neither she nor Harry had ever been unfaithful before and they had a marriage based on trust and honesty and good straightforward sex. When she first became aware that Tom was actively and seriously pursuing her – which took several months, as he had gone through most of the eligible women involved in publishing his books – she felt entirely secure in accepting his offer of a drink, and remembered asking him quite openly what he believed she could possibly gain by cheating on the perfect man by having an affair with someone who slept with any woman who'd let him. He hadn't answered and she'd forgotten she had asked.

'Oh Harry, I don't think the nursery likes it if you just swoop in and take them out without warning, it's not good for their routine and . . .' Another kiss.

'Hush your moaning, come and sit down with our babies while I make us some supper.'

Harry was not quite perfect, although he probably came nearer to it than most. A surprise only child of parents in their forties, who were by that stage convinced – and relieved – that their rare and joyless couplings would bring forth nothing more than an embarrassed silence in the ensuing few days, and who never quite came to terms with the shattering of their long-held misconception, his aim since the age of twelve had been to find a lovely woman, settle down and devote himself to her happiness and the production of a brood of lovely children. Cressida was rather more bad-tempered than he had counted on, but she bowled him over with her wit and cleverness as soon as he met her (on a blind date arranged by her colleague in permissions) and he found her consistently exciting in bed. She had even agreed to go one step further towards the brood by having a third child, which endeared her all the more to him. (Tom wasn't too pleased to hear of this particular plan, but since he and Cressida couldn't possibly have a child together and she was so keen to have another baby, he felt it would be unreasonable for him to put his foot down. Cressida felt rather disappointed at how quickly he'd conceded the point but knew he was being kind about it. Quite how their affair would have continued throughout and after the pregnancy hadn't been discussed very much at all.) Harry knew Cressida better than anyone but the affair with Tom had been conducted in what might be described as an exemplary manner and so even her best friend – which until then Harry had been – wouldn't guess the truth. And this in spite of the fact that his current academic research – Harry was a lecturer in psychology – was all about the Seven Deadly Sins and their contemporary counterparts.

The idea for Harry's research – which he planned to publish after giving a preliminary paper at the winter conference of the British Society of Psychologists, who had invited him to be a keynote speaker – sprang from an idle conversation with friends at a dinner party. Cressida's mother was babysitting Ben and baby Jemima, who was then six months old, and the happy couple – for they truly were – were enjoying a rare night out. Everyone had eaten plenty, drunk too much, and it was becoming voluble. The discussion ranged from politics to education to work to anecdote and finally to some general rambling on a topic about which all present had a dearth of knowledge but extra helpings of opinion. It began with some talk of superstition and lucky numbers, and particularly why the number seven held such significance. 'I mean, there are seven pillars of wisdom,' somebody said, 'and the seventh seal . . .'
'The dance of the seven veils . . .'
'Seven Dials. And Seven Sisters . . .'
'That thing about being the seventh child of the seventh child . . .'
'*The Seven Year Itch* . . . Or *Seven Brides for Seven Brothers!*'
'The Seven Deadly Sins,' interjected Harry with a suddenly serious tone. 'The number has significance throughout various religious and cultural systems, actually, including paganism, most of the eastern religions and the Judaeo-Christian tradition. In fact, though they wouldn't articulate it in quite this way, modern psychologists are still as fascinated with the seven deadly sins as they are with killing the father and fucking the mother.' Harry did have an unerring ability to spoil the party mood. Cressida felt obliged to lighten it up.
'Seven for a Secret – never to be told!' which only had the effect of putting a mysterious and uncomfortable end to the evening.

Undeterred, Harry was enthusiastic in the cab home. 'I remember doing something about this for my degree,' he told Cressida, who was almost asleep against his shoulder, 'and thinking it was absolutely fascinating but there was just too much work to do on it for that level and I'd already chosen the subject for my thesis. But now I could pose a really interesting contemporary interpretation of the sins, and their "good" counterparts, can't remember what they're called, the seven . . .'

'Cardinal virtues,' mumbled Cressida.

'Ah right, yes of course, you'd know that – well anyway, I think lots of work's been done on that already but there's probably an argument that even if you try to balance out the "sin" with the "virtue" – you know, if you try to make up for being lustful by being celibate, for example – well, it probably doesn't work like that. Maybe you end up with another sin entirely – I guess you might try to use a substitute, like food, and so become a glutton. Do you see what I mean? I don't know if that's what I'll find, seems a bit too neat and simple, but God, Cressida, this could be a really interesting piece of work. What do you think?'

She thought nothing, was already asleep and dreaming. However, Harry needed no encouragement and began to work on the subject the very next day. Beyond the obvious research, all he had to do was find a representative of each sin, someone who obviously had one of the sins in the ascendancy. Everybody, he guessed, must be capable of all seven to some degree or other. He needed someone whose defining characteristic might be one of the seven, even if manifesting itself differently in a modern context. And he wanted to look at the people he knew for this study; he had to examine these characteristics *in situ* not just in the overtly conscious conditions of clinical research. So Harry looked about him, and from that moment onwards every spare moment at the university where he worked, and many at home, was spent on this project. Unbeknown to them, everyone he knew – and many he had only met – had already been categorised following Harry's observations. Very occasionally he amended his opinion but usually he found his instincts on the matter surprisingly trustworthy. The most difficult one to pin down, he found, largely because it usually inhabited a necessarily secret world, was Lust.

2

Tom was sitting in the untidy kitchen of the house he shared with Nita and their various offspring, just outside Manchester, feeding Katie her tea and feeling a whole raft of unfamiliar and unwelcome emotions. While his work as a writer and critic demanded a certain amount of intellectual consideration, he rarely went head to head on moral issues and his brain felt ready to burst with all the ethical questioning he'd been putting it through after Cressida's revelation. He remembered the first time he'd had this particular piece of news broken to him. Nita had reached across this very table once her kids had finally gone to bed, clasped his large dry hand in her small sweaty one and burst into tears. Five minutes later she was still crying, but joyfully.

'I thought you'd be mad with me. I thought you'd not want me to have it.'

'I'll do whatever you want. If you want to have it, well – that's fine. Maybe that's what I wanted. Maybe we both did.'

'Oh Tom. I'm so happy. I thought you might leave me. I couldn't bear it, couldn't live without you. Perhaps you're right. I knew I always wanted more babies, maybe I've been careless about it. But now I know why. Now I know what's meant to be. Sweetheart, are you really happy about it? Tom?'

Tom was making some calculations. They were to do with his age (thirty-seven), Nita's age (forty-two), his current commitments (nil), his desire to have a child (quite high, although it had been until that moment an entirely unconscious wish), the possibility of her wanting to have yet more children (low) and the likelihood of his finding a woman with whom he actually wanted to live and breed (nil). The sums were necessarily vague and unexpectedly easy and he was smiling as he gathered Nita in his arms and kissed her.

'Time I settled down anyway, honey.' Fertility was even sexier than mere virility: overcome with a proud sense of his own fully functioning male organs, Tom took Nita over the kitchen table, being careful to avoid the kind of roughness which might endanger his progeny. She retired to bed with a mug of camomile tea, exhausted and relieved. Tom took a beer from the fridge, his mobile out of his pocket, and punched out a text message: How R U doing pet? Drink? He selected four recipients from his phone's memory; women ranging in age from twenty-two to thirty-eight, all of whom lived locally: one voluptuous alcoholic English housewife married to a friend; one tiny feisty Jewish Glaswegian accountant who used to help him with his tax returns; one tall skinny Nigerian bisexual model he'd chatted up on a plane to New York a couple of years ago, and a sweet little bookseller whom he'd deflowered fresh out of Dublin whilst teaching her on a residential course in Creative Theory. When he forwarded the message to them it didn't occur to Tom that he would meet with anything but positive responses, and he was right. He also thought of the selection as entirely random rather than anything resembling a portfolio, though he was aware he'd steered clear of other writers, who had usually proved to be more high maintenance than the quality of sex merited. His most recent affair had been with an unhappily married translator of Norwegian literature, fearfully approaching her mid-century, whom he had known for years and whose frequent attempts to make the move from crying on his shoulder to falling in his lap had finally proved successful. But she became troublesome after only three months of occasional lacklustre trysts, when she wilfully mistook the first signs of her menopause for an early miscarriage and became quite hysterical. Tom had found it difficult to extricate himself from a relationship he had allowed to develop largely out of pity and had only just managed to reduce his dutiful contact with her down to three phonecalls a week. No, this quartet was unproblematic, undemanding outside the sheets and unquestioning within them. Along with the odd suppplementary woman he'd meet at a party or a reading, it provided him with the raw materials for a varied and appetising sexual life during Nita's pregnancy and beyond.

But the day Tom heard about Katie's existence was getting on for three years ago. And now Cressida – who had come to mean more to him than he ever believed a woman could – had uttered the very same words. Irony was Tom's speciality; his first, unexpressed response to Cressida's revelation had been unalloyed joy, followed very shortly by absolute horror. When Nita had announced her pregnancy his initial, unspoken, response had been horror followed by an acceptance which, when Katie arrived, grew into his first experience of unconditional love. This was all the wrong way round. From the beginning of their affair Tom had been shocked by his feelings for Cressida and often wondered why since sleeping with her he never wanted anyone else, to the extent that he suspected her of emasculating him in some way (sex with Nita, which he viewed as a kind of fortnightly service agreement, didn't count). He had usually bowed out of anything resembling a relationship – which was not, by his definition, the same thing as the numerous friendships which involved the odd bout of casual sex – at a point when endearments still sprang easily to his mouth and he was able to blame his departure on the sudden return of a moral dimension he had never actually owned. He had also sworn to Cressida that he never fell in love and never pretended to and this claim soon became the basis of their lovers' tiffs, a phrase which belies the passion of such exchanges.

'You don't understand, Cress: I don't fall in love. I love, of course; in fact I *love* almost everyone. Fellow men and women. We have a shared experience, and we can take some pleasure in each other from time to time. That's what love means to me. But falling in love – nope. Did that once, years ago, and decided it wasn't for me. Then I met you and I couldn't help it – falling in love. But not with any of the others.'

'That's weird – I'd place "in love" much further down the scale than real *love*. Falling in love is easy; it's to do with romance and attraction and – short-livedness, I guess. Love is deeper, stronger, and it's on a firmer basis, you can fall in love with someone you don't know well at all but love can only happen when you do know each other.'

'Female claptrap, pet. How can you tie it to any notion of *knowledge*? Who really knows anyone? No, you and I both know what we mean when we talk about love, but it defies definition, and it has no finite value, just as sex has no single meaning.'

'Oh right, I thought we'd get round to this sooner or later. Just because I see having sex with someone as significant and valuable – Jesus, sounds like something religious and that's not what I mean at all . . .'

'Isn't it?'

Cressida feigned a yawn. 'Ah, too easy, Tom, to throw that one at me. Life with the nuns, Catholic schoolgirls blah blah, so yes, it colours my life but I've grown up since then, I've lived a bit myself, and not every judgement I make is on some kind of fundamentalist basis. I just mean that it can always have the same importance *if you want it to*. And that you don't have to walk around thinking of every person of the opposite sex as a potential conquest. I've just never wanted to have sex with someone I don't love.' Cressida paused and then frowned before continuing, 'Actually that's bollocks, I've felt like having sex with lots of people I don't love, and some whom I positively dislike, but I have always – refrained – because I don't want it to become some purely physical act I do with lots of people, I always want the intimacy to be emotional as well, and therefore yes, it does hold a certain value for me even if you can't actually *weigh* it.'

'I respect that view, but disagree with it entirely. Why can't you show my view some respect?'

'Because your view is that you can, and should, fuck as many women as you feel like fucking, whatever the circumstances, so whether or not I believe that we mean the same thing when we talk about love, for you it's in the context of having fucked too many women to even remember. Don't ever expect that to be something which makes me glad. Or even comfortable. Imagine if it was the other way round – how would you cope if almost every man I talked about was a previous lover? If all the men I spoke to and called friends knew – knew the *taste* of me. Imagine.'

'Jesus, you can be crude.' Tom found frank discussions about sex slightly discomfiting; he put this down to his working-class upbringing.

'No, I can *speak* crudely. Straightforwardly. You're the one who can *be* crude, who has been crude in the way you've treated sex. Just try to imagine it, Tom. For one minute. How would you feel?'

'Yeah, yeah. It would be no big deal, it wouldn't affect things between you and me. You say you love me, so that's fine, whatever your past had been I'd just not think about it.'

'Just as you can decide not to fall in love? That much control?'

'Precisely. And that's always worked for me.'

End of conversation, usually. Tom sounded almost purist about it all, whereas in fact he had often bandied the 'L' word about quite carelessly and it never meant the same thing twice. And he couldn't deny that Cressida's short and sincere list of sexual relationships, which now included him, was both flattering and reassuring. His reinvention of the past was partly wishful thinking, although he had also convinced himself, somewhere along the way, that he was essentially A Good Man. Deep down, Tom told himself, his attitude to sex, and therefore to women, was based on a code of fairness in which the women he bedded always had a good time and were never deceived about the nature of the deal. His intimate knowledge of so many female bodies had lent him a sexual confidence that made each lover feel that she was its inspiration; that during their lovemaking he was expressing something he felt for her alone. Nothing exhilarated Tom more than the early days of an erotic fascination in which he could re-create his sexual world again and again, until he had exhausted all possibilities and needed to move along. Still, the times they were a-changing, and Tom had to admit that Cressida had got him, undoubtedly she had got him. The time he spent with her made the whole of his previous existence, except for the arrival of Katie, utterly hollow. And the notion of having a child with her embodied everything positive and good he had ever thought about human life. Grand thoughts indeed, for a man so earthbound.

Tom often laughed grimly to himself at what he saw as Fate's most fantastic trick; making it be Nita who 'caught him out'. The conception of Katie occurred at the precise moment he lost sexual interest in Nita; the point in a relationship at which he usually began the countdown to his exit. He had endured the wining and dining element of their relationship and borne the tedium of their conversations only in order to maintain their explosive sexual adventures, and had been aware from the beginning that the intellectual chasm which gaped between them would eventually swallow whole even the best sex in the world. Nita was too enamoured to be suspicious, and besides, suspicion wasn't in her nature; she was too busy being grateful for small, unexpected mercies. When her daughters Felicity and Harmony (Nita was both a secret social climber and an unreconstructed hippy) were twelve and ten respectively she was a newly-divorced woman of forty who was, in theory, looking forward to life without the burden of Justin, her depressed and depressing ex-husband. In particular, she was keen to take up again her informal studies of Eastern religions which she had begun in her teenage years and failed to develop to any degree. But her putative freedom was shortlived; she met Tom Webster, respected writer and critic, at the first and only literary event she had attended in her life, within the year. She fell head over heels in love as she was wont to do with any man who spoke to her for more than five minutes at a time and a mere eighteen months later had given birth to Katie, alienated her pubescent daughters who really didn't need their mother flaunting her long-dormant sexuality in their fatherless faces, and became utterly dependent upon Tom in every respect.

What made Nita such a drag was, Tom believed, her lack of imagination. Her fantasies were about fields and blue skies and warmth. Cressida regularly dreamt of life-threatening situations in which she was personally responsible for the lives of potentially abused children, supposedly aided and abetted by a group of men who seemed to be the police but *who were not the real police*. When spring was in the air Nita looked up at the fluffy white clouds and took pleasure in the blossom; Cressida was watching the pavement for dead baby birds. This did not make Cressida a better person than Nita, but it did make her a whole lot more interesting. Nita's deepest thoughts, despite her wholehearted but dim-witted study of several shelves full of books on Eastern spirituality, converged at what Harry would describe as 'pick and mix Buddhism' – mostly rabid vegetarianism combined with damaging overuse of henna. If pressed, she would hazard a guess that the Four Noble Truths formed part of the US Constitution. Even so, when she batted her long-lashed eyelids at Tom during his reading, she should have realised, shouldn't she, that his interest meant nothing more than a sexual frisson and a gap in his timetable. She should have been more careful, if only for her children. But she was more deeply conventional than she would care to admit and was particularly excited at having bagged a fairly well-known writer, even one whose work she had never read. Tom remembered, wincingly, the night he saw as the turning point in their relationship.

One evening around six months after he and Nita had met, Tom, always a skilful lover, had surpassed himself utterly. Nita, having only ever slept with her husband – and not that much with him in the last few years – was so amazed at the things Tom could do to her body that she was overcome with gratitude. 'Oh Tom,' she sighed, 'when we do this I realise just how much you love me, how perfectly we fit together. I know how difficult it is for a man to take on a woman with children, especially someone older, and when you could have anyone you wanted, and I'm just so happy that you love me enough to do that for me. So happy.'

Alarm bells were ringing in Tom's head on a number of floors. Women's ability to mistake good sex for love was a constant source of irritation to him, though not sufficiently irritating for him to disabuse them of their error before embarking on one of his trademark sessions of fervent lovemaking, and in this case Nita had compounded her misunderstanding by assuming that he had in some way 'taken on' her entire life just by sleeping with her regularly. Some observers may feel that Nita's assumptions were justified, given her (misguided) impression that she and Tom were a 'couple', that he had considered her particular circumstances as a mother in some detail before embarking on the relationship (wrong: it never occurred to him that her children were anything other than a fact of her life and utterly disconnected to him or to her sleeping with him) and finally that his virtuoso lovemaking was a sign of how much he worshipped her (wrong again: Tom was a true Casanova and to make love convincingly was a matter of pride to him). So why did he not bow out at this point? We may never know; Tom certainly hadn't worked it out yet. But it could well have been a factor in Nita's subsequent contraceptive lottery.

And then there was Manchester. Tom, like both his younger brothers, was born and bred in Newcastle, raised by working-class parents who bestowed upon him much love, an ambition to 'make something of himself' and priceless plebeian credentials including the softest and most seductive of Geordie accents. He completed his education at Manchester University – English Literature, First Class Honours – and moved back there after a dozen years of London life began to take their toll on his pocket, his time, his mind and his career. Manchester gave him time to think, to write, and to avoid a great number of women whose faces, at least, had become a little too familiar. So, Manchester. Or more precisely a small conurbation about ten miles outside the city where Nita had lived for nine years. Another problem in the difficult relationship between Tom and Cressida, this small matter of two hundred miles. Their trysts had to take place within a strict time frame, dictated by his infrequent visits to London and her occasional need to travel on business. They had always held one another in sufficient trust to play this absolutely straight; not one risk of being spotted by mutual friends, or caught out without a convincing story, had been taken. But it was hard, and the weeks in between their meetings – usually afternoons in hotels which succeeded in rising above any whiff of seediness by their astonishingly frank eroticism, plus two memorable weekends at continental book fairs, off which they had both fed for the months in between – were full of poignant 'miss you' type conversations and emails, which inevitably took their toll. The love between Tom and Cressida would be categorised, by the people who value such categorisations, as 'true'. Of that there is no doubt.

While Tom and Cressida were playing their lovers' games and testing a number of moral theories in the field, Harry was sitting in his armchair defining and fine-tuning his own controversial treatment of the archetypal Sins; drafting and redrafting the most important, most high-profile speech of his career. Publication of the work was already almost certain; a good reception from his peers at the conference would clinch it. He began to think of the event as the 'launch' of his prototype book, potentially a life-changing moment. The world of academic psychology tended to be unglamorous; those who attracted any kind of wider interest usually did so by making wild claims based on dubious, and ultimately discredited, research. Harry now had the opportunity to open up debate on a subject which, if dealt with sensitively, could appeal to huge numbers of non-specialists and lead to lucrative deals with publishers, radio, television, US universities. It could gain him respect and recognition both within and outside the profession.

Harry was convinced that a secular inspection of the Sins of Pride, Envy, Anger, Lust, Gluttony, Avarice and Sloth alongside their corresponding Virtues, or 'good twins': Humility, Love, Kindness, Self-control, Generosity, Temperance and Zeal – would yield some fascinating insights into human nature and ancient attempts to suppress it as a form of social control. He strongly suspected that the Sins were a religious interpretation of mankind's naturally burning instincts, a construct designed by medieval church leaders to demonstrate their flock's distance from the creator and their own proximity to Him. Harry assigned the Sins a new, morally neutral name: Prime Motivators. He argued that the so-called Virtues sometimes caused more harm than good. He wrote passionately, with a growing conviction that this time he was really on to something.

3

Cressida was about to attend her meeting with Sister Mary, having made an appointment for the following afternoon. She caught the bus to the Willesden address given her by Dr Fisher and made her way, nervous, nauseous and blinking in the spring sunshine, to a large stuccoed semi-detached house. As she rang the doorbell she noticed that a plaque next to the entrance had been taped over, but before she could decipher the words beneath it, a solidly built woman of around forty in a navy skirt and jumper opened the door.

'Mrs Nelson?'

'It's Ms Nelson. But Cressida is fine.'

'Cressida then. Hello, I'm Sister Mary.' She had a soft Irish accent, and a tone that Cressida warmed to at once. The women shook hands.

'Hello, Sister. Thank you for seeing me so quickly.'

'Oh, I understand that time is of the essence, we try not to leave our ladies waiting long. Do follow me.' Cressida was ushered through to a reception area and left to wait. The hall was neutrally painted and characterless, rather shabby, and Cressida was relieved to see that there was nothing on the walls, no magazine rack, no piped music. Just as it should be. Sister Mary reappeared through the door to an adjoining room. 'Do come in, my dear.' The nurse sat behind a large desk and Cressida took a seat in front of it. On the wall above Sister Mary's head she was startled to see a pale cruciform of light wallpaper. Father, forgive me, she said to herself – relishing the melodrama and being ashamed of herself for it – for I know exactly what I'm doing. Sister Mary looked at some notes before speaking.

'Now then. I understand from Dr Fisher that you have just

missed your period, and that you are sure that you conceived – let me see – eighteen days ago. That's very precise!'

'Yes, I have been taking notice because my husband and I . . .' her voice faltered and dropped a little, 'my husband and I have been trying to conceive a third child – we started two months ago, this was the second cycle – and so I – I have been keeping a note of dates and so on.'

'But this isn't your husband's child?' Sister Mary's voice was kindly, patient.

'No, no I'm afraid not. My – my calculations about when I was ovulating must have been a few days out – I think it must have been a very long cycle which has never happened before – and so I – um – I – you see, I have been seeing another man and we met up eighteen days ago and we – had sex – and . . .'

'But how can you be sure this isn't your husband's child then?'

'Well, although we started trying last month, the plan was on hold this month because he was away for the – well, for what I thought was the relevant few days. Of ovulation. And we haven't – done it since his return. So actually, since my last period, the only man I've had sex with is – this other man. So I'm sure.'

'I see. Yes, that does sound rather – conclusive. Right. So, what are your plans?'

Cressida was startled. 'How do you mean, plans? I asked Dr Fisher to refer me for an – for a – termination. It's impossible for me to have this child. I won't pretend it's my husband's and I have other children to consider, my marriage . . .'

'You sound rather defensive, my dear. I wasn't asking for your justification, just your ideas about timescale and whether you can stay overnight and are aware of the different options and so on.'

'Oh. I'm sorry, it's just that I'm rather tense about it all, of course, and can't believe I've been so stupid and actually can't believe I'm here in this mess, having to do this awful thing and . . .'

'It's a standard process nowadays, Cressida. Probably an overnight stay won't even be necessary. And then you can forget all about it.'

'No, you don't understand, I do – I do love Tom. That's not my husband, that's this other man. And I do want to have children with him, I just can't, we always knew we couldn't, and so it just feels like everything is the wrong way round and . . .' She was crying now, uncontrollably.

'Cressida, this isn't your fault. You aren't to blame. The responsibility is shared.'

'No. No, the responsibility is not shared. This is my child, it's in my body, this is my fault and this is my decision. I am completely alone.'

Sister Mary reached out a warm smooth hand and patted Cressida's arm.

'No, dear. You're not alone. I am here whenever you need me.'

Cressida cried like a baby.

Later that morning she took the tube to work, still a little puffy around the face but otherwise much calmed. Entering the office, she interrupted a round of What Would You Rather Do? and joined in heartily, even proffering her own suggested options. The game speedily degenerated into Who Would You Rather Shag? 'My brother or your sister?' Cressida snapped at the most macho man in the office, and when, shocked to speechlessness, he failed to respond she pushed it further. 'A putrid old bag lady or a gorgeous pneumatic eighteen-year-old girl – who's dead?'

'How long has she been dead?' chirped the trainee copywriter gamely, but Cressida's original victim, who couldn't begin to understand the rules, was too appalled to continue.

'Jesus, Cressida,' he said, 'that's revolting. How can you even think them up let alone have the gall to say them? They're the product of a seriously perverted mind.'

'Sex and death, Roger, sex and death. That's what it all comes down to.' She was quoting Tom, who was quoting someone else, but she had never believed it until now.

As Cressida was inventing new and increasingly baroque inter-pretations of the game, Sister Mary was making a phonecall.

'Margaret? It's Mary. She left around an hour ago.'

'And?' Dr Fisher's voice trembled slightly.

'And – I don't think we'll have any trouble. She talked herself round. I didn't have to do anything but offer the poor woman some comfort. Still, we've actually succeeded! At last, it's been worth the effort!'

'Phase two completed then,' murmured Dr Fisher with a satisfied smile.

'How do you mean, phase two?'

'Well, phase one was sending her to you, phase two was your dissuasion, and phase three will begin when she presents herself for antenatal care. Of course.'

'Oh, I see. Phase two completed then.' Sister Mary sounded unconvinced but Dr Fisher terminated the conversation abruptly. She was still smiling.

Margaret Fisher was a woman who had attempted to relinquish her Life Plan slightly too late in proceedings to change course. Devised at the age of sixteen, shortly after her carefully executed and eventually successful pursuit of the most desirable boy in the lower sixth form, this involved an intense early romance followed by a testing separation during demanding medical training, topped off with a post-qualification marriage and arrival of a gorgeous boy and a beautiful girl whose mother would work two-and-a-half days a week in the village practice where their father was the senior partner, and spend her remaining hours cultivating their social, creative and cultural skills with admirable devotion. Her childhood sweetheart, Jim, however, gave up at the first hurdle and rather than train as a medic, chose to set up a lucrative business selling imported household cleaning products in their home town of Liverpool. Undeterred, young Margaret stuck to her side of the bargain and got through her entire five years of training before realising that the monthly visits from Jim were not progressing into serious commitment. She gave him an ultimatum, which he took, and bowed out, being sufficiently callous to marry the woman he'd been sleeping with for the past two years, who promptly produced twins.

Margaret's recovery period was painfully slow. Attempts to replace Jim with a succession of other potential mates proved fruitless; never a beauty, she had charmed him with the sheer power of her personality, but having utilised it to the full so early on it had failed to develop with her and all that remained was an angular frame covered tightly in skin which was too desperately hungry to be touched. Slim, personable, nicely turned out, well read, a lively conversationalist, she never failed to terrify every new man she met. All were subjected to an appraising glance which bordered on the psychotic, and which always fell floorward in disappointment. She had never had another lover.

At forty-two, Dr Fisher had given up on every aspect of her dream except one. To hell with finding the man, she could, and would, have the beautiful child of her dreams. Almost twenty years of celibacy had left her feeling like a wind-dried chicken in a Chinese restaurant window; her secret garden was concreted over, her womb abhorred the prospect of childbirth. So conceiving a child herself was out of the question. But she was dubious about the science of IVF and artificial insemination and wouldn't ask a friend to be a surrogate, even if she had one. And not for her the trials of fostering or adoption, being forced to compromise her ideals in order to receive one of the lower-grade children available to a single woman. She didn't want a mixed-race eight-year-old with learning difficulties; Margaret Fisher was going to have the baby she herself should have given birth to. For three years she waited for an opportunity, had several false starts and twice came very close, but now Cressida had presented her with an almost perfect set of circumstances. A child conceived by a healthy, intelligent mother with a history of successful breeding who did not want the baby but whose Catholic upbringing might militate against abortion and who, in any case, was deeply in love with the also intelligent and, what's more, creative, father, plus a husband who was far too reasonable and sensitive to demand a termination even though his wife was pregnant with another man's child: the situation couldn't get much better. The chances of Cressida changing her mind and deciding to terminate the pregnancy were slight now; this much was evident. But keeping the child – that was a different question. And one for which Margaret Fisher was keen and ready to provide the answer. Her shamelessly cynical use of Sister Mary, an old school friend whose violently pro-life stance had several times overcome her better judgement, can perhaps be forgiven when you bear in mind the sad and overwhelming circumstances of Margaret's obsession. Would Cressida provide the missing part of her life's jigsaw?

Harry would say that Dr Fisher was driven by Envy. For a life she should have had but was denied. And the objects of her jealousy had always been women like Cressida. Women who had all they ever wanted but who still, foolishly, ruined it all for themselves and everyone else. She managed to suppress her scorn by replacing it with what she imagined to be sympathy and care in her chosen profession (although really she saw the study of medicine as the path to power. By finding out how people breathe, grow, excrete, reproduce and die she could understand the mystery of existence. The phrase 'caring profession' hardly applied). But from her splendid isolation what she really wanted was to take control. If Cressida submitted to her control, just briefly, Dr Fisher would win her heart's desire.

Cressida's head was awash with lines of a script which seemed to be writing itself. She had often imagined breaking the news of her affair to Harry – to the extent that she sometimes worried she had unwittingly done so simply by repeating the words she dreamt nightly – 'Tom. Tom. I love you. Oh love. Oh Tom' – but simultaneously breaking the news of a pregnancy which did not belong to him had not hitherto occurred to her, and seemed like a crazy choice to make. Following her meeting with Sister Mary her right to choose seemed oddly irrelevant. Who, after all, had the right to choose anything in their lives, really? During that meeting Cressida had acknowledged something absolute: the future of her child could not depend upon the identity of its father. Perhaps what she really meant is that it must depend utterly upon the identity of its father. This conception was not the result of some aberration. She and Tom made love; this child was a symbol of their love. And in whatever way, she also loved Harry, that much was true. So she must tell him. The truth. Whatever that meant.

She sent Tom a text message asking him to call her that evening on her way home – the only time of day when, surrounded by strangers, they were able to talk freely – and got back to work.

Some more unpalatable truths were knocking at Tom's door at that very moment. He had noticed Nita becoming withdrawn and anxious over the last week but had put it down to exhaustion so when she asked him to sit down – at that kitchen table – he was all ears and no brain.

'Tom, I don't know how to say this . . .'

'What is it, pet? Are you ill or something?'

'No, no, I'm not exactly ill, I'm actually . . .'

Whenever Nita broached a serious subject Tom found himself hoping that she was trying to get rid of him. Somehow, he was convinced that the guilt she would feel at kicking him out would guarantee that she would move heaven and earth to keep Katie in his life, whereas if he left of his own accord she might make things very difficult indeed, and Katie was the only reason he was still at this kitchen table. How delicious it would be if Nita really did announce that she had a lover and wanted him to leave. But no, that wasn't going to happen. Nothing was going to happen that hadn't happened before, '. . . I'm pregnant.'

At the heart of Nita's zealous love for Tom and her devotion to the call of motherhood, there lay a great laziness. Her spirit lacked muscle; her soul was unformed; she suffered from a deadly complacency. Like an amoeba, she could unconsciously engulf whole beings by simply oozing, witlessly, over them. Tom was surrounded, and he could do nothing but surrender. He put his head on his arms and began to laugh until the tears arrived. The master of irony suddenly got it.

All Tom wanted to do was bury his head in Cressida's neck and weep with her, for the child they could not have together, for their star-crossed love and, mostly, for himself. He received her text message and called at the appointed time, his heart pounding. It was ridiculous that they had to talk like this. They should meet, in fact he was determined that this news, which he believed put the nails into the already fairly tightly closed coffin lid of their affair, should be told when they were in one another's arms. But if he spoke to her for more than a moment he'd be lost; she could always tell if he was bluffing. Too late for him to hang up, she answered the call. Her voice was small, quiet, tired: 'Hello, love. How are you doing?'

'Fine, fine. But what about you? Did you go to – that place today?'

'Yes. And it was – useful.'

'Good. Are you – well, will it be soon?'

'No. Because I'm not going to. I couldn't live with that knowledge, I simply can't do it, Tom. I'm having it. Don't worry. I'm not asking anything of you. I'm breaking our rules, I understand that. But you can have as much or as little to do with this as you like, because it's not conditional on your leaving Nita or even telling her about it, there are no conditions attached at all. I take full responsibility. Tom?' His continued silence confused her. 'Tom, what's the matter?'

'Nita's pregnant again.'

There was a long, long second when Cressida's breath simply stopped. He heard the hiatus. Then she caught it again, and slowly released it. She was thinking of what she could say. She was trying not to think about what she was feeling. She was silent for longer than Tom could bear.

'Cress, Cressida, my love, I'm so – I'm so fucking sorry about this. She's supposed to have a whatsit – a coil thing – fitted but apparently it was giving her some problems so she had it removed and "forgot" to mention it. It's the last thing I want, the last bloody thing I ever wanted.'

'No. No, the last thing you bloody want is my baby. I don't suppose you've sent Nita off to Manchester's own Sister Mary, have you? I'm the pariah. Well, like I said, this is nothing to do with you, and just as well since you're going to be up to your neck in Pampers yet again. But my baby – do you hear me? – my baby – isn't going to suffer because of you being an arsehole.' She clicked her phone shut and kept her eyes wide open all the way home.

4

Cressida's conversation with Harry was simply too painful to relate. Hours and hours of inarticulate, disbelieving, distraught questioning as the numerous tormenting facts of her shameful infidelity, her barefaced deceit, his utter gullibility, his foolish trust, his intense jealousy and finally her irrefutable pregnancy, heaped themselves upon his poor head. Finally, at three in the morning, they went to bed. To their marriage bed, to the family bed where their children toddled each morning, to the bed that was the only place they had to go. And, no longer allowed to hold out a caressing hand or snuggle in for warmth, Cressida curled up and wept silently while Harry stared disbelievingly into the dark, until they fell into their separate, fitful sleep.

Cressida took the children downstairs as soon as they woke, leaving Harry snoring on his tear-stained pillow. She gave them breakfast and sat with them in front of the television, unduly grateful for the early-morning children's programmes. She stared, red-eyed, at the screen where a quartet of barely humanoid creatures gambolled in garish colours. Having always found these characters faintly disturbing, this morning they seemed positively sinister, with their apeish features and incongruous props. When they lay in bed their heads were so large that they could only prop them up uncomfortably, and to Cressida it looked like a pre-schooler's parody of the Elephant Man. She couldn't bear to watch it any more; her eyes glanced around the room, trying to find something simple and pleasing to fix on. Jemima's doll's house was on the coffee table. But there was something wrong there too. All the soft-bodied dolls were sitting down at the table, but in order to fix them to their wooden chairs their flexible wired arms had been bent (by whom? Ben? Harry?) around the chair backs. A last supper for hostages, a communal force-feeding. Cressida rushed to the toilet and threw up, watched solemnly by two concerned little faces.

'Mummy, are you being sick?'

'No, I'm standing on my head and riding a camel.' This, the family's usual response to obvious questions, fell flat. 'Sorry, sweetheart. Yes, I've been sick. I'm not feeling very well.'

'Shall I get Daddy? Daddy will make you better.'

'No, Ben, let Daddy sleep. I'm fine now. Come on, let's play something. I know – Snap! Jemima, you too. Come on, baby.'

'Mummy's sick.'

'That's right, but I'm all better now. Come on.'

Harry emerged at eleven o'clock, bloodshot, pale, smelling of illness. He was in a state of shock, and could hardly bear to look at Cressida. His world had crumbled in the space of twelve hours – no, it actually crumbled in the space of ten seconds, since then he'd just been aware of the fact. The children were still playing in the sitting room. Cressida made tea and sat opposite him at their kitchen table. She waited.

'Why didn't you just get rid of it? And then you wouldn't have had to tell me anything at all. Then you could have carried on with . . .'

'I couldn't not tell you. No more than I could get rid of it. I have no excuses, Harry, not one. I wish I could think of all the reasons I've done what I've done, but there simply aren't any. I fell in love. Very heavily. And failed to put up the screens – didn't even try to put up the screens.'

The screens had been the subject of much discussion before their marriage. At the time, Harry was practising clinical psychology, which he found immensely distasteful and from which he fled to the safety of the university at the earliest opportunity. The parlous state of his patients' relationships and the endless merry-go-round of partners many of them got through terrified him. He never felt as if he came from the same species as some of these people. Being unfaithful was anathema to him, and he had assumed that Cressida felt the same. They had both agreed that the notion of Fate was ridiculous, that loving someone meant growing with them, developing that love, and that fidelity was an absolute prerequisite. And these facts meant that love was something you had to work at, fidelity was a state to be achieved by putting up the screens when required, when you sensed anything which might grow into a dangerous attraction for someone else. Cressida wondered how often Harry had needed to put up his screens. Perhaps not as much as she did, simply because he had a great knack of being oblivious. She could never be oblivious, however much she tried. She always knew.

Next it was time to tell Mother. Cressida took the day off work and drove to her parents' house. When their youngest daughter (Cressida was the eldest of three girls) had left home her parents had sold their large, rambling family house in Highgate to which they had moved from Leeds when Cressida was twelve, and moved into a large, rambling family house in Harrow, still easily within reach of all their daughters' North London homes. There had been talk of a bungalow, or even a new house built to their own specifications, but in truth, the change her parents longed for was an escape not from their house but from each other. And a large rambling house, complete with outbuildings, really was the best environment to effect long-term mutual avoidance.

Standing in her mother's excessively large and well-stocked kitchen (Patricia was Harry's stereotypical Glutton), Cressida quietly broke the news first of her pregnancy – well, that's marvellous, darling – and then of its provenance, which provoked a stunned silence. Followed by a curt, focused barrage of questions. And then, determinedly, 'I'll have it.'

'What?'

'I'll take it – the baby. I'll bring it up. You can't have it near Harry, and this other chap – well, even if he wanted to have anything to do with it he has a child and you have your two and all in all I think it would be better if I take it.'

'Mum, I'm not having it so that it can be taken away. Can't you see that? I'm not having it to make some sort of moral point about its right to live. The fact I'm having it means I'm keeping it. And in any case, what do you think Dad would say about your bringing up a baby now?' Even as she said it she guessed her mother's response. 'Your father wouldn't even notice, Cressida. As you know. He spends so much damned time in the lab now, that frankly I'd be glad of the company.' David Nelson had retired as a biochemist five years before but still took an active interest in certain long-term research projects and spent almost as much time at work, or at home in his study, as he used to before his retirement. It was true; he probably wouldn't care much either way.

'No, Mum, it's my baby and I'm going to keep it . . .'

'But how does Harry feel about that?'

'I don't even know if Harry has thought about it in that much detail. Harry's probably still wondering if he can have me sectioned. He thinks I'm insane.'

'Well, I can see why, darling, I mean this is shocking.'

'You're not shocked, Mother. Not a bit. Shocked maybe that I was dumb enough to get pregnant and am now ridiculous enough to have the baby, but not shocked at my having an affair. Are you?'

'No, that doesn't shock me. It's probably my own fault for calling you Cressida. Still, I expect I could have called you Chastity and you would have done the same thing. So you're right, I'm not shocked – or surprised.'

'Meaning what, exactly?'

'Meaning that I know you and I can sometimes feel your – frustration. About life. About how it all goes by and you can never get a handle on it and all the things and people you want to help and influence and push in the right direction just won't let you and then you realise you've spent years on them and completely neglected yourself. That's what I mean, Cressida. That's what I know.' Cressida decided not to point out that her mother had just offered some interesting self-analysis and instead curtailed the conversation.

'Then you will know, as well, that I would never have a baby and give it up. I've no idea, Mum, what's going to happen. It's almost refreshing. I love my children and I will love this baby; I have a job and part share in a house and a car; I have a husband and I have a lover. Only the last two bits are likely to change. For now I'm going to hold on to the others very closely indeed and see where the wind blows me.'

The lover was just then wondering what he was supposed to be holding on to right now. Katie, yes, he had Katie. His determination to live with her and be part of her upbringing came as a surprise to everyone who knew him, but he had always been aware of a hard-line streak in his attitude to parenthood. So even if Nita had wanted to terminate the pregnancy he would have tried to dissuade her. It's not about ethics, he would say, but about justice. Why punish the child for the sins of the father? Secretly, though, he thought it was about Fate. But this second time around? And at the same time as Cressida? What had he done to have the shittiest karma imaginable dumped on him now?

Cressida, meanwhile, needed a check-up. She went back to Dr Fisher's surgery, sheepishly.

'Well, as you can see, I decided to have the baby.'

'Indeed?'

'Yes. When it came down to it, I just couldn't go through with it. It suddenly seemed terribly unfair. I mean, in the end I just don't think my – situation – is bad enough to merit doing that. I'm healthy and have a job and a house and so on and it seemed – self-indulgent – to get rid of a baby I conceived just because I'd made a mistake.'

'And you – have strong feelings for the baby's father?'

'Yes, I suppose that's part of it. Although it looks as though he's not going to have much to do with it all. I don't think he's very pleased about my change of heart, and he's actually discovered that his – his partner – is pregnant as well . . .' Although she couldn't prevent a few stray tears from falling when she spoke, Cressida was enjoying the opportunity to share some of her recent woes with a disinterested professional. Dr Fisher seemed to be encouraging her confidences and it was an immense relief to tell the doctor the whole sorry story, finishing with Harry's announcement from the night before that he was going to stay with friends for a while.

Dr Fisher tapped the desk gently with her fingertips, inwardly digesting the good news, and decided that the time was right for her to push phase three along a little.

'How do you see the situation progressing? With your family, I mean. Do you think that your husband will agree to bring up another man's child?'

'Oh, I don't think so. I don't see how he could. Although then again, I don't see how he could live apart from the children. I mean, they're as close to him as they are to me, and I couldn't deprive them of him. So – so, I really don't know what's going to happen. Or even what I want to happen.'

'But you don't think this baby's father is going to be an integral part of your plans?'

'Doesn't look like it. Again, I don't see how he could. He has – responsibilities. I realise it may seem – no, I realise that neither of us has been very good at honouring our responsibilities but we do have them and we do value them. So it's not as if I think he *should* come to live with me and start yet another family. I mean, that might selfishly seem to be the best thing to do but I think we could end up with *everyone* being unhappy. We made a promise, when we started seeing each other. I said it was bound to end in tears and he said they'd better be ours – his and mine – and nobody else's. It didn't work out that way though.'

Dr Fisher looked sympathetically at Cressida. Was now the right moment? Worth a try.

'Cressida. I understand entirely why you have decided against an abortion. That is a choice that only you can make. But in doing so, it seems that you have put at risk some other things which are very important to you, like your family. I'm not suggesting you change your mind, but perhaps you need to consider ways in which the impact of your decision could be minimised.'

'I don't understand how it could be. What do you mean?'

Dr Fisher looked terribly wise.

'Well, you might like to think about what to do when you have had this baby. Would it be the right thing for you to keep it? To bring it up with your children, if that means depriving them of their father? And when the baby's father may not be around either. Is that really the best thing for you all? Including the new baby? Hmmm?'

'Do you mean put it up for adoption? Oh no, I think that now I've got this far – now I've decided that a termination would be selfish – well, that seems to be a commitment to looking after it as well.'

'A commitment at what cost though, Cressida? What cost to those you already love? Listen to me for a moment, and don't answer right away. I have a proposition for you.' Cressida looked across the desk blearily. 'Let me have the baby. Let me look after it. I am unable to have children and although I have tried to live with that fact it's been a great sadness to me. You know me well enough, I hope, to trust that I would offer only the best love and care for the baby. I would move away from the area and of course I could cover your expenses and . . .'

'Stop now.' Cressida wiped her eyes and looked ferociously at Margaret Fisher. 'That's enough. You can't possibly believe that I would hand over my baby to *anybody*. It doesn't matter how much you want a child; you can't just take someone else's and expect that to be a solution. You're a doctor, for Christ's sake, hasn't that taught you anything about human beings and mother-hood and – and – what women feel about their babies?'

'Oh yes, being a doctor. It's taught me that there are mothers whose only form of communication with their children is with a voice raised in constant anger – or who smoke throughout pregnancy. Or whose desire for their own sexual satisfaction overcomes all considerations for their children to the extent that they turn a blind eye to their boyfriend's abusive behaviour. That's what being a doctor has taught me. And I became a doctor to *make things better*. I could do this better than –'

'Than me? Is that what you mean?'

'No. Not better than you. But – as well as you. Like you.'

Cressida rose to her feet. 'You can't be serious. I could report you for this, you know, this is an outrageous way to . . .' Margaret cut in sharply, desperately, as her patient made for the exit.

'I know, I know, it's not within the code of medical ethics, is it? But how much of life fits into the right "codes"? I know it's unorthodox. But it would mean everything to me. Please, don't be angry with me. Think about it, perhaps discuss it with your husband or the baby's father. Or both. I can have tests – psy-chological profiling – I can get references – you can see my bank account – anything.' Cressida slammed the door. 'Anything.'

Unbelievable, thought Cressida. This previously unwanted pregnancy is becoming hot property. The little bastard isn't taking it lying down. Good for you, she smiled, good for you, my love.

5

Back home, Cressida ran after Harry as he opened the gate. 'You left this.' She held out his toothbrush.

'Thanks. I'll – I'll call you then.'

'Yes. OK. The kids didn't take it too badly did they, really?'

'Well, since we told them I'm working a long way away and will keep coming back to see them, I don't think we can count that as any great victory. When they realise that it's become a permanent arrangement they'll probably be less pleased. Ben especially.'

'Do you think it will be permanent?'

'I don't know. I don't know yet, Cressida. The subject of custody hasn't been discussed.'

'Custody? You mean, you'd try to . . .'

'Try to live with my children? Try to keep hold of the most precious – fuck it, the only precious – things in my life? Yes, Cressida, yes I just might try that. And if you move that – if you move your *lover* in, I certainly will.'

'That's not going to happen. That's not a possibility.'

'But he is your lover? You're not calling him your ex-lover yet, are you?'

'I don't know what he is. Nothing, at the moment.'

'Well, snap. We have something else in common. Something apart from you.'

It was an enormous relief to hear Harry being hateful. If he'd taken it all like a lamb Cressida would have been so angry at him she would have let him have it there and then. But bitterness, bitchiness – that was fine. She could cope with that. Good for Harry.

Even as he turned around to walk away Harry was regretting his outburst. He couldn't understand why Cressida had been unfaithful but felt it must be, somehow, to do with her dissatisfaction with him. And like most men he assumed that it must be sexual dissatisfaction, something to do with his performance, or size, or staying power, or just his body. But in Cressida's case it was something far less easily definable, and much much more to do with herself, and some reaction – call it chemical – between her and Tom. Try explaining that to a cuckolded husband. Harry was also thinking about revenge. There had been times in the past when he was aware of a female student demonstrating a more than usual interest in his seminars and lectures. His screens had always gone up at the first opportunity; not so those of many of his weaker-minded colleagues, at least one of whom had been known to position a toothbrush to peek over the top of his jacket pocket when attending student parties. Apart from simply not wanting anyone but Cressida (obviously, he had the odd ten-second fantasy, but never the intention of pursuing it, and it had never been even the vaguest torment to him) he always felt rather protective of these nubile girls – for they really were but girls – who exposed themselves so readily to so much potential abuse and heartache and damage. And pleasure. But there was one PhD student, a twenty-eight-year-old, Nicola, who was unlike Cressida in every conceivable way. She was slender, black, studious, beautiful, scientifically gifted and apparently humourless. Harry had categorised her as Pride, seeing in her steady gaze and long stride an aloofness built, he was sure, on the shoulders of her own feelings of superiority. She was also more self-aware and confident than her younger peers, and had not allowed her attentions to be shaken off lightly. Having been about to start shaking more dramatically, Harry was now toying with the idea of standing still and screenless and seeing what happened. That would show her.

Nicola was indeed interested in Harry, although not as interested as Sophie was. Sophie had been Harry's departmental secretary for five years and she fell in love with him the day they met. She also, conveniently, fell in love with Cressida, and the children as they came along. She was blonde and curvaceous, a stereotypical secretary from a fifties comic book, whose main hobbies appeared to be the constant growing of her hair and nails – activities which, as Cressida once pointed out to Harry, could be just as easily achieved by a corpse. Sophie would be thrilled to know how much time Harry spent thinking about her, though the context wouldn't please her overmuch: she was his model for Avarice. Desperate to accumulate love and approval, she overcompensated with a generosity that verged on the reckless. Sophie gave so much to everyone else she was careless with herself and frequently ended up penniless or heartbroken. Harry was in fact rather worried about her, as recently she seemed to be even more depressed than usual about all the things her life lacked, particularly a child. At thirty-two, Sophie had decided – just as Dr Fisher decided, but much earlier in her life and for slightly different reasons – to bypass the possibility of ever finding a perfect man – or even just a nice man who would love her and was still available – and focus instead on becoming a mother. She could do this easily enough in the old-fashioned way but was determined her child shouldn't be the result of some furtive and finally unsatisfactory sexual encounter (she'd never met someone like Tom) so decided that she would wield whatever power she had over the choice of putative father. She was already looking into available methods, regularly calculated her monthly fertile period, and was bang up to date on her rights regarding maternity leave and pay. But there was nobody she wanted to make a child with except Harry. Would he, she wondered as she filled in a mail-order form for a DIY Artificial Insemination by Donor kit, agree to help her?

With Harry gone, the house seemed more chaotic, the children were jumpy and Cressida was lonely. She took the week off work and the kids out of nursery, but wondered if being home all day in an anxious state wasn't even more disturbing to her children than if she were carrying on as normal. Cressida got around to calling Tom back – he'd been sending daily emails and texts begging for a meeting – and finally agreed to meet, though she couldn't see what they could possibly say to each other. Her mother babysat while they met in a pub they had never been to before.

'Hello, Cressida.'

'Hello.'

'You look – beautiful.' Tom had always been fearful that he might glimpse Cressida from a distance one day, coming to meet her after a tortuous separation of three weeks, and suddenly find 'that feeling' gone. Always waiting to see if the woman he'd been loving in her absence was the same as the one he was about to meet. Cressida, on the other hand, always looked to catch sight of Tom thinking, 'I'm waiting for the man I love to appear.' But now Tom was, as usual, stunned by the feelings that overcame him just by looking at Cressida. She had been waiting for her heart to skip its usual beat and was, therefore, better prepared for this meeting.

'Thank you. I don't have a script, you know. What is it we're meeting about today?'

Tom considered various approaches but dived straight in. 'I still love you, Cressida. I still love you more than life itself. You're in my head night and day; you're all I think about. Nothing can change that.' She nodded faintly in acknowledgement.

'Have you told Nita?'

'No.'

'Does she not even suspect something's up? How good a performance are you putting in with her?'

'She knows I'm not thrilled about this second child. But she thinks that's to do with money worries and not having finished this book.'

'Are you going to tell her?'

'What for, Cressida? So that she'll kick me out and I'll end up separated from my child? My children?'

'But you're prepared to be separated from the child you and I are having?'

'No. There's nothing I'm less prepared for. But this really does seem to be an either/or situation. Nita wouldn't just say, "Oh yeah, off you go to live with the woman you *really* love and the baby you're having with her, while I give birth to our second child, and you can visit regularly, that'll be fine." I mean, she has a vindictive streak. And who would blame her for being just faintly pissed off if I abandoned her and the girls and Katie and – this new one? I have no choice in this at all, you know that.'

'How would Nita feel if she knew about our affair? Don't you think that you should let her make her mind up about you once she knows the whole truth? Knowing you don't love her?'

Tom sighed, impatient now with Cressida's irritating obsession with knowledge and truth.

'It doesn't matter how she would feel if she knew – she doesn't, nor will she. Why try to second-guess that stuff?'

'I can see I've irritated you already. Didn't take long, did it? What you're saying is that you'd rather live a sham existence than be with me. When it was about Katie I could understand it. But now you're going to have another child *with me*. It evens everything up in some ways. The different factor becomes which woman you want, not whether or not you can see your child. And in any case, no way would Nita stop you from seeing Katie, she needs your cash and she knows you're a good father. You're dramatising it and making her seem monstrous. It's tempting for me to believe it, but in the end I'm sure she's got the interests of her kids at heart and she would never stop you from seeing them.'

'*Seeing* Katie isn't enough. How would you like to just *see* Ben and Jemima? If they lived with Harry and you *saw* them at weekends? Especially if you were in London and they were in frigging Manchester? I can't abandon Katie. You *know*, you absolutely *know* that all I want in the world is to be happy with you. But we can't be happy together, not in these circumstances. Our children come first.'

'Are you suggesting I'm not aware of that? I know what you're saying. I also know that you're ignoring the fact that you are just going to *see* our baby. If you want to, that is?'

'Of course I want to. But look – does this mean you and Harry are divorcing? I mean, have you two decided what's happening?'

Cressida paused. She felt exhausted; it was hard to remember how much she loved Tom during this particular conversation. When she first saw him, she had almost jumped up and kissed him and dragged him off to a hotel. But the mood had changed. Already knowing what his response would be, she answered, 'I don't know. But listen – just say we did divorce. And I was living alone with three children, one of them yours. What would you want our relationship to be?'

'Is this a trick question? Because obviously, what I'd want is to be with you whenever I could. I'd try to come down here more often – or maybe you'd get a job further north. I'll never stop loving you, or supporting you as much as I can, and of course I'd try to contribute financially, you know I could probably afford to without doing too much damage – up north – and – Cressida, why are you looking at me like that?'

'You are fucking unbelievable. You think I should settle down to being your occasional bit on the side, some dirty secret, while you live with your "official" family as if nothing had ever happened? You really think that's fair? You really think that's something I'd accept? So, from being married to someone totally devoted to me, who's a fantastic father and who's faithful and supportive and – perfect – you think I should become a single mother waiting for occasional visits from the father of her third child? I think it's clear what you want. To have your fucking cake and eat it. Well, not a chance. You just carry on convincingly fucking your dim-witted old bint so she suspects nothing – and why not stick your dick everywhere else you can too, like in the good old days? – and I'll be nowhere, do you understand, I'll be nowhere in your life. Me and this baby, we're getting out now. If you'd seriously ransom our chance of a future together to the absolutely unlikely prospect of being estranged from your – other children – well, that tells me a lot about your priorities. Just fuck right off.'

Well, that went well, Tom murmured into his coffee as Cressida left in tears.

Cressida knew that Tom was probably right about happiness. Better, perhaps, to let go of everything and see where you fall than attempt a salvage operation which could leave you facing every day with a truckload of guilt. She didn't even know whether setting up house with him would work, bearing in mind all the complications and his unimpressive domestic history, and she knew that her outburst had been unreasonable; there was no clear path to their happiness. But then, happiness had never come easily to Cressida. Anything smacking too much of happiness, especially in crowds, drove her to distraction. Public displays of any form of mass emotion either put her in mind of Nuremberg or left her in tears. She simply couldn't join in acts of communality. Didn't trust them. If all those people could be happy together – well, they could all become terribly despondent together too and that really would be unbearable. So sometimes she closed her eyes to the big picture and focused, out of necessity, on the bare essentials: who did she love and where did she want to be?

The pursuit of happiness had become a popular post-coital conversation topic for Cressida and Tom. He claimed not to be a seeker of happiness: 'I've never believed it to be attainable, never reached for it. The few times I've thought it's maybe going to come around it never has. Moments of happiness are all we can hope for – moments like these. Not to be scoffed at, of course, but it can never be a state of life.' While the wisdom seemed undeniable – after all, Cressida was only truly happy in the brief moments she was with Tom and even then only when she had forgotten, just for a few seconds, that she was not really 'with' Tom – it felt terribly defeatist of him.

'Surely it's something we all reach for? If we didn't, why bother living at all?'

'Well, why bother? I mean, that's right, I agree. Sometimes – when all this really gets to me – I do wonder whether everyone might be better off without me. Katie, Nita, you, my folks. I seriously do.'

'Ah, now that is the artistic temperament at work, or maybe at play. It's a terrible, egotistical, indulgent thing to say and it undermines everything important to you, including me. Makes it sound as though anyone who cherishes you is foolish or misguided, that you're not "worth" my love. You don't really believe that.'

'Sometimes I do, pet. Sometimes I really do.' They lay in silence for a while, he enjoying the effect of his morbid revelations, she waiting for it to wear off. 'I started a new book today,' he finally announced.

'But you haven't finished the old one!'

'I know, and shan't – can't – for a while. This has been blocking it, getting in the way. I feel so much better now I've realised why I've been so held back, so thwarted about finishing it.'

'What's the new one about?'

'Not sure really. I've got the outline of a plot, but don't know where it's leading. I think it's something to do with mothers and sons, originally enough.' Cressida felt a pang of disappointment; while she had always enjoyed discussing Tom's work with him, she was aware that none of it – seemingly not one line, or bit of a character or even incident or part of conversation – was ever connected to her. She knew about the greediness of writers, their tendency to cannibalise, to parody, to lift wholesale, so really, she sometimes thought, he could write just something which put her inside his work. Just one tiny detail, as a sign to her. It never even occurred to Tom that she felt left out like this. Early on in their affair, during the obsessive, euphoric first few months, he had kissed her and called her his Muse, which attempted compliment she rejected outright.

'Your Muse? No thanks. I've always thought it's an ignoble calling, Musehood. A bit like being an artist's model – they go on about them as if they're inspiration, as if they're significant, but they're just flesh. Just victims. They have things done to them which are then passed off as if they were somehow involved, but really they were only ever Objects. Even if it is with a capital "O".'

'Whoa girl, calm down, OK, you won't be my Muse. Sorry I suggested it.'

'Anyway, only poets can have Muses.'

'All right, I've retracted, let it drop now, pet.' Tom's amusement at her wrath was tempered by a little ruefulness; nobody had ever turned him down like that before. 'So. If not my Muse, what then? What do you want to be to me, pet?'

Cressida didn't hesitate. 'Your editor.'

6

Cressida's perfect husband had left his temporary digs with the express aim of blotting his copybook. Never in his life had Harry gone out quite simply with the aim of fucking someone. Every time he had ever pursued a woman, it was with the most honourable intentions. Of course, there was always the possibility of sex, but it had never been his sole aim, and certainly not on the first date. But all that was due to change. Tonight there was a big pre-exam party that everyone in his faculty was invited to. Usually on these occasions, Harry went for a quick drink, smiled at the requisite number of staff and students and then rushed back to Cressida and the kids, relieved to be sitting comfortably, drinking better wine, and enjoying a superior level of conversation. To-night, he was going to stay until the bitter end. But it wasn't going smoothly. It was ten o'clock already and there was no sign of Nicola. A lesser man would begin to look for alternatives but not Harry. If he was going to commit adultery by having a wild night of meaningless sex then it mattered deeply who his co-conspirator, however unwitting, was going to be. He waited, concerned at the slight sweat he'd worked up in his tweed jacket, and wondered if he should brush his teeth again, just in case.

Cressida's mother, Patricia, telephoned her.

'Well darling, have you thought about my offer?'

'You're not seriously still trying that one, Mum?'

'I thought that with Harry gone you may have – reconsidered.'

'With Harry gone it becomes even more important to me that I have my children about me.'

'Oh for God's sake, Cressida, grow up. Jemmy and Ben need Harry. This new one is a cuckoo in the nest. You're doing exactly what you always did, cutting off your nose to spite your face. Cressida? Cressida!'

It was the first time she had hung up on her mother in nearly twenty years. Needs must.

At eleven p.m. Harry was about to return sheepishly to Adam and Steve's, the friends who were putting him up. They had been not entirely unaware of Harry's plans for the evening – they recognised that excited spark, that attention to hygiene, that palpable dry-mouthed anticipation, and guessed accurately what its cause was likely to be. Adam was an old school friend who had suffered through his teens from a crush on Harry and, although that fire was now just about spent, in his bleaker moments he hated Cressida with jealous rage. For the five years they'd been together, Steve had been aware of this, and never more than when Adam reported the news of Cressida's atrocious behaviour with barely disguised glee, with which he quivered yet again when Harry left, booted and suited, for the party. The prospect of That Woman getting her comeuppance was almost worth the agony of imagining Harry with yet another lover. Steve, who liked Cressida enormously and knew that Harry doted on her, saw him preparing to approach the lion's den and could say nothing to warn him off, was not sufficiently close to Harry to intervene. So Adam sent his oldest friend upon the heady primrose path with a wink of conspiratorial encouragement.

Just as Harry was about to make the return journey, he caught sight of Nicola, wearing something tight and black, walking straight up to him. She was holding two opened beers and handed one to him. They drank. He was about to speak when she put her empty bottle down and said, 'Let's get out of here. We'll go to my flat.' He followed her.

Cressida answered a ring on the doorbell and found her mother, who kissed her briefly in greeting and strode through to the kitchen.

'Now, we'll say nothing about that silly show of temper. Put it down to hormones. Are the kids asleep? Good, then let's try to have a proper conversation, shall we?'

Patricia swooped rapidly around the familiar kitchen cupboards, shovelled ice into two tall glasses followed by a large slug of gin in each and tonic water which fizzed over the rims. Licking her fingers, she plonked one glass down in front of Cressida and sat opposite her. 'Now then, do you want to keep Harry?'

Cressida decided to grow up and give in. She sighed. 'I don't see how I can really, Mum. He's hardly likely to come round to this one. And who can blame him? I mean, it's a bit of a double whammy for him. I think that if I'd "just" told him I'd been having an affair we may have been able to – work it through, is what you're supposed to do, I believe – but presenting him with such tangible *proof* of my – adultery – is taking it one step too far.'

'Men are strange, Cressida. You'd be surprised.'

'Meaning what, Mother?'

'Meaning that someone like Harry, someone who likes his home comforts and his family around him and that kind of stability, may actually put up with quite a lot in order to preserve it.'

'Yes, I do see that, but I still think that there are limits. And in any case, why was I having an affair?'

'You tell me, darling.'

'I can't exactly. But I do love Tom. It's not that I don't love Harry, but I really do love Tom, in a way you can't –'

'Can't imagine? Do you think I can't imagine loving someone like that?'

'I'm sorry, Mum, but you have to see – you've been with Dad for nearly forty years and he was your first boyfriend, and people behaved differently then, and –'

'Bollocks.'

'What?'

'That's absolute bollocks, Cressida. Nothing's different. Falling in love isn't different. And there was sex then, you know, even pre-nineteen-sixty-bloody-three there was sex. Besides, your father *was* the first man I slept with – not quite my first boyfriend, thank you – but I think you're making some assumptions about me that may not be entirely accurate.'

'What do you mean? Mum?'

Patricia drew her breath in sharply then sighed and said, 'Three years after your father and I got married, two years before you were born, I met someone – Paul – you won't have heard his name mentioned – and I fell in love with him.'

'But what about Dad?'

'I fell in love with Paul – who was also married – and we realised very soon that we *should have* been together. We were a perfect fit. When he took me to bed I understood what making love could be like. Not that there was anything wrong with your father; in fact I'd been terribly happy about it all until then, it was just that Paul seemed made for me. It sounds ridiculous, but that's what we felt.'

'Not ridiculous. Go on.'

'He had a little boy – two years old – and unlike many men in those days, he did everything for him, absolutely doted on him. But his wife – well, they'd had to get married because of the baby, you see, although they had only been seeing each other for a few months. She sounded nice enough, but they were a mismatch in many ways, and although he never directly accused her of it he suspected that the pregnancy wasn't entirely accidental on her part. But he took the rap, did the decent thing – all the sorts of ideas you'd probably laugh at for being old-fashioned notions of virtue I expect – and although he didn't love her he would never leave her because of the boy, his son. I never actually tried to make him leave her. I sometimes wonder if I really wanted to, you know, life without your dad would have been very odd, but I used to hate the way he talked about the boy. He said the child was the only thing he loved more than me, and I was so jealous.'

'But Mum, that's what parents feel for their children, that's *right*.'

'I know that now. But not then. It's not something you can understand until you've had kids of your own, is it? And I had all sorts of romantic ideals about love finding a way. But there are some non-negotiable routes and they run through your children's lives. I thought that he and I could make a child, he could still see his little boy, it wasn't as if I wanted to separate them, and a child with me would have meant the world to him. But he was unbending. He had a responsibility he wouldn't take lightly, and he wanted to be the boy's dad all the time, give him breakfast, put him to bed and everything in between. I understand it now of course, and if I think of the scandal it would have caused anyway . . . well. So you see, I do understand you. Paul and I should have been together. But we couldn't be. And your father wasn't second best – we'd been so happy until then. But if I'd already had you – well, I don't know whether I'd have taken up with Paul in the first place of course, but I expect I would. It was very – extreme – what we felt, I mean – but if I'd already had a child – I would have felt just the same as he did. I was trying to – what did he used to say? There was a phrase he always used – oh, that's right; I was trying to create a parallel universe. One in which he and I had met at the right time and everything had happened as it should. But where we really were – the real world – had already turned and we'd missed each other . . .' Cressida was crying with her mother now. She held her hand.

'Mum, thank you for telling me that. I'm so – sorry. So sorry you had to . . .'

'There was no had to, you know. That's what I learned from it.'

'What do you mean?'

'We were entirely culpable.'

'But you fell in love, you were overwhelmed –'

'No. That's what we said, that it was uncontrollable, there was nothing we could do, it was bigger than we were. But that was bollocks too. We kissed, and it was such a perfect kiss we fell into it as if our course were set. But we set the course. And we should have held hands very tightly and looked at each other for a minute then walked away from one another. We could have done that. But we chose not to. Don't ever say you couldn't help yourself, Cressida. As though you're nothing but a bag of instincts. That's what our brains are for, after all.'

'Did Dad find out?'

'I told him. Paul and I agreed not to see each other, after nearly a year of running about and telling lies and fearing discovery, and I told your father at once. He was almost destroyed. I offered him the chance to leave me. But he decided he still loved me and wanted us to stay together and then we decided together not to put off having a family any more, so a few months later you were conceived.'

'Wasn't that a crazy thing to do? To tie yourselves into being parents when the marriage was so threatened?'

'The marriage wasn't threatened. I could never be with Paul. I was sure I would never feel that way about anybody else but was also confident that if it seemed about to happen I would be able to –'

Patricia paused and Cressida suggested, 'Put up the screens?'

'Sorry?'

'The screens. The shutters. Put up your defences.'

'Yes, yes, that's what I mean.'

'And did you ever feel that way about anyone else?'

'No. No, I never did. Just Paul.'

'Oh, Mum. Mum. What am I going to do?'

Patricia moved to the chair beside Cressida and hugged her. She stroked her daughter's hair until the tears had subsided but found the gesture so unfamiliar that she felt compelled to break the moment and said briskly, 'You really should cut your hair you know, dear. What did I always tell you?'

Cressida shivered and sat up, composing herself, 'Women over thirty shouldn't have long hair?'

'That's right. It's not appropriate. You won't be taken seriously.'

'There's no chance of that anyway. I still wear jeans you know, in spite of my great age.' Patricia pursed her lips, kissed Cressida dryly on the cheek and was about to go when her daughter began to sob again. She turned back, with a little shame at her brusqueness, and gave her another hug.

'Hush, love. Hush. You'll be fine. We'll be fine. You'll see.' She handed over a tissue.

Cressida blew her nose loudly, like a child, and said glumly, 'I can't see it ever being fine. It's too much of a mess. I'll never be fine again.'

'Oh yes you will, my girl. It might just take rather a long time.'

Back at Nicola's flat, Harry was taking rather a long time over making love to her. Unused to kissing and undressing someone from whom he was totally, and apparently mutually, emotionally detached, he found it at first almost too exciting; when she lay naked on the bed and looked at him expectantly it took considerable control not to just plunge in without further ado. But now they'd been through every mode of foreplay and were well over halfway through Harry's repertoire of positions, he was finding it difficult. His objectivity clarified his senses far too successfully; where was the haze which kindly enrobed writhing bodies in a rose-tinted glow of voluptuous glory; whither had fled the sound of the tide in his ears which imbued each sigh and grunt with a gracious harmony; why did the body of this woman, who was undoubtedly the most gorgeous, toned, flawless and desirable that he had ever seen, let alone fucked, leave him strangely unmoved? The ability – perhaps even the propensity – of the human male to mate satisfactorily with any member of the opposite sex within a certain, generous, age range is well catalogued. But, Harry was wondering, was it true? Were most men *like that*? Are their real sexual encounters with beautiful strangers as astonishingly arousing as the imagined version? He was beginning to doubt it. Turning Nicola – whose eyes had remained discomfitingly wide open throughout – on to her belly, he resolved to bring matters to a close with a sure-fire rear entry finale. Placing a pillow beneath her rump and one hand on each of her firm, curved, silken buttocks, Harry was astounded to realise that the only way this was going to work was to employ fantasy. He shut his eyes tightly and thought of – of what, do you think? He was well on the home strait by the time he realised that the image he had conjured, and was focusing on in near-desperation, was the larger, paler, wobblier, but infinitely more precious, backside of his wife. With the final thrust Harry broke through to a realisation of his double – no, make that a triple – deceit and plunged in to a desolate and joyless ejaculation.

More pillowtalk. Cressida and Tom used to spend hours discussing sin and goodness, particularly in the light of Harry's research which, being so wilfully and confidently reactionary, fascinated Tom. Cressida told him about a man she had worked with several years before with whom she used to have a light but increasingly intense flirtation. Their friendship began to take on the characteristics of an affair, their meeting for drinks began to be secret, their kisses goodbye on the cheek were trailing mouthwards. On one occasion they had deliberately drunk themselves into a state of moral limbo and snogged like teenagers before catching the last tube home in opposite directions.

'So what happened afterwards?'

'We referred to it once the following day, as a daft mistake, and then avoided each other for a little while. It took around six months to approach normality again and now – everything's fine, he's a good friend. And we're both glad that nothing more happened, because it would have been crazy. And we certainly wouldn't be friends now.'

'But I don't get it. You were keen on each other, attracted towards each other, and yet you just acted like adolescents. Why didn't you take it further? Why didn't he even try?'

'We were both with other people, we didn't want to mess up our lives – I knew I didn't actually love him though we had that kind of romantic frisson, and I guess from his point of view – well, I suppose it's because he's a good man. Just that.'

Tom was quiet; he felt sad but didn't know why and was angry at both the sadness and his ignorance of its cause. 'There you go again, equating being sexually unadventurous with being "good". Maybe he wasn't naturally very passionate. Maybe he had hang-ups about sex. Maybe – and this is most likely – maybe he was *scared*.'

'Scared of what?'

'He could have been scared of loads of things: Being found out. Failing sexually. Starting something he couldn't control. You.'

'For God's sake, why won't you accept that not all men are like you? Some of them are capable of exercising some control, you know. Some of them try to keep promises, and that is good, yes, I'd say that was certainly good.'

'But it's too easy an equation. Listen, someone who never fucks around might just be someone who never gets the chance – maybe they're shy or boring or ugly or whatever. Whereas someone attractive gets temptations thrown at them all the time. You can't say someone's good just because they obey certain rules regarding sexual behaviour which you have decided are the Right Thing to do.'

'What you're saying is true, in that of course it's all relative. And I didn't say ugly celibate people are good whereas pretty promiscuous ones aren't. But in this case – with Frank – he decided not to commit adultery simply because he was *good*. There are only two things, really, which make someone good: honesty and restraint. If you apply both of those to your life you're not going to go far wrong. That's what Frank does – and he is an attractive man, you've met him, he's not one of your ugly no-mates examples – and it's one of the reasons people like him. Someone pious and zealous about truth and restraint is obviously a nutter but people sense the difference, and a truly good man is a rare and lovely thing. Now, people like you too of course, but that's certainly not because you're good, it's because you're good company and witty and entertaining and well informed, and women like you because you've got that fantastic accent and you're sexy in some indefinably flattering way, and then finally because you're good in bed. But you're not "a good man". The things which good men do don't interest you, it's not something you're trying to achieve. Is it? Tom?'

'Sometimes I would like to be thought of as a good man. Just sometimes.'

'But you don't think that honesty and restraint are features of a good man?'

'You know my take on honesty. It can be brutal.'

'Which is precisely why you have to operate restraint, to make sure you don't have brutal truths to impart. I don't mean you should go shouting the truth at people – telling them their breath smells or nobody likes them – just that you should be truthful to yourself about how you behave and not have secrets. I don't know how you've managed in the past, keeping so many secrets simultaneously and never even tripping yourself up.' It wasn't just in the past; Cressida was sometimes aware that Tom was lying to her about trivia just to keep his hand in. Once she had discovered, through a series of accidents, that he had spent an afternoon in Manchester lunching and drinking with an ex-lover – a dull and dutiful few hours in fact, without the faintest glimmer of re-awakened desire on either side – rather than working in the library as he claimed. His excuse for having lied to her was fear of her jealousy but in fact, as she knew, the notion of telling someone the whole truth, all the time, terrified him. He had to keep something back, maintain some knowledge for himself alone. In the same way he rarely answered a factual question, such as where he was going that evening, in a straightforward manner, preferring to keep his options open with an unnecessary lie. This was his most slippery characteristic, and the one of which Cressida consciously reminded herself every time she dreamed of how their life together could be. She knew, too, that the slipperiness was part of his charm: she and Harry had married each other partly out of mutual admiration for each other's apparent certainty. He seemed so wise about the human condition, she seemed so sure about the world. Much of their marriage thus far had been spent discovering that they had both been duped; they were as much afloat on the same vague tide as everybody else, they were just capable of appearing to be steering rather than drifting. It was one of the few areas in which Tom did not practise deceit; he was painfully aware of his tendency to drift and Cressida found this one glimmer of self-knowledge oddly appealing.

'Ah well, duplicity is an art based on self-loathing, only the man who truly despises himself will ever be a success at it.'

'There, you see, you loathe yourself for it, you know it's not a good thing, you know it prevents you from being a good man.'

'And what about you, Cressida? Are you a good woman? Where are your honesty and restraint?'

'Down the toilet. Along with my moral fibre,' Cressida realised sadly. 'I'm not a good woman. Not any more.'

Tom had heard the quaver in her voice and turned to her. 'Come here, pet. You're my good woman. You're my good woman.'

Harry would say that Nita's fatal flaw was Sloth, whose flipside – unbridled Zeal – scared her so much during her tempestuous, obsessive and almost paranoiac teens that she guarded against it like the plague, and her spiritual complacency was the tragic result. However scatterbrained her approach though, the back of her head occasionally functioned in a focused manner and, just as Tom had made his calculations two years ago, so she worked out that two plus two was a lot more stable than two plus one. This new baby would seal it, she was certain. She was rather taken aback by Tom's reaction which seemed almost like grief, but was quietly confident that once the reality sank in his natural, excellent, paternal instincts would take over. Just as well, since Felicity and Harmony had barely spoken to her since hearing the news, seemingly embarrassed by it. And indeed they were, particularly Felicity, who knew very well that her mother's paramour had not exactly been exclusively devoted to her. News moves quickly around the playground and Tom was well known around the north-west and could rarely travel anywhere locally incognito. Although it was old news, it still held currency and tongues had, inevitably, wagged. Whether the girl refrained from mentioning this to Nita out of kindness, cruelty or indifference was unclear. But Felicity was now almost sixteen years old and Tom was an attractive man who had come between her and her mother.

To Cressida at her lowest, it seemed that Nita was getting the best of every world: mercifully unaware of her boyfriend's multiple infidelities, convinced of his devotion, expecting their second child and safe in the knowledge that he was her man. It was not really a position Cressida envied – in fact most of it stank – but the key elements were making her exceedingly jealous. She had Tom and Nita's home telephone number. She had been carrying it on a scrap of paper in her coat pocket for the last few days. Her fingers checked on its presence from time to time. Just one phonecall, a few simple words, and she could shatter Nita's dream. It was so tempting, but Cressida was holding off, not from any commendable ethical restraint, but simply because if Tom hadn't the guts to do it she didn't see why she should. She was missing Tom, almost unbearably. They had been in touch with one another every day for a year and a half but now the lines were down. She missed the banality of how are you, swapping baby stories, work gossip, the final tiny I love yous. More than this she missed the anticipation of meeting, the sweet secret afternoons of bliss in Tom's arms. She was in a torment, dreaming of him every night; she woke with her fingers damp between her thighs and was almost appalled at the unceasing erotic bent of her imagination. Early pregnancy had previously turned her off sex completely until around the fourth month. From then until full term, during both her pregnancies, she would regularly leave work early on some plausible pretext, call Harry, demand he make his excuses to join her and then tear the clothes off him as he walked through the door. This time around, the insatiable phase seemed to have struck early, with no satisfactory outlet. Cressida wondered why little girls were never threatened with blindness or hairs on the palms of their hands, and was painfully aware that she would gladly risk both in her futile pursuit of libidinal satisfaction.

Margaret Fisher was similarly engaged, but in her case it had been a way of life for so many years that she no longer thought about it. Around once a fortnight, she removed a black velvet drawstring bag from her knicker drawer from which she lifted a 9-inch dildo moulded from smooth, heavy black plastic, and employed it vigorously for no more than five minutes. She had tried every kind of penetrative sex aid in most available styles – various shapes, sizes, textures and built-in special features including one frighteningly lifelike rubber phallus which delivered a shot of viscous lubricant when she pressed a button on its base at the required moment. The effect was most disappointing: having only ever had intercourse with Jim using condoms, Dr Fisher had wanted to re-create what she considered to be the lost experience of receiving ejaculate unhindered but had been aware of nothing until, later, she turned over in her bed and found an unpleasant wet patch spoiling her best Irish linen sheets. Perhaps, she concluded, she hadn't missed much after all. And in any case, the thing had looked gruesome, ludicrous. Her present choice – discreet, quiet, reliable, effective – suited her down to the ground.

Tom and Nita were not having sex. They had not made the beast with two backs (a woefully inadequate description of Tom's frequently acrobatic sexual innovations) since she broke the news of her pregnancy. For the first time in more than ten years Tom was celibate, a fact more significant than it might sound. On the whole, not to have at least two desirable sexual partners lined up at any given time does not necessarily mean celibacy. The man in the street might consider himself approaching celibacy if he has not had a sexual encounter in six months, maybe. Or two years. Or possibly five years. Even then he may not use the term celibacy. It's too deliberate, too pessimistic, too *final*. But Tom realised he had reached a point in his sexual life which he never thought would happen and it was an unnerving experience. Now that he was not having sex with Cressida there was no need to have sex with Nita in order to convince her that he was not having sex with someone else. And he only wanted to have sex with Cressida. It was extraordinary. Even the longing he felt now for Cressida was more vivid and more tragic than the yearning he had always felt between their trysts. He *craved* her. Tom was finding out about losing love and being alone. Celibacy and isolation: his new bedfellows. He couldn't even talk to a friend, because he and Cressida had been so careful to ensure that nobody in the world knew about them. Besides, most of his friends were women – men tended not to trust him around their women; consequently his closest male friends were single, and incapable of offering more than paranoid incomprehension on the subject of Woman Trouble. And all of his women friends were, without exception, former lovers. Tom was developing an unusual sensitivity about this fact; another reassurance he was longing for was some proof that he was capable of forming a relationship with a woman which wasn't based, somehow, on sex. Apart from his mother there was nobody he could think of. It's not difficult to work out which deadly sin was in the ascendance in Tom's soul; harder though to comprehend the changes he was experiencing right now. The changes were obvious to Nita, who was anxious about them, and to the girls, who were curious.

'So what's up, Pop?' asked Felicity cheekily, attempting to twist her own Manchester accent into an unflattering version of Geordie.

'Oh you know. This and that,' responded Tom, refusing to take the bait. But she wasn't a girl to give up easily. She reverted to the harsher vowels of the north-west to ask, scornfully, 'And a bit of the other?'

'What did you say?'

'You can't fool me. Everyone knows. Everyone knows except Mum, and she's dumb.'

'Don't talk about your mother like that.'

'Like you'd care.'

'Fliss, I don't know what –'

'My name's Felicity. Only my friends call me Fliss.'

'Right, well, my name's Tom. Nobody calls me Pop.'

'Suit yourself, mardyarse.'

Felicity walked towards the door. Her thick dark hair hung in a heavy curtain to her shoulders. She was wearing tight jeans and swinging her hips precisely and deliberately. She was feeling as powerful as only a pretty sixteen-year-old girl can feel. Invincible. She turned back towards Tom.

No child likes to lose a father. The most ineffectual, unaffectionate, uninvolved absent father is still missed by his offspring. And Justin had been none of these things; he was loving, generous and close to the girls. Even when he was depressed, Felicity and Harmony were his world's focus and despite his evident failure to do things other fathers did – drive them to parties, give them pocket money, criticise the length of their skirts – they didn't want him to leave. Justin could barely cope on his own at first. Nita's coldness towards him was bad enough, but having to *visit* his own daughters was humiliating to a man whose mental state was already in turmoil. Sometimes he didn't turn up when arranged. At those times he was sitting in the small flat he'd rented, about two miles from the house he and Nita had bought together after his first promotion, staring at the floor and wondering how this had happened. His daughters sensed his misery, and their mother's irritation, and they knew where their sympathies lay. When she introduced them to Tom, when she left them for nights on their own, when she told them they were to have a new little brother or sister, when Tom moved in, when he argued with Justin, when Justin left the country, when Katie was born – through all these upheavals to their lives they had kept so quiet and calm that Nita had wondered if something might be wrong but was too indolent to enquire further. But Felicity had been coming out of her shell in recent months. And she still remembered where the blame lay. And had thought of the best, most appropriate style of revenge.

Felicity, looking determined, walked to where Tom was sitting at the table and stood very close to him. But instead of making him kiss her as planned she blurted out, 'You sent my dad away. You made him go all that long way away.' Tom was surprised; his assumption had always been that the girls were glad to see Justin go – Nita had told him of the catalogue of failed appointments and miserable outings which had characterised her ex-husband's relationship with his daughters. In any case, since the girls never referred to their father in Tom's presence he concluded they rarely considered him, except on the one occasion per year when he made the long trip back to Manchester in order to see them for a fortnight, and their annual one-week holiday together somewhere in Europe. They were always quiet about those times too. Had Tom given the subject much thought when considering his attitude to his own daughter, perhaps he would have reached a different conclusion, but he had paid little attention to Justin. Priding himself on what he saw as a lack of jealousy but which could be a lack of care, Tom had never given the idea of Justin much thought at all and had happily accepted Nita's version of events.

'I didn't send him away, Fliss. Felicity. He was messing your mother about, making arrangements and failing to keep them, letting you and Harm down nearly every week . . .'

'He was ill. Mum couldn't be bothered with him any more.'

'That's not a fair thing to say. She'd gone through years of coping with his – state of mind.'

'So did he. And just as he was getting better she said she didn't want him any more. And that meant *we* couldn't have him any more. And that wasn't fair. And I loved Mum, but when – when she got *you*. And had Katie. What were me and Harm supposed to do about that?' Real tears now. Felicity's plan had gone completely pear-shaped, she had too much to say which wouldn't remain unsaid for any longer.

'Don't cry, sweetheart. Felicity, pet, come here.' Tom stood up and put his arms around her. She tensed. Maybe this would work after all. As he patted her heaving shoulders, Felicity firmly pressed the length of her body against Tom's. She stopped sobbing into his neck and began to very gently kiss it. It took a while for Tom to realise what was happening, and as he did, Felicity's voice said clearly and determinedly into his ear, 'She's *disgusting*. You know she is. You've been with all those other women because she's so *disgusting*.'

Tom lowered his arms and tried to move Felicity away from him but she clung to him with a vengeance.

'You'd like to kiss me, wouldn't you?' she said, turning her face up towards his. 'You can if you like. You can do anything you like.' She held his right hand against her breast; her other hand pressed his backside so their groins were locked. 'You like me, don't you?'

Tom was almost paralysed with sheer surprise. And shocked at his own foolishness. And dumbfounded that he hadn't previously realised how Felicity felt about her mother. And kind of proud, both that he understood this was about a daughter and her mother rather than him, *and* wasn't even vaguely aroused at the idea of being seduced by this nubile girl. Very firmly, Tom took both of Felicity's hands and pushed her gently away. 'Felicity, you are a lovely girl and I'm very fond of you. I'm also very sorry not to have realised how hurt you were about your father. It was wrong of me not to take notice, and I will try to be more sensitive about it, with you and Harmony. Perhaps we need to talk about it. But you definitely need to talk to your mother, because maybe you're not taking some things into consideration. You shouldn't have to lay the blame at any one person's door, these things are never caused by just one person. Now, you've just been feeling very hurt and emotional and we can forget about what just happened because it doesn't matter at all and I will never refer to it again. OK?'

Things had not gone according to plan. Felicity had recovered her dignity and with it her anger. Her face was streaked with tears and twisted in rage.

'No, I'm not OK. How dare you push me away? From what I hear, you've not been doing too well recently around here. Maybe you're just too old. You're certainly too old for me. If you think I'd ever let you fuck me then you really are as stupid as you look. You carry on with the old bitch and keep your hands off me. Just fuck right off, d'you hear?' She ran to her room.

Tom suddenly felt sick. He realised he had an enemy.

8

Harry's attempt to lie in a relaxed post-coital embrace with Nicola was unconvincing.

'It's OK,' she said, 'you can go now.'

She had seen through him so accurately, and seemed so determined, that Harry didn't even try to argue. He got up, dressed, and just before leaving approached the bed where Nicola, looking less than proud, was watching him.

'I'm sorry, Nicola. That wasn't – that wasn't fair to you.' She smiled sardonically.

'Fair? Funny word to use. Listen, doc, don't worry about it. I'm fine. More fine than you. Just go now.' Nicola was disappointed that Harry had proved himself to be just like all the others. She had imagined her advances meeting with a gentle refusal, a courteous walk to her home, an embarrassed but kindly brush-off. She had believed Harry to be that rare thing, a good and faithful man, and had been counting on him to be the one who would resist her, and thereby reassure her.

It was now 4 a.m. After leaving Nicola's flat Harry had visited several bars and was more thoroughly inebriated than he had been since his student days. Although he had keys to Adam and Steve's house Harry didn't want to sneak upstairs in this state, couldn't bear facing them over breakfast the next day. He let himself into his department and spent five minutes having an uncomfortable waist-down wash with cold water and liquid soap, dabbing dry with crisp paper towels. He replaced his boxer shorts, entered his office, hung his jacket and trousers behind the door, settled back into his reclining chair and fell into a deep and troubled sleep.

* * *

At 8 a.m. Sophie came in to work. She had taken to arriving early simply because she never slept well and had nowhere better to be. When she saw Harry asleep in his chair, whisky bottle on the floor, surrounded by the miasma which only a body full of booze and misery can produce, she had a sudden flash of inspiration. The date was perfect. She had everything she needed in her bag.

She kneeled in front of Harry, breathing in his smell. He had always smelled good to her – always of himself, never of deodorant or, her pet hate, aftershave. In her experience men wore aftershave only to cover guilt. Harry's avoidance of the stuff, and the fact that even after a jog or game of squash his sweat was clean and appealing, was one of the many assets which would make him, in her eyes, a perfect father for her child.

Gently, Sophie removed Harry's penis from the flap in his boxer shorts. Softly, she began to lick its tip. It started to twitch and grow and Sophie worked quietly, taking more and more of its length into her mouth. Harry groaned but didn't wake. She began to suck, faster now. Sophie was performing the blowjob of her life. All her love for Harry, her desperation at her loneliness and her anticipation of carrying out the master plan in this undreamed-of manner combined, and it was stupendous, she was playing it so expertly you'd half expect his cock to produce music any moment now. Shame he was asleep. Sensing that Harry wasn't far from ejaculating, Sophie carried on her expert oral frottage while reaching in the bag on the floor by her knees and taking out a large syringe. Harry's hips were beginning to move in contrary-motion to Sophie's lips, his occasional moaning had become a rhythmical grunting, until finally he woke, arched upwards and came into Sophie's waiting mouth crying, 'Cressida!' Hungover and confused, he looked down to where Sophie knelt, cheeks bulging. 'Sophie!' She tried a sheepish smile but it was difficult with her mouth full, so took the syringe, spat efficiently into the tube, gathered up her bag and rushed off to the Ladies muttering, 'Sorry about that, Harry.' While Harry put his drained penis away, trying to work out what had just happened, Sophie was on the floor of the disabled toilet cubicle (the only one with enough room to lie down), legs in the air, inserting the syringe as far inside her vagina as it would go and releasing its contents carefully. She lay with her feet up on the handrail for several minutes and then very carefully got up.

When she re-entered the office Harry was sitting at his desk, fully clothed, head in hands. She stood in the doorway, legs crossed. 'Harry. I'm sorry about that. I'm – I saw you there and you looked so sad and – I wanted to – you know, do something nice for you and –'

'But Sophie, I was asleep. You – you – took advantage of me.' He didn't know quite how true this was, so it sounded a bit hysterical.

'No harm done,' said Sophie brightly. 'But I do think I'm feeling a little – under the weather. Do you mind if I go home?' Harry thought she was behaving extremely oddly, and noticed she was walking strangely too – taking tiny steps instead of her usual hip-swinging stroll. What could be the matter with the woman? Feeling embarrassed and ashamed by events of the past twelve hours, he waved Sophie off then turned his mind to Cressida (from where it had never really wandered far) and particularly to how he might feel about bringing up another man's baby. He set off for Adam's house to collect his belongings so that after his morning lectures he could return to his family.

9

'A Sister Mary to see you, doctor. She doesn't have an appointment.' Dr Fisher told the receptionist to let her enter. What could Mary want now?

'Come in, Mary, sit down. Now then, what can I do for you?'

Sister Mary was shaking with anger. She was a proud woman, fiercely defensive of her dignity and her reputation as nobody's fool, which title she no longer deserved.

'Margaret. You told me that you would refer all your patients who request abortions to me –'

'Only those I thought might be talked out of it, Mary –'

'Yes, well, that was the idea. But I thought it odd that there have been so few. And that they have all been so – similar. All educated and intelligent, all already mothers of healthy children, all white –'

'Have they really? What a strange coincidence.'

'It wasn't coincidence. I've realised what you've been doing. You don't want to save the lives of unborn children; you just want a child of your own. You've been trying to practise your very own method of – of *eugenics* –'

'Don't be ridiculous, Mary. You're getting hysterical.'

'But I'm right, aren't I? You wanted me to talk those women out of abortions so that they – one of them – would give you her child? Because – because you've failed to get a man who can do that for you, even though you had the best – the most lovely boy in the school, and made such monstrous demands on him that it was no surprise he was unfaithful, after all you'd put him through over the years and –'

'You're jealous. You're jealous about Jim. Christ, Mary, how long have you been carrying that particular torch? Jim was a loser. He didn't cut the mustard. I've not found a man who could.' Margaret realised there was no point denying her friend's accusations. 'Do you blame me for trying to get a child in the only way open to me? I wasn't lying, I *was* sending them for you to dissuade, I –'

'You were getting me to lie. Running around covering the plaque on the convent door, hiding pictures of the Pope, taking down all the crucifixes, God forgive me, just to convince those women they were seeing a nurse. And then the ones who wouldn't be dissuaded – making me send them back to you so you could – arrange to destroy their babies. I started to think it was odd, that these women were all from such similar backgrounds. I started to look at your records –'

'You had no right to do such a thing! How did you –'

'Never mind about that. There are people who are genuinely sympathetic to what I'm trying to do.' Dr Fisher could guess precisely which of her hatchet-faced receptionists had cooperated with Mary's requests for data. 'And I found that in the last three years, since we've been doing this, in addition to a surprisingly high number of terminations for your patients, there have been two women who were patients of this practice whose babies were adopted. And numerous babies born to single women. Some of them *must* have considered a termination, but none of them got referred to me. So I looked at the details more closely. In almost every case, these women were either not English, first-time mothers or mothers who had a child with a disability. So I worked out what you were doing and what you were making me do to help you. And I'm appalled, Margaret, appalled at how you've treated me. You've probably been gaily sending women off for abortions who really *could* have been dissuaded, but whose babies didn't hold enough currency for you. All because you couldn't find a man to match Jim. I know that's the truth, whatever you say. It's monstrous, there's no other word for it.'

Margaret Fisher wasn't in the mood for this kind of criticism. Her best-laid plans had been scuppered and the last thing she needed was some crazy cleric accusing her of wrongdoing.

'Have you quite finished, Mary? Because I think you should go now, before I call the convent and let them know what you've been up to. Whatever your intentions, and doubtless they've been the best, it wouldn't look good in the papers, would it? Loose cannon Sister Mary puts the fear of God into vulnerable women?'

'You – you bitch!'

'Tsk. And thank you for letting slip your feelings about Jim. I'd never have guessed. It's hilarious to think you were keen on him. We used to laugh about you, you know. Guess what your nickname was? Sister Mary. Prescient, I think the word might be. It was obvious you weren't going to find a man; Jesus, the nearest you were going to get was being a bride of bloody Christ, and he'll have anyone. Now, I shan't be sending anyone else your way, I shall have to employ different tactics but believe me, I will get what I want. You can go now.'

Sister Mary had nothing left to be proud of. Even her work saving the babies had been a farce. And Jim, lovely Jim, whose stolen photo used to form the centre of her adolescent fantasies, Jim had laughed at her. Winded and wounded, she walked out. But she'd be back.

She left Margaret Fisher feeling more than a little guilty. Even though Sister Mary wasn't what you'd call an object of envy, she'd always carried a certain aura of goodness about her. And Jim hadn't laughed at her; in fact he'd always been rather defensive of her, as he was of all easy targets. Mary was right about Jim, too. She, Margaret, had acted foolishly and she was paying for it. Perhaps her scheme had been closer to a kind of madness, a monstrosity, than she had cared to admit. And perhaps it had been easier to be a prey to envy than to come to terms with her own monstrosity, and her own perceived failures. Perhaps, even, Margaret realised, she was going to have to learn to love herself in spite of it all. Now that would be progress.

The next day Cressida received a note that the doctor put through her letterbox: *Please forgive my presumptuousness, foolishness and interference. I have come to realise that my longing for a child has less to do with wanting to be a mother than with wanting what I felt I should have. But it's not a question of 'should' or rights and I shouldn't have treated it in that way. I am sorry to have caused you more distress at what must be a very difficult time in any case. And I wish you all the very best with your life, whatever happens in it. Margaret Fisher*

Cressida knew nothing about Sister Mary's pact with the doctor and considered the note slightly over the top, but assumed it was well meant. She wrote a card in reply saying it's fine, no problem, no harm done, and posted it through the surgery letterbox, thinking that one more person acting unusually didn't make that much difference to what had become a farcical situation. She didn't know the half of it.

10

When Cressida returned home that afternoon, pushing Jemima in the buggy with Ben walking by her side, they all saw Harry's car parked outside.

'Daddy!' shouted Ben, thrilled and throwing himself at the front door. 'Dad, you're back!' Harry opened the door and was struck by this little whirlwind of excitement who was shortly joined by his sister as soon as she'd been released from her pushchair. He held their tiny bodies close to him and closed his eyes in sheer joy. Cressida followed them into the house and put the kettle on.

It was only after bath and bedtimes that they got the chance to talk to each other. Cressida began.

'So why are you back? And under what conditions?'

'Let's not talk about conditions. Please. Except possibly – the human condition.'

'Right, you can stop that right away. Keep your psychobabble to yourself, Harry, for God's sake.'

'I'm sorry, I didn't mean it in any professional sense. Just that talking about "conditions" starts to sound like – like legalese. So please, let's talk to one another as – as ourselves.'

'OK. I'll begin again. Why are you back?'

'Cressida, I've missed you so much these past few days. I don't know why this has happened and I can hardly bear to think about you – with someone else – but it hasn't made me not love you. I think – no, I know – that I still love you. I don't know where that can go, and if you want it, and how long it would take for things to – be good again – but if you wanted to try and thought it might work, well – I would. I would, please. You and the kids mean everything to me, it would take more than jealousy – and believe me, I am jealous, insanely so – to make me throw in the towel –'

'But the baby? Are you saying –'

'Wait. I have something to tell you first. My own confession.'

Cressida's first thought was Sophie. She had always been aware of how Sophie felt about Harry, though she never felt threatened by it, or even disturbed. But it would make sense – Sophie notices Harry's not going home, he's lonely, looking for revenge, they go for a drink, things go on from there. So she asked quietly, 'Sophie?'

'What? Good God, no.' Harry modified this. 'Well, not exactly. I mean – listen. Let me explain.' Deep breath. 'Do you remember me telling you about someone in my tutorial group, a girl, erm, a woman called Nicola?'

'The academic high-flyer who looks like a model? The one on the last Christmas party photo in your office?'

'That's the one. Well –'

'You didn't!'

'I'm afraid so, you see –'

'Harry, you fucked that beautiful woman whom the entire teaching staff spend their spare time drooling over?'

'Well yes, but Cressida, I'm so sorry and – Cressida, what are you doing? I don't understand, why are you *laughing*?'

'Oh Harry, I'm sorry, I didn't mean to laugh, but it's just remarkable, I mean *how*?' Harry's masculine pride was feeling the tiniest bit wounded by his wife's amused reaction to what he thought would be bad news.

'Cressida, it was awful, I just didn't want to – you know – well, I thought I did at first and she's always made it clear she was interested so I thought – right then, what's to stop me now? – but then it just went wrong and I kept thinking about you –'

'You felt guilty?'

'No, not guilty. I just thought about you. Because you're the only woman I want. Because I love you.'

Typical, thought Cressida, a little ungenerously. Harry has adulterous sex with a stunning and desirable woman but it doesn't make him feel better, even at the time. What is this man, a saint?

'Oh Harry. What are we going to do with you? It's not funny – although it is remarkable, I mean, that girl could get anyone she wanted and she seems so – organised and ambitious about everything. I mean, if she'd seduced the head of department I could see it as a possible career move. But she doesn't stand to benefit from having sex with you – apart from in the obvious way, love, of course. I'm surprised, that's all.'

'So you're not jealous?' Harry asked a little plaintively. She considered this carefully and was about to say that no, it didn't make her feel jealous, when she had a sudden mental picture of Harry and Nicola in bed, she saw the places where their flesh merged and their mouths against each other, and she felt a little stab in her chest and her palms pricking.

'Yes. Yes, I am jealous actually. And I think I'll get more jealous the more I think about it.'

'Good. Well, I don't mean good, but if you didn't care much at all that would have been – well, that would have been not good. But that's not all.'

'What do you mean? There was someone else as well? How busy have you been in four days, Harry?'

'It's not exactly like that. But after – after Nicola – well, it was awkward and I didn't stay and I was drunk so didn't want to wake Adam and Steve so rather than go back to theirs I let myself into the office and fell asleep. But then when I woke up, it was – I was – Sophie was –'

'Was what? What was she doing?'

'She'd been – giving me a blowjob.'

'What! In your sleep?'

'Yes, well, I did wake up – at the end – but it was too late by then. And I was – well, perturbed, as you might expect – but then she just spat the – spat it out and went off at great speed. Later she said she'd felt sorry for me and had done it to make me feel better or something, but then she went home for the rest of the day – embarrassed I suppose, I certainly was – and so of course I haven't seen her since.' Harry had been too blearily hungover to see precisely where she spat *it* out otherwise by now he would have worked it out.

'That's extraordinary.'

'Yes. But you do believe me, don't you, Cressida?'

'Oh, I believe you all right. You couldn't make it up, could you?'

'No, I don't suppose I could. But – do you think we might try to make everything work again?'

'For the children?' Cressida spoke in heavy quotation marks to which Harry, in his earnestness, was oblivious.

'For them and for us.'

'I don't know, Harry.'

'Are you still seeing Him?'

'Haven't since – since I told him The News. Well, we met for a drink – and only a drink – a few days ago, but things have become even more complicated. His partner's pregnant again.'

'No! So – do you think he's going to – I mean that you and he are going to –?'

'Unlikely, I'd say. So Harry, it's not an ip dip sky blue thing, I'm not sitting here choosing between two men. I'm just thinking about what's for the best, what can be achieved in these circumstances, how could anything work at the moment. I mean, another man's child, Harry, and maybe a man who will want to see it and whom I wouldn't prevent from seeing it. And with whom I've been having an affair. It's not an easy situation to comprehend, let alone live with.'

'I know. I've thought about that. It might be hard, although you know I like babies. As for the Other Man, well, if I knew for sure that you weren't lovers any longer then that might be something I could cope with. Can't guarantee it. But maybe we could try?'

Cressida was wondering whether she could ever 'just see' Tom and not want to make love with him. She doubted it. But what choice did she have at this moment?

'Let's think about it a bit more, Harry. But in the meantime, stay. Stay with me and the children.'

'Thank you, Cressida.'

'Oh no. Thank you.'

They exchanged brave smiles.

Up in Manchester a frosty atmosphere pervaded the hitherto only repressedly unhappy household of Tom and Nita. Since his run-in with Felicity Tom had been trying to tread carefully, but he still couldn't feign pleasure at the pending new arrival and Nita sensed, for the first time, that not only was her plan of how to keep Tom permanently (maybe even marriage! she had thought) going badly wrong, but both of her daughters were openly hostile towards her. Felicity spent most of her time out of the house going to clubs and parties that Nita felt she really should know more about, and Harmony barely talked. Exhausted with running the house, albeit haphazardly, and dealing with quite severe morning sickness, Nita finally caught up with Felicity when she was coming downstairs for some camomile tea to help her sleep and her daughter was coming up to her room after a night out. Felicity looked a mess; her make-up (too much of it) was smudged and she reeked of cigarettes and beer.

'Felicity, what's the matter?

'Give me a break, Mum, I've just got in from a late party, that's all.'

'I don't mean now. Although I do wish you'd tell me where you were going from time to time. I mean just what's the matter? You don't talk to me, you've hardly spoken two words to Tom in as many days and you and Harm seem – well, seem to be – unhappy. Is something wrong, love?'

It was too tempting. Felicity could divert attention from what she'd actually been up to. She'd been seeing more of Dave the twenty-eight-year-old DJ than was entirely appropriate; only two hours earlier he had taken her outside the nightclub where he worked and bent her over the car park wall for a thrilling, if not very tender, two minutes of lovemaking, after which they shared the cigarette which hadn't left the corner of his mouth during the entire process. It wasn't precisely how Felicity had imagined her first romance but it did, at least, feel like first-degree real life. It was also her chance to dump Tom in it. That would show him. She started to cry a little and her mother prompted her, 'Tell me, love. Tell me what's wrong. I'm worried about you, you know.'

'Oh Mum, I can't.'

'Yes you can, you can tell me anything. Try, love. Come on now, try.'

'Well – it's – it's Tom.' More tears now. 'He – he tried to – he *touched* me.'

'What do you mean? You mean, he tried to – what are you saying, Felicity? What are you saying about Tom?'

'I've just told you – he put his hand on me – on my chest, and tried to kiss me and then said you were out until later so we had plenty of time and – and that it was about time he did it to someone who – whose tits weren't sagging – and –' She trailed off, expecting to fall into her mother's arms. But Nita's reaction was the other kind of grand maternal gesture. She slapped Felicity hard on the cheek.

'Liar. You little liar. Tom would never do that. You little bitch, you're trying to come between us, I've always known you were jealous. Since your useless father left you've been nothing but trouble. I've tried my best with you and Harmony, tried to give you a new family, but no, you just wanted me to be unhappy and *all yours*. How dare you say such things about Tom. I'll not hear that rubbish, do you hear me? I'll not hear it.' She rushed back upstairs, where the rest of the household was waking to what had become her screaming. 'That little bitch!' she shouted as Tom caught her on the landing. 'She's accusing you of touching her up. Little bitch!'

Tom pushed past her and ran downstairs to find Felicity a sobbing little heap in a kitchen chair. Nothing had turned out as it should. By now she should have been wrapped up in her mother's sympathetic embrace being told that she was always her little girl. But that wasn't going to happen. Hearing him approach, she wiped her face with the heel of her hand and controlled her crying. She turned her tear-stained, panda-eyed face, livid with her mother's fingerprints on one side, and smiled at Tom's appalled expression.

'Good job it isn't true, isn't it? Because she wouldn't have believed it. Wouldn't even listen. Anyway, I'm off as soon as I can be. So don't worry, she's all yours. You can have her. And she still doesn't know about what you've really been up to. You're as much as she deserves.'

Harmony came into the kitchen and sat with her sister. She told Tom, 'You can go upstairs to her now. It's OK, I don't hate you. It's not really your fault. But we don't like it here any more.'

These were not his daughters. Although he had tried to be fatherly to them it had been a failure. If he truly loved their mother, if they hadn't heard the rumours about him, if he hadn't

74

put the cuckoos in their nest in quite such a cavalier manner, if he hadn't rowed so openly with Justin for what was nothing more than macho posturing, maybe they wouldn't have needed to fight for her quite so much. And now he was being told, quietly, by a fourteen-year-old girl, that he had won. Won a life with Nita. And he felt more sorry for these two children than he had ever felt for himself, which was a considerable feat of compassion.

'She does love you, you know,' he tried, but it was no use. He and they knew where Nita's loyalties lay and they knew the worth of her love. He retreated, defeated.

11

Sister Mary was in her cell (a perfectly comfortable, plainly-decorated room) at the convent trying to pray but with little success. These days she thought of her attempts to pray as akin to dialling up the internet. With a little patience she could be online in a minute or so and keep the connection open for as long as she liked. Occasionally it took several attempts, which Sister Mary refrained from calling server problems since that sounded a bit impudent but which she was not sufficiently naïve to put down to excess traffic. Few people, she knew, regularly travelled the super highway towards their Creator. But tonight she was well aware that the impediment to connecting was her pride. Her pride had always made obedience rather difficult – poverty and chastity were less problematic – and was sufficiently overweening to allow her to believe that Margaret's proposed baby-saving plan would work due to her own intelligence and attention to detail. Now she felt ashamed at her part in such a shoddy affair, and especially at her own gullibility. So she was back on her high horse. Harry had a point about this reversion to type, didn't he? Anyway, Mary gave up on her attempts to get in touch with the Lord and instead sat on the edge of her single bed and seethed at how foolish she had been made to feel and how successfully Margaret had conned her. That woman should be struck off the Register, at the very least. How could she, Sister Mary, make sure that some punishment was meted out to the doctor without reflecting back upon her? Reluctantly, she had to accept that this was not possible. She had been gagged. Margaret was out there in the world preparing to fulfil her selfish plan at someone else's expense. Was there no justice? Mary thought there should be, even if she had to make it herself.

* * *

Margaret felt so bad about the whole situation with Mary that she did the unthinkable – turned, albeit briefly, to the comfort of religion. Having not attended mass since the age of eighteen, she hadn't a clue where to go for a high-quality confession, so drove around a ten-mile radius and eventually chose an attractive old church well away from the surgery, to avoid bumping into anyone who knew her. During her search she was appalled to see that most of the Catholic churches were either pre-fab huts which looked unlikely to weather the next strong breeze or concrete monstrosities whose modernist stained-glass windows illustrated little more than geometry. But by the time she found an architecturally acceptable church and waited, kneeling in a pew, breathing in the familiar smell of incense and furniture polish, she had regressed a couple of decades and was already feeling that old familiar anticipatory warmth. Her turn for confession arrived.

'Bless me, Father, for I have sinned. It is – twenty-five years since I made my last confession –' She sensed a jerking movement behind the curtain. He was awake then, she noted with relief. Possibly hoping for a murder or at least some petty crime. 'I did wrong to God when I – look, actually Father, I don't really feel it's helpful to just list things. What I'd really like is to explain something to you.' She was surprised when he began to speak – he had an Irish accent, which was far from unusual, but he was evidently a youngish man, with a deep, strong voice.

'Would you like to make a face-to-face confession, my child?'

'What? Good heavens no. I mean – they don't do that nowadays, do they? Good Lord. Sorry. Goodness. Umm, no, no I don't think I could do that. If you don't mind, I'd rather just blather on on my side of the curtain, if it's all right with you.'

'Fair enough,' he sounded amused. 'But it's not actually so terrifying. It can make the experience more *human*.'

'That's precisely what I don't want. Humanity, I mean. You see –' and Margaret launched into her long and detailed explanation of her life plan, its failure, her subsequent attempts to secure a child of her own and her current feelings of guilt, largely concerned with the ill-used Sister Mary. She glossed over precisely how she used to choose the women whose babies Mary would endeavour to save. She realised that in fact what she had seen as her right to have a child could quite possibly mask some distinctly unappealing recessive prejudices, and she wasn't going to tell a strange man about those, priest or no. When she had finished the priest asked a surprising question.

'Wouldn't it have been easier to find another man with whom you could produce a child?'

'Of course it would. But I never seemed able to – after my first boyfriend, Jim, after we split up I think I felt, oh, lots of things including betrayed, desperate, despairing – you can imagine – and I never really got over that. So men seemed to be quite scared of me, they seemed to sense those things, which is odd really, since men are supposed to be emotionally illiterate, aren't they? Oh, I'm sorry, I don't mean that the way it sounded, I mean less emotionally literate than women. You know. But they saw through me. And I didn't. But I was still utterly determined to find a perfect mate and marry him, I didn't want to just – you know – just use a man to produce a child. And after a while, all that side of things – seemed to – well, to dry up.' She was also glossing over the velvet bag in her knicker drawer, but who can blame her for that small omission?

'And yet, considering the amount of anguish your interference in several women's lives has caused, perhaps using a man to conceive a child would have been the lesser of two evils? Hmm?'

Times have moved on, thought Margaret, were priests really supposed to say things like that? Although, she conceded, he had a point.

'I suppose so. But I thought it was always wrong to – well, you know, extra-marital sex and so on.'

'Ah, *wrong*. Not a helpful word, my child. Where would life lead us if we spent all our time looking round the corner for what might be wrong? There are no absolutes. It is perfectly possible to behave in a way which may once have been referred to as sinful for the very best of reasons.'

'Really?' Margaret was fascinated. This young man was most persuasive, obviously intelligent, and his lovely Dublin accent was terribly attractive. She was enjoying a stream of wicked thoughts which she really ought to confess but wasn't about to, and tried to remember if confession had ever been this much fun in the past.

Vague memories of crushes on young parish priests or visiting missionaries began to stir. Those asexual men in long black dresses whose very unavailability caused whole pews full of schoolgirls to cross their legs tightly on Holy Days of Obligation. It all came flooding back to her. 'But as a priest, surely, you are supposed to show people the one true way, you can't have them wimbling around all over the spiritual shop?' she asked, lapsing into the animated colloquial speech of herself as a young woman.

'As a priest, I have to think – what will make this woman happy and fulfilled? What does she need which is missing in her life?' His voice was very low now, his mouth evidently close up against the grille as he asked, 'What can I give her?' Margaret swallowed audibly.

'And what do you think – what do you think you can give me?' she whispered. In answer the curtain was drawn back. She got off the kneeler, which swung back against the side of the enclosed confessional box like a gate. It was almost pitch black as she felt the priest's hands take hers and lead her carefully to where he was sitting. He lifted his cassock and put Margaret's hand around what even she recognised as a prodigious erection. She gasped quietly then shut her eyes tightly and allowed the priest to position her; with remarkable deftness he pulled down her tights and knickers to her ankles then, moving her closer, placed the front two legs of the chair over her underwear and slowly pulled her down on to him. Close to fainting, she orgasmed as soon as he entered her and then proceeded to enjoy an entire series as they rocked silently to and fro. He gripped the seat of the chair to minimise the sound of wooden legs grinding on flagstone, she bit his shoulder to prevent herself from crying out, and finally he pulled her down with both hands so firmly, and was inside her so deeply, that she felt as though her diaphragm was being stretched. He came with a shudder. They remained clinging to one another in the dark. Margaret wanted to fall asleep on his lap. But the priest moved her firmly up and off, turned her around and guided her gently back into her side of the confessional, closed the kneeler and replaced the curtain. Only then did she open her eyes and become accustomed to the half-light.

'What is your name, my child?' asked the voice behind the curtain.

'Margaret,' she whispered.

'God be with you, Margaret,' he said, without irony, as she pulled up her underwear, took a deep breath and left the confessional, walking past a small group of waiting penitents, mostly women. So, she was thinking while she made her slightly wobbly way up the aisle, it really does make one feel better. I feel totally – shriven. And he didn't even give me a penance.

That's what she thought.

12

Felicity and Harmony were leaving home. Justin had been getting his act together; holding down a good job. He was even engaged – to Kyria, a thirty-six-year-old textiles artist whose chaotic family – Irish on her mother's side, Maori on her father's – seemed rich and cheerful in contrast to his own small and dysfunctional family group. When he arrived for his annual June visit – this time accompanied by Kyria – he announced that he was considering a return to the UK. The girls' clamour to move in with him clinched it and Kyria was happy with the idea. She knew how much he missed his girls and as her own first marriage had ended after two traumatic miscarriages followed by a prognosis that she would not conceive again, she was keen for him to fulfil his paternal duties with the kids he already had. His firm had offered him a lucrative transfer to the north-west of England and Kyria could work anywhere, so it was decided. The girls would live in their rented cottage in the countryside a few miles from Nita's house, as originally planned, and then after their holiday they would remain there with Kyria while Justin returned to New Zealand to make arrangements for the move. All of these plans were agreed with an extraordinary level of calm. Felicity explained to her father that she and Harmony felt rather in the way now that their mother was about to have Tom's second child and they thought it would be better all round if they didn't live there any longer. Besides, her unsuitable boyfriend had dumped her for someone younger so there was nothing at all to keep her at home. Harmony, mean-while, had worked out that the attention she craved could only be forthcoming from her dad. Both girls hit it off with Kyria, whom they had not previously met, instantly. After discussion about schools and exams, the whole plan was agreed. The girls wanted the new arrangement to begin right away – to get out from under their mother's feet, they explained, since she had enough to cope with during this rather difficult pregnancy. So off they went.

Nita was distraught. Whatever her failings, and she had undoubtedly failed her daughters in ways too numerous to count, she didn't want them gone from her. Her lovely girls. They all used to be so happy. As she got used to the idea though, she began to cheer up a little – which she put down to good karma but was really her hormones kicking in. She and the girls hadn't got on well for a while, perhaps this would ease their relationships. And now she and Tom and Katie could wait for the new arrival just like – and she couldn't help letting this slip into her mind – just like a proper family. Tom, surely, would be pleased to have her and Katie to himself and it might make him look forward to the new baby.

But Tom was stunned by what had happened, and by how responsible he felt about it. Unlike Nita, he had reached an understanding about how her daughters had felt over the past few years and he was guilty for his part in it. Especially his attitude towards Justin, who had been dignified and helpful, never pointing the finger of criticism at either Nita or Tom, and who obviously loved his daughters as much as he, Tom, loved his Katie. He wouldn't forget the look on all their faces when they finally walked away. They hugged one another, overjoyed, before getting in the car where Kyria waited in the driver's seat. And they didn't look back once. Tom and Justin even had a brief conversation alone – the first since their blazing row three years before – in which Tom tried to convey his hopes that the girls would be happy and his regrets that he hadn't dealt with their unhappiness better. Justin simply said, 'What could you do? How could you know my girls? Do you think someone else could feel for your Katie like you do? Would you like to think of another man looking after your baby? And when she's ten, twelve, sixteen, she'll still be your baby, believe me. I'm past laying the blame, there's just no point. But having my girls back with me is the best thing that could happen to me. Kyria understands that, you know. And that means she's the second best thing that could ever happen to me. For the first time since I left here I'm a happy man. And I don't think you are, Tom. So don't beat yourself up about my children; take good care of your own.'

Neither of them mentioned Nita. Tom wondered if perhaps he should try to defend her, though against what he wasn't sure, but decided not to. It would sound ridiculous for him to tell this man – who had known her more than seven times as long as Tom had known her – any sort of home truths about Nita. Justin was right, Tom saw, he was indeed a happy man. A contented man. Kyria was a delightful, relaxed presence who behaved easily and naturally on every occasion. His daughters longed to be with him. Tom realised he was jealous of Justin.

As he, Nita and Katie returned to the house after waving off the happy party, Tom saw that life was unlikely to improve significantly in the near future. While he believed he had made peace with Felicity, she had left something to remember her by in any case. A note was propped up against the teapot on the kitchen table, with 'Mum' written on it in Felicity's handwriting.

'Oh look, bless her, I thought she was a bit quiet saying goodbye. She must have found it difficult after – after everything. But she's left me a note.' As Nita opened the envelope Tom took Katie into the living room to settle her in her playpen. He was fairly sure about what kind of information the note contained and was getting Katie out of the firing line. But no shocked exclamations emerged; Nita didn't demand he come at once. Maybe Fliss had said goodbye with good grace. Tom walked casually into the kitchen half expecting Nita to be washing up or making dinner but found her, much as he had found Felicity only two weeks before, a sobbing heap in her chair. The note was specific; giving names, times and stating evidence. It also listed all the people who knew. Of course, it wasn't exhaustive – nobody had been as busy as Tom – and there was no mention of Cressida, but it was bad enough. After a brief dalliance with the notion of denial Tom realised he might as well have been caught *in flagrante* and would have to own up. Nita just looked up at him, waved the note weakly in his direction and asked, 'Why, Tom? Why? With all these women. I know two of them, you've brought them into this house, they've held our Katie. How could you do that? Why have you done this?' Since it was a question he had never asked himself, Tom was at a loss to explain.

'Look, Nita, I know it's bad, but none of it meant anything. None of them were – important – to me. I didn't *love* any of them.'

'If you'd loved me, you wouldn't have done it.'

'I don't think that necessarily follows. Look, I realise it's – painful – for you, and I apologise, I really do. But we have very different attitudes towards sex, don't we?'

'Do we? I don't know. We've never discussed it, have we? You knew I'd only ever been with Justin and I knew not to ask any questions. I thought our attitude to sex was the same – it's something we do with each other because we love each other.'

'That's true, Nita. That's right.'

'Then why do you do it with other women?'

'Because sex and love aren't the same thing. And these women – some of them are good friends I've known for years and –'

Nita's usually warm Manchester accent hardened into a harsh staccato. 'Friends! Do you have to fuck your friends? Don't you see, Tom, friends are by definition the people you *don't* sleep with?'

'By your definition, Nita. Not mine. Sex can mean everything to me or it can mean nothing. Sometimes I just wanted to – fuck someone. Not to hurt you – it has nothing whatsoever to do with you and is no threat to you or to our life, don't you see?'

'Are you completely fucking stupid? You think that this isn't a threat?' She waved the paper in his face.

'That might be. But the information it contains was unknown to you, couldn't hurt you, had no impact on you. Until Felicity decided she wanted you to know.'

'My own daughter. My own daughter and her friends talking about you in the playground. Humiliation, that's what it is. And what about our child – our children?'

'I have never done anything which might hurt them. I am devoted to Katie and will be devoted to this new baby. Nita, you know how I feel about Katie.'

'Do you think it will be good for her to hear what her father was like? How he treated her mother? What he thought about women?'

'For Christ's sake, Nita, I haven't assaulted anyone. You make it sound like I'm a bloody rapist. And I can't live my life in a way that I think will make good reading for my daughter when she's old enough to understand. My sex life is my business, nobody else's.'

'But my sex life has been your business and nobody else's,' wailed Nita.

'I know, pet, but that's your choice. Listen, we've never discussed this, have we? We've both made assumptions about each other.' Tom realised a possible way out of this. 'And take a look at those dates. When is the last one?'

Nita scanned the list. 'Almost two years ago.'

'Precisely. Now what does that tell you?'

'You've – stopped?'

'Of course I have. I just had a wild time when we were expecting Katie, I guess I was scared of being trapped and all that sort of stuff –'

'And after she was born.' Nita was working out the dates and wasn't going to be fobbed off so easily.

'There's no excuse, and I'm truly sorry that you're hurt, but believe me, there's no need to worry. None of it means anything to me. Not one person on that list means anything to me.'

Nita wanted so much to believe him, and on this point he did sound utterly convincing. On this point he really was telling the truth. She looked at the list again. Then she scrunched it into a ball and threw it in the bin. It would take all her powers of forgetfulness, but she would do it.

'Tell me you love me, Tom.'

'Honey, of course I love you. More than anything. You know I do.'

'Only me?'

'Only you, pet. Nobody but you.'

'And you won't ever –'

'Never again. I don't want anybody else.'

A cock might just as well have crowed at this point, as Tom knew only too well, and it wouldn't have been his own. But to be thrown out by Nita now would certainly mean the loss of his children and he did what had to be done, including leading Nita by the hand upstairs and making tender love to her while Katie played happily downstairs. Unlike Harry, Tom didn't usually find this too difficult. In fact, if he knew about Harry's problems he would hoot with derision. Any man, surely, could convincingly fuck a reasonably attractive woman whatever the circumstances, provided he wasn't too addled by drink, though sometimes that actually helped. But this time he found the entire experience repulsive. He longed for Cressida's touch so much that he too climaxed with her name on his lips. But that's where it stayed. Tom's mouth was, by necessity, closed.

Had Nita questioned him more specifically about his sexual habits, he would probably have tried to define himself as a feminist, or as near to a feminist as a man can get. Women were equals, in value and in capabilities, and he enjoyed their company. Particularly when they had no clothes on. He would even describe his attention to his lovers' sexual pleasure as a mark of his respect for their gender and their equal right to satisfaction. However, it was probably more a mark of his self-respect; Tom knew that for a man to get a reputation as a boorish womaniser was undesirable, but as a great lover – well, that's an unbeatable accolade. In any case, the love you make is probably round about equal to the love you take, so if she's having a good time it's more than likely he is. As for any emotional content – he truly believed that the large number of female friends who had readily become lovers and might, until the last couple of years, have continued to be occasional bedfellows, all felt as detached about it as he did. Maybe one or two of them did. Amongst the others – not always intelligent but rarely stupid, confident, often high achievers – some thought his occasional returns were a sign of great and uncontrollable passion and were immensely flattered; some were utterly unaware of the existence of other lovers in his life at all (they didn't know the rules) and yet others were simply in love with him and found it difficult to resist the charm he exuded every time he returned. Even now, there were at least half a dozen women who would gladly welcome him back into their lives in the false hope that he might stay this time. Because, each of them told herself, nobody could make love to her with that fervour and care who wasn't in love with her. Why bother? Why indeed? Tom was deluded and deluding in his attitude to sex; it represented something so important about himself that there hadn't really been room for anyone else in it. Each conquest was approached with the energy and obsessiveness of a man in love; was it surprising that the objects of his affection sensed the strength of his feeling and each jumped to the apparently obvious conclusion that it was aimed at her? And was it any less surprising that the arrival of Cressida turned his world on its head and left him reeling?

Because he was a man who read books, on the rare occasions he wondered at all about his behaviour the word that sprang to his waiting mind was *anima*. While humans should obviously control some of their urges – to murder, for example, or to rape, or any other form of violence – surely it's positively unhealthy to curb the sexual urge? And if a certain moral relativity can be applied (what the eye don't see . . .) then surely any man in his right mind will take what sexual opportunities life offers him. Perhaps Tom spent so much time in Apollonian pursuits – his writing was undeniably classy – that his personal life was bound to verge on the Dionysian. He would like that take on it. So Tom never thought about his sexual past in terms of the great difficulty he had in saying goodbye. Ever. To anyone. Or that the fact he never said a final goodbye was his way of leaving a multitude of doors open for his re-entry at some later, lonely date.

This is not to suggest that Tom was cruelly deceiving and seducing hundreds of poor innocents. On the whole, they were women who were old enough to know better – his track record on age was not too bad; certainly no actual minors. He did appreciate good conversation, at least. And he was occasionally aware that somewhere, in his pursuit of older women, was the assumption that they would not become pregnant too easily or willingly. Although Nita had disproved that theory pretty conclusively – and many of them had slept with him in full knowledge that he was about to become, or already was, a father. However, even here Tom did a little truth-turning to his advantage: Cressida remembered talking to him about his domestic situation shortly before they became lovers. She knew about his baby daughter but had heard little or nothing about the mother, and in fact the word at the office was that it was someone he barely knew, some brief fling which had gone badly wrong.

'Are you with the mother?' she had asked him.

'Sort of.'

'What does that mean?'

'Well, we're both bringing up Katie. And I spend most of my time there.'

'So you mean you are together?'

'I suppose so.'

Had his first answer been less vague, it's possible Cressida's shutters would have come up so far that Tom's inevitable pursuit might have ended in failure. And in some strange way, Tom's response *was* honest, but honesty *per se* had never held much value for him and he simply answered the question in a way that was supposed to leave the door a little open. Which of course it did. For Tom, truth operated on a kind of stock exchange; investments could go down as well as up. Truth may be a valuable commodity one day and a complete liability the next, you needed to buy and sell it at the right time.

Even when he realised that the way he felt about Cressida didn't fit into the Lust plus Friendship equation which had applied to almost all of his previous relationships (sometimes it was just Lust) Tom didn't re-examine his history. He didn't want to go there. He was beginning to suspect that as well as being rather more deceitful than he had admitted (just because something isn't said doesn't mean it can't be assumed. He might not think that regularly sleeping with a woman and saying he loved her equalled any kind of commitment to fidelity, but he did realise that it wasn't a wholly unreasonable assumption for someone to make) he had actually been in some ways exploitative. These bright modern women couldn't ask if his intentions were honourable, they all used birth control effectively and for them to wait too long before going to bed with him suggested either a chronic STD, an unhealthy religious obsession or, worst of all, frigidity. Tom was so wholeheartedly committed to the art of lovemaking that even if they embarked upon it with a sensible (cynical) attitude, by the end of it they were convinced there must be more to it; it just wasn't like any casual sex they'd had before. So the late twentieth century had been something of a brave new world for a man like Tom, and just unfortunate for the ladies that there weren't many Harrys around.

Although Cressida had Harry and still fell for Tom. Ah yes, but it was different with Cressida.

Nita did some more sums and saw clearly what she must do. After forcing Tom to swear eternal fidelity (if truth held any sway with him he'd have crossed his fingers, but it didn't so he did it with a sincere expression and holding her hands) she suggested they 'start again'. They would be a proper family. Tom saw no choice but to concede. He counted himself lucky that she didn't know about the one woman who had actually posed a threat to her, or the baby she was expecting. But he was going to have to see Cressida again before he went out of his mind.

13

Having Harry back in the house was distinctly odd for Cressida. She was a more natural soul-searcher than Tom but her motivations and impulses seemed so confusing that she found few, if any, answers. While she still felt guilty about her adultery, she didn't actually find the guilt compounded by her pregnancy. And although she still couldn't decide what, precisely, her feelings for Harry were, she was finding it terribly comforting that he was around. The kids were much happier, she was back at work, nobody else had offered to take her baby away at birth, so all in all she was approaching serenity. Except for her thoughts about Tom. She was still driven wild at the thought of him and knew that they had to meet soon for what might be their final conversation. This thought drove her even more wild. What could they possibly do?

Returning to work plonked her rudely back into the outside world. The office offered a strange mixture of escapism – by devoting time and thought to her work she had less time to fret – and exposure – in a couple of months' time her secret would be an obvious fact and she wasn't sure how she was going to play it. So much depended on Tom, and on Harry, and on the future they decided between them.

Harry had already broached the subject of what the new baby would be called.

'Do you want it to have its father's name?' he had asked.

'Haven't thought about it.'

'Or your name?'

'That might make more sense. Although it wouldn't be very good in terms of family togetherness.'

'Cressida, I don't mind if you want it to have my name, like Jem and Ben. Especially if – well, if I sort of am going to be its father.'

'Harry, you're talking almost as if you're looking forward to it!'

'Well, it's interesting, you know. I've noticed since coming back that I sometimes forget it's not mine. Because we were – well, you know, we were planning a third and so I was sort of expecting the news and then the news came but was rather different from what I was expecting and yet – and yet, it isn't. It's the same piece of news. More or less. I'm just bothered about you being well and happy now.'

'You really are a fucking saint, aren't you? I don't believe you can sit there and say that.'

'I know. I don't believe it myself sometimes. And I don't feel in the slightest bit saintly. But it really does feel sort of similar to the other times. Because it's you, I suppose. By the way – I was wondering – well, had you told Him that you and I were planning to have another?'

'Yes. I'm sorry if that sounds awful, Harry, I suppose it is. It really is only our business. But it – well, it sort of had to come out really. I mean, it affected . . .'

'Hmm, yes, I can see that it might. But how were you going to be sure it was mine anyway?'

'By making sure I only – slept with you while we tried. I know, it sounds awful now, I don't know how we – I – could have thought it was a good idea. We couldn't be final about it, you see. So I was going to get pregnant and then we hadn't really decided what we would do but I suppose we would have carried on. After it was born. Christ. It sounds *despicable*. And so arrogant. How could we possibly think . . .'

'But you did sleep with him again.'

'Yes, because I knew I wasn't pregnant and then you went on that trip and we were already finding it difficult to cope –'

'Jesus, Cressida, it must have been all of two months without.'

'It just seemed very final, so the opportunity arose and we took it. And I must have had a freakishly long cycle, though how I've no idea.'

'Cressida, you are sure, aren't you, that it's not mine? I mean, might you not really have had a period – remember, you had a tiny bleed for the first two months with Ben?'

'Sorry Harry, I'm sure. It was definitely a period, nothing light about it. And I actually did a test just to check. I know it's not much consolation, love, but if I had been pregnant I really wouldn't have – seen him again.'

'In some small way I suppose that is a kind of comfort. But look, this thing with names and everything. And just – announcing it to people. How are we going to play it? It may sound selfish but I'm not at all keen on everyone knowing it's not mine. If we're going to bring it up I'd rather they think it was mine.'

'I'm not going to tell the child lies, Harry.'

'I'm not suggesting that. And some people will have to know the truth. But maybe we can keep it from being general knowledge?'

'Maybe. We'll have to work all that stuff out.'

'And actually, while we're on the subject – I'd rather we knew what was going to happen by the time it starts showing, because I'm not keen on everyone knowing you're expecting Tom bloody Webster's baby and that I'm hanging on just in case you decide to let me help you bring it up. Sorry.'

'No need to be sorry. I realise that. I need to talk to Tom, don't I?'

Cressida was waiting for him at the station. As soon as they caught sight of one another they knew what was going to happen and had no intention of stopping it. Kissing hard and quickly, they walked into hotel land around the corner, booked a room in the first place they came to and went straight to bed. If clichés were ever appropriate, it was here. For both of them, it was like coming home. They even rallied enough to play their favourite lovers' game of Innocently Rude Quotations (Cressida won with a line from *Alice* – 'eat me').

So our lovers were reunited. Temporarily. Hours later they emerged from the hotel and went to a bar. The time had come to speak, fully clothed and sensibly. The time had come for them both to put their cards on the table.

'Tom, I think about you all the time. I only want to make love with you. I don't know what I'd do without you.'

'I feel the same, you know I do.'

'So. What do we do about it?'

'Honey, what can we do about it? The non-negotiables – the kids – are still there. Even more of them than before.'

'But what about our child? What are you going to do about that?'

'I've told you already, I take full responsibility, I'll go to the birth, I'll contribute financially, I'll visit whenever I can . . .'

'Even when I'm still with Harry? How will that work?'

'Are you definitely going to stay with him then?'

'Funnily enough, that's exactly what he asks about you. And I've had to tell him I don't know, that we need to talk about it, that we haven't decided what's going to happen.'

'Ah.'

'Meaning?'

'Well, you just make it sound as though I've suggested there may be a change of plan and there simply can't be. Nita's utterly alone now – Fliss and Harmony have gone to live with their dad – I'll explain about all that later. It's been hell – and she is, after all, going to have my second baby. And there is still Katie.'

'You talk as though Ben and Jemmy don't exist. Do you have to keep reminding me about this?'

'Yes I do, because you're talking as if you and I have got a choice in this, and we still haven't.'

'I have lots of choices. What if I said I didn't want you to have anything to do with this baby? That I wouldn't acknowledge you as the father?'

'I'd be hurt. Very hurt. Christ, Cressida, a baby with you is the thing I've wanted most since we started. Not like this, but still, a baby with you. Don't you think I want to be a father to it?'

'But if you think that being with me would make you less of a father to Katie, how does that work? How can you be a father if you're not there? Isn't that what you're always saying? Isn't that why you'll never, ever be with me? Or is it just your excuse for that?'

'It's not a bloody excuse and you know it. Katie's already here. She'll soon have a brother or sister. That's two children. Then there are your two. They already have a father. How can it possibly work? Sweetheart, don't cry, please.'

'There must be a way. There must be something we can do. I can't bear this.'

'It will – settle. I can't bear the idea of you not being in my life, you know that. And I swear, I'll do my best, I truly will. I just can't leave Nita.'

'What?' Cressida pounced. 'That's the first time you've said it like that. Not Katie. Not "my family". But Nita? The woman you swear you don't love?'

'I don't love her like I love you. But I have some – affection for her. She's the mother of my child. Children.'

'Her ex-husband doesn't seem to feel the same way.'

'I'm not getting into comparative discussions. I just have some responsibilities towards her as well as the kids.' Tom was convinced that Nita needed him for more than simply bankrolling her family; he was sure that without his presence she – and therefore his children's wellbeing – would begin to fall apart. Holding Nita up had become part of the package for him.

'It's a bit fucking late to start having those sort of compunctions, isn't it?'

'Possibly, but there you are. I can't help that. I haven't got a magic wand, because if I had, believe me, I'd wave it to go back in time by – ooh, about seven years, and we'd meet and fall in love and I'd propose on the spot and we'd spend the next twenty years fucking like rabbits and making dozens of babies together. Just ours. But I haven't got a wand. And therefore I haven't got a hope.'

'Seven years ago? I was already married to Harry by then.'

'You'd have left him for me.'

'I don't know if that's true, Tom.'

'So if it's not true, what have we been doing? What have we just done?'

'I'm not absolutely sure. Listen. We are going to have to stop sleeping together. Aren't we?'

'I suppose so.'

'So that was the last time, OK?'

'OK.'

'The last time ever in our entire lives. Do you understand?'

'How can we possibly say that –'

'The last time. Agreed?'

Tom waited, sighed, then said, 'Agreed. But Cressida –'

'No buts. Listen to me. I am going to go back to Harry. I am not going to tell him what we did today. I am going to say we agreed that you would visit the baby on a regular basis but that our relationship is over and I want him and me to have a go at putting our marriage back together.'

'Is that what you want?'

'I can't have you, Tom. You've made that clear. And – don't take offence – Harry is a better bet in every respect. If I'm not sleeping with you, time and biology will eventually win and I'm sure that Harry and I can make it all work – sex as well – if we want it to. Tom, I used to be so much in love with him. And everything between us was so good.'

'Better than us?'

'Don't ask tasteless questions. We're not intimate any more, Tom. We have no lovers' rights. We are the biological parents of this child that's going to be born. That's all.'

The words had so frequently formed themselves within Cressida's head in the past few days, one of the many fantasy conversations she imagined in detail, that it was hard to believe she'd actually said them. Both she and Tom had mentally rehearsed The Parting many times over, but these circumstances were never part of the scenario. Having to part but still having a child seemed like a disastrous combination of denial and responsibility. Cressida would cope with it – that's why she was the one who had to say it – but for Tom it was too unnatural to comprehend. He understood that Cressida was being brutal because she needed to be but still couldn't quite believe that she meant it. She was regaining her self-respect, letting Tom know that if they weren't going to be together they were no longer lovers, she would not be duplicitous for a moment more if the rewards of duplicity were insufficient. Sadly, regaining her self-respect felt a bit like losing far too many other important things, but she couldn't afford to think about that right now.

'Goodbye, Tom.' He didn't answer. 'Tom!'

'Right. Goodbye, Cressida.'

'I'll be in touch in a few weeks. After the scan, probably.'

'Right.' The scan. A photograph of their baby. He remembered seeing Katie as a twelve-week foetus; she looked like a baby and moved, regally, like a seahorse. He fell in love with her just for being alive. 'The scan – can I . . . ?'

'No. I don't think that would be appropriate.'

'I can't look at your belly any more, is that what you mean?'

'Not just my belly, Tom. You heard what I said.'

'But the birth, I must be there for –'

'You are joking? Shall I have you and Harry there together? You can take it in turns with the camcorder.'

Another man was going to see the baby he and Cressida had made before he did. Another man would see his baby put to his lover's breast before he did. Tom was overwhelmed by an unfamiliar wave of nauseous, prickling, heart-stopping jealousy. Cressida saw it, paused, wondered for a moment whether he was about to have a change of heart, then sensed him control himself. She almost cried but was getting better and better at not crying. 'In any case, Nita's due around the same time, isn't she? You'll be busy enough.'

'Right. I suppose so. Well – hope it's all – OK.'

'Yes. Goodbye, again.'

'Goodbye.'

Watching Cressida walk away, with the air of a woman who would not turn back, Tom was aware that he might just have made the greatest mistake of his life. But he was a stubborn man, not used to either changing his mind or pleading, and put the thought away with all the other difficult ones, then left for the Manchester train.

14

Sister Mary's repeated attempts to 'get online' to God over the past fortnight had failed utterly, which only fuelled her sense of being alone in the world – along with her growing impression that if justice was to be done it was she who would have to deliver it. Unsure of exactly what she was going to do, but with a bag packed ready for anything (she thought) she lay in wait for Margaret amongst the dense shrubbery which shielded the doctor's house from public view. Stalking someone who worked regular hours and had no social life should have been an easy matter; surgery would be over by now and Margaret was due home any moment. Three hours later the nun was still waiting. Having already nodded off once, and feeling increasingly damp, Sister Mary admitted defeat and left the scene feeling dejected and somehow less set on revenge than when she first camped down in the privet.

Instead of returning home after work, Dr Fisher had made a return visit to church with an even more specific agenda than last time. That morning she had opened her diary at the surgery and noticed the little red asterisk which appeared every twenty-six days and denoted the first day of her pleasingly regular menstrual cycle. She realised that her familiar pre-menstrual symptoms had not emerged over the past few days. After morning surgery she took a urine sample, dipped in a test stick, looked pointedly at the wall for the requisite two minutes and then glanced back at the incontrovertible evidence of her pregnancy. Getting her house visits over with as quickly as possible, she had sat in the park near her home and grappled with the situation for an hour. Half an hour in, her mental calculations and deep anxieties were submerged by an unfamiliar but overwhelming sensation that she took several minutes to identify. Then it came to her. It was joy.

She was overjoyed. And with her joy came an accompanying gift of tears, which dropped heavily on to her lap and made passers-by stare, not bothering her in the slightest. Thirty minutes of cathartic weeping left her feeling physically weaker than she ever remembered feeling, but so emotionally powerful that she knew she could fly if she only thought about it for long enough.

Quite why she needed to inform the priest of his impending paternity was not clear, but she was determined. Margaret composed herself, tidied her face and hair, prepared the list of things she was not going to say and the (much longer) list of comforting assurances she would make, largely to do with money, i.e. the fact she was not demanding any. In truth, she wanted the priest to know because she had nobody else to tell and the news was too exciting to keep locked up. She also wanted to see how her baby might look.

Approaching the pews by the altar, where a scattering of sinners waited their turns, Margaret asked the man nearest the back which priest was hearing confession.

'It's Fr O'Donnell tonight, my dear.' That must be him, but she needed to check.

'Is he – quite a young man?'

'Ach no, dear, he's the parish priest and he must be seventy if he's a day.' Margaret felt bitterly disappointed that she might not be able to see him that day, but at least she could find out his name and come when he was next due to hear confession, or even arrange a meeting before that.

'There is a younger priest, isn't there? He heard confession about a fortnight ago, he had an Irish accent and –'

'Ah.' The man's expression was sombre. 'Ah yes, we did have a young chap to help out while Fr O'Donnell was in hospital.' He lowered his voice, 'Prostate, you know? Terrible business.' Margaret nodded sympathetically. 'But he's left now, he was only here for two months. To be honest with you, my dear, he left under a bit of a cloud.'

'Oh?' Margaret's heart was beating hard enough to choke her.

'Aye. I don't like to spread rumours but it seems that he was – well, y'know – quite a one for the ladies. So it seems. Quite a one for quite a lot of ladies, if you know what I mean.' Margaret felt only a little disconcerted – what did she expect, after all? She wasn't planning on proposing marriage, simply finding out a little more about him. Her joy was so unalloyed that a small unpalatable truth wasn't going to upset her. Besides, now she was curious.

'Oh dear. How do you know that?'

Her informant was animated now, there was a twinkle in his eye as he explained, 'Well, the story goes that he was actually having – *goings-on* – right in the confessional! That he would talk the ladies into letting him "help" them or some such tale and then – *take advantage*.' Margaret's memory gave her heart a vivid jolt, which caused a corresponding pang between her thighs, and she had to control what can only be described as a smirk and replace it with a look of shocked concern.

'How did it – come to light?' she asked.

'Ach, it was a terrible thing.' The old chap shook his head with great relish. 'He was "hearing the confession", shall we say, of a certain lady of the parish who had been getting more and more devout ever since he arrived – I tell you, lady, you used to get a handful of folk coming in of an evening, but shortly after he arrived all the front pews would be full of women, we should have guessed something was up; thought it was something to do with the Easter cycle but it was more a question of sap rising I'd say – anyway, this lady – once they'd done the business and she was about to go he gave her his blessing – but got her name wrong!'

'Oh dear, so then she knew she wasn't the only one – but then why would she tell –'

'She knew all right, but it gets better. I mean worse. You see, the reason he'd got the name wrong was because she sounded exactly like – oh, and I expect she *felt*, heh heh – exactly like her sister.'

'They were twins?'

'Oh, better than that, better than that, m'dear. He realises his mistake and corrects himself, or so he thinks. But that's the name of her *other* sister.'

'Triplets?'

'Precisely so. But he'd never seen 'em together; in fact probably never *saw* them at all. So he must have been confused something awful. And the lady is so mortified and enraged that the priest has been dandling all three of 'em that she belts out of the confessional, pulling her knickers up as she goes, so I've been told, though I had the great misfortune to miss the spectacle, and screams blue murder at her sisters who are sitting there nice as pie waiting for their turn at the "confessional". When they twig what's been going on they run in and drag the poor chap out of there, frog-marched him up the aisle they did, and by the time they were in the car park they'd been joined by other members of the fanclub who were similarly deceived.'

'What did they do to him?'

'Fortunately for him the menfolk got him out of there before they realised what the women were telling them, otherwise they'd have all swung for him. He locked himself in the presbytery and called the police who came and broke up the mob. The next day he was gone.'

Margaret imagined herself telling her child this story and still couldn't help feeling buoyant. She was determined to track this man down and tell him the news face to face, if only to demonstrate that she was not like the ladies of the parish and that there were no hard feelings. What passed between them was of no matter to her, their wordless tryst gave her the thing she wanted most and she couldn't help but feel that God had moved in a mysterious way.

'What a story!' she exclaimed. 'Where has he gone now?'

'Oh, back to Ireland I believe. They'll probably stick him in a bog parish and leave him to rot, or send him overseas. A shame really, he was a bright young man. But you can't behave like that now, can you?'

'Certainly not! Well, thank you for telling me the story, Mr –?'

'ó Ceallacháin, Padraig ó Ceallacháin.'

'Thank you, Padraig. And what did you say the name of the wayward young priest was?'

'Oh, that was another problem – nobody could ever say his name, I don't think I can even remember it, you know.'

'But he only left a little while ago! And surely, an Irish name . . .'

'Ach, he was Irish all right – brought up in Ireland anyway – but his folks weren't Irish, that's for sure. Now wait a minute, it'll come to me, Un-something. Uncomber. Something like that.'

'That's unusual. Where's that name from?'

'No idea, lady. Like I say, I could never pronounce it and nor could my Niamh. Funny spelling, it was. Our Aoife – that's our oldest granddaughter, you know – she could say it beautiful. Or was that little Siobhan? The youngsters can remember that sort of thing, they teach them at school I wouldn't be surprised. Hold on a mo, it'll be on the parish noticeboard –' Margaret was practically sweeping him aside on her way out of the church. 'No need to rush off, dear, look, it's almost your turn, only me and Mrs Connor to go before you.'

'I'm not in the mood,' whispered Margaret. In the porch, on the parish noticeboard, she found the ragged copy of the parish magazine dated three months earlier with a special feature about its locum priest, whose half-page photograph beamed serenely at her. 'We are delighted to welcome Fr Joseph Kojo Nkromah who will take on all of Fr O'Donnell's duties in the parish for the next two months.' Fr Nkromah. From Dublin. Via Ghana.

The following morning Sister Mary was surprised to receive a call at the convent. She wasn't expecting anyone to telephone – in fact, since she and Margaret stopped scheming she had no contact with anyone outside and was also keeping away from her colleagues as much as possible. Her Mother Superior had noticed the change in the usually cheerful nun and was already preparing to have words. It had also been noted that Mary had not been to confession recently – normally a weekly event – and when a nun doesn't make her weekly confession it can only be because she finally has something worth confessing. Mother Superior had seen it all before but was nevertheless surprised that one of the most exemplary sisters appeared to have fallen prey to the outside world. The signs had all been there – secrecy, shiftiness, an excessive interest in everybody's timetable. It was not impossible that Mary had been seeing someone on the premises; she had frequently volunteered to stay behind when the nuns were out on their visits to the sick and to the home for single mothers which they ran. All in all, it was obvious that something fishy was going on and something fishy usually meant sex. Words must be had.

Mary went to the front hall and picked up the receiver. 'Hello. Sister Mary here.'

'Mary.'

'Margaret! What do you want? I hardly think –'

'Mary!' This was so impassioned that the nun remained silent. 'Mary, please, listen to me. I need to talk to you. I know I've behaved like a complete shit to you and have been absolutely terrible about all this baby business, but please, I have to talk to you. I've no one else.' Mary sighed, almost in pleasure, as she recognised her professional response overcoming her instinct to hang up.

'Of course you can talk to me. Shall I come to you?'

'Yes, please. To my house. I'll give you the address, it's –'

'I know it. I'll come now.'

Mary asked permission to leave the convent for a few hours. Eyebrows were raised when she would not give full details of her appointment. 'I have a friend who needs to speak to me. She sounds troubled. I have done my domestic duties this morning and feel that I am needed there.'

'What about your prayers, Sister? You haven't been in the chapel today.'

'I feel that helping this friend is more important than prayer, Mother.' The eyebrows were on a level with the hairline now, 'And I will be in chapel this evening. All evening. To make up for it.'

'Very well. I shall see you there. You may go.'

'Thank you, Mother.' Mary took the convent car – an ancient green Austin Allegro, donated by a worthy of the parish whose teenage son had discarded it after several scrapes and small crashes had utterly ruined its already decrepit bodywork. Having been given the task of cleaning it, Mary had found taped to the top of the glove compartment a small sealed bag of cannabis resin which she had removed to her apron pocket whilst completing the cleaning. Then, when what was left of the upholstery shone and she had painted over the rusted exterior with the wrong kind of paint in a contrasting shade (terracotta eggshell; it was all they had), she had carefully replaced the bag in its original position, believing that it was important to be prepared for any eventuality.

She drove to Margaret's house, stopping en route at a newsagent's to buy some chocolate digestive biscuits, a disposable lighter, a pouch of Golden Virginia and a packet of large Rizlas. Carefully ignoring the slightly trampled privet hedge that had been her shelter the previous day, she rang the doorbell.

A pathetic sight greeted her eyes: Margaret Fisher in disarray. And yet, despite the pathos there was also something attractive about the lack of control, of care. It was Margaret as Mary had never seen her before, it really *was* Margaret. Unwashed hair, dark circles around her eyes, bitten nails, wearing tartan pyjamas, and with an expression so raw and unmediated that Mary's gut instincts instantly moved in line with her sense of professional duty, both of which propelled her towards Margaret whom she took in her arms and held fast. Once the first bout of weeping subsided she sat her down on her sofa, made a pot of tea, put the biscuits on a plate and brought in a tray. By now Margaret was curled up in the corner holding a tissue to her nose and sobbing raggedly. She accepted a mug of sweet tea and nibbled at a biscuit before remembering she hadn't eaten since yesterday lunchtime and promptly munched her way through four of them. Then she breathed out long and deeply, and slumped. Mary began.

'So what is it, Margaret? What's got you into this state?' She was brusque but caring; there was no saccharine in her approach.

'I'm pregnant.' Mary spilled her tea all over the coffee table. As she busied herself with clearing up she heard the whole story. When Margaret had finished, her expression tragic, Mary was puzzled.

'So, what you're saying is that you were very glad when you thought you were pregnant with the child of an anonymous priest with whom you had one bout of casual sexual intercourse but now that you know you weren't the only one he was playing horsy horsy with in the confessional you're utterly appalled?'

'Don't play the innocent with me, Mary, I don't give a damn about how many women he had, for God's sake. You heard his name. Nkromah. Fr Bloody Nkromah!'

'And so?'

'And so, he's *black*. From Ghana. I'm pregnant with a baby who's going to be – mixed race.'

'How could you not tell he was black when you were – doing it? And you thought it was going to be half-Irish anyway.'

'That's not the same and you know it. It was bloody dark in there and I had my eyes shut the whole time. I don't believe it, Mary, you're smiling. Damn you, how can you treat me like this? I thought you were supposed to be one of baby Jesus' little messengers, for Christ's sake, you shouldn't be mocking me.'

'Oh, I think you've already had a visit from one of baby Jesus' messengers, don't you now, Margaret? Can you blame me for finding it slightly amusing that this has come to pass?'

'Come to pass? Come to pass?! You're even talking like the frigging bible now. Mary, this is terrible, can't you see?'

Mary's voice hardened. 'What's terrible is your attitude. You don't mind getting knocked up by a nameless priest but now you know his name's "foreign" it's a different matter. You should examine your attitudes, Doctor, because from here they look thoroughly racist.'

'Racist? How dare you! I'm not racist, it's just that this baby was supposed to be mine. To look like me. To not beg questions. Don't you see?'

'What, so if you suddenly give birth to a white baby nobody will even wonder who the father is, is that what you mean? They'll all think – oh look, Margaret Fisher's such a clever woman, she's managed to create a child all on her own, isn't he just the spitting image of her, isn't that grand?'

'You're being ridiculous. You know what I mean. Fewer questions would be asked if it were white.'

'Complete rubbish. You're just trying to find excuses for your outrageous racism. The irony of this can't be lost on you, Margaret – you, who've been trying to steal – yes, steal is the word I'll use – from another woman – finally get your own baby and then want to give it back because it's not going to share your *skin tone*. Don't you think that's fantastically *sick*?'

'You're coming over all County Cork, Mary, did you know that? That means you're losing control.'

'No, it means I'm talking to you from the heart. Talking in a way I haven't talked in years, not since my family first came to bloody Liverpool and I was supposed to forget County feckin' Cork and pretend to be someone else entirely.'

'Mary!'

'Don't Mary me. Admit that I'm right. You get the one thing you supposedly want most in the world but that isn't good enough for Margaret "Adolf" Fisher.'

'How dare you! And what are you doing?' Mary had taken the hash, tobacco and Rizlas from her bag and was rolling a small but perfectly formed joint.

'Oh, I dare all right. You're a wicked dried up old bag, Peggy Fisher – oh, you'd thought everyone had forgotten about Peggy, didn't you, well nobody ever did call you Margaret except to your face – and you should be pleased that your dream's come true. And accept that it's come true in a way over which you had no control. Go with it. Be happy. Here,' she lit up, 'have some of this.' Margaret looked doubly shocked.

'But the baby –'

'Ach, a tiny bit of a puff isn't going to harm the baby and you know it. Have some.'

Margaret took the joint and had a small, expert drag. She handed it back.

'It's been a long time. I didn't know you –'

'Oh, now and then, just when I was at school. Thought you'd be well used to it, being a doctor an' all.'

'Practising medicine only puts you in touch with legal drugs. I could have all the methadone I could handle but finding a spliff when you really need it . . .' They handed the joint between them twice more. Margaret began to giggle.

'Imagine my mother's face. When she sees the baby.'

'Jesus, it'll be worth it just for that. What will you tell her?'

'I'll tell her I fucked a man I'd never even seen. But it's OK – he was a Catholic.' The women rocked with laughter.

'Tell her he's a top Catholic. Tell her you went for the Pope but a stand-in priest was the best you could do.'

'Then I'll tell her I'm going to put his name on the birth certificate. So that people won't talk.' Margaret was shrieking with laughter.

'Then you can tell her his name!' sobbed Mary. 'But you can say she needn't worry, he won't be visiting, because he's fighting paternity suits brought by the Beverly Sisters!'

'And Bananarama!'

'And every last feckin' member of the Nolans!' Margaret and Mary laughed until they cried, then they cried for ten more minutes and finally fell asleep at opposite ends of the sofa.

Waking up two hours later, they fell upon the remaining biscuits and ate all they could find in Margaret's sparsely stocked kitchen: four stale rice cakes, a lump of Wensleydale cheese and an entire pack of cornflakes, which they ate with a sparse sprinkling of tinned evaporated milk. Mary ran Margaret a warm bath and tidied up while her patient soaked in the tub. A shout came from upstairs.

'Mary!'

'Hello?'

'I haven't got a clean towel here, can you bring one up from the cupboard under the stairs?'

'On its way.'

When Mary entered the bathroom her friend was standing on the mat. Margaret took the towel and wrapped it around herself slowly, looking at the woman standing, transfixed, in the doorway. Then she let it drop. She moved closer.

'Mary.'

'You're so *slender*.' Mary placed her hand, ever so gently, on the side of Margaret's waist, where she had been fixing her gaze ever since she entered the bathroom. She moved it away abruptly. 'I'm sorry, I –'

Margaret replaced the hand. It began to move, to stroke, falteringly at first but then in great sweeps along and around and across the doctor's body, tracing the bones and muscles, performing an instinctive exercise in sensory cartography, finding a route to remember and revisit. As she felt the hand firmly cup her breast Margaret wanted to explain something.

'He didn't touch me. Not my skin. He fucked me but he didn't *touch* me.' Mary nodded. 'Have you ever –?' Mary shook her head. 'Do you think we –?'

'Hush,' said Mary. 'Hush now.' And leaned in for a kiss.

15

Sophie asked Harry if they could meet privately, away from the university. He was anxious at first, wondering whether she believed that they had embarked upon a relationship of sorts, but realised that even she couldn't be that deluded about the nature of their one sexual encounter. Perhaps she wanted to clear the air. Or apologise. He could hardly refuse. They went to a coffee shop half a mile away where Sophie, normally a fiend for double cappuccino, ordered fruit juice. Harry brought his espresso and her juice to the table.

'Bit of a health drive then, Soph?' he smiled but she didn't return it.

'Something like that.'

'Jolly good. Right, now, I assume you want to talk about the – um – the incident of – what can it be now? – three weeks ago? Before you say anything, may I suggest that we put it all down to –'

'No. Sorry, Harry, sorry to interrupt, but actually although it *is*, sort of, about the "incident" it's a bit more complex than that. You see, I'm pregnant.'

Silence. Harry looked a little surprised, but not at all perturbed. 'Well, congratulations are in order, I'm sure. And of course, nothing will ever be said about – what happened – to the, well, to the father. Erm – do you mind me asking – are you *with* the father, Sophie?'

'No I'm not, Harry. Because you are the father.' Harry was looking confused but still not actually worried.

'But Sophie – how can I put this – you know this, I'm sure – you can't actually *conceive* by – erm – by . . .'

'Of course I didn't get pregnant just by giving you a bloody blowjob!' Sophie's indignant tones rang out around the small café which became unnaturally quiet as their fellow customers stopped turning newspaper pages, chatting amongst themselves and even chewing. 'I mean, I didn't even swallow!' she continued, drawing a whistling snort from a man to her right who simultaneously inhaled all the crumbs from his croissant and whose subsequent fit of choking mercifully cloaked the rest of their conversation, to the chagrin of everyone else present. 'I spat it out, didn't I? Into a syringe. And then I impregnated myself. And it worked. Do you understand now, Harry? Harry?'

He was very pale and his hands were trembling when he put down his cup. Sophie thought he looked more surprised than she had imagined he would be. 'I'm really sorry if it's a shock, Harry. But I shan't ask you for money or anything – really, I'm going to bring it up myself and everything and shan't expect you to have anything to do with it, and of course I won't actually tell anyone –' Then she realised that he was trembling not with shock but with anger. His white face became livid as he said, through a clenched jaw and with an expression she could never imagine seeing on his handsome, amiable face, 'You silly, silly fool. How dare you? How dare you steal a child from me!' Sophie tried to brazen it out, though she was beginning to feel scared.

'Hey, come on, that's going a bit far, don't you think, doc? Look, you're my ideal man, OK? I've never known anyone I've liked as much as you, you're perfect. I thought you'd be – flattered.'

'Flattered? Flattered that some daft floozy who can't hold down a relationship with a man for more than a fortnight decides to *steal* my bodily fluids because she has decided that she wants my baby? You can't seriously think this would be anything except a terrible – a *shocking* piece of news.' Sophie tried to digest this response. She had assumed he wouldn't be glad – certainly not glad like she had been a few days ago when the test showed that it had actually worked – but she didn't think he'd see it in such dramatic terms.

'Are you worried about Cress? That was the one thing I thought about – afterwards you know – because I'd never do anything to hurt her, you know that, but I thought she doesn't even need to know about this . . .'

'Oh I think she does, Sophie. I think she does. It's remarkable timing, Sophie, do you know that?' Sophie looked blank. 'Yes, perfect timing. You see, by the time you give birth Cressida will have had a third child. That's right, she's pregnant. Did you not think that might be a possibility, when you were making your great plan? Or would it have made no difference anyway?' It was true, thought Sophie, that for some unfathomable reason the fact that Cress was pregnant too made the situation a very great deal worse. She was beginning to feel less than overjoyed about her pregnancy. Such short-lived happiness. She stumbled out, her eyes filling with tears, and left Harry staring at his coffee.

Cressida took the news remarkable calmly, and was more concerned at Harry's rage than at the possible outcome.

'Do you think, Harry, that you might be so angry because this sort of evens things out? Before you interrupt, I am not making any comparison between my having an affair and your being sexually abused in your sleep, OK? But the outcome – the pregnancies – are the same, aren't they? Suddenly we're both having babies with other people. Christ, it's almost funny.'

'What? So do you feel happier, now that we're "even", is that what you're saying?'

'No, not at all. I think it's appalling. And just because I'm having someone else's baby I don't see why you should have the right to just rush off and do the same.' Harry began to protest. 'I'm joking love, in a grim sort of way, but I'm just worried that you'll do something mad. And though I think she's been an absolute arse, I do feel sorry for Sophie. I mean, she's hopeless. How is she going to manage?'

'That's precisely my concern. If she'd told me she was pregnant by *anyone* I'd be worried for her and for the child. But the fact it's mine will make me absolutely terrified for its wellbeing. Not that she's a bad girl, she's just –'

'She's thirty-two and you're still calling her a girl.'

'Precisely. She's – hopeless. What do you think I should do?'

'Nothing, for the time being. Apologise for being mean to her. Invite her round for tea.'

'You are joking now.'

'No. If she's going to have your baby she'd better feel as good as she can about the whole thing. I'll help her.'

'Who's being a saint now then?'

'A very practical sort of saint. Look, Harry, this whole situation is an utter farce. This just adds to the pot. I mean, how many bloody babies are involved in this? And not one of them conceived at the right time by the right people. It's absolutely crazy.'

The newly formed household of Justin, Kyria, Felicity and Harmony had enjoyed several weeks of calm contentment. This was, naturally, about to change. Kyria had missed two periods and realised that the impossible had happened. What timing – she and Justin were planning to marry in six months, the girls had just escaped their pregnant mother and were unlikely to welcome being confronted with a pregnant stepmother, and the subject of children had already been closed, dealt with, resolved. And yet, what a miracle! Kyria hugged her secret to herself and prayed that this child would live. She had hardly dared hope when the first period failed to arrive; put it down to the stress of the move. But she'd been aware of her breasts feeling tender. And she hadn't felt like having sex as often as usual. Following this second no-show Kyria knew, absolutely, that she was pregnant; no need for a test. She called her sister in Wellington, who was so excited that she squeaked inarticulately down the line for a good thirty seconds but was finally forced to swear not to tell a soul until Kyria had seen a doctor. Not even Justin would know until then.

While she sat on the edge of her bed pondering these things in her heart, there was a knock at the door and Felicity entered. Kyria snapped out of her reverie and smiled at the girl, then saw her face.

'Fliss, what is it? What's the matter?' Felicity was pinching a small white plastic stick between her thumb and forefinger. Her little hand shaking, she held it up for Kyria to see the two clear blue lines across its tip.

'This is the matter. I can't believe it; after the first time he always used a condom and everything, and we only did it six times. I can't believe it.'

'Dave?' The girl nodded.

'I missed my last period but that's happened before and I was so stressed out at home, I thought it was just something to do with moving out and arguing with Mum and everything. But I've never missed two. And that's when I knew.'

'Have you told Dave?'

'No chance. I hate him. This is nothing to do with him.'

'Fliss, sweetheart. Don't worry. I'll help you.' The girl's face crumpled into tears.

'But Kyria, what am I going to do? I'm about to start my "A" levels. I don't want a baby, I can't have a baby.'

'What do you want to do, love?'

'I can't have it. I can't have it.'

'OK, OK. I think we need to see a doctor and then we'll take it from there. Fliss, sweetie, don't worry. We'll sort this out.'

'Don't tell my mum, Kyria. Or dad.'

'I think you'll want to talk to your mum, Fliss love. Maybe not right away, but in a day or two, I'm sure –'

But Felicity was adamant. 'No. Not Mum. I'll talk to my dad. Will you come with me?'

'Of course I will, darling.' It looked as though Kyria's news had been superseded, and she decided to keep it to herself until Felicity's situation was resolved.

How many pregnancies? Count them: Cressida and Tom, Tom and Nita, Sophie and Harry, Margaret and the good father Nkromah, Justin and Kyria, Felicity and Dave . . . But what's this? Only six? Fear not; patience is a virtue (although not one which features in Harry's scheme of things) and it will be rewarded. That much is guaranteed.

BOOK TWO: Evolution

Why must you tell me all your secrets
When it's hard enough to love you knowing nothing?
We're living four flights up
But I swear right now it feels like underground.

from 'Four Flights Up', Lloyd Cole and the Commotions

1

What began as a whisper is turning into a full-blown rumour and it won't be suppressed. The hot news in the office is that Cressida Nelson is pregnant but – get this – *it isn't Harry's*. No, the sound from the ground is that she's been having it off with *Tom Webster*! You'd think she'd have more sense, wouldn't you? I mean, a *writer*. One of our writers. But then the really crazy thing is that Tom's girlfriend – you know, that woman up north who trapped him a couple of years ago – *she's* up the stick too. Isn't that incredible? I mean, has nobody heard of contraception?

Four miles north of Cressida's central London office the university psychology department is alive with revelations. Sophie Diamond is pregnant and – you're not going to believe this – *it's Harry Shepherd's*! By AID apparently. I know, you can't imagine it, can you? Talk about weird. But the really bizarre thing is his wife's pregnant too! Yes! And someone told me that the baby she's having isn't Harry's! It's some writer's she's been having an affair with, quite a well-known one I hear. I mean, this is the twenty-first century, there's just no excuse for it, it's not like they're sixteen-year-olds, is it?

Just around the corner from Cressida and Harry's house the Queen's Park medical practice is buzzing with scandal. Have you heard about Dr Fisher? Well, she's *pregnant*! No, she's not been seeing anyone; it's a complete mystery. But someone told me that she'd just picked someone up, some bloke. You can't imagine her having casual sex, can you? Well, let's be honest, you can't imagine her having any sex at all, she's such a grumpy old bag most of the time. It's unbelievable, a woman of her age, and in her position. Anyway, she's still working at the practice, completely brazen, and I heard – this is the strangest bit of the whole story and I'm not sure if it's true but they say that she's now living with – and I do mean that in the biblical sense – *a nun*! A *female* nun. So she has sex with some chap she doesn't know and then turns into a bloody lesbian. Bizarre!

Felicity is half a dozen miles away from her old school yard but her ears are burning all the same. Did you hear about Fliss Montague? You know she was seeing that Dave from the club? Well, he shagged her over the car park wall and now she's *pregnant*! Yeah, that's why she left school. *And* her mum's up the duff again, even though she's really old and that Tom Whatsit she lives with is a right dirty old git. He shagged Miss Tyler who used to do Art, you know. Yeah. Anyway, my mum says she wouldn't be surprised if he'd been fiddling around with Fliss as well and it's his baby. And Janey Barker from 5F says it isn't true cos Dave was already going out with *her* but Matthew Hardwick saw Fliss and Dave cos he's fancied her for years and he was following her (I know, what a fucking psycho) *and* Karen D'Rosario emailed Harm Montague to ask her about it and Harm didn't reply, even though Karen's supposed to be her best mate, so that's how we know it's true. *And*, as if that wasn't enough fuck-ups all happening at once, Fliss and Harm's real dad has got his girlfriend pregnant too! Nightmare!

Gossip. Not one of the deadly sins and, therefore, not a feature of Harry's research. But the prevalence of careless whispers in his life – the sidelong glances as he walked along the corridor; the persistent pose he glimpsed through glass, of hands clapped to mouths, eyes bulging; the stifled giggle as he entered the seminar room; the slack-jawed regard of the student who was clearly not concentrating on his lecture – hurt him. Damaged him. And he was gradually coming to the conclusion that the pain he felt was no longer due to the truth of the gossip but was caused by his new view of humanity. Even the most sympathetic of his colleagues – those who listened, nodded, spoke quietly and encouragingly to him – subtly betrayed their fascination with his predicament;

revelled, somehow, in the knowledge that he was within the scandalous tangle and they were safely outside, looking in, or down, at him. Harry had spent all his life on the periphery, observing what everyone else was up to, and he was much discomfited by this reversal. It made him feel like an animal in a zoo. There was no cover, no shade. Thoughts of the captive animal were never far from Harry's thoughts now, he was beginning to feel nervous about his state of mind; he was beginning to wonder if he weren't becoming a little *fanciful*.

2

Cressida stretched out in bed, one arm raised above her head, the other reaching down to cup the firm curve of her growing belly. She yawned widely, turned on to her side rubbing her eyes and let out a long, growling groan, 'Harry, love, I know it's hard but please try not to let it get to you like this.'

'But it must be just as bad for you – worse, because everyone knows, everyone sees it. How can you be so calm about it? It can't just be your bloody hormones. It's hell, Cress, even worse than this – mess. You and I seem to be working our way through it, God only knows how, but everyone else – they just want to see the show. We're a story for them.'

'Of course it's a story. Don't you think you'd be the same, if this was happening to someone else? It's fantastic, they're having a field day. These things aren't supposed to happen, we're all so damned sophisticated but hey look, here are some people who don't know the rules and see how convincingly they've fucked up. Come on, love, it's all pretty basic, isn't it? Flawed human nature always makes the best stories. Doesn't it?'

'You make it sound Shakespearean. I don't think their interest is literary.'

'Shakespeare's interest wasn't bloody literary. What I mean is, in the great beasts-versus-angels struggle it's always more juicy if the beast wins from time to time. If the rude mechanicals play to type.'

'Beasts. That's right. That's what it makes me feel like. Cress, I've been imagining myself as this animal in a zoo that's actually rather like the people who are watching it. But they don't see that and they can't hear what it's saying even though it speaks their language and I feel – it feels – like everything it does, even the most natural, necessary things – every time it breathes or swallows or moves, they're all disgusted and horrified by it, and it just terrifies me . . .'

'Sweetheart, you are an animal, and so are they. That's all we are. Animals with choices.'

'That's a terrible thought. A terrifying thought.'

'Is it?' Cressida sounded unperturbed as she got out of bed. 'Oh, it's not too bad I don't think. Look, love, I'm sorry, could we talk about this later? I need a pee.'

While she didn't share Harry's painful tendency to think too much on every event, Cressida had been carrying the burden of her predicament fearfully, until she concluded that the combination of anxieties was simply too much for anyone to bear and promptly dropped her worries into the ether. She had simply thrown up both her hands at the crazy cat's cradle of her life and decided to let nature take its course. She and Harry had agreed to take an approach which involved neither telling lies nor broadcasting their situation to the nation but they soon discovered that the latter course would at least have given them some control over the circumstances in which the news spread, for spread it did, like a virulent chromatography of deepest beetroot, diluting irregularly to an uneven pink blush, covering and overreaching their circle of friends, family, colleagues and eventually neighbours, local shopkeepers and former school pals from all curves of the globe:

Hi Cress, Greetings from Oz!!! Long time no e, so sorry I haven't been in touch for ages darling, but I changed jobs a few months ago <and> moved house, so it's been absolootly crazy Down Under! Anyway, I just got the most amazing email from Mark S – he'd been talking to Juanita D and she told him your News. Wow! Just wanted to say that I'm thinking of you at this difficult time and that – well – I'm here if you need me! It would be great to talk!!! Hugs, Suki xxx

It was these latter additions to the outer circle that irritated Cressida the most. The stares from old dears in the newsagent's were less intrusive than the handful of careless, probing emails she received from foulweather friends. Having for years dismissed English reserve as an excuse for emotional illiteracy, at work she now sought out those middle-aged males who would no more mention her increasingly visible pregnancy than they would discuss their prostate operations with anyone other than their consultant. With their protection and her own survival instinct, Cressida created a thick caul for herself, allowing her to move unharmed through the gawping crowds.

She also drew her first family around her. Before the news was allowed to break more widely, Harry took Ben and Jemima for a lunchtime outing while Cressida served soup and bread and wine to her mother, father and two younger sisters and, while they slurped and mopped with their usual gusto, carefully explained what was happening. As she talked, an eerie silence fell upon the group. Spoons were laid down until she finished speaking. And then all hell let loose.

'Jesus Christ, Cress, I don't bloody believe it! How can you be so stupid!' This was Beth, younger than Cressida by eight years, and constantly in imagined combat with the shadow of her academically-gifted, gainfully-employed, happily-married and generally popular big sister. It was almost a pleasure to see her having made such an almighty mess of her perfect life. 'And what about Harry and his secretary? Do you really believe that happened? I mean, come off it, were you born yesterday or something?'

'Oh that's not fair, Beth! You know Harry wouldn't lie about something like that. And as for – all this – well, it could happen to anyone. I think you're just – remarkably brave to go ahead with it all, Cress. I don't think I could do it.' This was Polly, who was thirty-one and known mainly for being unlucky in love; she was aware that what she mostly felt was toe-curling jealousy at Cressida's unerring ability to attract men and conceive babies at the drop of a hat.

But Beth wasn't giving up, had already begun to smirk as she said, 'I suppose the choice facing you now is – Tom's dick or Harry's?' She giggled with such mirth that Cressida was smiling despite herself, even as her hand hit the table and her mother interrupted.

'That's enough, Beth! Look, girls, let's not discuss the whys and wherefores. Cressida has explained the situation and what we need to do now is give her and Harry all our help and support.

And make sure that Ben and Jemmy aren't too much put out by everything that's happening round them. Isn't that right, David? David!' Cressida's father had resumed eating and his soup was almost finished. Soaking up the dregs with a great hunk of buttered bread he gave the matter some consideration before answering.

'Cressida, you're a slut. That writer chap ought to be shot. Your husband is an arse who should've horsewhipped you instead of sitting in his bloody office writing about Sin. Ha. Writing about it, note. He's such an arse that the secretary story is probably the truth. And so now there are two little bastards on the way. Well, the world goes round all the same and one puking brat is much the same as another. Good luck to you all, I say.' He popped the bread into his mouth with satisfaction and raised his glass. 'Eh, Cress? Good luck to you.' Everyone relaxed and smiled.

'Thank you, Daddy,' said Cressida, relieved. 'More wine anyone?'

3

Sophie was being cheerfully upbeat about what to Harry seemed an untenable position. The glances and whispers in her direction made her feel like the main attraction and, unlike Harry, that was what she wanted to be. Being talked about in hushed voices seemed more like a taste of recognition than humiliation and she was convinced that the tone amongst both male and female colleagues verged on envy. The women who had previously treated her like a flighty girl now had to sit up and take notice and were already proffering maternal advice on how she should stand, what she should eat, even how and where she should give birth. She felt as though her body was taking over not only her own existence but that of everyone with whom she came into contact and she welcomed the sensation, open arms at last preparing to close around someone who wouldn't leave in the morning, astonished at her own nonchalance when the physical realm overtook her; when she vomited each morning, when she rubbed her aching calves, when the small unfamiliar flutters in her abdomen stopped her in her tracks.

But Sophie's tiredness and physical symptoms were not due solely to her pregnancy. For several months she had experienced a tingling in her arm, which she put down to lying badly in her sleep. Once she had lost her vision for a few minutes and the accompanying headache had convinced her that she had suffered a migraine for the first time in her life. These incidents had been forgotten in her excitement about the baby and when, at three months pregnant, she suddenly fell over for no apparent reason, her concern was only for the child she carried and not for the cause of her fall.

Cressida had been true to her word and invited Sophie to eat with her and Harry very shortly after Sophie's first visit to the antenatal clinic. The women compared their respective weight gain, due dates, Rhesus factor and food cravings with such apparent enjoyment that Harry felt both left out and outraged. Sitting back in his chair, he felt obliged to point out the ludicrousness of the scene. 'Here is my wife, who is going to have her lover's child instead of mine as planned, and here is my secretary who is going to have my child through no fault of my own. And they are talking about *whether or not they can drink coffee*.' His wife and secretary looked at him, smiled briefly and then turned back to each other. It scarcely needed saying, their shared look implied, but we're doing our best, getting on with it, covering well. How else can we cope with this?

Sophie's widowed mother, who lived in Hampstead, was seventy years old and not in good health. She had been upset to hear she was to expect a grandchild and not a son-in-law (Sophie didn't mention the child's father and the question wasn't likely to be asked) so relations between mother and daughter, never brilliant, were decidedly strained. A brother, older by six years, was a New York banker. Indeed, it seemed he had been born a New York banker and was no more distant in New York than he had been in the bedroom across the landing at home. Thus, alone in the world apart from a wide circle of featherbrained friends, Sophie began to look on Cressida – two years her senior – as a mother figure, and Cressida allowed her to do so. She saw how Sophie's long-held feelings for Harry were sincere and overwhelming and felt that the girl deserved kind treatment, if only because she loved her husband with an intensity Cressida feared she herself could never regain. And besides, her own mother was proving to be invaluable, and it seemed unfair that Sophie shouldn't receive some similarly useful support from the people who were, in a way, her only family. It was Cressida who advised Sophie, after the fall, to see a doctor, and Cressida who subsequently held her hand in the specialist's office to discuss the tests that had thrown up some worrying results. But for now, Sophie was remarkably contented and Cressida was coping heroically well.

Harry had seen Cressida's anger channelled into a fierce protection of their children, both of whom sensed only the tenderness beneath it. And he had sat helpless while Patricia fed herself with her daughter's pain, taking great floods of tears and gulping sobs into her heart until Cressida's aching shoulders calmed and sank, the weight removed. Even Sophie's avarice seemed focused on preparations for her baby's arrival – not filling up on the aggressively marketed props of new parenthood but collecting her thoughts, reading up on the subject, ordering her mind and ensuring that everything was in its place. Perhaps, Harry was beginning to think, our tendency towards one particular characteristic or Prime Motivator defined both the positive *and* damaging aspects of our personalities. Inspired once more, he began to write.

4

Tom had not written a word since he last saw Cressida, apart from the contents of several dozen emails addressed to her, many of which he never sent. Letters, too, the old-fashioned kind, in envelopes, which he never even considered posting. He shredded them as soon as the envelopes were sealed. With neither the mammalian acceptance which buoyed up Cressida, nor the intellectual reawakening on which Harry fell back, his confidence was at its lowest ever ebb and his failure to get a response out of Cressida lent all his attempts to get on with his novel, or indeed his life, an air of doom. If he couldn't communicate successfully with the woman he loved, how could he own the arrogance to trade any more words? This was unusual; at previous low points in his emotional life Tom had successfully sublimated an aching heart into page after page of beautifully turned prose, until it became a positive advantage to feel like shit for a couple of weeks. But his heart wasn't simply aching; it was thudding heavily and unrelentingly, marking out the dull, empty seconds of his life. Even holding Katie failed to give him the perspective he longed for; he knew he adored her but it gave him no pleasure. While he had become reconciled to the fact that he and Cressida would never be together, Tom had never countenanced her being outside his life and he was finding the loss almost unbearable.

Nita, believing that she knew the full extent of Tom's infidelities, and that they were too long ago to be relevant to his change of mood, was horrified at what she assumed to be his anxiety about the new baby. The all-new family life she had been planning was not meeting expectations. For one thing, she missed her girls and was upset by their reticence. Felicity never spoke to her, just sent the odd note, and it wasn't only because of the information about Tom that she had left and to which Nita, carefully, never referred. Nita tried, to her own surprise, to hold out an olive branch.

'Harm, love,' she had said, 'if it doesn't work out living with your father – you know you and Fliss can always come back here. Any time. You know that, don't you?'

Harmony had instantly injected a cheery tone into their chat. 'Oh Mum, we're doing fine and anyway we don't want to get in the way when you've got so much to do there getting ready for the new baby. Honestly, we're fine, we're having a great time.'

'Fliss hasn't been in touch much.'

'She's – working. Getting ready for next term. That's all it is, Mum. Don't worry!'

Unable and unwilling to delve further in any direction, Nita fixated on the child she carried. She decided that all would be well if she gave birth to a boy. Whatever Tom said on the subject, she was convinced that all men, deep down, wanted a son and if she managed to produce one it would make Tom's commitment to her absolutely secure. Consulting a few of her hippy books on Eastern mysticism, she scoured the patchouli-scented pages and tracked down some relevant chants to make a boy child. She practised them secretly, religiously, strangely confident of their efficacy.

Since adolescence, Nita had been searching for a foolproof code for living – a mantra, a connection to some spiritual plane she had never been able to reach. Brought up in Manchester by her terrifying Aberdeen-bred grandmother and eternally-cowed mother, until the age of fourteen she was led to believe that her father was a) Italian and b) dead. It was only when a letter with a Bombay postmark arrived addressed to Nita, spelt Neeta, that this myth was exploded: in fact her mother had taken up with an Indian student who stayed long enough to name his daughter, but no longer. When confronted, her mother just sighed while Grandma cursed, and swore the child had been misled for her own good. It was discomfiting enough for young Nita to find that the provenance of her coffee complexion and raven locks lay further east than she had believed, let alone the fact that her name was not actually a shortening of the mediterranean Anita she had always assumed (she had never set eyes on her birth certificate). The news contained in her letter was that part, at least, of the Father Myth was true; her father was dead and had remembered his lost English daughter – as he thought of her – in his will, with a bequest of £5,000 to be kept in trust until her twenty-first birthday. At twenty-one Nita blew the lot on a trip to India with her boyfriend Justin, who was studying Geography. In a very short time they got through a number of relationship traumas, a few bouts of dysentery and all the cash, at which point they returned to Manchester. He got an IT job while she was taken on by a private school, where she taught English as a foreign language, mainly to people who had come from all over India and its environs to learn it, a situation which Nita, typically, thought of as being apt rather than ironic. Soon after their younger daughter started school, the insincerity of his lifestyle struck Justin in a dramatic fashion. His resulting depression, lasting five years, took the final spark of nomadic ambition out of his wife, whose reaction to their eventual separation and divorce, driven entirely by her, was one of unbridled relief. She had thought that she would never be happy again. Then she had met Tom.

Eventually, Tom telephoned Cressida at work.

'You know I can't talk here,' she said lightly, casually, avoiding sibilants but still sensing the ears of her workmates prick up with attention.

'I must see you. If you say no, I swear I'll come and drag you out of there, and . . .'

Cressida cut him short impatiently, 'All right. Tomorrow lunchtime. One o'clock at Dante's.'

'I'll be there.'

'See you then.'

Quite what Tom hoped to achieve by meeting Cressida was unclear even to him; all he knew was that without the prospect of her blue eyes before him he was stumbling, emotionally and physically, like a man struck with grief. Once, he had tripped while going upstairs and, inspecting the fresh graze on his knee, he had been aware that while to some extent it reminded him of being seven again, at that age he would have jumped up, wiped off the blood with a snotty tissue and carried on. Now he just felt like crying for his mam.

The lovers hadn't met for almost three months and great changes had worked their magic on them both. When Tom saw the swell of Cressida's belly in which his child lay, he almost knelt at her feet. When she saw his pale face and red-rimmed eyes, she almost drew his head to her breast. Perhaps that's what should have happened, although it would have been a mite too gymnastic for the small Italian restaurant Cressida had chosen specifically for its intimacy. Only she knew that it was where her pregnancy had been confirmed – the toilets were downstairs in the brasserie basement or, as the sign at the top of the stairs indicated, 'L'Inferno'. But here they were on the ground floor, in 'Paradiso'. The first floor was where the proprietor and his family lived and Tom had, in happier times, scolded him roundly for missing out the 'Purgatorio' altogether which, he insisted, if the speed of service were anything to go by, would have been a more appropriate name for the dining room. Joe Dante had thrown up his hands and waved his tea towel in mock horror, before returning to the kitchen and whispering to his wife, Maria, that yet another English customer was banging on about That poem, and he was sure as hell going to have to get around to reading it one of these days, or just change the name of the damned restaurant to Giuseppe's and be done with it.

Tom's faint hopes that he and Cressida might end up in bed were dashed as soon as the two of them resisted their initial urge to grab each other and composed their unmade faces into something approaching neutrality. They didn't speak until they had ordered food and Cressida asked for a large glass of Chianti, at which Tom's eyebrows raised instinctively and hers lowered into a mind-your-own-business frown. He sipped his beer and, as the caller of this meeting, tried to frame his feelings into words. He had believed it would be easier than email, but that was when he imagined seeing himself reflected in Cressida's limpid gaze. Now she scarcely looked at him for any length of time, and when the food arrived – miraculously quickly! – she concentrated disproportionately on twirling spaghetti round her fork as he stammered his way through various different ways of saying I miss you. Finally he was silent. Cressida took a large mouthful of wine, looked him in the eyes and swallowed deliberately, reminding

Tom of her unique ability to slow a second into a moment: for someone who thought, spoke and usually moved at great speed, she had a surprising trick with time which seemed to him like a microscopic rewind – blink, the moment's passed, but then open your eyes and you're still in it. It had elated him at first; now it seemed fearsome.

'So what are you saying, Tom?'

'That I still love you as much as ever. That I can't live without you. That I miss you like hell and can't do a damned thing not knowing whether I'm going to see you again.'

'I heard all that. I've read all that. So what's new?'

'You seem – a little *callous*, Cress. Don't you hear me, can't you hear what I'm telling you?'

'Yes, I hear it. And I don't feel callous, don't mean to be callous. But I need to understand what you want me to do about it.'

'Don't you love me any more?'

'You know I do. As much as ever.'

'Well, that's a bloody relief. I thought for a moment –'

'What? That I didn't love you? But I've always said I love you. You've always known it. That's never been in question.'

'So – we love each other. As much as ever. And miss each other unbearably.'

'Yes. All of that is true.'

'So – can we see each other again? I don't mean we have to start – making love again, not if you don't feel like that, but can we still meet and talk and be with each other?'

'You're not saying you want us to be together?'

'Cress, we've been over all that, I have no choice, I *can't* be with the woman I want to be with and you know all the reasons. But we can be together somehow. I know it's compromised, but it has been for nearly two years now. I can't have you out of my life, it's sheer misery.'

Cressida wished she smoked, so that she could take a long drag and blow it gently into Tom's face, but she had to make do with a deep intake of breath before she said the one thing she had never overtly said before.

'Tom. I love you too. And I want to be with you. I would be prepared to make the changes – in time, and carefully, and always thinking about the children – I would make the changes which meant we could be together. But to come this far and revert to meeting up every fortnight – even if we only hold hands – Christ, especially if we only hold hands – I can't do it, love. I'd do anything for you, have never wanted anyone like I want you, and feel as certain as a person can feel that those things are never going to change. But I want you to be mine, and I want to be yours, properly. There's been so much scandal that a little more wouldn't hurt and there is *always* a way to work everything out even if it's awful at first. We need to be brave. But, if what you're asking is can we remain lovers, then the answer is no. For my babies, and my own dignity, I need to draw that line. And I'm longing for you to walk over it, love, but I can see already that you won't take that step. I'm not punishing you or playing hard to get, I'm just telling you how much, and how, I love you. If it's so unbearable to be apart, why don't we make sure we aren't? And if we don't have that courage, why make a mockery out of something that has been very beautiful? You must see that.'

'You are trying to make me reject you.'

'Isn't that what you're doing?'

'No! Never say that! Cress, don't ever think it.'

'I know you love me. I also know you're rejecting me. It's terrible that the two can co-exist, but there you go. Harry and I are trying as hard as we can but I can't pretend to be as hopeful as I was last time you and I talked. There was a certain amount of bravado at play. So I see a possible future where I'm on my own being the main carer for his two children and your baby. And you are two hundred miles away with a woman you don't love and your two children. You know, your attitude to your kids reminds me of the girls in fourth form at school who got pregnant because they were Catholics and didn't believe in contraception. You take one bit of the picture and hang on to it like it's a talisman, whatever is happening over the other side. Standing by your children is a fine and natural thing; but bringing them up in a home where the parents are so mismatched could end up doing more harm than good.'

'Cress, I don't want to get into statistics, but some people reckon kids would rather their parents stay together even if they row continually.'

'You think children are always the best judge of that? Ask them when they've grown up and look back and realise the reason their parents stayed together was *their fault*. Can't see that being very productive. Anyway, when I think of the state we're in I start to feel hopeless, which I can't afford to do. At least if I know truly that you are rejecting me – don't flinch – then I can try to make the very best of what I have got instead of always dreaming you might come to rescue me.'

'Cress,' Tom moaned, 'my children –'

She patted her tummy, 'This one too, Tom. Inside me. Had you forgotten?'

5

When Felicity told Justin her news at first he felt murderous. His impulse was to go and find this Dave and punch out his lights, do him over, teach him to leave little girls alone. Then he felt guilty at having left his little girls alone, to be exploited by marauding DJs while their mother cavorted with her new man. Then he felt murderous again, this time towards Tom whose attempt to take his place as father and protector had so clearly failed. Then he felt murderous towards Nita for her evident neglect of Felicity and her lack of interest in where her daughter was, and with whom, at nights. Then he felt more guilt until eventually he sensed a great low sliding woomph of pain in his chest which metamorphosed into acute grief for his little girl. By the time Felicity, scared by the few seconds of silence during which she couldn't read her father's face, said, 'Dad. I'm sorry,' he was ready to take her in his arms, stroke her hair and tell her that everything would be fine. It soon transpired that for sixteen-year-old Felicity being fine meant being not pregnant. Adamant that her mother shouldn't know – at least not until after she'd had her own baby – despite Justin's pleas that she tell her, Felicity turned to Kyria who accompanied her to the doctor and arranged a termination as soon as possible. The pregnancy was into its ninth week, just like Kyria's own. And apart from her sister in New Zealand, nobody was any the wiser.

Justin was worried that Kyria might feel unable to offer her help. While they had never discussed the issue specifically, he had a general idea, probably inferred from conversations with her prolific Irish/Maori family, but also in the knowledge that her own infertility had given her much pain, that she wouldn't be comfortable about Fliss's decision to terminate the pregnancy. For himself, Justin saw the situation very clearly: his daughter needed help and this was the nature of the help required. Had she chosen to give up school temporarily and have the baby he would have been equally supportive. But for Kyria, he understood, the lines were more tangled.

'Kyria, love.'

'Hmmm?'

'Listen, you don't have to have anything to do with this. This Fliss business. If it upsets you. I mean –'

'I know what you mean. But it would upset me more if I didn't help your girl, honey. Truly. Let me help.' Justin was relieved.

'Thank you. I try, but I never know what to say, and a girl needs her – a girl needs another woman for – this sort of thing.'

Kyria smiled in spite of herself. 'Did you worry I might try to make her change her mind? Offer to look after the child myself?'

Justin blushed. That was exactly what he'd worried about. 'I suppose so. Not that you'd be unkind to her. Just that you'd – find it too difficult.'

'I'm fine. She'll be fine. And we need to remember Harmony in all this too. I swear to you, Jus, I'm glad I'm here to do it. Truly I am.'

On the morning of the abortion, Kyria discovered that she was losing a little blood. Just a tiny bit of spotting. An absolutely normal phenomenon in early pregnancy. Possibly caused by stress. And exactly the way her two miscarriages had begun. There was nothing to be done; Fliss needed her strength today so Kyria stared at her glistening eyes in the mirror while pushing the fingernails of each hand into the palm of the other, composing her face into a mask of calm. She took Fliss to the hospital, sat with her while medics came to take blood, check her temperature, talk through the operation, and gave her cheek a kiss and her hand a final squeeze as she lay on the trolley ready to go to theatre.

'Kyria,' whispered Fliss with difficulty, 'I'm doing the right thing aren't I? I'm not doing – something bad?'

'Of course you're not, honey. You're doing fine. You're a fine brave girl and this is not going to be the main thing you'll remember about your life. I promise you. OK?' The girl smiled tearily. 'And I'll be here when you come round from the anaesthetic, all right? Don't worry, everything will be fine, you'll see.'

Felicity nodded, comforted, and was wheeled away. Kyria controlled her tears and said an unconscious prayer for the small lost soul while she waited for Fliss to return.

But that night, with Felicity relieved and exhausted and sound asleep in her room, Kyria went to bed having seen that the tiny spots of blood were still appearing. Justin awoke in the night hearing her sobs. 'Kyria. Love. Is it the baby? Are you upset about Fliss? Oh love, tell me what's wrong, is it the baby?' When he deciphered what she was telling him through her crying, and realised that yes, she was crying for the baby, but not only Felicity's, he understood what she had done that day for his daughter and for him and even while he joined in her tears he was rejoicing at having found this woman. Justin was not of a philosophical bent but his mental suffering had provided him with gifts as well as arrows and the most precious amongst these was an innate respect for love. He knew what he and Nita had thrown away – nothing great or overwhelming, nothing spectacular, but a shared life, a quiet love and a usually happy family – and was determined to hold on to every precious drop of it in his new life.

The tears were without cause; Kyria's first scan, at ten weeks, showed an active, minuscule being with a regular heartbeat which lit up as an intense white dot on the ultrasound screen. 'Tinkerbell!' murmured Kyria to Justin who sat at her side. This foetus clearly had no intention of departing early and though Kyria continued to lose a little blood every four weeks until the sixth month of her pregnancy she was confident that Tink would hang on in there. At fourteen weeks the couple told Felicity and Harmony both the date of their wedding and Kyria's due date, which was not long after Nita's.

'That's great news! Well done, Dad! And Kyria of course.' Harmony was genuinely delighted. Felicity was working out the timing of events and when she hugged her stepmother-to-be she was as glad to discover that there would still be a baby after all as she was in the knowledge that it wouldn't be her own. In the midst of their celebrations, all four of them were aware that this announcement was being enthusiastically welcomed while Nita's last two pregnancies had met with horrified responses. Felicity and Harmony, catching one another's eye, missed their mother for the first time since they had left her six weeks earlier. Thus an impulse to take the first tentative steps on the road towards reconciliation was sparked and the girls called Nita that evening to arrange their first return visit the following weekend.

6

Tom was away on a British Council junket in Prague, so Nita had the girls to herself. There was a happy reunion with Katie and loud exclamations at the size of Nita's bump, which at almost five months already looked large on her small frame. A great wave of relief fell over the household and they enjoyed two days of quietly, gently, easing themselves back into one another's lives, taking walks during the warm summer evenings and needing to say very little. On their last night, with Katie and Harmony already asleep, Felicity told Nita about her pregnancy and its termination. Battling with an intense jealousy that her lovely girl had depended upon another woman at a time when she should by rights have called for her mother, Nita spoke wisely and softly to her daughter and hid her own pain. Sloth was nowhere to be seen; Nita exuded a tranquillity, a soothing calm as she rocked Felicity in her arms.

'Mum, I'm sorry I didn't tell you, I just felt so confused about everything.'

'Shhh, love, I understand. I haven't been here for you recently, I understand.'

'And Kyria's really nice, Mum, she wanted me to talk to you but I wouldn't and I know she and Dad discussed calling you anyway but I told them I'd go away if they dared to do it.'

'It's all right, love. I'm glad you had Kyria with you. And glad for her and your dad too. I really am. I've missed my girls, you know. It's been very strange here without you and our Harm.'

'I thought you'd like it better if it was just you and Katie and – him.'

'I suppose I did too, love. I thought we'd all be happier. But don't blame Tom for everything. If there was a rift between me and you it wasn't him that put it there.' Felicity remembered the note she had left and began to apologise but Nita interrupted her. 'Don't worry about that. I suppose I'd have found out one way or another, those sort of things never go away completely. And we discussed it, he didn't deny it. But it was a long time ago now and though I'm not saying it was easy to let bygones be bygones that's what I've had to do. Do you see that, love?'

'Mum, there's another thing too. You know when I said he'd touched me?' Nita felt a little sick but didn't stop her rocking. 'Well, I just made it up. It wasn't true. I got mad with him and I suppose I was jealous of him and angry at you for getting pregnant again – and it was after – Dave and everything – so I thought of the worst thing I could say about him. Like a test for you, you know?'

'Not one I passed with flying colours, love, was it?' Nita sounded wry now but was in fact hugely relieved. She hardly seemed to know Tom these days, it wouldn't have been the greatest surprise in the world to hear that he had tried something on with Fliss but it would have made the prospect of the next few months even more exhausting than she already found them.

'I don't blame you. It was a terrible thing to say about anyone. Listen, Mum, me and Harm don't mind Tom. He's just not – Dad. And not that interested in us. How can he be, we were already too old when you started seeing him, he was always going to seem like an added-on thing to me and Harm. Especially because Dad was ill and it didn't seem fair to make him leave us then. Oh Mum, I didn't want to make you cry, I'm sorry.'

'It's just that you sound so grown-up and sensible, Fliss, and I've not been very sensible. About your dad – I can see how it seemed, but I just couldn't go on any longer. Didn't have any help with it and couldn't see any light at the end of the tunnel. For five years we were just treading water and I couldn't bear it any longer, lost all hope. But I'm happy for him now, Fliss, I truly am. I think he and Kyria will have a good marriage and I'm glad for them.'

'Do you wish you were still married to him?'

'No. No, I wish we'd worked harder at it but I think that at the time I couldn't have. And I love Tom. I know he's not perfect, but I love him very much.'

'How is he?

'Still down. It's funny, he's been like that since you left. We've all been miserable, haven't we?'

'Maybe he thinks it's his fault we left. Tell him it isn't, won't you? And tell him I'm sorry about – about everything I did before I left.'

'I will, love. Thanks for that. He'll appreciate it.'

Despondent at being turned down yet again, and so firmly, by Cressida, Tom certainly did appreciate Felicity's apology and yet it hardly dented the carapace of his misery. He was slowly despairing of ever finding his way through the all-encompassing unsatisfactoriness of his life, and started to feel obliged to shore up any bits of his crumbling world that could feasibly be salvaged. Returning to Nita after her weekend with the girls, he was aware of a new mood in her. She promptly stopped attending her pregnancy yoga classes, only went swimming once a week and took the bus to work rather than walking. While she rested her body, her mind was working overtime; she was tearing through novels on the bus journey, reading the books from Tom's shelves which she had previously ignored and putting aside her own collection of herbal medicine dictionaries and self-help manuals which had been the subject of much mockery from him over the three years they had known each other. In the evenings she took Katie for rambles in the nearby countryside to pick wild flowers which she later identified at home, read a broadsheet newspaper, started to attempt the cryptic crossword and bombarded Tom with questions about religion, philosophy and the literary classics which started off at beginner level but eventually sent him to survey his shelves for the books in which he would find her answers. While wishing to applaud her intellectual efforts, Tom realised that they made him feel uneasy. It was all so uncharacteristic of Nita, to focus her mind on such a variety of subjects and to attain any depth at all. It was so far removed from the way they had lived that it began to represent, for Tom, a moving apart. He began to fear, not quite consciously, that he was becoming less central to Nita's life, that a vague threat loomed over him which he had to vanquish if he were to hold on to Katie. And since he had given up Cressida for Katie he was prepared to fight for her any way he could.

'Nita. Shall we get married?'

'What! You're joking! What brought this on?'

'Aren't you pleased?'

'Well – yes, I suppose I am but mainly I'm – very, very surprised. We've never discussed marriage.'

'I know, but I thought it was something you'd like to do and now seems to be a good time – I mean, we can wait until after the birth if you like, but now that we're about to have two children and so on, I thought it might be – a good idea.'

'Bloody hell. Look, Tom love, that's a lovely thing to ask but I need to think about it. Oh love, you look all dejected.'

'What is there to think about? I mean, I thought you'd be pleased.'

'Oh, I'm ever so flattered, don't get me wrong. And I really will think about it. It's just that – if we're OK now, why change anything? But listen, I'll give it some thought and we can talk about it again. Just tell me, why do you think it's a good idea?'

'The kids – you know, to put it all on a legal footing and so on.'

'Aren't you supposed to say it's because you love me?'

'Pet, of course I love you. I wouldn't be asking you to marry me if I didn't, would I?'

'It's so – sudden. You know what I mean. I fell in love with you so quickly, Tom, but then I fell for our Katie and so who knows what would have happened if I hadn't? Do you understand? It's as though we've never had any normal life together, any quiet choosing to be with each other sort of time. I don't mean anything particular by that, just that I don't want to fall into something else. I'd rather jump into what happens next. Give me some time to think, love. Just a little bit of time.'

It's hard to say who was the most shocked by this exchange but in both cases it was Nita's response that caused the surprise. She could scarcely believe that as soon as Tom offered her the one thing she had been aiming for it suddenly seemed less attractive. And he felt extremely nervous about why on earth she would turn him down. Her disingenuous explanation of 'falling pregnant', for all its colloquialism, wasn't lost on him either, they both knew that it had been no accident. But mainly, Tom felt anxious and a little insulted. He tried to take it calmly.

'Nita, of course you must think about it but think about this too: I've never asked anyone to marry me before.'

Until the age of twenty-five Tom had slept with four women: he had met his first girlfriend, Lucy, in a nightclub. They were both seventeen and they went out for a year and a half, at which point he left Newcastle for Manchester and the relationship fizzled out. During his first year at university he had an extremely brief series of encounters with Suzanne, a girl in his Victorians tutorial group, which he had hoped would last for rather longer, and a three-month affair with Shabnam, his then best friend's glamorous Iranian girlfriend, which was sexually thrilling but finally depressing and which Tom finished, much to her disappointment. And then in the second year he met Bronwen, with whom he fell in love and lived for three years. The two university years were idyllic; they played at home-making, made inventive, enthusiastic love for hours on end and became the Arts faculty's golden couple, both achieving Firsts (hers was in History although she, like Tom, planned to write), both attracting a wide circle of friends and both evidently set for great things. On the eve of their graduation, as Bronwen lay in his arms, Tom asked her to marry him and she instantly said yes. They would wed when each of them had a book deal.

Once they left their circle of friends and set up together in a shabby rented flat in Shepherd's Bush (Tom was aware that writers had to live in London; that was the main Rule), they began to founder. Bronwen was temping in the daytime and doing bar work four evenings a week. Tom was writing. After six months during which she paid the rent and he continued to write, Bronwen, who had always been of a lively, good-humoured disposition, began to change. She was justifiably resentful of Tom's zero contribution to the household – not only did he provide negligible amounts of cash gleaned from poorly-paid bits of journalism and copywriting, but he also failed utterly to lend a practical hand on the cooking and cleaning front. Bronwen was exhausted and unsupported which triggered not only unprecedented levels of bad temper but also a hard line in physical violence. Shocked by her new aggression, Tom readily accepted her accusations of negligence and began to play a more active role, taking on a part-time clerical job, which he detested, and wielding the mop and hoover on a regular basis. Neither the temper nor the violence diminished though – once the dam had been unblocked there seemed to be no stopping the deluge – and every couple of days Tom would find himself nursing a cut cheekbone or a bruised shoulder. Although she was almost his height, Bronwen should have been no match for him but she never pulled her punches and he, well-brought up young man that he was, never dreamt of hitting her back. Scrap that: he dreamt well enough, he would just never do it. Behind the vicious creature with hard fists and pinching fingers Tom could still see her beloved face saying yes to his marriage proposal and the thought of sullying it with a blow was anathema to him.

It was clear, however, that Bronwen's feelings about the marriage plan had changed and when, one New Year's Eve, she fractured his wrist with a well-aimed saucepan, thrown from the bedroom door, ostensibly in punishment for his inability to satisfy her sexually (her demands had become increasingly dramatic and Tom was rarely able to relax sufficiently and thus hardly ever ejaculated, a failure which enraged and insulted her), Tom realised that the relationship was over. He spent the next fortnight drunk and the following four months finishing what was to become his first published novel. The postcard he sent to Bronwen – who had stayed in their flat while he slept on friends' floors – telling her about his publishing deal and wishing her well in her endeavours – was returned to him with 'Fuck You' scrawled on it in purple eyeliner. Tom didn't have sex with anyone except himself in the aftermath of Bronwen for almost four years, until he was twenty-five, at which point he decided to take matters into his own hands or rather, stop having to do so. Not all women were like Bronwen, he knew, but none of them – not one – would ever be given the chance to diminish him as she had done.

And so. He wasn't being entirely truthful to Nita about the marriage proposal. While Tom sometimes liked to shock his lovers with tales of Bronwen's brutality – she had become a well-known children's writer, getting her first series of books accepted only a year after the split and so her name was a familiar one – he was careful to share it only with the most sensitive of souls and on at least three occasions its judicious telling had opened previously impenetrable arms, and subsequently legs, to him. Or he told the women who had no convenient outlet for the story – the married ones who weren't on the literary circuit mostly. He had told Cressida too – just because he told Cressida everything – and then wished he hadn't because her response had been completely unsatisfactory.

'Do you think she might have been jealous that you were more successful?'

'What!'

'Don't jump down my throat. I just mean – well, maybe she was insecure about her writing and you were getting bits and bobs here and there and –'

Tom cut in sharply, 'I don't believe you're saying this. She *beat me up*. For fuck's sake, why are you looking for excuses for her?'

'Not excuses. Just trying to understand. I'm not excusing her, it's appalling behaviour, I just wondered –'

'Well, don't just wonder. OK? There aren't two sides to this story. She was a bitch and she treated me like a dog. OK? If you love me you must see that, Cressida. You must.' Cressida looked away, exasperated at her lover's ability to become passionate about the past to such an extent, when she saw that there was so much to inflame her in the present and the future.

She was the only woman he'd told about the marriage proposal even though in his own reworking of the history it had never happened; he had extrapolated backwards and convinced himself that he had been wary from the start; conscious of a psychotic streak in Bronwen which ensured he never surrendered to her utterly. This was self-delusion, he had been madly in love with her, in a way which now seemed to be merely a prototype for the way he loved Cressida, but which had been love nevertheless. So at the moment he told Nita he'd never proposed before, he actually meant it, although he realised his mistake a moment later. Not that it made any difference.

And now that Bronwen had returned to occupy some space in his brain, Tom realised that there were lots of things about her that reminded him of Cressida. They were both quick-witted, sardonic, several steps ahead of him at times, and he loved it. They both gave themselves up to him and yet still controlled him during lovemaking in a way he hadn't encountered with any other woman; a subtle combination of surrender and imposition which was entirely instinctive. And they both loved him with a passion which sparked its twin in him and which meant that to seriously countenance pursuing and making love to another woman filled him with something like disgust. Bronwen's strident North Welsh accent was nothing like Cressida's faint hint of Yorkshire (being of a contrary nature, she had hung on to her faint Leeds accent with enormous care, defending against any hint of creeping south-erliness) but regardless of the vowel sounds there was some lilt to the tone, some quality in the voice, which held the same appeal for him. Come to think of it, their colouring was similar too – light brown hair, fair skin and blue eyes – and even their build, which was curvier and taller – their shoulders almost level with his own – than the women he usually went for, who tended to look rather more like Shabnam, and indeed Nita, being small to the point of fragile, dark-haired, dark-skinned, dark-eyed and – though Tom would never admit this – usually in some way exotic. The arm he placed around the skinny shoulders of his typical paramour had something colonial about it, even as it seemed to protect. Especially as it seemed to protect. Bronwen and Cressida were also at least as clever as he was. Nobody else had been.

So Tom's Prime Motivator didn't kick in until he was twenty-five, a full-grown man, before which his activities in the Lust department were hardly unusual. What would Harry make of that?

Perhaps he'd try to journey further back into Tom's history; as far back as we can: why not to the instant when he slithered from his mother into the world next to the motionless little body of his twin sister? Tom didn't need to remember the moment; he'd imagined often enough the expression of grief on his mother's face as she stared at the still limbs of her firstborn child then picked up the dead baby and held her close while the midwife gathered up her living, breathing, kicking younger brother and took him away until the opportunity for a maternal welcome came around. Which it undoubtedly did, as the grief was tempered by joy, but Tom never quite lost the feeling that he was an interloper; his survival seemed due not to luck but to some sneaky trick he'd played *in utero*. Throughout his childhood and adolescence, all his hard work and good marks and creative endeavours failed, he was sure, to compensate his mother for her loss, which he rarely thought of as a loss he shared but one for which he was entirely responsible. And yet the urge to search for his missing half was as terrifying as it was powerful, which might partially explain why he so rarely found a girl he could take home to Mother, how the compulsion to hunt, to collect women was stronger in him than he would ever acknowledge, and how seductive it was to pursue women who were entirely Other, whose eyes could never be reflections of his own. Tom had once misquoted Cressida during one of their quarrels and she had snapped at him, 'I didn't say that. You must be confusing me with someone else.'

Without thinking, Tom had replied, 'No! The only person I ever confuse you with is me.' It had proved a surprisingly effective *non sequitur*.

7

Margaret had been unwilling to have a scan unless there was any suggestion that something was wrong. Like many doctors, she had an unhealthy scorn for the machinery used to treat the common man or woman and so she was already fourteen weeks pregnant when she finally decided, encouraged by Mary whose excitement clearly exceeded her own, that now was as good a time as any to have a look at this baby. The pregnancy was making her feel grossly distended, continually exhausted and blissfully content, and as she settled herself on to the couch and allowed her belly to be covered with gel by some junior technician she marvelled at how far she'd come.

'Now then, Margaret,' lisped the young woman in a kindergarten tone which would have made the pre-pregnancy and pre-Mary Dr Fisher wince but which now made her feel cared-for and special, 'let's have a look at your baby, shall we? It's a fine bump for sixteen weeks,' she murmured as she slid the blunt-headed scanner over Margaret's belly and then without pausing for breath added, 'Ah, that'll be why. Look at this, Margaret.'

The doctor turned her head to scrutinise the screen, and almost choked. Bobbing gently in the gloom were two embryos. Tiny movements of their limbs made ripples in the surrounding liquid and every few seconds they seemed to almost touch for a moment and then move away, apparently oblivious of one another.

'Twins!' squeaked Margaret.

'Jesus, Mary and Joseph!' exclaimed Mary, crossing herself automatically. Then she saw the tears on Margaret's face. 'Peggy. Margaret. It's OK, my darling, it's all right. We'll manage. We'll manage.'

But the expectant mother shook her head and began to laugh.

'Of course we'll manage. Mary, this is wonderful. This is abso-fuckinglutely wonderful.'

The technician blinked nervously as the women hugged and then all three turned back to watch the babies swimming their primordial dance in leisurely, suspended animation.

Margaret had never questioned her longing for a child very deeply, assuming it was something to do with a desire for 'proper' family life. When she was six years old her father, Dr Greene, a consultant anaesthetist, left their home in Guildford to live with his mistress, a nurse, who was about to give birth to his child. Margaret's mother was seven months pregnant at the time, and two days after her husband's surprise departure she gave surprise birth at home to a second daughter who lived for twenty-eight hours exactly. This was the mid-sixties and the elderly family doctor, who had attended the birth wielding his forceps un-necessarily, signed the death certificate with a sigh then, on his way out of the door, spotted the silent child watching him from the top of the stairs and beckoned her to him. Young Peggy was shocked when the doctor's moist red lips approached her ear and he hissed. 'And woman shall give birth in pain. It's a terrible business. Don't forget. Study, my girl. Study and you will escape your lot. Now, you must be a good quiet girl and look after your poor mother, d'ye hear?'

The girl nodded blankly as she watched the doctor open the front door, leaving her with her distraught mother and the tiny corpse of her sister, whom the undertaker had trouble separating when he arrived an hour later, at the doctor's behest, with a little wooden box and a length of white silk. Her father was attending the birth of his son, Stephen, when his baby daughter's burial took place. Many of the mourners, particularly members of the proud father's family, found their social skills uniquely challenged when they attended Stephen's christening two months later. By then, though, Margaret's mother had returned with her daughter to her home town of Liverpool and a few years later married Solomon Fisher, a local man fifteen years her senior, but had no more children. Margaret never saw her father again and although her stepfather was kind to her, and legally adopted her, they had little in common and both Solomon and her mother saw her academic achievements as the perfect way to get her out of the house. Small wonder that the girl developed a strong desire for normal family life along with a deep-rooted fear of the same. And yet at the time of the scan she felt nothing but delight.

Sophie's scans and antenatal check-ups had proceeded well but on hearing about the worrying symptoms she reported, her GP had referred her for a series of urgently carried out tests in various hospital departments, culminating in a consultation with a neurologist. Unclear about what the tests were for, and still in a sublime state of happy expectancy, Sophie asked Cressida to go with her to see the specialist. They sat side by side as the neurologist talked them incomprehensibly through the results, ending with the sinister question: 'Have you heard of MS, Sophie?'

'Um, yes, I think so. That's the one where you feel down all the time and can't be bothered, isn't it?'

'Well, not exactly, I –'

'Oh, I'm sure it can't be that, in fact I've never felt more bothered, and I'm certainly not depressed or anything, so –'

'Sophie, I think you mean ME.'

'Isn't that what you said?' Cressida held Sophie's hand.

'No. No, I'm talking about MS. Multiple sclerosis. Does that mean anything to you?'

'Multiple sclerosis? Like Jacqueline Thingy?' Sophie's eyes filled with tears and her voice rose to a strained pitch. 'But I can't have that. That kills people. I can't die, I'm having a baby.'

'I realise this must be a shock but please let me explain. Jacqueline Du Pré is a famous example of someone who suffered an extreme form of MS, what we call "galloping" MS, for obvious reasons, but not all cases are the same. The way in which it affects each person is different. There are lots of different symptoms and levels of extremity and life expectancy –'

'Oh God.'

'What I mean is, you're right to think about your future with this baby. And there's no reason why you shouldn't have a perfectly normal pregnancy and birth and many many years –'

'Oh God.'

'– left to you. Now, you're not going to be able to digest all this information at once so I'm going to give you some written material which you can read at your own pace, and then I'll ask you to make some further appointments in my clinic. We will inform your GP who will ensure that everyone involved in your ante- and post-natal care is aware of your condition.'

'Why do they need to know? Will they catch it?'

'No, it's not a disease in that sense, not something infectious. It's just important that the medical staff caring for you know you have MS and take it into consideration when prescribing any kind of treatment. Although normally, I must stress, you will need exactly the same kind of treatment as you would if you didn't have the condition. Do you understand?'

Sophie sobbed an affirmative and trotted out of the building and into the car park, with Cressida's arm around her, clutching a small sheaf of pastel-coloured photocopied sheets and a few leaflets in her trembling hand. Once in the car she grabbed Cressida's arm and said dramatically, 'Promise me, Cress, that if anything happens to me you'll take care of this baby.'

'Oh Sophie, don't worry, you're going to be able to look after this baby, there are all sorts of things you can do and like the doctor said you never know how seriously you're going to be affected, you might never even have an attack again.'

'Yes I will. I just know it. Please Cress, promise me.'

'I promise.' Cressida seemed to have no choice but to make the vow, although as she did so it was with a fervent hope, and not for wholly admirable reasons, that she would never have to honour it.

Cressida took Sophie home with her and as Harry opened the door expectantly she threw herself into his arms, sobbing her apologies for unwittingly putting his baby at risk in this way. Cressida explained what the doctor had told them and Harry felt an enormous anxiety emerge, fully formed, from somewhere inexplicable within him. It was the first time he had actually connected Sophie's bump with himself, but it was little more than an embarrassing prospect until it was so obviously threatened. And he recognised a deep concern for Sophie too, she who was so affectionate and loyal and now carried his third child. Much as he loved Cressida, he began to entertain idle daydreams about the life he could have had with someone as doting and straightforward as Sophie. Well, to be precise, the life he could have had with Sophie.

This didn't happen in front of the children. Ben and Jemima remained sanguine in spite of the adult maelstrom whirling above their heads. At four and three years respectively they understood most of what went on and, provided they maintained pole position in the lives of their parents, were generally unfazed by it. Tears and arguments had been kept entirely out of their path and, while their sense of Cressida's sadness and Harry's suffering naturally entered their skin by osmosis, it was always accompanied by their sense of love and so they were protected, mostly, from damage. It was fun, in any case, to see Auntie Sophie so much and the prospect of the new babies – first Mummy's and then Auntie Sophie's – inspired, as one might imagine, a whole range of creative and educational play.

8

Just as Harry was beginning to feel calmer about the ludicrous turn his life had taken, and even beginning to look forward to the births of his wife's child by Tom and his own baby by Sophie, the seventh baby turned up. Not exactly on his doorstep, nor quite at his feet, but very definitely on his conscience.

He had heard no news of Nicola since the night of their unfortunate sexual liaison, save a brief memo from the departmental Registrar telling him that Ms Mackenzie had decided to take a couple of months off to attend to some family business and then work on her thesis at home. Harry toyed with the idea of sending her a note of apology but had no idea what he could possibly say and so left the matter alone. It wasn't as though he didn't have enough to think about already, and possibly leaving a little time and space between them would make matters easier when they did meet again.

Nicola had different plans, though. The morning after that fateful night she had made some important decisions about her life and the direction it was taking. Several changes were urgently required. She also recognised a strong desire to see her mother, to feel at home, and to extract herself from the university, at least temporarily, in order to consider her next move.

Nicola's late father, Arden Mackenzie was a Coloured South African, the result of a brief affair between a black housemaid and a white student, whose promise to take her away with him to Europe crumbled as soon as parental pressure of a monetary nature was gently applied. Young Arden never met his father, but thanks to an anonymous monthly cheque his mother was able to save up enough cash to buy her son a decent further education after a strong start at the local Mission school. At twenty-two, Arden left the home where he lived with his mother, just outside Johannesburg, for London, armed only with a law degree and various vigorously wriggling sacks of guilt about leaving his mother and his country at what proved to be a particularly difficult time for both. He threw himself into the new liberties – compromised liberties to be sure but these things are relative – of metropolitan life in the free world. Tall, handsome, hard-working and a persuasive talker, within three years he was a junior partner in a respected small law firm owned by an ex-colonial with yet another guilt complex, earning enough money to send generous sums home to both his mother and the ANC, though the sacks never did quit their wriggling, and spend the remainder on living the bachelor lifestyle to the full.

Nicola's mother, Bathsheba D'Aguar, left Guyana with her parents and six older siblings in the early 1960s and trained in London as a nurse. When working in the A&E department of a city hospital she treated Arden who had been admitted unconscious and bleeding, the victim, it appeared, of a violent and probably racist attack. When he recovered consciousness and was interviewed by police the young man confirmed that yes, his assailants had been white and no, he could neither give descriptions of them nor think of any reason why they should have attacked him. But later, as Bathsheba, with the gentlest hands he'd ever felt on him, busied herself with his wounds behind the cubicle curtains, Arden was overcome by a double blow: an intense pang of conscience and the unfortunate effects of concussion, and whispered woozily to the little nurse that it was only one man who had beaten him – he was no fighter despite his six-foot-four-inch frame – and that it was because he, Arden, had slept with the man's wife. Bathsheba tutted quietly and said in her soft accent, which kept more than a hint of the musical Creole she had spoken as a child, 'That's a bad thing you did. But it's still not right that he hit you around like this, nope, that's still not right.'

Arden chuckled flirtatiously through his medication. 'Well, to tell the truth, nurse – should I call you nurse? Do you have another name?'

'Nurse is just fine.'

'OK, nurse, to tell the truth he didn't hit me just because of that. It was because of something I said about his wife.'

'Oh?' Bathsheba's curiosity was uncontainable. So was Arden's giggling.

'Yes, you see she had told him about our affair – if you can call it that – and so he'd come to have it out with me man to man. And I'm afraid I told him he was welcome to her.'

'Oh.'

'That's right. And he said – what do you mean? – so I told him that I never wanted to see his wife's fat white arse again.'

'And then he hit you, right?'

'That's right.'

'Did he hit you as hard as this?'

'As hard as what?'

'As hard as this.' Bathsheba's healing hands applied a stinging slap to Arden's cheek, opening a wound near his mouth and providing the final blow to a loose upper molar. 'Don't you ever dare speak that filth again. About any woman. Seems to me like you need some respect and maybe that man found the only way you're gonna find any.' Pulling the cubicle curtains smartly behind her with a decisive swish, Bathsheba exited while Arden spat his tooth out and stared at it, white and bloody in his palm, thinking – that's a strange way to fall in love. Younger than him by ten years, plump, pretty, spirited and capable of taking moral charge of him, she was perfect.

Bathsheba's first three babies were girls, then she had three boys. There was only one tricky patch, a late miscarriage, when Bathsheba was forty-four, which sent her into a long depression during which her young sons were puzzled at their mother's behaviour and her older daughters realised that the lost baby was never to be referred to. Then that period in turn seemed to segue into the Change until Bathsheba realised that she was in fact pregnant again and she gave birth to Nicola, her beloved surprise, her baby.

Being the seventh child of a seventh child was a terrible burden for a bright, sensitive girl. If there was one thing Nicola could accurately predict it was her own utter lack of prescience. Had she accepted that first sight was more than most people achieve –

think of her parents falling in love – she would never have expected to attain second. But her continued inability to harness the power she believed she had been born with left her frustrated and ashamed, to the extent that she could not talk about it to her family. The first time she learnt of the infamous saying, when she was seven years old, Nicola had run to her mother to ask whether that meant she was Special, and Bathsheba, keen to imbue her daughter with all the confidence the world would require of her even if it did demand a little bending of the truth – assured her that it did indeed make her extremely Special and Powerful. This only verified for the child what she had always suspected; some sense of being treated differently, of being in some respects an outsider, which had worried her in a vague, uncommunicable way. Now that she understood, she believed, the reason for this feeling of otherness, Nicola waited to feel the power course through her veins and tested her second sight on a daily basis, but never felt the slightest bit special and became convinced that she was a failure as a seventh child. The most obvious effect of all this anxiety on the girl was to render her trust in her own instincts almost utterly useless; consequently she found it difficult to make the leap of trust required to form close friendships. Arden's death from cancer shortly after her sixteenth birthday exacerbated her sense of isolation. Nicola was strikingly beautiful and coolly aloof, the conquest every boy in school – in fact, every straight male in school, from headmaster to first former – dreamt of making. Science, certainty, the study of the finite, became her benchmarks and she concentrated her academic efforts in Maths, Physics and Chemistry. She scorned superstition and religion, knew perfectly well that she shouldn't believe in old wives' tales at her age, yet clung sentimentally and secretly to her belief in the myth of the Seventh Child. During her two years as star pupil of the Sixth Form at her local comprehensive, where all of her older brothers and sisters had already marked out a shining path of achievement which Nicola simply flew over without noticing it fading beneath her, she undertook deliberate, almost cynical experiments to test what she was convinced was her lack of instinct: with an air of extraordinary detachment she entered into a series of short-lived sexual relationships with older men, two of whom were her teachers and all of whom found themselves overawed in her presence. Vain, irresponsible, their erotic imaginations paralysed at adolescence while their limbs lolloped towards middle age, it was unsurprising that none of Nicola's early lovers impressed her much. Later, at university, she became involved with men her own age and found in these experiences both more physical satisfaction and mental equality, but she would never have described herself as having fallen in love. This bothered her, and her desire to find an explanation for it soon superseded her quest for love itself.

She began her higher education studying Chemistry at Cambridge, but during her wide and diligent reading on the whole gamut of scientific studies she discovered Psychology, the subject in which she would, surely, find the precise truth about the mind, particularly her mind, and its evident failings. She had then taken a second degree, financially supported by her mother who had been left very comfortably off by Arden, and then her PhD. It must be said that the world Nicola had inhabited for all of her adult life was a rarefied one, and possibly not the best environment for the lonely voyage of discovery she had embarked upon.

Nine weeks after the night with Harry – nine weeks which had given Bathsheba constant joy and her daughter only an occasional headache as she learnt how to relax, how to be waited upon with good grace, and how to sleep for hours on end – it was dinnertime, and Bathsheba was busy in the kitchen.

'Almost ready my darlin',' she shouted through to the dining room where Nicola's PC was set up on the table. 'Your favourite; fried chicken with rice and peas.' Nicola's favourite had actually been, for several years, chilli crab linguine, but she'd been very well brought up and never mentioned this.

'Great, Mamma, I'll tidy up here and get the table ready. Just us tonight?' More often than not a selection of the ever-growing Mackenzie family came round to eat with Bathsheba; she mock-grumbled that she had to cook more now than she did when her kids were small.

'That's right, honey, just us. Here we go.' She set a plate in front of Nicola, piled high with steaming food.

'Mmmm, smells fantastic, Mamma!' Nicola leaned over and took a deep breath, which hit the back of her throat with unusual force and caused an equal and opposite reaction from her stomach.

'Honey, what's wrong?' shouted Bathsheba as her daughter ran, hand clutched to mouth, to the downstairs toilet.

Nicola reappeared and sat down, puzzled.

'Sorry, Mum, I don't know –'

'I know,' interjected Bathsheba. 'I know. Let me see your eyes.' She took Nicola's face between her hands, stared for ten seconds before letting her hands drop and said, undramatically, 'You're having a baby, aren't you?' She saw in an instant that this was news she was telling. 'Oh honey, you didn't know. You didn't know. Sugar, what's been happening?'

Bathsheba got the expurgated version, which boiled down to an unfortunate alcohol-fuelled liaison with a tutor that had obviously gone badly wrong contraceptively.

'But weren't you – you know, using something?'

'Of course, Mum, that must have been the problem – you see, I had been using a coil –'

'A coil! A bit of metal in your womb which scrapes the babies out of it every month? My daughter, having a coil?'

'Mum, it seemed like a good idea, better than fiddling around with a cap or stuffing my body with hormones – but anyway, listen, I decided it wasn't efficient enough so I'd changed over to the Pill. And it should have been fine, but there must have been something funny about my cycle, because obviously the Pill hadn't taken effect. I realise now I've missed at least one period but thought it was something to do with the Pill –'

'But what about safe sex? You think I know nothing, but I see the telly. You should have had a condom.'

'No, it's OK, I would usually, but he's married –'

'Married!'

'Yes, and has only slept with his wife for the last – I don't know, ten years or something, so there was no risk of disease or anything.'

'He told you that and you believed him?'

'Yes, he's a nice bloke.'

'A nice bloke!'

'Look, Mum, he's a nice bloke but we both got drunk and did something very silly and – anyway, hold on a minute, I'm the one that's found out she's pregnant, why am I having to offer you the words of comfort, hey?'

'Because I'm your mother and very soon you're going to know what that means and then you'll –' Bathsheba fell silent.

'Then I'll what?'

'Nicola – you aren't going to – you are going to *have* this baby, aren't you?'

'I honestly don't know, Mum, haven't thought about it, I mean, Jesus –'

'Uh-uh!' Even *in extremis* blasphemy was banned in Bathsheba's house.

'Sorry, I mean, well, this is a bit of a shock. I need to think. Need some time.'

'How long gone are you? Why didn't you notice before?'

'It must be – it was just before I got here, so nine weeks I suppose. My periods haven't been regular these past few years –'

'It'll be that womb-scraper that's made them go wrong.'

'Whatever.'

'Don't you whatever me, my girl. Just before you came here? Is that why you came? My baby, is there something you're not telling me? Did he – did this man *rape* you? Tell me, my honey, is that why you came here?'

'Partly,' replied Nicola truthfully. 'Oh Mum, don't cry, I don't mean I've been raped or anything like that, I mean yes, what happened made me want to come back home for a bit – but this is just my own stupid fault and some really bad luck, OK? And it will be all right, whatever happens, I'll be fine. But you need to help me, OK, Mum? Will you help me?'

'Oh sugar,' wept Bathsheba. 'My baby. Come to Mamma.'

9

Nita was learning lots of things fast. Yet she never seemed to be in a frenzy and was managing to maintain the air of peace which had come upon her when she cradled Felicity in her arms. Sloth, apparently overtaken by tranquillity, the Sin providing the Virtue. The impression of ease was aided enormously by the size of her belly, which forced her to move slowly, majestically, like a little galleon. But she felt it within, as well, and most particularly she was aware of a clarity to her thoughts, an ability which she had never experienced before to separate what might be termed her head from her heart. So she saw within her love of Tom all the loneliness of a divorcee approaching middle age with children on the brink of adulthood, who feared the prospect of living alone. She saw the attraction of his modest but tangible fame, and especially of his intellectual achievements, and understood how her misguided perception both of his desirability (he wasn't that famous) and her own fading charms (which were actually more changing than fading; she just hadn't noticed) led her to deceive him in order to conceive Katie. She didn't waste time pondering his multiple deceptions and insincerities, they were not her concern right now, although the knowledge of them increased her feeling of regret for having been instrumental in holding on to a man who really didn't want to hold on to her. She saw that she – anyone – deserved better and that he had sacrificed his freedom for their child, and not for love of her. She felt shame at having tried to exert so much insidious control over matters which obeyed no controls. She decided to forgive herself these attempts at control. And, finally, she saw that she would have to do something about it.

When Nita was seven months pregnant she asked Tom to sit down at the kitchen table and hear her out. She told him what she had seen, silencing his initial attempts to interject and refute and calmly stating everything she knew. For Tom, it was one of the most shattering moments of his life; the realisation that all his work to dupe Nita had failed. Followed by the realisation that his work had been simply to dupe Nita. Yes, to stay with Katie, of course, but the work that was required was to make his life into a constant lie. Even though he had kept secret his love for Cressida, about which Nita still knew nothing, he had failed in his duplicity, had wasted over three years of their lives pretending. And now Nita was the wiser. Now Nita was, remarkably, the stronger. Now Tom was about to be dumped.

'. . . and so you see,' Nita finished, 'there's nothing more you can say about it. I love you as much as I ever have, but I haven't really known you, have I? And I see that you don't love me and that's no way for us to live. I won't live like that any longer.'

'But to keep the family together. Nita, I realise things haven't been perfect between us, but everyone needs to make compromises, don't they? No relationship is perfect, is it? And as for the children, they need –'

'They need honest parents. They need truth. And they need calm. You and me together doesn't allow for that. I've already messed my life up once and I am not going to do it again.'

'What, you call breaking up a second family *not* messing your life up?'

'In this case, yes. Because I need – I *want* – more than this. I don't mean I want another man, I think I've tried that bloody merry-go-round once too often. I mean I want to live *with myself*. And the way things are between us, I just can't. I'm sorry, Tom.'

'I must live with my children. I will not allow you to take Katie away.'

'I'm not going anywhere. And if you stay in Manchester you will see her every day. I don't mind if you stay living here, at least for a while. But not as my man. For God's sake, Tom, as if I'd ever take her away from you, or you away from her. You're a very, very good father and she would hate to be apart from you for any length of time.'

'So you're suggesting we live in the same house? How in hell is that going to work?'

'I'm not sure it will, it's just there as an offer.'

'Nita. Don't you – don't you *want* me any more?'

'No. Not really. I mean, sleeping with you has been one of the best things in my life, but now I see how it's been – really see it – it's changed how I feel about it. I couldn't be your lover any more.'

'Please, pet. Please, I do love you, I know I haven't shown it very well but I –' Tom's voice failed him as, finally, reality bit. Hard. 'But – but nothing. You're right. I'm sorry. I'm very, very sorry.'

'That's OK. I'm sorry too. Truly, Tom.'

If Harry's sin/virtue theory is going to work out, the upside of Tom's lust should be – what? His love? Too vague. Maybe his love for one woman, his ability to harness all that physical yearning and use it to make one woman deliriously, eternally happy? Maybe. But it looks like he's missed the boat, both ways.

Not that Cressida and Harry were making each other deliriously happy. By five months into her pregnancy they had made a few desultory attempts at lovemaking but neither had their heart in it and had given up halfway through. Having moved past the phase of passion – be it passionate love for someone else or passionate jealousy of someone else (Tom managed to be omnipresent, unwittingly) – they were both simply exhausted. Cressida's libido backed off and Harry's confusion about his feelings for Sophie moved into the space she'd left. At least it made him appreciate how it was possible to even *think* of infidelity, which he had never previously been able to imagine, but any empathy that gave him with Cressida was outweighed by the guilt it entailed. Sophie, meanwhile, was so used to loving from afar, and so in awe of the kindness she had received from her beloved and his wife, that she hadn't the faintest clue that the very change she had dreamed of for so many years was slowly taking place in Harry's mind. Her illness preoccupied her too; she had suffered blurred vision on one more occasion since the first and was following a careful diet, taking gentle exercise and working fewer hours. Harry could hardly refuse this last request, although his workload was ever-increasing, particularly as the date for his Seven Deadly Sins lecture was only a few months away and he was beginning to feel distinctly wobbly about his central premise.

Despite being fearful of what might happen to her and, more pressingly, her baby, Sophie was determined not to allow that fear to affect everything she did. Cressida's promise was her insurance policy; if anything happened to her the baby would still be cared for, so she set that batch of neuroses to one side and concentrated on taking care of herself. For Sophie, this meant finally learning to respect herself, to take herself seriously and to change the habits of almost a lifetime. The only person she could talk to about the changes in her life was Cressida, to whom she tried to explain.

'Nat was always Mum's favourite. It was a really difficult birth, and touch and go that he would survive, so she wasn't supposed to have any more kids and she and my father doted on him. So when my father died suddenly and she found herself pregnant with me she must have been really shocked. I just don't think she accepted me.'

'Oh Sophie, surely she did? It must have been difficult at first, but I'm sure she was glad to have you.'

'You'd think so, wouldn't you? Even though it must have been difficult. But whatever I did was never good enough. We weren't that well off – my father was a businessman on the way up and his death was unexpected, so he hadn't really made provision. But Nathan got a private education and skiing trips and all the clothes and books he wanted, and my mother always said it was so that he could follow in his father's footsteps, move in the right cicles and everything, but that didn't apply to me. I went to the local comp and never had anything new. I know lots of people feel hard done by but I really wasn't given the same advantages, I'm not just imagining it.'

'Maybe she'll feel differently when she has a grandchild,' proffered Cressida half-heartedly. 'Maybe she's just one of those people who's not very good at showing their emotions.'

'Maybe.' Sophie looked unconvinced. And well she might; she didn't know that on the day of Nathan Senior's funeral, a combination of grief and valium had led her mother, Vivienne, to partake of a night of bitter pleasure in the arms of Josh, her late husband's youngest brother. When they awoke he saw that she looked every year of the thirty-nine she boasted and bowed out gracelessly. Sophie was the resultant second child (supposedly) of

Nathan Diamond – conceived posthumously, even when such scientifically advanced procedures were unheard of – and the truth about her paternity could not be revealed, to her or to Josh. Thus Sophie had grown up with the phrase 'Nat's father' ringing in her ears, convinced that had she only been a better, a more loving, a more peaceable, a brighter and happier child, she might have heard her mother talk about 'your father' with the same yearning sadness.

Sophie's avarice involved holding close to her whatever she possibly could, especially men who might love her, whether they might be father or brother or lover, and the pretty things, the handbags and shoes and clothes which constant scrimping for her brother's bright future had denied her – not for themselves, but as though they might be gifts from mother to daughter, as though these little purchases were maternal messages of comfort and of love.

10

Nobody who knew Cressida would instantly describe her as an angry person, but if someone had asked if she was an angry person the instinctive answer would have been yes. This split was due largely to the fact that Cressida was rarely angry *to* people – her colleagues, her secretary, her friends never felt in the firing line of her anger although its constant subdermal simmering could easily make them nervous, and yet they were all aware that she was angry *about* things. From grammatical errors to the Third World Debt, Cressida was in the habit of exhibiting the most terrifically angry responses to newspaper articles, television headlines, the blurbs on the back of book jackets and the outpourings of any politician, bishop or other spokesperson for whatever kind of faction they might represent.

When she was five years old the family holiday featured a visit to a wishing well.

'Make a wish, darling,' said her mother, handing her a coin. Throwing in the penny, Cressida closed her eyes and dared to wish for the two things she most longed for.

'Wings and a willy,' she whispered fervently. Both symbols of freedom, routes out of the queue. For someone so apparently at ease with the corporeal, Cressida had been wishing her way out of her body – its mortality and its femaleness – ever since, one way or another. Little Cressida had felt herself quite alone when she made her wish – her eyes were tightly shut and she was concentrating hard – so her whisper was less modulated than she meant it to be, and was clearly audible to Patricia, who understood her little girl's desires but never let on she'd heard.

Patricia came from a long line of discontented women who had sacrificed a decade or more of their intellect and ambition on the altar of the family only to discover that their reward wasn't quite as fulfilling as they had been led – or had led themselves – to believe. Cressida was born during the early years of a happy marriage (and, as she now realised, her birth had been a reaffirmation of the marriage after Patricia's affair) whereas her sisters' births coincided with the busiest period of their father's working life when their mother was taking a break from teaching. They remembered tension and shouting; for Cressida her earliest family memories were of a happy young couple beaming at their beloved child. Her ambitions always included finding someone with whom to re-create that charming scene; thus all her early experiments with men were fated to be carried out on the unconscious basis of finding a nice one to marry.

As she moved through school Cressida learnt that her five-year-old wishes had been wise ones. The wings she gave up on once she stopped believing in the Tooth Fairy. But she wouldn't quite relinquish her hold on the willy, realising at nine that the clever boys in her class were not as clever as she was but were granted, nevertheless, more air time, more room for manoeuvre and more tolerant chuckles from teachers. Messy handwriting, an unwillingness to play the guitar at school assemblies and a refusal to be paint monitor were qualities which were welcomed in bright Mark and quick Peter but frowned upon in disobedient Cressida. Her experiences at her Catholic comprehensive school in Leeds proved similar; every well-formed girlish sentence was greeted with an unenthusiastic nod from the teacher, whether male or female, while the most gauche and thoughtless comment from the boys was met with attention, praise and, most notably, an expression of sheer relief. Her London sixth form showed a slightly different slant; a pretty girl saying not much at all could extract an exceedingly encouraging response from male teachers; a plain girl of whatever intelligence met with little but world-weary impatience. There weren't many pretty girls who were intelligent *and* talkative, at least not in public. One or two teachers displayed a genuine disinterest in the gender of their pupils, and there was an inspirational English teacher who made it her life's work to get the clever girls talking, but on the whole the experience of education was a disappointing and frustrating one.

Cressida despaired of the fact that this bubbling pool of gender politics, in which the males seemed worthy of either scorn or pity, was supposed to hold the blueprint for her precious image of happy family life, would eventually have to yield up the man worth devoting herself to, but she never quite gave up on it all, somehow, working out for the best. When she left home for university she exuded a bossy big sister charm which attracted a select series of lovely young men to what developed into a kind of Boyfriend School; they were put through their paces and expected to shape up to their responsibilities from the start. Time and again they failed at an early hurdle – usually the question 'What would you do if I got pregnant?' to which nobody except Harry ever gave a satisfactory answer. Oddly enough, the young men still strove to please her; almost as if they were grateful for her taking the trouble over them, and none of them ever dumped her, or were unfaithful to her; she was always the one who ended the relationship. Perhaps they were scared.

Harry was the most successful Boyfriend in every way, although, even before meeting Tom, Cressida had begun to feel that he had an overly-reverent attitude towards her, especially in bed. When she and Harry made love she felt *worshipped*, a sensation which was partly pleasurable but also disturbing to her; sometimes she wished he were a less caring and careful lover. Sometimes she just wanted to feel *fucked*. Without consciously considering it in these terms, when she had agreed to meet Tom for their first tryst she was convinced that she was embarking upon a short-lived and sordid affair which would teach her to hold on to the good things she already had; almost as though the experience would set her back on track. But she soon discovered that sex with Tom was far from any kind of worship: their lovemaking inhabited a secret world that was usually wordless and always dark, even on the sunniest afternoons, and was such a basic, free and satisfactory transaction that Harry's reverence repelled her and she had no desire to return to being adored in that way. 'Can't you just bloody do whatever *you* feel like doing,' she once demanded in exasperation at the solicitous attention her husband was bestowing on her prone body, 'as hard as you like?' Harry, surprised, had tried to oblige but his heart hadn't seemed to be in it and Cressida felt embarrassed and self-conscious; two sensations which never impinged upon the raw and far more outrageous sexual shenanigans she got up to with Tom.

Perhaps Cressida's confusing life as a girl at home explained her future behaviour towards men: her scientist father habitually demonstrated all the grand passion and blind faith of an artist while her mother taught the great texts of English Literature as though they were little more than pleasingly formulaic arrangements of language (her Arthurian time charts were legendary in the school at which she taught once her own daughters were older). Maybe it's obvious that Cressida might be angry about what you could call mixed messages. And why she might be vulnerable to the charms of a man like Tom.

She was still giving Jemima night feeds when their affair began and she remembered as pivotal the moment when, after sucking gently at her breast for a full minute, Tom trailed his tongue along her skin from nipple to earlobe and whispered, 'Baby, your milk tastes so *sweet*,' before kissing her open mouth to show her. She couldn't help but admire the resourcefulness with which he made use of the materials to hand – his easy changes of pace in response to the fluctuations of her body so that whether she was menstruating, ovulating, lactating, gaining or losing weight, he always relished the opportunities with which she presented him – which gave her a sense of physical emancipation that no amount of considerate stimulation could ever hope to achieve.

Quite how all this resolves what lay behind Cressida's anger is not clear, can never be clear, but it's a clue nevertheless.

Harry still didn't have a clue. His research was beginning to founder, he was concerned that the whole paper might be nothing more than his own neuroses laid bare for all to see. Yes, he'd created elegant arguments for the positive sides of Avarice, Sloth, Anger and the rest – but where was it leading? Having begun to write with optimism and even certainty he was no longer sure about either the basic premise for the document or his ability to discover its journey's end. And he was aware of the painful omission in his cataloguing of characteristics. The name Harry Shepherd didn't appear under any of his seven indices; incredibly, it had never occurred to him to consider himself as a man with a Prime Motivator. As a man like other men.

When Harry was six. Or, no, it could go: When Harry was eight. Or ten. Or thirteen. Picking out a moment is impossible, there was no one defining experience. Instead, there was a slow war of attrition, being fought by his parents, against his spirit. Resentful of the unexpected addition to their unhappy home, his mother and father, who would define themselves as decent people, determined to do everything they could for the education and advancement of their son. Only the best for little Harry, who excelled in examinations and sport, made a few close friends and was never the slightest bit of trouble to anyone. Oxford was a foregone conclusion and his parents were very satisfied indeed. But when he decided to study Psychology they realised that however hard they had worked to give Harry all the things he needed, however much they had discussed the pros and cons of Medicine, the Law and Business, outside influences were about to jump in and ruin everything. Their attempts to dissuade him from taking the path which would inevitably lead to his turning into everything they despised (essentially, a man with a beard) came to nought and his mother became convinced that he had fallen under the influence of drugs, women or some Rasputin-like figure at college. After all they had done for him, their only son had thrown it back in their faces and gone off to study the workings of the human mind. He would, his mother said with a tight-lipped sigh (her speciality), be neither use nor ornament. Even the fact that he remained clean-shaven was not enough to change his parents' minds and so against their hand-wringing wrath Harry had employed the mechanism that was their strongest gift to him, and simply cut off from them. Not socially, not physically – he continued to visit, he introduced them to Cressida, invited them to the wedding and so on – but fundamentally. They didn't even notice.

Now that Harry had begun to see himself more clearly, although still at a distance, he thought it was easy to see how Pride was his downfall.

11

Harry was following the lines between past and present, now and then, back and forth – his fingers were beginning to trace them; with a frown of concentration, tongue peeking out from the corner of his mouth, he started to make sense of the shapes and the sounds, the wavelengths along which his life ran, his own evolution. Still anxious about his impending lecture, still not convinced of his intellectual ability to pull himself out of the abyss and make the right impression in front of his peers, he nevertheless felt increasingly fearless about what he was discovering. Examining himself had developed from being a terrifying inward glance to a steady, satisfying gaze at Harry in the world.

Living with Cressida, who throughout the middle and later months of her pregnancy, in the heat of an Indian summer, had practically gone feral, was helping him enormously. To simultaneously comprehend what was happening inside her body and see her instinctive responses to it – which were mundane, trivial, thoughtless and mainly focused around drinking huge quantities of iced water – became Harry's great joy, his insight into the overlapping circles of beast and angel and therefore into life itself. Prime Motivators apart, he started to find his habitual contemplation of the complexities of human existence almost relaxing; they seemed to perform a kind of dance in his mind's eye which he enjoyed watching but didn't dream of interpreting. Whatever his views on the big picture though, his own life wasn't becoming any easier. He was still in turmoil about Sophie, Cressida was acutely aware of the situation and only Sophie remained oblivious, though even she was starting to find Harry's behaviour towards her odd and the secret was becoming dangerously close to exploding from its box. Only Harry's habitual retentiveness kept the latch closed, for the time being.

Any hopes Harry had for settling in to his strange new life with its concomitant benefits were dashed one warm, windy November morning when he went to the university early. It was Wednesday, a day when he didn't have any morning sessions, and he planned to spend the free time working on his lecture. He had travelled by bus and as he sauntered through the car park outside the faculty entrance he noticed a woman piling crates of files into the boot of her car. Just as he passed she dropped a box; Harry raced across and, as she bent over the escaping papers and he leaned forward to help, was shocked to realise he was looking at Nicola's elegant nape, from a poignantly familiar angle. Focused on saving her work, Nicola didn't realise she had any assistance until she turned around and bumped Harry, who was by then standing motionless and aghast, with her heavily pregnant belly.

'Nicola.'

'Shit!'

'Nicola, you're . . .'

'Shit shit shit.'

Throwing her rescued papers into the boot along with several armfuls of fallen leaves, Nicola moved purposefully around the car and heaved herself into the driver's seat while Harry, coming to from his reverie, tried to dissuade her from leaving. But short of dragging her from the car there was little he could do to stop her. He gabbled a series of questions, apologies and assurances at her through the closed window, and even when she had reversed without looking to see if he was in her path and swung the car around towards the exit he hadn't given up. 'Nicola, I know it's mine, please stay to talk to me, tell me how you are, Nicola, I'm sorry, is it mine? If it's mine I don't mind – I mean, I'll help you, Nicola, it's OK, I'm having a baby already with Sophie and my wife's pregnant too so it's fine, another one is fine, and it will be OK and please stop, Nicola, please stop, if it's my baby . . .'

Nicola's main concern as she sped out of the university gates was for Harry. The one thing she had wanted to avoid – Harry gaining any knowledge of her pregnancy – had happened despite her carefully planned early arrival on a morning he wasn't usually in the faculty. While she didn't keep in touch personally with anyone from the university, she remained by default on a round-robin email list which sent regular gossipy bulletins to all its members and so she had heard the rumours about Sophie and Cressida fairly early on. By that time she had already decided against terminating the pregnancy and any thoughts about discussing the situation with Harry were rejected once she heard of the weird and not very wonderful position he was already in. Since discovering her pregnancy she had done little but work on her thesis and attend antenatal appointments, while her mother fussed and cooked and cared for her, and had thus enjoyed the most relaxed and easeful six months of her life she could remember. Bathsheba was thrilled at the prospect of her youngest child having a child of her own and she and Nicola planned to care jointly for the new baby, with grandma taking over its daily care once mother found a suitable job. As for the birth, Bathsheba would be there in the dual capacity of mother and midwife, with Nicola's sisters doing stints as required. Her close family offered all the support and love she needed, Harry was evidently in a bad way baby-wise and she wouldn't want for money, so Nicola had decided, out of kindness and with some relief, that he wouldn't need to know about yet more impending paternity. She intended to bring the child up with full knowledge of who its father was and had some vague idea of writing to Harry in a few years' time, calmly explaining what had happened and enabling him to meet the child. Bathsheba privately thought this idea was rife with problems and had almost called Harry herself to let the cat out of the bag but hoped that on seeing the baby Nicola would be more prepared to come clean and allow an early meeting of father and child.

Time was moving on, towards December, when all seven babies were due. All of the expectant mothers conceived their respective babies within a month of one another, first Nita, then Cressida (yes, it happened that way round), Kyria, Nicola and Sophie (within nine hours of each other, as we know) and finally Margaret. Their due dates, because of the likelihood that the twins would be delivered at thirty-six rather than forty weeks, were somewhat closer.

Kyria, who had by now married Justin in a tiny, perfect ceremony attended only by Felicity, Harmony and Justin's two closest friends, was excitedly awaiting both the birth of her child and the arrival of a large portion of her family from New Zealand, who had decided that they should postpone their visit until after the birth and thus celebrate the creation of an entire family in one fell swoop. In spite of her regular bleeds and rampant indigestion, Kyria had been so thankful that this child was surviving that she spent the uncomfortable late months of her pregnancy in a benign daze: Justin would return from his more than satisfactory new job to find his delightful new wife lying on the sofa surrounded by discarded bits of textiles (she couldn't be bothered with weaving at the moment, after a flurry of activity in her middle trimester she had become uncharacteristically, overwhelmingly indolent) just holding her bump and beaming widely.

'You look beatific, angelic,' he would say, kissing first her belly, then her mouth.

And she would smile slowly before correcting him richly and roundly in her antipodean drawl, 'Darling, I look horrific, idiotic. But do I give a damn? I do not. So thank you for your kind words, and will you now go to that kitchen and make me some damned food, I'm hungry as a horse.' Justin would practically skip to the kitchen to do as she asked. They were still in the rented house; following the girls' reconciliation with their mother he had a feeling that they might not want to stay with him and Kyria for ever and was waiting to see which way the land lay before committing to buying a place. In their first frank conversation since well before their divorce, he and Nita had discussed this possibility, in the light of what Justin referred to as her 'recent difficulties' with Tom. Although Nita had told her ex-husband that she and Tom were no longer together Justin was dubious – he hadn't seen the new Nita up close and wondered if the split was just a temporary blip in what had always seemed a slightly tenuous arrangement in any case. He had never warmed to Tom, unsurprisingly, but had seen him with Nita on several occasions and always felt, quite objectively, that it was a mismatch, but could see how much Nita both adored and depended on him. Still, nobody knew how that one was going to work out and just to be safe, just to ensure that the girls weren't put under any kind of undue pressure, he felt it better to stay put for the time being. Besides, the cottage was beautiful, easily affordable, and Kyria preferred to stay under the care of the excellent local midwives, and look forward to giving birth in the tiny cottage hospital nearby; the hassle of moving would be too much to cope with for all of them.

Margaret and Mary were as excited as schoolgirls about the nearing births. The nursery in Margaret's house was tastefully decorated and kitted out with two of the best of everything. They went to Liverpool together to tell Margaret's mother the news that her daughter had inadvertently conceived twins with a black boyfriend who had left the scene shortly after their conception without even knowing about the pregnancy. Frankly, she was so glad just to think her daughter had successfully got it together with a man at all, she wouldn't even have minded a Protestant by this stage, so getting two grandchildren into the bargain would be like Christmas coming twice that year, and it was so nice that Mary O'Neill had become such a good friend, although it was a shame she had lost her vocation. This was the official line, which the lovers had agreed in order to spread the shocks out over a period of time. In fact Mary hadn't lost her vocation, but had decided to honour it in a different fashion and in any case could hardly remain in the convent. In her final interview with Mother Superior, the older nun, always proud of her blood-hound instincts, had been unable to suppress a triumphant snort at hearing just how fishy things had got.

Having spent most of her professional life trying to convince expectant mothers that the best place for labour was in a hospital, Margaret had become a disciple of the home-birth gurus and although she went along with the advice from the doctors caring for her (a post-forty primagravida expecting twins was never a combination likely to be warmly welcomed by the medical profession) she had her own secret plan which not even Mary was party to.

Nita was prepared to let Tom attend the birth of their second child if he insisted, but had made it clear that she would prefer him to look after Katie while she gave birth in hospital accompanied by a friend. Since telling him that their relationship was over she had suffered not one regret and Tom saw that pleading would have been useless, even if he had managed to swallow his pride once more and beg for another chance. It was clear that even without knowing about Cressida, Nita had gathered enough information and reached enough truths to defend herself against any attempted reconciliation. Tom, who was by now in a constant state of low-level depression, much more tedious and painful than the writerly bouts of gloom he was used to, was beginning to rethink how he had played this particular game, wondering whether he should have found the courage to make a life with Cressida. He saw now that what Cress had said to him about access to his children was right, and realised what she had refrained from saying – that she wasn't the only threat to his living with his children; there was always the possibility that Nita would find out about some infidelity, or simply twig that his assurances of love were becoming increasingly hollow. He had assumed so much control over too many lives, had made arrogant assumptions about his place in other people's existences, and instead of living happily enough as a family with Nita and his precious children while continuing his thrilling affair with Cressida, which would have been his ideal situation, he was left with a beloved three-year-old who stayed with him two nights a week, and two expected new babies who would never see him in bed with their respective mothers. More agonising than even these terrible circumstances was the knowledge that he would never see himself in bed with Cressida again. His longing for her grew deeper and more painful by the day but their only contact was a few factual emails about her antenatal appointments and the odd stilted phonecall.

Still, Nita was feeling stronger and happier having made the break and even the thought of living alone with Katie and the new baby held no fears for her. Fliss and Harmony would come for Christmas in any case, and Tom would certainly do his bit practically so Katie would be well cared for. And she would be living honestly, openly, independently. A whole world of possibilities awaited her.

Harry continued to pay his solicitous attentions to Sophie. One evening, as they sat drinking tea side by side on the sofa in her tiny Kilburn studio flat, Harry noticed how Sophie's thick blonde hair curled up on one side of her head and under at the other. And how she moved her hand, every thirty seconds or so, to tuck the curly-up side behind her ear, displaying her smooth, pale neck and her soft jawline. He put their cups on the floor, turned to her and kissed her lips very softly.

'Sophie, you must know that . . .'

'Ssshh. Please don't, Harry. Cressida . . .'

'Cressida knows what I feel about you. She's the one who's always encouraging me to come here. I don't mean encourage, I mean she sort of gives me permission, or reassurance. She cares about you too, and it's almost as though she's glad that – well, that I feel – this way – towards you.'

Sophie blushed. 'Even so, I'm too guilty about that kiss already. Whatever you say Cressida's been too good a friend to me and your family is too much of a family to me for me to feel comfortable about this. Do you see what I mean?' Sophie was shocked at her own sensitivity. She had never cared much whether her lovers were married or not and now here was the man of her dreams kissing her and she was fending him off. Dammit.

'Yes, of course. And I'm not suggesting that there's anywhere for this to go. But I wanted you to know.'

'Thank you. It makes me very, very happy, Harry. And sad, too. But mostly happy because this baby has the perfect father, and it's sweet to think that we could have made a baby in the normal way. Do you see what I mean?'

Harry nodded, kissed her once more and then sat her back on the sofa, unrolled her pregnancy tights, pulled down her support knickers and kissed the insides of her thighs.

'Harry, have you listened to a word I've said?'

'Mmm-hmm.' Harry's mouth was full. Sophie began to protest faintly but then leaned back and closed her eyes. By the time Harry emerged and, moving up her body, kissed her again, this time in question, she answered by wrapping her legs around his back and pulling him inside her. A short while later they lay in an uncomfortable heap half on and half off the sofa and began to laugh as they struggled to sit up.

'Actually, I'm even happier now you know,' she giggled, 'funny that, isn't it?' Harry's smile crumpled into a rictus of pain and she held him as he cried. 'Don't worry, my love. It's OK, it's fine. You're a good, good man and I love you. But listen – I shan't ask you to do that again. All right, my love? All right, Harry?'

His head lay on Sophie's shoulder a little longer and they both gazed at the gas fire, he wondering whether in fact Lust was his Prime Motivator, or even Avarice and how could he possibly make any sense of his lecture now, or his life, and what was he to do about Nicola who wouldn't answer his letters and who had gone ex-directory, while Sophie was carefully planning precisely in which tiny clothes she would dress their baby first.

And then there was Cressida. Still strong and optimistic; still weak with hopeless love for Tom. In the same minute she could swoop from contented daydreams about what their baby would look like to a quick bout of weeping that Tom wouldn't be there to see the birth. Or much afterwards either. Having sort of written off the possibility that she and Harry would ever be a happily married couple again, and simultaneously, with perhaps too objective a generosity, worked out a future whereby Harry and Sophie could get together and they could all live with their children in close proximity, Cressida found it especially painful to contemplate a life where Tom was a minor player. The news that Nita had dumped him – which he imparted in a mumbled phonecall – came first as a shock, then a thrill and finally a gloomy realisation that if he asked her to be with him now it would be because he had lost Nita, and even Cressida's much-dented pride wouldn't stand for that. She just hoped that Tom realised it too. Which he did. Sort of.

There was a world outside. Wars, famines, earthquakes, acts of mass destruction, illnesses, deaths, births, elections of new governments, changes of laws, schooldays, holidays, birthdays, hospital visits, the weather. And these putative parents were, to their different degrees, involved in, and aware of, what was happening outside their own front doors, or families, or heads. It's just that their lives were progressing inside far smaller worlds within worlds within worlds. There were a few unifying moments – when the TV news was so bad that people watched it all the time and each of our mothers put a hand to her belly as if to block her child's eyes and ears against the loud unsightliness of the world. Otherwise, the pregnancies continued on their parallel lines until two weeks before Christmas.

BOOK THREE: Genesis

Oh what are you doing Sunday, baby?
Would you like to come and meet me maybe?
You can even bring your baby.
Oh.

from 'Disco 2000', Pulp

Monday

Sophie sat in a four-bed NHS ward, wearing a back-fastening hospital gown whose missing ties caused it to gape from nape to thigh so that when she walked down the corridor everyone in her wake got an eyeful of backside. For several hours she shifted uncomfortably in this garment of stiff white cotton, clutching the two edges together behind her when anyone came past and twice backed into the toilet glancing rapidly from side to side as though besieging the ward in reverse. But once she was given her pre-med she forgot completely about the gaping and sat bare-backed, patting Harry's hand absent-mindedly as she waited to be wheeled into the operating theatre.

She had developed the symptoms of pre-eclampsia and, bearing in mind her other health problems, her doctor had advised an early caesarean, around three weeks before her due date. Harry hadn't mentioned their sexual encounter of a fortnight ago to Cressida, who was in any case too preoccupied with her own final month of pregnancy to care much about anything except feeding her children and putting her feet up as much as possible, and they had not repeated it. Even so, when Harry told his wife that he would like to be present at the birth of Sophie's baby, Cressida's infamous blinking trick discomfited him considerably.

'So, even though I'm already overdue by a week and could go into labour at any point, you are going to be there when Sophie has her caesarean?'

'I'd like to be.'

'What happens if I go into labour though, Harry?'

'Well, your mum's on call for the kids . . .'

'I didn't mean what happens to Ben and Jemima, I meant *what about me?*'

As her pregnancy progressed, Cressida's affection for Sophie had become strained as it took Harry's attention away from her. She wanted to voice some kind of disapproval at his solicitous treatment of the woman who had, after all, stolen his semen for her own use, but since she herself was carrying Tom's child there was little moral high ground she could occupy and so she kept uncharacteristically quiet. She also felt partly to blame, having actively encouraged Harry to keep any eye on Sophie in the full knowledge that he might like to keep more than an eye on her, a possibility that irritated rather than dismayed her. Protective of her own body and its cargo, Cressida's basic instincts were beginning to play cuckoo to the baby birds of tolerance.

In the combined excitement of the impending birth and the thrilling secret she shared with the man she loved, Sophie hadn't noticed the change in Cressida. Obsessed with her baby and her MS, Sophie hadn't spent much time at all considering Cressida's motivations, though in the beginning she had been suspicious, for Harry's sake, that some kind of escape was planned, imagining Tom arriving one afternoon and bundling Cress and the kids into an unmarked van before driving off to a secluded hideaway where they would remain until they had forced Harry to arrange a quickie divorce giving his wife all his worldly goods and eternal custody of their children. After that exhausting scenario had played itself out in her head, Sophie made it her business to avoid thinking about this terrible, romantic, just about possible but highly unlikely, turn of events and simply accepted Cressida's maternal kindness, advice and support, never forgetting that this woman had chosen to sleep with another man when married to Harry Shepherd and must, therefore, be mad. So the women had carried on as friends, both trying not to get bogged down in the legal and practical side of their respective, conjoined, predicaments until they absolutely had to.

Harry was adamant about being with Sophie for the birth, assuring Cressida that if he got the call to come to her then he would respond at once. The fact it was taking place in an operating theatre rather than a labour ward made the situation much easier – had Harry opted to be birth partner to a squatting, grunting, open-legged Sophie the consensus of opinion would probably be censorious; as he was simply going to watch his child being born surgically, nobody raised an eyebrow.

Naturally, Harry had considered his position from all angles – some old habits really do die hard – and his recent voyages of self-discovery hadn't been sufficiently edifying for him to relinquish his tendency to ponder. He became aware that while he assumed he was seeking peace of mind, in fact he was seeking answers which might have quite the opposite effect. He was growing concerned that the date for his big lecture, which was only a few days away, would arrive and find him paperless. Even apart from his problems with the lecture itself, the timing had become disastrous. If both pregnancies had gone according to due date, Cressida's baby should have been born almost a fortnight ago and Sophie wouldn't be giving birth until nearly three weeks hence. But in fact the expected labours had encroached upon his pre-paration time as well as his thought processes and he could no longer see where his theory was taking him. Laying open the Cardinal Virtues as useless and replacing them, as antidotes to the Sins, with the Sins themselves, had seemed like a neat solution to the moral problem his definition of Prime Motivators had posed: everyone had one of the Seven in ascendance, but don't worry, if it goes too far in one direction and you become a sex-crazed maniac, a twenty-five-stone slob, a friendless recluse or any other kind of psychologically challenged ex-member of Society, you can just activate your very own personality swingometer and – hey presto! – end of malfunction. Provided it doesn't swing too far the other way, you understand. Once he'd nailed this theory Harry gave himself a couple of days off for good behaviour but returning to it and reading the paper at an imaginary lecture in his office, he saw, in his mind's eye, his own crucifixion by a baying tribe of angry colleagues, outraged that the man who called Faith, Hope and Charity 'trite' had spent three years on research which demon-strated – what? That people do bad things, which we used to call sins, owing to personality traits that could manifest themselves as either strengths or disorders. Three years. For that. There had to be more to it, something to drag all his work, his theories, into focus – maybe a quick peek at original sin – The original sin – was in order. And what better opportunity to consider the originality of sin than by studying the newborn? Harry's response to looming professional disrepute was flailingly inadequate but he was still hanging on in there.

When the trolley arrived to take Sophie down to theatre, Harry accompanied it. Giving her a warm kiss on the mouth before local anaesthetic was administered, he went off to wash his hands as requested and then returned to stare pointedly at the air above Sophie's abdomen while the surgeon began to discuss the procedure on which he was about to embark. Somehow, in the excitement, Harry had forgotten his deep-rooted squeamishness and dislike of hospitals. Cressida had given birth at home on both previous occasions and planned to do so again, so although these had indeed been bloody, messy events, they took place against a domestic backdrop that made them less starkly horrific. The fact that Cress had remained just about vertical and active throughout had also helped combat his own tendency to slump at the sight of blood, as did the occasional call to hold her hand, massage her back or murmur encouraging words in her ear – an oft-repeated trio which Cressida requested entirely to make Harry feel at ease throughout what she knew must be an ordeal for him. But here was Sophie, out flat, all but covered in sheets, and above her stood a green-clad man wielding a flashing blade. Harry felt the tingling at the back of his neck which augured nervous vomiting or a dead faint, and sensibly sat down on a chair a few feet from Sophie's head, well away from the action.

The night before, and against both his own instincts, such as they were, and Cressida's advice, Harry had called his parents and explained, truthfully, that the child his wife was expecting was not his but that his secretary was due to give birth to his baby the next day.

'I see,' said his mother eventually.

'I realise it's rather a lot to take in, and it is all a bit complicated. But I thought it was important that we weren't pretending; we certainly shan't be pretending to the children.'

'By "the children" do you mean Benjamin and Jemima?'

'I mean them *and* the new babies.'

'I see.'

'Right-o. Well, now you know what's happening.'

'Yes. Yes, I suppose I do.'

'And you'll explain it to Dad?'

'I will tell your father, of course.'

'OK. Thanks, Mum. Erm – wish me luck . . .'

'Goodbye, Harry.'

Harry instantly regretted having told the truth and realised that, far from being shocked or distressed by his news, his mother just wished he hadn't imparted it. Honesty to him was all-important; to his mother it was not a vital aspect of life, particularly if it confronted her with unpalatable facts. So, Harry thought, surprised, even those who hear the truth can long to hear lies. Laying himself bare, getting the truth off his chest, was only worth the effort if the listener valued both truth itself and the courage it took to tell it. He hadn't known that before.

As the surgical team talked over her and she slowly lost sensation from the waist down, Sophie was wondering what the future might hold. She was almost certain it would not hold Harry, at least not in the way she had held Harry on her sofa on the happiest (soon to become second happiest) day of her life. For all her dizziness, Sophie Diamond had a sharp enough wit and could think with clarity when she needed to. She had rarely called upon the ability in the past, since her early attempts to make sense of her lost father, distant mother and alienating brother all ended in tears and for her own safety and sanity, it was easier to blur the lines. She was thinking much more about her mother too. Vivienne had telephoned Sophie twice in the past month – remarkable for a woman who usually never made contact with her daughter at all and who responded lukewarmly to all attempts by Sophie to maintain some form of relationship. Sophie sensed that her mother was fascinated, utterly against her will, by the notion of becoming a grandmother. Sophie had been troubled by terrifying dreams for the last two months and believed, she didn't know why, that mending the rift with her mother would keep them at bay.

Indigestion had been a problem as well, and Sophie knew these two interruptions to her sleeping pattern were almost certainly linked. Thank goodness we have brains, she thought, to help us out of these holes.

Five minutes after entering the operating theatre, their heads spinning in a mire of moral quandaries, Sophie and Harry both felt their attention turn sharply to what was happening in this life. The surgeon was so deft and the tension in the room so overwhelming that Harry completely forgot to pass out and as the bloody, struggling body of his baby was lifted from Sophie's womb, he burst into silent tears instead. Sophie smiled as she blinked at her child under the bright lights of the theatre and held out her arms. Cord cut, weighed and cursorily wiped, the little body was laid upon Sophie's chest and it was Harry who edged her nipple towards its open mouth to latch on and suck drowsily, shocked at the dry light world outside.

'Harry,' said Sophie quietly, glancing down at the dark head at her breast, 'meet Marlon.'

There was a moment when Harry struggled with the notion of silence, but only a moment – which was nevertheless long enough to give the staff who were stitching up and clearing away at the bottom of the slab the chance to digest and respond at the same time, so Sophie's announcement was greeted with a veritable chorus.

'Marlon?!'

Harry recovered himself first. 'I mean, Sophie, it's an unusual name nowadays, and of course everyone just thinks of Brando, and are you really sure that . . . ?'

Sophie was unperturbed by the response; despite sporting a deep abdominal wound and being unable to move her legs she had never felt more confident or more powerful and she and her son inhabited a shimmering bubble of quiet joy which even universal mockery could not puncture.

'I always said to myself that I'd call my son Marlon. And it is after Marlon Brando so it doesn't matter if that's what everyone thinks of. Marlon Diamond. It's beautiful. He's beautiful.'

'Marlon Diamond!' shouted the surgeon from the scrub room where he was removing his gloves with a resounding snap and calculating whether or not the blood spots on his bowtie would be visible to the next patient. 'Sounds like a spiv! Don't buy a watch off that baby!' Sophie sighed dismissively as the staff sniggered. The Chinese midwife who had held her hand while the boy was born smiled at her, patted the child's bottom and whispered low, 'Marlon Diamond. Sounds like an angel.'

Although nearly three weeks premature, Marlon weighed in at a respectable 6lb and after some perfunctory checks confirmed his excellent state of heath he was returned to Sophie who hadn't lost sight of him for a second. Harry didn't exactly feel left out, although the Marlon had come as a shock, but he saw at once that Sophie and the boy formed a single unit. The aura around them was diffuse enough for him to enter and leave it as he pleased, but it was almost tangible. Harry, of course, *had* thought about the future, had even imagined himself and Sophie trying to make a go of it once everything and everybody had calmed down. But now he understood that this new Sophie – determined, confident, undeterrable – was to him both more admirable and less loveable than the woman he had begun to fall for. The features of Sophie that had warmed his heart were connected to what he perceived to be her simplicity, with its accompanying spontaneity and loyalty. And his heart had been warmed at a time when Cressida was leaving it out in the cold, when it yearned for love like the skin on his back ached for the heat of sunlight in bleakest midwinter. But this Sophie had instantly acquired a fully developed set of maternal traits that made her careful, cunning, competent and ruthless. The physical effects of motherhood, which had enslaved her body for nine months, were retreating and being replaced by the – what? – angelic? Hardly – emotional? Rational? Harry couldn't work out what had kicked in to effect the change but it seemed to be something essential to Sophie. And it didn't leave room for him, nor did he want it to.

As Harry stood watching his son fall asleep at Sophie's breast the surgeon re-entered the theatre.

'Doesn't Daddy want to have a hold now?' he asked cheerily.

Both parents looked up and said quickly and quietly, 'No.'

'Not just yet,' said Sophie.

'No, that's fine,' Harry replied happily. Marlon was beautiful. He looked completely unlike Ben and Jemima had looked when they were half an hour old, which Harry found oddly comforting. And he knew that he already cared deeply about the child and would grow to love him dearly. He also knew that the boy was indisputably Sophie's.

At afternoon visiting time Cressida waddled in with flowers and grapes. It had been a supreme effort for her to prepare herself for the visit, and she was worried that Harry's beaming pride and Sophie's dogged adoration would have her in tears. It had been difficult to gauge much from Harry's phonecall after the birth except for his amusement at the baby's name, so Cressida was hugely relieved to see that Harry looked mostly hugely relieved and Sophie looked blissfully smug, both of which she could easily cope with. And, although she couldn't swear it, Cressida was quite sure that the link which had been strengthening its hold between Sophie and Harry was not exactly broken but hardly of international safety standard either. There was no dancing spark, there were no mooning glances, all she could sense was a gentle mutual respect and affection, as if they were two people who worked together and were fond of one another but had never become especially close.

'Oh Sophie, he's absolutely gorgeous. Isn't he, Harry?'

'He's a beautiful boy, that's for certain. Here, Sophie, can Cress hold him?'

'Of course she can. Careful now, don't wake him.'

Sophie handed Marlon to Harry, who was about to put him in Cressida's arms when he remembered. 'Actually, I haven't held him yet myself, so if you don't mind I'll just hang on to him for a moment.'

'You haven't . . . oh, right. Sure, I can wait my turn, you give that lovely boy a cuddle.' The women's eyes met and each knew the other understood that the first time Harry had held his new son was to present him to Cressida. Sophie smiled as her friend took the little bundle from her husband and cooed, 'Well, Marlon Diamond, hello there. Hello there, lovely boy.'

Tuesday

Cressida was eating apples like there was no tomorrow. Pregnancy cravings – *pica* – had never affected her in the past but this time around she couldn't get enough apples. They had to be English, preferably Cox's Pippins or, at a push, Russets. Once or twice she had managed Braeburns but would generally scour markets and greengrocers until she found the right variety, then buy up several pounds at once. Strangely, she could remember the precise moment the craving took her; in a moment of weakness she had been about to call Tom but, as she ummed and ahhed, and twice dialled his mobile number but hung up before it rang, she was overcome by a desire to eat an apple. It wasn't just the taste she was after, it was the whole experience of holding the smooth globe in her hand, polishing it and then crunching a large bite into its side leaving a reddish-green imprint of her teeth around a white flesh wound. She would then munch loudly and without manners, turning it on its horizontal axis until the classic hourglass of the core remained. Holding the stalk she would demolish it, pips and all, in three careful bites, leaving just the dried brown stick, like the leg of a persistently tough insect, between her fingers. During November she began to eat the stalk too, folding it in half, looking around to make sure Harry wasn't watching, and swallowing it down with a mouthful of water. Her bowels had never performed better.

It was while she was reclining on the sofa eating her fifth Pippin of the day at ten thirty on Monday evening – a few hours after seeing Sophie and Marlon at the hospital – that she began to sense the early stages of labour, getting stronger quickly. Waiting until she had washed down the apple stem, she kicked the newspaper behind which Harry sat and, as he lowered it, said, 'Hope you're not jaded with the birth experience, love. Because, if I'm not mistaken, you're in for your second one in as many days.'

Harry was already worn out but had the grace to smile encouragingly, 'Plan A in action then?'

'Yup, reckon so.'

Harry called Patricia, got Ben and Jemima out of bed and wrapped up in dressing gowns, each holding a carefully packed little suitcase, while Cressida kissed them both goodbye, told them to be good for Grandma, and that all being well they could come back to see her and their new baby brother or sister the next day.

While Harry rushed off to the late-night store for supplies of chocolate and frozen peas – the former for consumption, the latter for application to pressure points – Cressida, by now pacing the front room, getting started on her sixth apple and breathing noisily and rhythmically, telephoned Tom's mobile. He answered from sleep, in a daze.

'Uuugh?'

'Tom, it's me.'

He woke up sharply. 'Cress. Are you OK? Do you need me to –'

'No, calm down. Just to let you know, labour's started so it will all be happening over the next few hours, or the next day, or whatever.' She was met by several seconds of silence and it took her as long to realise why. 'Tom. Stop crying. How dare you cry now, of all times?'

'Oh pet, I'm sorry. This is terrible. I want to be there, honey, I've missed you so much and . . .'

'Enough. You could have been here. Well, probably not here. You could have been at the birth of our baby, you know that.'

'Don't start that again, please, it's torture.'

'Don't you start talking about torture. You don't know anything about torture. Right now, I'm contemplating a bloody painful process which is going to take place between my legs and to be honest the only person I want to share that process with is you, but you have decided, however you want to portray it, not to be here. So I think I know a bit more about torture, OK?'

'Baby, I'm sorry, I'm sorry, I –'

'I've been thinking a lot about you recently,' Cressida said wildly, biting into her apple with relish, 'and I've realised what you are, or what you do anyway.'

'What do you mean?' Tom thought that she sounded just slightly insane.

'You're a snake in the grass, deceiving everyone ever so quietly all the time, but what you're offering, what you're using to tempt with, isn't fruit from the tree of bloody knowledge; it's the precise opposite. You're saying – eat this, taste this, fuck me – and you'll get nothing, you'll get blissful ignorance, you'll duck every issue and not even notice. Don't you see that?'

'Cress, pet, you don't know what you're saying, it's making no sense. I haven't deceived you, have I? I've never deceived you.'

'You may not have been unfaithful to me – within the parameters blah blah – but you did deceive me. By talking about love and making it sound like what I mean by love. And you deceived Nita in the same sort of way, but now she's realised and I'm stuck here, in limbo, in ignorance, just wanting you. You're like an oblivion. And you make that moral wasteland you occupy some kind of paradise, nirvana itself, but that's not what life is about; it's just the most terrible *self*-deception. And one by one everyone realises it and moves along but you're going to be stuck there, spinning the lies and believing in them and trying to sell them along to the next person, woman, whatever. Kiss me and opt out of truth. Make love with me and start to believe in the shoddiest kind of moral relativism. Love me and forget everything you know, all the good simple things like happiness and contentment, and swap them for my version of cynicism. Do you see? Tom! Tom?' Still he wept. 'Listen to me, stop blubbing! It's the last thing I need. Just shut up and wish me luck, OK?'

Tom pulled himself together long enough to say a quiet, 'Good luck, pet. I love you so much,' to which Cressida responded with a snort which could have been a sob and hung up, as her contractions began to get stronger.

By the time Harry returned, Cressida, who had put the phone down on Tom and wept passionately and without self-pity for five minutes, had assumed a squatting position. He ran to her, dropping his shopping on the floor as he helped support her.

'Oh shit.'

'It's OK. Just call the midwife now. But it won't be long.'

Cressida's previous births had been long but straightforward. This time she had the distinct impression that the baby was in a hurry. She could sense her cervix dilating, was aware of the strength of her contractions increasing by the minute. Cressida had always fancied the idea of giving birth in water, but decided that getting an inflatable pool wasn't going to be worth the effort. Now, though, it became a desperate urge.

'Upstairs!' she commanded as soon as Harry re-entered the sitting room, having found the midwife's mobile on answerphone mode and left a barely coherent message upon it. Taking two steps at a time on each out-breath (by now they were exhaling in unison), the pair got upstairs with huge momentum and Cressida barely found the energy to shout hoarsely, 'Bath!' at which Harry rushed into the bathroom and turned on both taps to their full power. Cressida, meanwhile, was pulling off the outsize T-shirt and leggings, and flinging them wherever she pleased. She managed to untie the armoured bra which accommodated her greatly increased bust but needed Harry to tear down her elasticated support pants. Before he had checked the temperature of the bath or turned off the taps Cressida had flung herself over the edge and was kneeling in the water, breathing yet more heavily.

Both Harry and Cressida had imagined this moment – if the long drawn-out process of labour can be described as a moment – with increasing levels of anxiety. Cressida, who hated to think of Tom's baby being born without his hands there to welcome it, put her faith in the knowledge that she would be experiencing an immense physical diversion from her worries, with its own rhythm and regulations which would inevitably take her mind away from Tom. Harry didn't have the luxury of labour to fall back on and was terrified that all his well-controlled feelings of jealousy and rage would somehow be obvious to the new arrival whose first minutes in the world would be marred by his brooding presence. Cressida's faith was the very opposite of blind, and well-placed; her focus was entirely upon her baby's complicated exit from her womb and arrival in her arms. Harry should have shared it, because as soon as he saw Cressida kneeling in the bath, forehead sweating, eyes closed, mouth pouting comically as she huffed and puffed, the moment became all, and the history – with all its pain and trauma and surprise – faded farther into the distance as a new story began.

Even so, Harry still found time for a little existential angst, which only took him a second and could generally be fitted into any thought-process before he could say boo. Seeing Sophie with Marlon had exacerbated his concerns about the basis of his Seven Deadly Sins lecture. And now, looking at Cressida preparing to give birth in a more strenuous and medically uncontrolled manner, he was able to express for himself which elements of his professional life were troubling him. While his work concentrated on the theoretical and educational aspects of psychology, it all pointed to various types of analysis and therapy in whose efficacy, given the right circumstances, he believed very strongly, although he was personally uncomfortable in their practice. The role of the analyst had always seemed to make enormous sense to Harry as soon as he began to learn about the profession: he or she was providing the nearest an adult can get to unconditional love, that is, an acceptance of whatever the patient wished to say, and however he wished to say it, however disturbing, incomprehensible or downright indulgent it might be. But of course, this acceptance was only possible if there was a certain necessary distance between analyst and patient, if the former remained something of a mystery to the latter. What this boiled down to, thought Harry, was that an analyst offered the kind of love a mother has for her child but that love existed only in theory, it was virtual, it had no place in the world. The love was a *representation* of mother-love, and dependent upon there actually being no bond at all between analyst and patient. Or, more simply, the analyst portrayed himself as an *unknown mother*. This paradoxical notion, coming in the midst of so much known motherhood, began to border on obscenity and Harry was hugely perturbed.

More pressing matters interrupted Harry's shocking train of thought when Cressida, between bouts of panting, demanded more apples.

'But darling, you're not really supposed to be eating right now, you know. Not actually in the middle of labour. I mean, what if . . .'

Cressida cut him short with a snarl, 'Get me the fucking apples, Harry. I *know* it will be OK, I *know* this baby isn't going to be delivered in an emergency operation during which I'll choke to death at the hands of the inexperienced anaesthetist, so Get. Me. The. Apples. OK?' Harry rushed downstairs and did as he was told, putting his head out of the front door and scanning the street for any sign of the midwife before clambering back up to the bathroom.

During his twenty-second absence, Cressida delivered a plea that sounded like a prayer. She groaned quietly, 'Tom. Please. Love us. Love me and our baby. Tom. Please,' stopping abruptly when she heard Harry's foot on the top stair. Her labour, approaching its second stage rapidly, was providing her with the same kind of pain she normally experienced during the first days of her menstrual cycle; an overwhelming cramp which could bend her body double while crystallising her mind.

Kneeling in the bath gave Cressida the perfect opportunity to keep Harry away from life's most inconveniently dramatic physical process, although that wasn't in her mind when she jumped in, and the situation suited them both – no need for her to find little jobs for him to perform and no expectations weighing heavily on his shoulders. Apart from handing her apples Harry had no specific role and that suited him fine. Tom, alone in his rented Manchester room, was pacing the floor in panic.

At 3 a.m., just when Harry was about to leave a third message on the midwife's answerphone, the front doorbell rang. As he sprang to the bathroom door Cressida shouted for him to stay. Kneeling up in the bath and clutching tightly to the rail with one hand, she moved the other down to feel the child's head emerge and she held her breath as her vagina slowly, slowly expanded to allow it through. Then the body slithered down and Harry joined Cressida in catching the slippery mass. With a great sigh, Cressida squatted and then sat in the bath and scooped the baby into her arms, while Harry gently cleaned blood from its limbs. He tucked the strands of Cressida's hair which had escaped her clasp behind her ears and they both gazed down at the big navy blue eyes, which now opened in astonishment, as Harry and Cressida breathed a first hello.

Cressida returned to real time with a gasp. 'Harry, the door!' The doorbell had not stopped ringing for five minutes. Harry rushed down to answer it and found a breathless woman bustling in apologetically while rooting through her bag. Taking one look at his spattered and bloody appearance she tutted, 'Goddammit! That's the third one I've missed this month. Bloody traffic. Up here, is she?' and bounded upstairs.

By the time Harry had reached the bathroom the midwife had cut and clamped the cord, weighed the baby, pronounced it satisfactory in all aspects and returned it to Cressida to await the afterbirth, then decided that the best action she could take would be to make a pot of tea. She patted Harry on the arm as she passed him, saying, 'A lovely girl. Well done.' Harry knelt by the bathside and wiped Cressida's tears.

'A girl.'

'Yes. Isn't she lovely?'

'She's beautiful. Cress, what's her name?' They both assumed the naming would be Cressida's responsibility alone and so it was.

'This is Grace. Harry, meet Grace.'

'Hello, Tuesday's child. Hello, baby.'

'Oops, hang on, Harry, here comes the placenta. Hold her for a minute, would you?' Harry managed to ignore the slather and slap which followed and gazed into the baby's eyes while Cressida cleaned herself wearily. The midwife reappeared to 'check her over' and was impressed to report not even the slightest tear.

'Back to normal in a couple of weeks. Bet you're glad to hear that, eh?' She elbowed Harry in the ribs and received a weak smile in reply.

Wearing knickers almost up to her armpits, bleeding on to a gigantic sanitary pad which curved from her navel to the small of her back, Cressida sat in bed and held out her arms for the baby. Harry handed her over and watched her begin to suckle.

While Cressida and Grace slept, Harry telephoned her parents, his own, and various friends. He also left a text message for Sophie explaining his likely absence from visiting time later in the day. At nine a.m. mother and baby woke and he brought tea and toast upstairs, then left the room saying, 'I expect you have a call to make.' Cursing her husband for his faultless sensitivity, and kissing her baby for the hundredth time that morning, Cressida called Tom's number. It took an age for him to answer – after pacing the floors of his new rented flat he had begun to drink and had finally collapsed on to the bed at seven a.m. convinced that his lover and baby had failed to survive the birth experience and that any moment now he would receive a call inviting him to a tragic double funeral. So when he did answer, the sheer sound of Cressida's voice filled him with an immense euphoria, which diminished when he discovered that The News was almost six hours old.

'So you didn't think I needed to know right away? Cress, do you realise how worried I've been?'

'Sorry. There wasn't a moment. And then I slept. It was quite tiring.'

'Oh pet, I'm sorry, I didn't mean to say that. Look, are you OK? And is she – Grace – how's she?'

'She's absolutely beautiful, Tom. A beautiful girl.'

'I'm longing to see you. And her. Both of you.'

'How is Nita getting on?'

'They're thinking of inducing her.'

'Poor Nita. Well, you'll need to stay up there till then I guess?'

'Yes, but Cressida, I'll be there as soon as I can, truly I will, I can't wait.'

'Looks like you'll have to. Good luck with the next one, Tom. And I mean that.'

It sounded like she really did, which irked Tom. He didn't want her to be upset, but she could have sounded a little less over the moon, a little more as though she missed him. He envied Cressida the love affair she had embarked upon with his child, all the more because it was denied him. Even if he had denied himself.

Later in the morning Ben and Jemima returned home noisily, beating their grandparents to the bedroom and falling upon the baby with gusto. Cressida's parents followed with flowers and fruit and Harry brought champagne with which the four adults toasted the arrival of Grace, proffering tipsy fingerfuls of bubbles for the children to lick. Carefully, Harry arranged the children on the bed and gave them each a turn at holding their new half-sister before passing her into the waiting arms of Patricia, whose eyes were shining.

'Hello, gorgeous girl,' she whispered. 'Cressida, she looks so like you did when you were born. Doesn't she, David?'

'Hmmm.' Her husband studied the tiny face gravely, then broke into a beaming smile as Grace opened her eyes. 'Yes, I think you're right. Completely different to how Ben and Jemmy looked, isn't she? Hardly surprising really. Oh dear, I mean . . .'

'David!'

'Mum, it's OK. He's right. Unsubtle but right. But it's true, Ben and Jem looked so much like Harry, from the beginning, whereas Grace looks just like my baby pictures.'

'Nature's way,' said her father significantly while her mother rolled her eyes in irritation. The children began to clamour for the treats they had brought with them from their grandparents' house so Patricia volunteered Grandpa to take them downstairs and divide the spoils. When he was safely out of earshot she gave Grace, who was beginning to mew, back to her mother and apologised.

'Harry, Cressida, I'm so sorry, you know what David's like, I realise this must be so difficult for you both and –'

'No, it isn't really,' smiled Harry.

'What do you mean?'

'Well, I mean it doesn't feel difficult. Not to me anyway. What about you, Cress?' She looked up from watching Grace feed and shook her head. 'In fact, it feels to me just like the other two felt like. Being there with Cress was the same. All the wonderful bits were the same. And out came this beautiful baby. There's nothing about her that's – imperfect. Look at her. There just can't be. Do you see?'

'I suppose so. Yes, of course. Of course, Harry.' Patricia was so close to tears that she hurried downstairs muttering something about putting the kettle on. Harry sat next to Cressida and stroked the baby's foot, marvelling as always at the softness of newborn skin, the miniature perfection of the bone, blood and flesh that it covered and the vibrant pulse of life beneath it.

'Harry, did you mean that? About thinking she's perfect?'

'Yes. I absolutely meant it.'

'Isn't this strange? What do you feel about it?'

'Just the same as the others. Almost the same as the others.

I'm a bit more nervous, maybe. It *is* strange, not at all what I expected.'

'It may not last,' she warned. Harry grinned,

'That's my doomladen girl,' he said encouragingly. 'Don't get happy, whatever happens.' Cressida laughed ruefully.

'I *am* happy. In the weirdest way. But I *am*. You just confuse me sometimes, Harry.'

'It's immensely simple, love. I've just fallen for her completely. I've fallen for Grace.'

There are some wounds that refuse to heal and Cressida knew where hers was hidden. But hidden it was, out of the picture, Tom was nowhere to be seen. And few injuries exist which the winning duo of time and babies fail to ease at least a little. Over the past three years her love for Harry had changed so much she scarcely recognised it, could not have named it. But now she saw it clearly, glimpsed in the mirror a mother with a new baby at her breast and a father curving his arm around them both. That had to count for something. That had to be what Grace required, what Grace demanded. That had to be a blessing.

Wednesday

Nicola and Bathsheba were looking forward to the baby's birth so much that the rest of the family laughed at their enthusiasm; Nicola's brothers claimed it would all be too much for their mother to take, and her three older sisters were humorously open in their envy.

'Mamma never showed this interest in me when I was having *my* first!' pouted Christine, the oldest sister, now in her early fifties and expecting her own third grandchild in four months' time.

'Nor me, nor me. She was too busy working,' agreed the next.

'But just 'cause it's her *baby* . . .' chimed the younger of the three, scornfully.

'That's right,' protested Bathsheba, 'she's my baby girl, and you've got your own. You just wait, when your littlest one is about to have a baby, you just wait and see!' Nicola sat serenely amongst them, arms cradling her bump, smiling at their mock-arguments and thinking how fortunate she was to have these fine sisters, this grand mother, who kept no secrets from one another.

She was a fortnight away from her due date and, apart from her shock meeting with Harry in the car park a few weeks before, all had gone smoothly. Once she had decided to keep the baby and worked out with Bathsheba how they would deal with its arrival, she had felt strong, happy and easeful throughout these final few months of pregnancy. A residual fear had been that her mother, an experienced midwife with a dislike of unnecessary intervention in a natural process, would want her to give birth at home. Nicola didn't have that much confidence in her body; wanted the re-assurance of machines and white coats and procedure. When she plucked up the courage to tell Bathsheba she intended to give birth in hospital and began to explain why, her mother said soothingly, 'Baby, don't worry about that.'

'But I do worry, Mum, I just feel I can't do it at home, I'd be too scared and I could actually *make* it go wrong –'

'Nica, I meant don't worry that you're not pleasing me. You must please yourself, honey, nobody else. As long as I'm with you it's where I want to be. And however you want to do it, that's fine. Remember, I had all of you in hospital – in those days that's what we did. And I managed to avoid compulsory caesareans! You mustn't worry about upsetting your silly old mother, do you hear me, young lady?'

'Thanks, Mum. I do want to do it all as naturally as possible – maybe gas and air but nothing else if I can manage. But I'd like the option of other things, just in case.'

'That's fine, my darling girl. That's fine.'

The day after Cressida gave birth, Nicola confessed to her mother that, even after she had decided not to terminate the pregnancy, she had wished, until the fourth month, that she might miscarry.

'I know it sounds awful, Mum, and I'm so glad I didn't. I just thought I wouldn't be able to cope with it, that it was something – imposed upon me. In a way it was . . .'

'Every time I found out I was pregnant I wished I wasn't, honey.'

'Mum! I thought you wanted a big family.'

'I did. And in a minute or an hour or a day – or sometimes in a month – I was glad to be expecting again. But at the time – even if you've planned it – I think it's a strange thing to accept. That *thing* taking up space in the middle of your body. And so nearly every woman, if offered the chance to not be pregnant – would take it. Nica my love, don't look shocked. I don't mean they'd all get rid of their babies. I mean that if someone offered to wave a wand and make them go back a fortnight and then wake up and not be pregnant, most of them would take it. Because at the beginning you're not ready. Then you get your hormones and you get your mother going on at you and your man coming over all proud and all your friends being excited and little by little you welcome the invader. Make it part of yourself. So don't feel bad about those thoughts you had. Just be glad they went.'

'I just felt guilty remembering when I went for the twenty-week scan and there was that woman who'd had hers and they couldn't find a heartbeat – do you remember? And even then I thought she was overdoing it, crying and so on. I thought – she's young and she had a child already so it isn't as if she's infertile, and these things happen. I was so callous. I mean, *halfway* through the pregnancy. Of course she was distraught.'

'It's a hard thing to bear. It was the worst time of my life, the very worst, when I lost a child, and I already had six children.' Nicola looked confused as Bathsheba went on, 'And I'd thought that six was enough so when I lost number seven I thought I should just accept it as one of those things and move along. Everyone else needed me, your father was upset but more for me than the loss of the baby. But I needed that baby. I'd felt it kick inside me; I'd dreamed of what it would look like, I'd worked out where the hell it was going to sleep in that houseful of people. So I should have made a fuss and wept and wailed like it was my first, my only, baby I'd lost, but I just pretended it wasn't precious. Me and your father went through the worst time after that, he couldn't understand what was wrong with me. It was post-natal depression but you couldn't call what happened a birth and I never even held the baby, which I could, should, have done.'

Nicola was dumbstruck for a moment and then burst out with, 'Mum, why have you never told me about this before? And the others – some of them must remember – why hasn't it been talked about?'

'It's the one thing we never did talk about, honey. Maybe I should have been more open with everyone else, but it's only the girls who would remember – your brothers were all too young to know what was going on – and in the end Arden and I kind of worked it all out between us. I wouldn't allow it to be talked about and everyone just went with it – and I was feeling much better but a hell of a lot older and then I found out I was pregnant with you, so I thought – well, I guess I thought I'd put everything into looking forward to your arrival, that was how I'd be healed.'

'And did it work?'

Bathsheba smiled as she remembered. 'Did it work! I remember just after you'd been born and your dad came into the ward – men didn't come to the births then, remember, I did all seven of you on my own – and he kissed us both and asked what I thought of you, and I just looked at your little face and said "This is my eighth wonder, Arden honey, the eighth wonder of my world." We used to call you that sometimes privately – "the eighth wonder has got ten grade A GCSEs" he said when he called me at work that day – but not in front of the others. Or you. So yes, Nica, yes, it worked.'

'So – I'm your eighth child? Not your seventh?'

'Well, that's how I think of it. My lost baby was just over twenty weeks old, I knew her – it was a girl – already. The day I lost her is in the calendar I keep in here,' she patted her breast, 'the one where all your birthdays go. The same calendar.'

'But all this time I've thought I was your seventh child. You know, of a seventh child.'

'Honey, I remember you asking about this years ago but you were too tiny to understand about a lost baby and it seemed so important to you I just didn't know what to say but I wanted you to know how special you were so I just – went along with it. And you were special. Are. The cleverest, most beautiful girl in the world. Honey, you look surprised. This seventh child business – I don't believe a bright girl like you could really be taken in by fairytales for all this time. Did you really think it was true, honey? Nica?'

'Sort of. Not the fairytale bits. Just – the fact of being the seventh. Your seventh. Even if I didn't *believe* in the myth, I did believe I was the seventh child of the seventh child. I can't believe nobody's ever told me . . .' Nicola was shocked at finding out that the premise on which she had based so many of her decisions, and on which she had blamed her subsequent disappointments, was a false one. And that the people in the world to whom she felt closest – her mother and sisters – had been lying to her for nearly thirty years.

'Honey, I'm sorry if I –'

Nicola cut Bathsheba short, 'Don't worry, Mum – it's just going to take some getting used to, knowing you lost a baby and everything. And a lot of sorting out, getting it straight in my head.' She tried to sound cheerful. 'You never know, maybe it's going to let me off every hook I've hung myself on so far.'

'Do you want to tell me about it, child?' Nicola controlled the urge to let fly; she needed time to digest the news and she was aware that her unmediated anger and pain would upset Bathsheba more than they would solve anything. But the conversation would have to happen, and its significance would be too enormous for her to comprehend just now. Once Christmas was over and the baby was born, that would be a better time to start talking about such a huge, confusing deceit.

'Not yet. But I will, when I've had a good think. Come on, let's dry our eyes and get shopping!'

Every Wednesday morning Nicola drove her mother to the supermarket, early to avoid the crowds, for their weekly shop which now included constant additions to the baby hoard: nappies, bathing oils, lotions, breast pads, sleepsuits and dozens of muslin squares which Bathsheba swore Nicola would thank her for even if she mocked their purchase now. She also bought such great stocks of food it was as though she was preparing for a barricade rather than a birth and this time Nicola tried to dissuade her from storing up so much work for herself.

'Mum, we'll never get through all this stuff!'

'Your brothers and sisters and all their families will come round, we'll have to have something cooking all the time, you know that. And if this baby comes between Christmas and New Year we're not going to have much time for shopping all over again, are we, not with a new baby on our hands.'

'But folks will bring things with them. Honestly, Mum, you're doing too much. They'll feel guilty if every time they visit you're there slaving over the dinner. You know the girls will bring stuff.'

'It's not the same. They'll be our guests. Besides, you need to keep your strength up, we have to have plenty of brain-food and muscle-food in the pantry, for your own good and to make milk for the baby. None of that powdered crap!' she cried passionately as they passed the tins of formula.

'Mum, keep your voice down, will you?' Bathsheba's expertise in midwifery was of the most basic and useful kind; she could not comprehend why any woman whose breasts were in good working order would choose to overlook what the Good Lord giveth and feed her baby powdered cow's milk, and she didn't care who knew it. As they reached the rice aisle Bathsheba remembered her stocks were low. She bustled off and leant down over a catering-sized pack of long-grain, preparing to swing it into the trolley which Nicola wheeled alongside her. She swung up but it never went over. She lost her grip on the bag, which broke when it hit the floor and sent rice flying, as a seizure took hold of Bathsheba's upper body. Unable to breathe, she stared at Nicola in shock, clutching at her coat and trying to gulp the air. Nicola ran to support her mother as she fell, choking.

'Help me!' she screamed, as they both slipped on the spilled rice, Bathsheba's full sixteen stone bearing down upon Nicola as they fell heavily. 'My mum! Help me!'

Seventeen-year-old Dave the shelf-stacker on the next aisle, in an uncharacteristically acute moment, recognised the urgency of her cry and ran to its source but when he rounded the corner and saw the heavily pregnant young woman kneeling on all fours in a puddle of liquid screaming, 'Mum!' to the still open-eyed but now motionless body lying amidst the long-grain rice, his first-aid training all but fled.

'Don't panic,' he tried hopefully. Then, inspired, 'And whatever you do, don't move. In case of internal injuries.'

The paramedics were loath to take Nicola to the maternity ward in the same ambulance which would deliver her mother's body to the mortuary, but trying to separate them would clearly cause more stress to the already hysterical Nicola. Attempts to get the names and numbers of next of kin out of her proved useless, although they had at least found her name on the cards in her purse, so one crew member was working her way through the mobile phone she had found in Nicola's bag. It so happened that at that particular hour on a Wednesday all members of her family were either on the school run or at work, and leaving a worrying message on random answerphones was not the usual procedure for the emergency services. But by the time she reached the letter S, the paramedic was desperate. Shepherd, H the phone said. Although she could never explain why, Nicola had programmed Harry's mobile number into her phone a few months ago. Just in case, as she thought. The paramedic received no reply – Harry was still marvelling at day-old Grace and had switched his phone off – but the young woman had by now decided that the situation required a diversion from standard procedures and left a panicky message asking him if he was the next-of-kin to a Nicola Mackenzie, and if so could he contact the labour ward at St Mary's Hospital urgently. It wouldn't have helped enormously if Harry had responded at once in any case; but since he only used his mobile to talk to Cressida or Sophie, both of whom were currently necessarily stationary, he kept it turned off for days, and by the time he did call, shocked and anxious, it was conclusively too late.

Meanwhile the woman's colleague was trying to calm Nicola, who knelt on the floor of the ambulance holding Bathsheba's hand, which an hour before had smoothed her daughter's hair back from her brow and was now a dead weight. Bathesheba's immaculate plaited chignon and Nicola's jaw-length dreadlocks were studded with a confetti of rice grains. The ambulance man put his hand on the distraught young woman's shoulder and said, close to her ear, 'Listen to me, love. There's nothing we can do for your mum now. She's gone, love – but you're still here and so's that baby and I think you know your mum would want you and her grandchild to be safe. Wouldn't she? Your waters have broken, you've had a fall, and everything's happening a bit fast. But it will all be OK, it will all be fine. You have to calm down, love, take some deep breaths, let's do some deep breathing, shall we?'

All good stuff, but Nicola didn't even seem to register that someone was talking. Had she not been pregnant they would have sedated her by now but talking her round was the only path open to them in the circumstances. He tried again. 'Nicola. Nicola, listen to me. If you carry on like this you're going to hyperventilate. Do you understand? You need to take some deep breaths. You have to fill your lungs. Nicola!' For the second time in his career the man administered a shocking slap to the face in order to short-circuit the hysteria. The first time it had worked magically, like in the movies; now his patient fell to her side at the force, righted herself instantly and continued with her panicked breathing. The ambulance man felt first guilty and then foolish as he caught the raised eyebrows of his colleague, who had given up finding a live person at the end of the phone and was now leaving messages wherever she could.

Although almost entirely unaware of the efforts being made to help her, Nicola knew, somehow, what she was doing. The still small voice of calm was talking in her head, but at a whisper, which was drowned out by the tides of grief and fear which were clearly audible, as though a conch was being held to her ear, an effect which the slap, with its ensuing numbness, only reinforced. Every few minutes she saw herself, was ashamed of her uncontrolled terror, but the knowledge that her mother was gone and her own baby traumatically on the way was too awful to bear – peace, stillness, calm, anywhere she could hear the world, were places to be avoided, and her own rhythmical shrieking – too breathless to be keening and pitched too high to subside into sobs – helped stop her ears. She was also in pain; her shocked body had decided to eject the baby from it and would do so, even in the face of all the emotional resistance she could muster. So as Nicola shrieked and moaned, her cervix began to dilate and her baby's head pressed down hard into her pelvis. Her shallow breathing prevented its progress, already impeded, since the premature breaking of her waters, by the usual complications of a dry labour. A quick slap on the cheek had been a laughably inadequate diversion; so now agony stepped in and pulled off its old trick of making people sit up and take notice. A strong contraction pushed the baby's head down hard against the insufficiently opened cervix and the pain came not in a wave but in a bolt which made Nicola's body scissor convulsively and her eyes clench as though against a flash of lightning. She emerged from the jaws of her wild-eyed frenzy to fall seamlessly into the grip of a suffering so acute she wished herself back again but couldn't find the way. The ambulance reached the hospital and wheeled in its live patient, kneeling on all fours on her trolley, at high speed. Nicola's dramatic entry to the labour suite, via three corridors whose wipe-clean walls echoed with her atavistic screaming, induced a sharp intake of breath in all who heard it and delayed two births, which had been proceeding at a healthy pace, by at least an hour each.

Nicola's oldest sister, Christine, had responded to the answerphone message as soon as she emerged from the basement of the library where she worked and felt her mobile vibrate. She telephoned the maternity department at once, but her call came one minute after Nicola's arrival, just when the ambulance crew were apprising nursing staff of the full situation, and she spoke to a nurse who had only just come on duty and knew simply that a traumatic early labour had been admitted. So Christine jumped in the car and organised a telephone relay to let the family know that Nicola's labour had started early and that she would join their mother right away but that someone should fetch the suitcase, which Nicola had already prepared, from the family house. When she arrived in the labour-ward reception and asked for Nicola it was evident straight away that something was wrong. The nurse on duty asked her to wait and rushed off to whisper in another nurse's ear, who then also scuttled away.

'Where is she? Tell me now and I'll go to her. What's all this whispering about, take me to her now!' Christine demanded.

'Excuse me, I'm afraid it's not possible for you to see Ms Mackenzie right away, she is having some difficulties and . . .'

'What kind of difficulties? You don't understand, I'm her sister and I promised her I'd be there, she's already got her mother with her and I want to be there with them. Now let me see her!'

At the mention of Nicola's mother the young nurse had looked around desperately, willing for the return of her colleague, preferably with the ward sister, but nobody came.

'OK,' said Christine, placing her hands on the nurse's desk and leaning down until their eyes were level, 'just tell me where she is. Because if you don't, I swear I'll go in every bloody room in the labour suite to find her. You do believe me, don't you?'

'4D,' said the nurse with a gulp. Christine didn't even stop to thank her.

In 4D Nicola's screaming had stopped. A generous dose of pethedine had taken her mind off the pain to some extent and now the consultant had recommended an epidural since it was clear that this labour would be long and bloody even if Nicola were cooperating with her body. When Christine burst into the room she saw the anaesthetist preparing to place the canula into Nicola's spine and shouted, 'Nicola! What are they doing to you? What about your birth plan? And where's Mum?'

Her little sister's eyes looked blankly at her, peering from her wet, swollen face and then closed as she submitted herself to the operation of numbing her body from the waist down, which was, at least, a start, although from Nicola's point of view it was the wrong half first. A nurse approached Christine and put a hand on her shoulder.

'You're her sister? My name's Abena Matthews; I'm a midwife. Please can you step outside for a moment, we need to have a word.'

After Christine had set the family relay off on its well-worn track once more, this time with the awful news of Bathsheba's death as well as Nicola's problematic labour, she braved the labour suite again. Speaking through her own tears, she offered words of encouragement and comfort to the weeping Nicola, holding her sister's hand throughout the three hours of labour during which she could neither feel nor assist in the birth, the episiotomy, the application of forceps, then the ventouse which pulled forth the baby, the stitching up and the moment when Nurse Matthews held the newborn child in front of Nicola's streaming eyes and said, 'Look. A lovely healthy baby boy. Well done, Nicola, you've done so well. Do you want to hold him?'

Beneath a white sheet, Nicola lay open-legged on the table, her vulva a mess of blood and stitches where the scissors and steel instruments and the baby had all done their work. She was numb. She stared briefly at the baby, whose eyes were struggling to open, then turned her face to the wall. Her sister urged her to turn around.

'Oh Nicola. He's a lovely boy. A beautiful boy. Don't you want to look at him?' Christine wanted to slap Nicola into consciousness, to shake her into life again, but Nurse Matthews caught her eye in time. 'I'm sorry, Nica love. I'm sorry. You've – you'll probably want to see him later, you must be so tired and – it's been – it's been so difficult for you. I'm sorry, honey, here, let me wipe your face.'

While Christine tended to her sister Nurse Matthews took the baby into a corner and held him in front of her, waiting for him to open his eyes again. This time she wanted him to see a face with love in it, which was his right from the beginning. And when the child braved the lights again she met his stare with a gentle smile and a quiet, 'Hello. Hello, little baby. Welcome to the world,' and those words are almost always accompanied by tears, so how could he possibly guess that they weren't the right kind, and that they weren't his mother's? Abena Matthews kissed the baby's head, swollen and misshapen from the ventouse which had pulled him from Nicola's body, and went off to find a bottle.

The Mackenzie family's protective instincts were in turmoil. Whether to go first to their dead mother or their suffering sister was an important decision and not simply a question of hierarchy: as the oldest son pointed out, there was no actual *use* in going to Bathsheba now, but then what *use* was there in all crowding in to see poor Nicola who probably needed peace more than anything else? After consulting with Christine by phone they were less sure about what Nicola needed, though still convinced that it couldn't possibly involve a visit *en masse*. Finally it was agreed that the men would go to the mortuary and make the necessary arrangements there while the two remaining women would join Christine on the ward. They found her sitting, crying, in the interview room which hospitals keep for just such occasions.

'I've just been to see her,' she sobbed, 'and she won't even look at him. At first she was just so out of it that I don't even know if she understood what was happening. But then she seemed to come to all of a sudden, started to talk to me about Mum and what had happened and everything. And then just said, really calmly, that she didn't want to see the baby and that she wants to have him adopted.' Christine's audience was stunned. 'And then I said to her that she might not feel well enough to look after him right now but that I'd be happy . . .'

'Me too, of course,' said both other women at once.

'. . . yes, that any of us would be happy to have him at first, while she's getting better, and then when she felt well enough she could get used to him nice and slow. But she said she doesn't want him in the family. That all he'll do is remind her of Mum dying. She seems totally lucid about it and has already told the people here that's what she wants. They're telling her not to rush into anything right now, of course, but the woman I spoke to – she's a social worker I think – said that Nica probably has some kind of post-traumatic disorder which could last for months, and that she seems very calm and certain, although she's obviously not like her usual self. So she thinks she might not even change her mind.'

From the moment they knew of their mother's death, the birth of Nicola's baby had been seen by all of her siblings as a sign of hope; the ultimate memorial to Bathsheba would be her eagerly awaited grandchild arriving in the wide world on the very day she departed it. The notion that the baby too would be lost to the family had never entered their heads. But having emerged unscathed from the traumatic labour, it was unthinkable that he would not then be welcomed by his mother and her brothers and sisters. They each imagined Bathsheba's response to such a rejection which brought home yet again her absence, and the alternate layers of sorrow, bewilderment and grief became compressed and weighed heavy as stone in all of their hearts.

Nicola was tearful at their visit, talking only about the terrible moments in the supermarket and referring not once to the birth of her son. She behaved as though she had been admitted to hospital for a routine operation on the day when, tragically, her mother had died. Her sisters, longing to see her make some connection with the child but fearful of upsetting her, didn't mention him either. The youngest, who had brought Nicola's lovingly packed case full of sleepsuits and nappies, took it with her to the toilet and put all the baby items into her own bag to hand over to the nurses later, taking only Nicola's nightclothes and toiletries back out to her. After fifteen minutes of quiet, strained talk, Nicola announced that she wanted to sleep and would they mind leaving her now. The last thing she said confused them all: 'Do you know what the very worst thing is? Mum only told me this morning that I'm *not* her seventh child. Can you believe that? Can you believe that nearly everyone knew except me and that all my life I've wondered why I never know anything until it's happened? And sometimes not even then? Can you imagine?' There was no answer.

The two sombre groups met outside the maternity block, once Bathsheba's sons had made arrangements for bringing her body home before the funeral, which they would need to organise. At least they felt useful – members of their little party who had visited their sister were more clearly distressed by what seemed to them to be an unnatural and hopeless situation. After agreeing a rota of cover for Nicola at the hospital all six went to see their new nephew and found the nurse who had given him his first look of love, who this time handed the child to each of his uncles and aunts for a little more, and then placed him carefully back in his cot in the premature baby unit, his first home, since Nicola didn't want him in a crib beside her bed and there was no other place a newborn could be accommodated without his mother. As the family left the ward, Christine noticed how he dwarfed the four other babies on the ward, how he was noticeably stronger and more active and yet how, in a moment, there would be nothing around him, no eyes upon him except for professional ones. The premature babies were surrounded by gifts and cards and rarely without a mother or a father keeping watch over them, willing them to thrive. Nicola's baby had no need of such wishes but was the more vulnerable nevertheless.

A nurse looked in on Nicola later and noticed that, although she was lying unmoving on her side, her eyes were still open and she still wept. She looked through the unpacked case on the chair beside the bed and suggested a 'freshen-up': 'Get yourself out of that horrible hospital robe and into these cotton pyjamas – they look nice and cool. Or I could run you a bath with some of this aromatherapy stuff. Come on, love, you'd feel so much better.'

Nicola shook her head. The nurse put the contents of the suitcase into the bedside table and gently patted her motionless shoulder. 'Just press the button if you need anything, love. OK?' Her uncooperative patient nodded and the nurse left her with a sigh. Nicola curled around her flabby, empty belly, bleeding on to a hospital pad stuffed into disposable knickers, and felt drops of colostrum, the rich first milk of early motherhood, leave her breasts and soak the thick white fabric of her gown. The aching sensation of let-down made her body stiffen with fear and disgust; she scratched at her breasts through the rough cloth until her nipples were raw and the ache was replaced by a slow burning. She closed her eyes and kept them shut until the morning, although sleep didn't come for hours. Nicola was sure that if she opened her eyes and looked down, she would see that her milk had turned to blood.

Thursday

Nita's baby was almost two weeks overdue. Her belly had looked outsize on her slender five-foot frame for the past three months; now it was ludicrous, a joke. It jutted out so far in front of her that she regularly misjudged distances; consequently the bump had twice suffered the indignity of having lift doors close on it, and on three occasions had reached people to whom Nita was being introduced a moment before her outstretched hand, much to everybody's amusement. During the past week Nita had developed an itchy rash consisting of raised red hives over her legs and torso. In addition, her ankles were swollen and her thick dark hair was shedding constantly, so when the doctor said, regretfully, 'I really would advise an induction at this point, Nita,' she almost kissed him. All of her three previous pregnancies had followed a similar pattern – few unpleasant symptoms, a neat, well-rounded bump and a natural birth very close to the due date. Katie had been born at home and Nita's original plan was to do the same again and avoid the hospital at all costs, but when making the plan she could not have imagined the desperation she felt about getting this baby out and was much relieved that, all being well, she would be back home for Christmas and could begin to shrink back to normal size. The timing was also good for Felicity and Harmony, who had begun to spend most of their weekends with their mother and who were to spend the school holidays with her over the festive season.

Tom came to fetch Katie at 11 a.m. and found Nita waiting, recumbent on the sofa, for the arrival of Louise, the friend from work who was to be her birth partner.

'Jesus, Nita! You look –'

'Hideous?'

'No, no, sorry, I meant you look – utterly enormous. Even bigger than a few days ago. And you look – kind of – red.'

'I am kind of red, Tom, as in I'm kind of covered with these bloody hive things which itch to buggery and yes, I am utterly enormous. Anything else, while you're at it?' What really astonished Tom was how old and unattractive Nita suddenly appeared to be – surely she hadn't looked like this when she was about to have Katie? Surely he would have remembered *this*? But he refrained from voicing his surprise.

'OK, I'll start again. How are you feeling?'

'Kind of red and enormous actually. And dying to get this lazy baby out of me . . .'

'Lazy?'

'Well, what does it think it's doing in there for God's sake? It should have come out a bloody fortnight ago. If left to its own devices it'll probably just stop in until the weather gets better. Or until it can walk. Or, the day after it's born it'll leave for university.' Nita's humour had taken an ironic twist which Tom had noticed creeping up after he left her. That in itself, he thought, was quite ironic. 'I actually started having contractions last night, they got to about five minutes apart and then the bloody things stopped completely. Unbelievable!'

'Here's Louise now,' he said, seeing a car reverse up the drive. When Nita told him that one of her colleagues was going to be there at the birth he had hoped fervently that it wouldn't be either of the two he'd slept with and who hadn't got on Felicity's list, which, fortunately, Louise wasn't. Although, Tom was thinking as she tapped the window and waved at Nita, who began to heave herself, groaning, off the sofa, she was actually not at all bad looking. For five seconds he weighed up her sexual potential before the memory of Cressida crossed his mind. That was one second more than the appraising glance he had given Katie's playschool leader the previous week had lasted. And counting. He opened the door and let Louise into the front room where she helped Nita with the final lurch to standing.

'Hello, you poor old thing. My God, look at you! That skin! Time that baby was out and no mistake. Up you get, lass. Now, where's your case?'

Louise's reassuring voice instantly made Tom and Nita think how glad they were that it was she, and not Tom, who would be there at the birth. Competent, experienced and unflappable, with a fine line in consciously gritty northern humour, her mere presence showed up all of his shortcomings. Preparing for the birth of their second child was helping Nita and Tom become accustomed to their separation. After kissing Katie goodbye and giving Tom a rucksack full of little clothes and a long list of unlistened-to instructions about her care, Nita allowed Louise to bundle her and her overnight bag into the Nissan while Tom strapped Katie into his new silver Saab, to which he had treated himself with a view to raising his spirits, which it had done quite effectively for almost a whole day. Tom and Katie waved as the red car set off on its journey into Manchester.

'Well, Katie pet. What would you like to do today?'

'Playground.' Tom sighed irritably then tried to cajole Katie out of the tedious playground idea with fake and unconvincing jollity.

'Oh, not the playground again, pet! What about going back to Daddy's house and getting a video? I haven't seen the Tigger movie all the way through yet, how about that, sweetheart?' Tom's attempt to mask his dislike of playground duty didn't fool his daughter for one second, but she didn't really mind. The experience of her daddy's mind being elsewhere went hand in hand with spending time with him, always had done. While Tom had, since very shortly after her birth, put the *idea* of Katie first, and certainly cared for her more than he cared for any other human being, the older and more demanding she became the more difficult he found it to remember that sense of awe she used to inspire in him. Holding his tiny baby, helpless in his arms, had been like standing on an Olympic podium – Tom Webster, you have won gold. And as she developed – began to smile, sit up, crawl, shuffle, walk – each achievement was another blessing, another remarkable reflection upon his paternal skills. Then she began to talk and Tom's heart was fit to burst with pride each time she said his name, 'Da-da', which she said at least a month before attempting 'Ma-ma'. The sweetness of her voice, the freshness with which she approached each new sound and meaning, touched him to the core, brought tears to eyes whose crying had for years been focused on what they found when they looked inside. Looking outward and being moved by his baby's smile made Tom feel more connected to the world than he had done since everything went wrong with Bronwen. And when he fell in love with Cressida it seemed that even more of those connections were being reawakened, he was aware of longing simply to see Cressida or to talk to her, not as a substitute for making love but as an end in itself. He was taking pleasure in the knowledge of another human being, enjoying intimacy that was not confined to sex. But now, and Tom wasn't sure whether the timing was merely coincidental or deeply significant, since both ceasing to be Cressida's lover and Nita's boyfriend he had felt some of the joy of fatherhood diminish. He couldn't say whether the change was due to living apart from Katie or not being able to see Cressida, or a combination of the two. It didn't occur to him that it could be something to do with Katie's growing independence; at almost three she was voluble, demanding, overwhelming and frequently bad tempered. He felt less useful to her, more distant from her and was afraid of being too harsh or too soft, of setting too many boundaries or of giving her too much freedom. And the rewards of fatherhood seemed less obvious. When she was a year old he spent hours enjoying repetitive games of blowing raspberries on her soft little belly or playing 'This little piggy' with her tiny toes. As she grew, the pressure of responsibility suddenly seemed much heavier and less pleasurable. The eternal round of municipal playgrounds, soft-play centres, clanging music groups, low-grade pizza restaurants which catered for children and banal chat with other parents being dragged around the same circuit made Tom long for metropolitan life, for bars and cinemas and late-night gigs and people his own age to talk to.

All this Katie sensed, but she was nearly three and in need of a playground.

'I want to go to the playground!' she screamed.

'Right. Playground it is.' Tom shouldered his responsibility and off they went.

On the maternity ward, Nita was beginning to regret her earlier enthusiasm about induction. Dr Krishna – late forties, attractive, no wedding ring – had been perfectly charming to begin with, but she had gone off him the moment he ruptured the membrane to make her waters break; it had felt like the most shocking invasion and the rush of warm fluid had embarrassed her. As someone who used to consider herself a child of nature, this pregnancy had already severely jolted Nita's self-image and it wasn't over yet.

'We'll give it about four hours, Nita,' the doctor told her, 'then if nothing happens up there – well, I'm going in.' He winked and sauntered off, confident of the effect he never failed to make, especially on his older ladies.

'Now he's what I call dishy,' whispered Louise, looking for the shape of his backside through the white coat but having to content herself with the width of his shoulders.

Nita huffed and puffed. 'I think he's disrespectful. Going in indeed!'

'Disrespectful! Nita! How old are you? I think he's got a lovely manner. Better than one of those old blokes with bowties you normally get. God, if I'd had Dr Krishna waiting for me I'd have made the effort to get to the bloody hospital instead of having our Alex on the bathroom floor!'

Nita attempted to smile. 'Sorry, Lou. I just feel frustrated that I can't do this on my own. It was fine with the other three, but this time I'm all uncomfortable and huge and this rash is so itchy all the time. I know there's all this stuff about it being difficult for older mothers, but I'm only forty-four and I have kept in shape, it's not like I'm an overweight smoker who's never given birth.'

'I know, love, I know. But it's not like they're making you have it early, is it? I mean, you are two weeks overdue. And it's not doing you any good, is it? You're doing the right thing, love. Now, why don't you read a magazine? Or shall I massage your feet?'

'Bless you, Lou. I'm fine for now. Look, this is going to take hours, I can't feel a thing happening. I really don't mind if you go home and leave me to it till this afternoon.'

'Not a chance. Bob's got the kids all day and I'm staying put. Besides, it's fun here – checking out the blokes. I tell you, there are some lovely-looking men that work round here, it's not just the doctors. Wonder why hospitals attract them.' At this she smiled broadly at a well-built porter pushing a wheelchair past the door.

'Lou! Control yourself.' Nita took the first magazine from the towering pile on the table and began to flick impatiently through it while Louise continued to keep an eye on passing talent.

Tom and Katie sat glaring at each other over what remained of their pizzas.

'But I want that olive!' wailed the child.

'You've had all of your own olives and most of mine. This is my last one and I'm having it.' Tom's voice was slightly too loud. A woman at the next table tutted and her husband smirked.

Katie shouted louder now, 'I want that olive. It's not fair.'

Controlling the urge to pop it into his own mouth, Tom sulkily pushed the plate containing the desirable olive towards Katie, who grabbed it triumphantly. He was angry at himself for caring so much about the damned olive but it was, after all, a matter of principle, and he was angrier with Katie both for making him look stupid in public and for wanting, so badly, the last olive. His last olive.

'There,' he said to her quietly as she chewed happily, 'I hope you're satisfied.' This wasn't fair either, especially as Katie had played down her natural sense of triumph with good grace. Her mouth turned downwards and her lower lip wobbled. She looked at Tom ferociously and said, loud and clear, 'I don't like you. You're not my friend.'

'Fine. See if I care.' Katie set her mouth and Tom asked for the bill. Katie began to cry and her crumpled little face, just a moment ago so composed, reminded her father of how she looked as a baby.

'I'm sorry, pet. Sorry for being so grumpy. Come here, lovely girl and give me a cuddle.' Katie clambered off her chair and on to Tom's lap. As he wiped her eyes and blew her nose on the restaurant napkin he kissed her and asked, 'Are we friends again then, pet?' and was ridiculously relieved when she nodded. They left the restaurant, exhausted, and he drove her back to the house where they fell asleep on the sofa watching *Dumbo*.

Dr Krishna was not at all pleased with Nita.

'There's no movement here at all!' he said, slightly impatiently. 'I think we'll need to set up an oxytocin drip.'

Nita shuddered. 'Couldn't I have a pessary – a prostaglandin pessary?'

'Not now your waters have broken. That could take us till tomorrow and I'd be worried about infection. No, I think the drip is our best option. That'll get things moving all right.'

Once the drip had been set up it occurred to Nita that 'things' might well start moving but she was unlikely to be one of them. The drip line was too short for her to walk far from the stand containing the bag of saline solution, which in turn was positioned to work best for her in a sitting or lying position, neither of which she had any intention of doing. She had assumed that once labour was successfully induced she would be free to move around until the second stage of labour, at which point she would probably squat. The presence of the stand, the bag and the line into her arm made her nervous and the hospital's atmosphere began to cloy; for the first time in any of her pregnancies she started, ever so slightly, to panic. Louise asked a nurse if the position of the drip could be changed and was met with a pursed mouth and a terse, 'I'll see what I can do.' At this point it occurred to Louise that it could well be up to her to ensure that certain things moved in the right direction for her friend. Nita was relying on her for support and that's what she would get. With quiet determination and a reassuring pat on Nita's shoulder, Louise set off to find Dr Krishna.

Tom woke up before Katie, to the sound of television fuzz. He pointed the remote control over her head and switched it off. His left leg felt numb and his back was at an uncomfortable angle, but the moment was such a rare one, and his little girl so fast asleep, that he remained still. He gently kissed her hot crown and craned, pouting, to put his lips to her cheek, marvelling at its downy perfection, her beauty undiminished by her double chin and the line of dribble stretching to his shoulder. While Katie's mother awaited the first signs of labour anticipating some kind of blessed relief, Tom was thinking about his other child, about Grace. He wondered if he would ever take her in his arms and feel her sleeping gently on him like this. He wondered how he and Cressida and Harry would deal with the situation, whether jealousies and insecurities on all sides would keep her from him. And most of all he wondered how it would have felt to be with Cressida while she gave birth; he thought of his arms being the first to hold the baby, his face being one of the pair which made up her first view of the world, and he thought about lying side by side with Cressida with their baby sleeping between them. He could see her face so clearly, imagine the precise expression of tired, triumphant love she would bestow first upon the baby and then on him, one of those moments where she could make time pause for a heart-stopping second.

Then there was the baby who would be born today, Katie's little brother or sister. What could he possibly feel for the child born of a woman whom he had never loved, never chose, never pledged himself to and with whom he now no longer lived? He remembered how doubtful he had felt about Katie's arrival, his anger at being forced into fatherhood. But at least he was making some kind of a go of it with her mother, albeit in his faithless fashion, at least he was at the birth in some official capacity which was recognised and respected. This week he had been barred from the births of his two children. What kind of a man, he thought, could be so abhorrent that the women who bear his children refuse his presence at the births? This was a simplified and melodramatic version of events, he knew, but there was a satisfying self-pity to be had in defining this moment so brutally. As Katie stirred, waking, Tom's entire body felt hungry for Grace. He longed to hold her and kiss her, to change her nappy, to bathe and dress her and show her to the world. Without knowing it, he began to hold Katie more tightly to him and it took an irritated struggle and a sharp dig in the ribs for her to let her father know she couldn't move.

'Where's Mummy?' she asked sleepily.

'She's in the hospital, pet. Remember? She's gone with Louise to help her have your new brother or sister.'

'I want Mummy.'

'I know, darling, but we can't see her yet. Maybe later today, OK? And maybe we can phone her. I'm sorry, pet, but the doctors are looking after her at the hospital and she's quite busy until the baby is born. But soon she'll be home, soon she'll be home.'

'I want Fliss.' Katie had taken to asking for Felicity or Harmony quite regularly, and although Tom knew she sometimes also asked

Nita if she could see her half-sisters he always took it as a reflection on his own inadequacy. Despite his oft-repeated insistence, to Cressida, and himself, that keeping his family together was his top priority, Tom had spent a great deal of time at home holed away in his office, writing. Or listening to music, surfing the net, emailing Cressida . . . while Katie's practical care, her feeding and bathing and dressing, had often been done by Fliss, or occasionally by Harmony, as well as Nita. They had nurtured her and played with her every day while Tom had come in for the 'specials' – the bedtimes when he would sing her to sleep with melodious renderings of his favourite country music, and a wide range of folk songs and nursery rhymes from his own childhood, or the dramatically entertaining storytellings with which he would beguile her. He did change the nappies and heat the food, he wasn't exactly lazy about his duties, but if Nita or Fliss or Harmony was around, which they usually were, more often than not they did the basic tours of duty. There were always feasible excuses – he was tired from doing a reading or travelling abroad or writing till 5 a.m. (having wasted a day and started working at 10 p.m.). Nurturers earn no glory but acquire a natural authority which Tom, though he couldn't or wouldn't express it in this way, suspected he lacked.

'Fliss will be here soon, love. And Harmony. They'll come to help look after Mummy – and you're going to help as well, aren't you, my love? She'll need you to be a big girl and give her lots of help to look after the baby.'

Katie frowned. 'I don't want a new baby.'

'I'm sure that you will, pet, as soon as you see it. It will be a big change but it will be a lovely change.' Tom wished he was more certain of this, wished he felt further than he did from echoing his daughter's sentiments about the new arrival. 'And don't forget pet, you're always mine and Mummy's baby. Always.'

'But I'm a big girl!' She was indignant. Tom laughed, beaten.

'You'll always be whatever you want to be, honey. Is that better? Hey?' Katie smiled. 'Come on, pet, let's get some tea.'

The oxytocin was beginning to take effect. Nita's contractions began and in only a couple of hours were already quite violent. Her panic had not entirely subsided and now she felt that matters were getting out of hand; the labour seemed to be progressing without her. Louise had persuaded Dr Krishna to reposition the drip to allow more freedom of movement, but it didn't alter the power of the drug, which was now dictating an unnaturally fast pace to proceedings.

'Please can you take the drip out now?' begged Nita of the midwife as she came to check her blood pressure. The nurse looked doubtful.

'Your cervix is only about three centimetres dilated, love. We wouldn't normally stop the drip till you're at least five. If then.'

'But,' said Nita through gritted teeth, 'these contractions are too strong!'

'Do you want some pain relief?' asked the nurse brightly.

'I wouldn't *need* pain relief if they weren't so strong.' She broke off to breathe through a contraction which felt like an explosion. Thirty seconds later she resumed, 'And I have to keep going to the loo every twenty minutes because this bloody drip's filling my bladder and it *hurts*.'

'I do think pain relief might be the answer. Let me get Dr Krishna.'

Louise felt helpless. If she were a man, she thought, even an anxious putative father, the doctor would take more notice of her. As it was, each time he approached Nita's labour suite his expression made no secret of the fact that he thought Louise's requests were unreasonable. Dr Krishna appeared in a hurry, accompanied by the nurse, who ran to keep up with him.

'Now, Nita, I hear you're having rather a lot of pain?' Nita was unable to answer at that point. 'Now then,' he continued kindly, 'I understand that you are keen to avoid too much intervention, but you must realise that sometimes it's necessary, for both your health and the health of your baby. It's rare for a woman of your age to go through labour unaided; you must understand that just because your previous births were straightforward, it doesn't mean this one will follow suit. I think you'd feel a lot better if you had some pethidine at this stage. And it's a shame, I think, that you decided against the epidural a little earlier on, because that could have been a real help. So,' he sighed, 'are we going to try some pethidine then?'

Nita curled into a squat, grimacing through another painful contraction, and looked imploringly at Louise, who took a deep breath and said, calmly, 'Dr Krishna. This is a woman who has had three natural births. She used gas and air in all of them, except for the last one, less than three years ago, for which she only used a TENS machine. The drip is causing her to have violent contractions and her cervix is not dilating. She is concerned not only that she is not going to have the strength to cope with the contractions but that they are harming her baby by forcing it down on to her pelvis without even the protection of her waters, since you broke them six hours ago. So she doesn't want pethidine. She wants you to remove the drip and let her labour at her own pace.'

Dr Krishna looked surprised. He murmured to the nurse who verified that the monitoring equipment, another unwanted intrusion, showed no signs of foetal distress.

'Nita. Is this what you want?'

Almost in tears now, Nita gasped for air and yelped, desperately, 'Yes!'

'Very well. But I must warn you, you could be in for a prolonged and even more painful labour and – what's that?'

At the end of Nita's cry something had appeared between her legs. Leaning down, she closed her hand around a small foot. 'It's breech!' she shouted, surprised. 'How the hell did that happen? It's been head down for two months.'

The doctor gave some staccato directions to the midwife who ran off along the corridor.

'What's the matter?' asked Louise, worried by both the speed with which the nurse was retreating and the tone of Dr Krishna's voice.

'It's a footling breech, and since the cervix isn't fully open but the contractions are strong it's going to be very difficult for her. We can't possibly allow this to go on any longer. We'll have to perform an emergency caesarean immediately.'

Nita, breathing heavily, heard him clearly and protested, 'No! You're going to take me off the drip anyway – just give me a chance and I'm sure it'll all happen and –'

But a trolley surrounded by two medics and two porters was already trundling towards Nita, and with a one-two-heave-ho they lifted her from her knees and on to her back, causing her to shriek with the agony of the baby's weight against her spine.

'Let her kneel!' shouted Louise, running beside the trolley as it sped off towards the lift. 'Can't you see, you're just making it worse! Let her kneel!' she screamed as the lift doors closed in her face.

Nita was acutely aware of everything that was happening but utterly incapable of participating in it. Her trolley came to rest in the operating theatre, by which time Dr Krishna had reeled off what was going to happen to her. She could barely raise a protest when the drip was finally removed from her hand and the canula refitted with another line. She felt a stinging sensation in her left hand as the general anaesthetic was administered and then lost consciousness.

Of course, the knowledge that his second child had already been born was not something Tom cared to share with anybody. But Martin, his youngest brother, was staying with him that evening after a work meeting in Manchester, and once Katie had gone to sleep at 7.00 p.m., around the time Nita was fading Lethe-wards, he finally indulged in some unrehearsed revelation, fuelled by the generous quantities of beer his brother had brought with him. Martin listened, appalled, to the story of Cressida and Tom with an expression of growing disdain and when he heard that their child was born, that the ultimate manifestation of their infidelity was actually out in the world, he responded with scorn.

'You tosser. Tom, you absolute tosser.'

'Cheers, Martin, for that supportive comment.'

'Supportive bollocks. You've been playing around with women for years now, me and Mike never understood what got into you, or how you did it, and we used to be a bit jealous. But then I met Kim and she's fantastic, she's what I want, all I want. So the way you go about it, well, I thought, it's shit after all. There's no happiness there. Still, fair enough, if that's how you want to play it, it's a free country. But babies aren't free and you should've been more careful about where you stuck it, you daft twat.'

'The point is, though, that I'm not that much of a tosser. I may have been gullible and yes, careless, but I've stood by my mistakes,

I could've run out on Nita when she told me about Katie but I never did.'

'Yeah, but you still fucked other women, didn't you? You can't say the family's your main thing when in fact you're shitting all over the family.'

'I wasn't shitting over anybody. If Nita hadn't found out . . .'

'You're unbelievable! Don't you think what you've done is *wrong*?'

The extent to which Tom's path had diverged from the one followed by his brothers, which was in itself not dissimilar to the journey of their parents' lives, was summed up in this question. The Webster family members were not, on the whole, moral relativists. There were good things to do and there were bad. There was a right way to behave and a wrong way. If you wanted to be a good man you behaved right. Simple as that.

'Mart, what's the point of making some kind of moral judgement and labelling something as "wrong"? Where does that leave me?'

'It leaves you in fucking tosserville, mate, that's where. Two women up the stick who shouldn't be. Your own family broken up – even if it should never have been a family, if what you say about Nita is true – and another one maybe on the edge of breaking up. And two new babies whose dad isn't around. And is a tosser.'

'I don't fucking know why I told you any of this, guess I thought you'd listen sympathetically, give me some support, share in my troubles a bit . . .'

'A trouble shared is a trouble doubled, mate. What did you expect, advice? Sorry, Tom, I don't have the right kind of life experience for advising you. I've lived in the slow lane – do my job, married my girl, had my kids, footie on a Saturday. Never managed to live the life of Riley like my big brother. But, funnily enough, I'm well relieved about that. About not living up to your shitey standards.'

Martin was rarely so loquacious. Tom was wounded by his dismissiveness, his lack of sympathy, his refusal to look outside the moral framework of his own little world. His confident happiness in the simple life he'd chosen.

When Nita came round from the anaesthetic fifteen minutes later she was at first only aware of the pain in her lower abdomen and it took her a few seconds to work out where she was. Then she remembered and, panicking again, turned around to find Louise by her side holding a wrapped bundle and beaming widely. Nita's throat was so dry she couldn't speak but Louise understood the croak and brought the baby's face next to hers. 'It's a boy, Nita love. He's absolutely fine. A tiny bit blueish at first, but now look at him, he's pink and perky and ten out of ten.'

Nita smiled with relief and kissed the little cheek, still flecked with her blood. A nurse helped her raise her head and drink some water, after which she coughed and demanded to sit up, which she did, painfully, with assistance. Then she put the baby, wincing at holding all seven and a half pounds of him, to her breast where he began to suck. She smiled at Louise.

'Well. That was – dramatic.'

'Nita love, I'm so sorry I couldn't have done more to help you. Once they'd decided to do the caesarean it all happened so quickly and I just got shoved out of the way. I had to fight my way in here once they'd done the op.'

'You were grand, Lou. Couldn't have done anything more. I'm really glad you're here, truly I am. But they wouldn't have had to operate if they hadn't put me on that damned drip, I'm convinced of it.'

'Don't bother about that now, love. Just relax and rest and enjoy the baby. What's his name, by the way?'

Nita had wished for a boy from the beginning but now remembered why, and how futile her hopes had been. She realised she would have to be careful not to hold this against him, his unwitting fulfilment of an ill-begotten wish, and kissed him, quickly, in instant forgiveness of the sins of his father. 'I think I'll call him Jack. That was my grandpa's name. I don't remember him. He died when I was small but he was married to my grandmother for thirty years and if he put up with that old bitch for so long without killing her he was a bloody saint.'

'Nita!'

'It's OK, Lou, I'm not mad. Well, I'm not crazy. But I am angry about Dr bloody Krishna and his attitude. Don't worry, I won't get into a strop now, my belly's too tender for that. But once I'm home and me and Jack have got settled back with Katie, I'll be giving him a call to tell him exactly what I think about his medical intervention.' She sighed and kissed Jack again. 'Would you call folk for me, Lou? There are phones in the reception bit. Here's a list and a bag of change. Why are you laughing?'

'It's just that you're so well organised. You've brought a bag of change for the phone when you've come into hospital to have a baby.

'So?'

'So, I was just thinking of what it would be like if men were the ones having the baby. Cos even now, it's still the women who think of things like that. I bet if Tom was at home now you'd have put Katie's meals in the freezer and left him instructions for the washing machine.'

'Don't make me laugh, love, my stitches'll give out. Tom wasn't that bad, and I'm hardly Superwoman, but I know what you mean. Listen, Lou. I'm really, truly glad it's you here. You've been fantastic.' Lou squeezed her friend's hand and went to make the calls.

'Is that Tom?'

'Louise? How is she?'

'It's all fine. A lovely boy – Jack, seven and a half pounds. She had a pretty bad time. The induction was slow, then they put her on a drip which brought on the contractions too fast, then there was foetal distress so they did an emergency caesarean –'

'But he's OK – the baby – he's all right?'

'Absolutely fine. They both are.'

'Nita must be exhausted.'

'She is, but she's really angry too. She thinks the doctor made bad judgements and it sounds like she's going to complain. I tell you, you'd never believe she'd just had surgery, she's so full of energy and force. She's amazing!'

'When can I visit?'

'It's late now. How about leaving it till the morning and bringing Katie with you then? Nine-ish.'

'Are you sure she wouldn't prefer it if I came now? My brother's staying here, I can leave Katie with him and –'

'No. No, I think she needs a rest. Leave it for now.'

Tom agreed, a little too readily for Louise's liking. But then nothing he did was going to make her change her extremely low opinion of him and the way he had treated Nita.

So, Tom thought, I have a son. It didn't have a ring to it which he particularly admired, wasn't something he aspired to. He felt almost guilty that this element of his manliness was nowhere to be found, when so many other testosterone-inspired features of his personality were all too much in evidence. One of which was his immense relief at not having been present at what sounded like a traumatic birth. Beneath it, he recognised his guilt at even feeling relief, and remembered Martin's scorn. It was true that he didn't feel worthy of being present at the birth, either. If circumstances beyond his control had denied him access to Grace's entry into the world, he had nobody but himself to blame for his absence from Jack's arrival.

Tom went to bed early, in preparation for the inevitable six a.m. start to the day with Katie, leaving Martin morosely watching television. As he lay, uncomfortably awake, he wondered what Jack would look like. And what he would be like. Tom hoped that this son would be a mother's boy and the very act of hoping it made him despair of ever being able to fall asleep alone and not long for – for Cressida, is what he would say to himself, but a quieter voice subverted the echo which became – for company. Whenever he fell asleep alone Tom longed, more than anything, for company.

Friday

Kyria's body clock had changed radically; once happy on six hours' sleep, in the middle months of pregnancy onwards she tended to go to bed at nine in the evening, get up at around two in the morning to make peppermint tea and eat a small snack, treading the fine line between appeasing her nausea and provoking her indigestion, then return to bed and snooze until around nine. The habit remained long after the nausea had left her. This morning, she had woken up at seven, when Justin came back into the bedroom after his shower. The sensation of having a small dolphin thrashing around vigorously in her abdomen had become more acute after her early-hours snack and she felt a prolonged series of tightening sensations. When Justin brought her tea and the news that Nita had had a boy called Jack she didn't feel like mentioning them to him, and thought that, in any case, they were bound to be nothing more than Braxton Hicks.

She got up shortly after Justin left for work at eight. He was dropping Felicity and Harmony at the bus stop for their journey through Manchester to Nita's house. The girls were excited about seeing Jack and keen to be there to help their mother once she left hospital. By the time Kyria kissed them and wished them a happy Christmas the tightenings were becoming cramps.

'We'll see you in a fortnight, Kyria. We'll be back before that baby's out, don't worry. Take care. Bye!' She was tempted to mention feeling peculiar to Fliss, but she couldn't possibly hold the girls up when they needed to get back to their mother, so she waved them all off with a smile and made herself some more tea and toast before taking a brief shower. Swinging her legs over the edge of her bath and supporting her belly made her feel even more elephantine than usual and she laughed out loud at the sight of her enormity in the bathroom mirror. Drying herself seemed to be a pointless waste of energy, especially since Justin insisted on keeping the central heating on full power all day for her benefit, so she walked, naked, gently up and down the landing, humming to herself and going through her mental checklist of all the jobs she needed to complete before the baby was born. She was so busy humming and thinking that when an enormously powerful contraction overwhelmed her she was surprised to find herself kneeling over the laundry basket, which was fortunately full of bedding waiting to be washed. Her body had responded so quickly and naturally to the contraction that the urge to take up the position had been entirely unconscious and it did feel, as she slowly stood up, that she had for a moment not been there.

'Shit. I'm not all here this morning,' she said, out loud again. 'And now I feel like Alice. Curiouser and Curiouser. I'd quite like to shrink a little, actually, but that's not supposed to be happening for another three weeks so I really don't know what's going on. Ow!' Another contraction beset her, which she instinctively breathed through. For a moment Kyria considered calling Justin, who would just have arrived at work, but decided against it. She was enjoying her own company, and there seemed to be something almost magical about this morning which would be lost if anyone, even her beloved husband, shared it. Besides, she corrected herself, it wasn't as if she were actually alone. Far from it.

Two hours later Kyria was wandering around the house enjoying various new symptoms of labour, each of which was arriving in the right order and affecting her in an interesting, unfrightening way. She was in the sitting room now and the TENS machine whose four pads she had attached, with some difficulty, to her lower back an hour or so ago, was turned up to level four of ten. Its rhythmic thrumming tickled her between contractions and she turned it to a high-speed boost when the pains reached their peak. She had taken the time to dig out her favourite compilation tape, featuring selections from her personal collection, eclectic in its variety but utterly consistent in its ability to invite derision from Justin, who despaired of Kyria's musical preferences, and Fliss and Harm, who found it hard to equate their witty, artistic, perspicacious stepmother with this kind of music. These were mainly the softest of soft reggae, banal classical pieces underscored with handclaps and a nostalgic section of New Zealand sounds ranging from Kiri te Kanawa singing well-known arias to recordings of the local fauna. 'Girl, I'm gonna make you sweat,' she sang enthusiastically, trying to strut in time to the music but managing only a convulsive waddle, 'sweat till you can't sweat no more . . .' Catching sight of herself in the mirror over the fireplace she laughed heartily. 'Fuck's sake. This is contemporary bloody dance! Put me in a black leotard and I could be Arts Council funded.' During a heavily percussive rendition of Vivaldi's 'Summer' from 'The Four Seasons', she turned the dial of her TENS machine up a notch, to number five, and kept it on boost for sixty seconds. After a long outward breath she felt winded, more from the effects of the machine's vibration than the contraction itself.

'Jeez. It's like being attacked in the lower back by a really hefty hummingbird! Looks like this is it, girl. Looks like this baby really is on the damned way. OK, honey,' she patted her abdomen, 'hold your horses, we're going to call your daddy.' She laughed again, gently but not for long as once again her concentration was dragged back to the centre of her body. She moved her legs apart a little, then a little more, until she was leaning heavily on the sofa with her knees on the carpet, as wide apart as she could get them. She got a towel on the floor just as her waters broke with a warm gush, at which point she called Justin.

'Jus?'

'Kyria! Are you OK? What's the matter?'

'I'm fine, but honey, this baby's on its way. Tinks isn't going to wait.'

'Oh God, I'll be right there, love, hold on–'

'No, don't go, love. I mean now!'

'You mean–?'

'Noooooooooow!' The handset fell from between Kyria's shoulder and chin as she moved her hands down to catch the slippery body leaving her own at speed. Justin was terrified at the other end of the line.

'Kyria! Speak to me! Listen, I'll get an ambulance sent round now and – oh God, baby, please, speak to me. Kyria!' He listened, hearing Kyria's voice talking softly and then, he could swear, a tiny mewing sound. It was difficult to tell, since there was also a great deal of background noise. Still holding the baby between her legs, Kyria leaned forward and put her mouth to where the handset lay on the sofa.

'Right,' she breathed heavily, 'here's Tink. I'm going to put him on to you.' Justin, still straining to hear over what seemed to be a loud chanting, heard a rustle and another murmur from his wife, then definite baby sounds up close to the receiver.

'Kyria! What's going on?'

'Hush. Don't shout. Say hello to your son.' The baby began to wail.

'My son. Oh God. Oh baby. Hello, baby, this is your daddy. Welcome to – well, just welcome. My son. Jesus. Erm – I'm sorry I missed you coming out but –'

Kyria leaned into the handset and interrupted, 'OK, OK, that's enough for now. I'm going to feed him now, Jus. Before you leave, can you call the midwife unit and get them to send someone round to cut the cord?'

'Kyria, you sound – so calm. Are you sure you're OK? I don't – I don't believe this.'

'I am calm. It was lovely. So peaceful. It all happened just like it should, though it was a bit bloody quick, and it was like a dream. I did mean for you to be here, but I kept thinking – it's got to get worse than this. This can't possibly be it. And then it was! But time for you to share it now. Come home, love.' Justin was stunned. Colleagues nearby had realised what had happened and were staring at his delighted, weeping face, the men with an affectionate scorn which masked their own shining eyes and the women with shameless tears of their own.

'I'm sorry I was a bit slow on the uptake, love, I was shocked, so worried about you, and then there was this terrible racket going on in the background and –'

'That terrible racket, my so-English husband, was the friggin' Haka.'

'My son was born to the sound of the Haka?'

'Quit talking and come home. Me and Patrick are waiting.'

'Patrick! What happened to Christopher?'

'No idea. I was still expecting Tink. But this one is most certainly Patrick Montague, I knew as soon as I saw him. Now stop arguing and come home!'

Justin phoned the midwife then almost skipped from the office, accompanied by cheers and a round of applause that followed him all the way to the car park.

Saturday

After washing up the breakfast dishes Mary bustled around the house collecting items for Margaret's suitcase. She chose three freshly laundered nightdresses and the new blue dressing gown they had picked out last month. Then some comfortable elasticated clothes; leggings, T-shirts, a sweatshirt, along with two new nursing bras and a generous supply of knickers. She filled a sponge bag with toiletries; miniature bottles of gels and shampoos and creams which she had been collecting for weeks and another bag with the less glamorous accoutrements of motherhood; nipple cream, sanitary towels, breast pads, disposable pants, fragranced wipes, lip balm. Wrapped in tissue were four little sleepsuits and vests plus a pair of hand-knitted cardigans; one yellow and one green, with matching bobble hats. A pack of newborn nappies took up one corner of the case. Placing two soft baby towels and a fluffy bath sheet on top of the case, Mary smoothed everything down with a sigh of satisfaction and went to see how Margaret was getting on upstairs.

'Peggy! You're not even dressed yet! We should be leaving in twenty minutes.'

'I'm not going.'

'What?'

'You heard me, Mary. I'm not going. And don't call me Peggy.' Margaret was kneeling on all fours on the bed, leaning over the newspaper and sipping peppermint tea. She looked calmly pleased with herself. 'I'm not having a caesarean. These babies will come out in their own good time and I don't want to have an operation.'

Mary looked anxious and impatient. 'But sweetheart, you know that the doctor is concerned. It is twins, and you are over forty after all.'

'Stuff and nonsense. I'm fit and healthy, they're both head down and because they're twins they'll be smaller than singletons. I'm not going in, Mary. It will happen here.'

'You've been planning this all along!'

'Possibly. Don't look all hurt, love, I just didn't want to worry you. But you know I'm bad enough about hospitals at the best of times. I really don't want to give birth there in any way but especially not with all that – cutting. There's absolutely no reason to do it.'

'They're expecting us to go in–'

'Mary, it's not like school. They won't take a register. They'll probably be glad of the extra bed. Truly, I'd prefer it this way.'

Mary was scared, both at her lover's defiance of medical authority and at its potential repercussions. 'How will we manage? We can't possibly–'

'Don't worry. I'm not suggesting we do it on our own. I've got a private midwife on call. She's been around a couple of times already, her name's Abena and her mother's from Ghana and she's absolutely lovely.'

'You've been seeing someone behind my back!'

'What an accusatory tone! Mary, of course I arranged her visits for when you wouldn't be here, I had to keep it quiet and I'm sorry, but I really didn't want you to worry. But I don't think we'll have long to wait – I've been experiencing the early signs of labour for almost forty-eight hours now and they're beginning to hot up.'

'You didn't tell me!'

'I'm telling you now. No need to panic. Abena will be here in a few hours and all will be well. Truly. All will be well.'

When Abena arrived, at around noon, Margaret was well into the first stage of labour. The midwife quietly checked her blood pressure and temperature and asked how she felt.

'Aren't you going to check my dilation?' asked the doctor.

'No need. You've got a way to go and the last thing you want is my fingers up you time and time again,' the midwife joked, causing Margaret to glance up at her lover and smirk. Mary looked shocked and went to make a pot of tea. When she returned, she discovered that the decision to have the babies at home had been kept secret even from the midwife. Abena was expecting to accompany Margaret to the hospital and assist in a natural birth; she was anxious that her patient was taking independence a step too far. Once it became obvious that neither her advice nor Mary's pleading was going to change Margaret's mind, Abena explained that she couldn't possibly assist her patient under the auspices of the private midwifery practice which employed her, which simply didn't carry the insurance to undertake risky home births.

'So you're going to leave me to it, then?' asked the doctor, already sure that the answer would be no.

'I will stay. But I will stay as an individual person helping a labouring woman, I can't represent the practice. Do you understand?'

'Yes, thank you, Abena.'

'And you will have to sign this form which states that I have advised you go to hospital but that you have refused.'

'I understand. Here, let me do that now.'

'Right,' said the midwife as she tucked the paper into the side-pocket of her bag and rolled up her sleeves, 'let's get to work.'

The mother-to-be was feeling pleased with herself. Once the shock of pregnancy, followed by the shock of her feelings for Mary, had been numbed by the march of time and necessity, she had made a private vow to tell her babies all they wanted to know about their father. Remembering how lack of a father had affected her throughout her life, she was determined that they should never feel that they had been abandoned by him, and therefore she needed to give them the truth, or its bare bones, as soon as they could understand it. And at some point she would need to flesh it out with whatever details she could find so, while trying to trace Fr Nkromah via the Church, she undertook some research into the country of his birth. Even if she never found him, or if he never replied to the letter she planned to send when she did, at least the children would understand both why he was not present and where he – and therefore, partly, they – came from. In the process of learning about the country's historical and cultural heritage, she was trying to imagine the time when she would take her children to reclaim some of it for themselves. Still uncomfortable about her attitude to race, Margaret felt slightly fraudulent when she conjured up the image of herself and her two brown children arriving in the red dust of an African airstrip. Despite numerous attempts to develop her daydream, this was as far as she ever got, and even then she saw herself wearing a khaki divided-skirt suit with a foldaway traveller's hat, as though she were about to embark on a mission in the Congo. Still, she was doing her best with the language and learning a lot about the politics and felt that she was as prepared as she possibly could be for questions, particularly as none were likely for at least the next couple of years. She had even ventured a twenty-minute walk westwards from Queen's Park into the heart of Harlesden, a territory she generally avoided, where she had asked a bemused hairdresser to teach her braiding. She sat, pale and attentive, amongst the glamorous black girls getting their nails done, who advised her how to care for her babies' hair and skin; what to tell them about their father's country; even what music to play to them and where they should go to church. Amid the laughter and shouting of the young women, Margaret realised that they were playing games with her and was aware of what an incongruous sight she must seem, but she listened nevertheless and managed to pick the sound advice out of the more ludicrous suggestions she received.

Abena had been an accident. Not even Margaret's assiduous gleaning of all things Ghanaian could have found her a midwife of the right nationality. As soon as they met Margaret felt soothed and happy that this woman would deliver her babies; she knew for certain that Fate, or something like it, had delivered Abena to her. She didn't know that Abena divided her working life between the midwifery practice and the hospital and had attended the delivery of Nicola's still-unnamed baby only three days previously, nor that since then she was overcome by sorrow every time she thought of that tiny boy whose mother had left the hospital without him two days after his birth, without so much as a backward glance.

Even now, as she focused her mind on the matter in hand, Abena had to filter out concerns for what she had begun to think of as the lost child. Her patient was in good shape, breathing well through her contractions, moving loosely and comfortably around the room with sufficient adrenaline to make her eyes shine and her heart beat strongly enough to face the experience of birth. Both babies lay head down, all previous tests, examinations and scans suggested an absolutely normal presentation and Margaret's own health was probably better than ever before, now that she was regularly benefiting from Mary's love and cooking and cutting back radically on her evening gin and tonics. Without relaxing too much, Abena permitted herself an air of calm and comfort that surrounded and supported Margaret, who was positively enjoying this culmination of eight months' remarkable growth and development. Her contractions were progressively stronger and closer together and she felt, if not exactly in control of the situation, at least *at one* with it. She and her body were going on a journey and it felt like they were holding hands. It felt like soon she would just *be* her body, a prospect she anticipated with a thrill; to escape her brain, flee her mind and be overcome by a physical sensation unlike all others, based not on sexual abandon or drug-induced transcendence (not that she'd ever had much of either until fairly recently) but on something more primal, less selfish, simultaneously earthy and miraculous. She couldn't wait.

She didn't have to, or not for long, because the gradual progress of her labour had made advances where it mattered; her body was preparing itself for the birth in ways of which she was unaware. All she knew was that she was embarked upon a process which swept her up in its wake and when, seven hours after Abena's arrival, she felt the urge to push, she was still sufficiently fired with hormonally-produced painkillers and ecstatic expectation to need nothing more than words of encouragement and Mary's strong hands grasping her own. Kneeling on the sheeted floor of the bedroom she panted and strained, not without pain, but without any sense of debilitation.

'Put your hand here,' ordered Abena softly, and Margaret felt the head of her first child crowning at the mouth of her vagina. 'And now hold your breath – gently – gently – and slowly, very slowly let it out. Don't push this, let it happen. Let it happen to you.' The midwife's voice was low and insistent, her words became a narrative which turned into a song and Margaret's sigh as the head slid out was a long-held note of helpless satisfaction. It was echoed by Mary, who caught the baby's body as it slithered out of her lover's, and who for a moment could do nothing but stare, amazed and delighted, at the already struggling infant.

'It's a boy, Margaret. A little boy. Look!'

But before Margaret had time to do more than look surprised and draw breath, her second, smaller twin was born on the tide of her sigh. Abena, who had already cast an expert eye on the first baby, swooped up the second and examined her quickly. This body was still, no sign of her brother's flailing arms and curling fingers. She scooped mucus from the child's mouth, then sucked more from her nose. She laid the tiny girl on the sheet and massaged her thorax. Then she held her by the ankles and delivered a sharp slap to her buttocks at which the little girl coughed and mewed and finally cried.

'This one is weaker,' she said. 'She may be OK or she may have something wrong with her. I don't know. You'll have to take her to the hospital.' Margaret, who was holding her son, held out her other arm for her daughter. Mary looked distraught at Abena's words but the new mother nodded as she folded the twins in her arms and kissed them.

'But not right now?' she asked and Abena nodded.

'Not right now. If there's something wrong it's a slow thing.'

'What do you mean?' asked Mary, shocked, but Margaret looked at her calmly and explained, as she helped the boy latch on to one breast and tried in vain to help the girl follow suit.

'You know I didn't have amnio or CVS. So it was always possible, bearing in mind my age, that my babies might have some – handicap. There are all sorts of conditions, some of them very mild, which babies can be born with. But she's breathing now, and her responses are OK, aren't they, Abena?' The midwife nodded seriously. 'So there's nothing we need to do right now but we'll need to keep an eye on her and maybe take her for some tests in a little while.'

'Tests for what?' asked Mary anxiously.

'A few things. Down's syndrome is one of them.' Margaret and Abena each held one of the little girl's hands and opened it, casually. They both saw the telltale single crease in the palms and their eyes met knowingly. Abena cupped both of the baby's hands in her own and kissed them while Margaret stroked the girl's cheek with her nipple to stimulate the feeding response. 'My little Ama,' she whispered. 'We need to be very careful with you.'

Mary was so surprised at the calmness with which Margaret had taken the news that her daughter might not be completely healthy that she didn't hear that the child had been named for a second or so, at which point Abena was already saying, 'Ah. And so her brother is Kwame?'

'Of course,' smiled Margaret.

'How did you know that?' asked Mary, confused. 'Peggy, have you already chosen the names without telling me?'

'Not exactly. But in the Ghanaian communities that speak the Twi language children are usually named after the day of the week on which they are born. So the girl's and boy's names for Saturday – which is Memeneda – are Ama and Kwame. Good, I liked that pairing. And I'm relieved I managed to avoid Monday.'

'Why?

'Because their father's name is Kojo, the male name for a child born on Monday, and I'd have had to name the boy after him, which would have been a little strange.'

Mary was beginning to relax, enough to gently mock the babies' provenance. 'Now then, Monday's child would be – what? – fair of face? I suppose you couldn't tell that in the dark?' It was Abena's turn to look confused – Margaret had told her the father was Ghanaian and no longer in the UK but no more – as Mary grinned and continued, 'Abena, what's the male name for Friday?'

'Kofi.'

'Now Peg, are you sure he wasn't Kofi?' Margaret knew what was coming and was already laughing gently. 'Because he was certainly loving and giving, wasn't he, fairly prolifically so by all accounts?'

Abena left the new household two hours later, having cleared up, weighed the babies, advised Margaret about care for herself and the twins, left a pile of superfluous leaflets and helped Kwame and Ama latch on to their mother's breast, though even her experience and Margaret's determination were not much of a match for the little girl who seemed to want nothing more than to sleep. She had opened her eyes only once, looked into the gaze of her mother and then closed them again, but it was long enough for both Margaret and Abena to notice the epicanthic fold on each eyelid which confirmed their earlier suspicions. Kwame, on the other breast, was still sucking, and had objected noisily to the five-minute interruption to feeding time when Margaret took a quick shower. Mary found the double feeding session innately comical – it looked as though Margaret were brandishing two rugby balls in preparation for an unusual try, and realised that their queen-sized bed would prove only just adequate.

'Abena, thank you. You've been wonderful, thank you so much.'

'You did the hard bit. Congratulations, I'm very pleased for you, Margaret. Now, contact your own doctor, and I'll see you tomorrow. Don't worry, I'll let myself out.'

'They're quite pale, aren't they?' commented Mary, kissing both babies' feet in turn.

'They'll get darker as they get older,' said Margaret wisely. 'Even if both parents are black the baby can be quite light-skinned, the pigmentation changes once they're ex-utero.'

'You are such a feckin' scientist,' said Mary, shaking her head, 'and I love you,' she added.

'You too. Us too.' Weary after the labour, worried, for all her matter-of-factness, about Ama, and aching from her first experience of breast-feeding both babies at once, Margaret looked radiant, contented, and ten years younger.

Sunday

After such a busy week a day's rest would surely be in order. But there is no rest for the wicked, or for anyone else much; only the new babes are allowed a moment's respite; all seven of them waving their limbs, pursing their lips and sinking in and out of dreams which consist entirely of being in the dark and emerging into the light, then returning, then re-emerging. Over and over again. Only Ama isn't waving her limbs much. And Baby Mackenzie, Nicola's unnamed boy, is doing all his waving without an audience.

In fact he did have a frequent if surreptitious audience of one. Abena, Margaret's midwife, came into the hospital on Sunday, her day off, on the pretext of needing to complete some paperwork but actually, as she knew only too well, to see the little lost boy. Abena had no children and could see no chance of ever having any, so was in the process of registering as a foster mother. She used to dream of looking after a tiny baby who would stay with her for several years while its mother was in prison for drug-related offences and who, on release, would see how happy her child was and thank Abena for all she had done then leave quietly, tears in her eyes, allowing Abena to become the child's true mother. It had taken Abena a month or so to consider and reconsider the implications of her dream – she knew the dangers – and she concluded that her wishful thinking would not be an obstacle to her happily fostering older children on a short-term basis, that the dream was a threat to no one, and that she was right to offer care in this way.

She picked the baby up and walked around the Special Care baby unit, humming gently while burying her nose in the soft folds of his neck and breathing in the milky baby animal smell of his skin. Hearing someone come into the unit she turned and recognised Christine. Her instant expression was one of guilt but she saw right away that there was no need.

'Hello. It's Abena, isn't it? You remember me, Christine?'

'Of course. Has – has his mother . . . ?'

'No. The only way she'll talk about it is to say that there must be an adoption immediately. She insisted on going to our mother's funeral yesterday and now she wants us to agree to sell the house as soon as possible – the house where she and Mum and the little one were going to live – and she just won't talk about him at all, except to answer yes or no to simple questions, like, will you allow one of us to look after him until you've had time to rethink? To which the answer is always No. She forbids it.'

'Do you think that with time she might change?'

'I just don't know. She's adamant. She's fine when she talks about Mum – distraught but not weird. But about the baby – I don't get it, if she were in complete denial I could sort of understand it, but she's treating the whole thing as though he's just an unfortunate incident which needs to be dealt with.'

'So what are you going to do?'

'Well, I can't bear the idea of not leaving some doors open to Nicola. No way will we have him adopted. But we are wondering if we might look into something more short term, like fostering. If that would be possible.' Christine was looking at the nurse shrewdly when she asked, 'What do you think, Abena?'

'I think you know what I think. I think you know what I'm feeling about this little boy.'

'I think I do. And is it something you've thought about before?' At this point Abena told Christine about her previous fostering plans and how she would dearly love to look after the child. She could get some parental leave at first, and then would start working part-time, perhaps even try to get a childcare job which meant she could be with her foster child most of the time. All of these matters she had already thought about but now, focused on this real baby, they began to make absolute sense. The child's aunt watched the nurse's eyes shine and her hand stroke the baby's back as she spoke, evidently trying to control her eagerness. For a moment, Christine was anxious about her hunger for the boy, but quickly understood the craving to be entirely natural. She left the hospital half an hour later, having given her nephew a long cuddle, with Abena's telephone number in her pocket.

It hadn't been too difficult for Tom to invent some reason to go to London on Sunday. Nita was at home being waited upon by her older daughters, who were having great fun with Katie and cooing over Jack and it was clear that Tom's presence wasn't needed. He took the train, and spent the entire journey feeling sick with excitement and fear. Not only was he going to see his child, he was also going to meet Harry for the first time ever and, most terrifying of all, he was going to see Cressida after almost five long months. It was inconceivable, he thought, that they had survived such a long and upsetting separation. He had begun every day of it with such a heavy heart, and yet, it had carried on beating, he had carried on breathing and writing, eating less and drinking more, missing Cressida and aching for her voice or her look or her touch for hours on end at first, then for several minutes every hour and now mostly for the odd painful moment of the day. Tom was irritated by this diminution, it seemed he was insulting himself, that his memory didn't have the *cojones* to keep her by him night and day, that his own mind was quietly allowing the pain to recede, little by little. Being at home alone with his loneliness was proving unedifying – rather than seek to understand his motivations and decisions Tom used the time for alternate bouts of self-pity and guilt. Feeling more isolated than ever, he failed to remember that at times like this the first thing he would have done was reach for some woman's number. Or that the point in his life at which he had thrown in his lot with Nita had been a deliberate effort on his part to quell the loneliness once and for all by living with a tolerant, doting woman whose intellectual prowess could never threaten his own. Even making some connection between his feelings for Bronwen and his love for Cressida hadn't given him any clues; he had reached such a fatalistic position on all life had to offer that he was taking it lying down, couldn't even raise his head to see what might be coming and decide whether he should duck or hold out his arms.

Armed with an A–Z, he took the train from Euston out to

Queen's Park and thence to the three-storeyed terraced house which Harry and Cressida had bought the year they married, which was, coincidentally, the year before house prices in the area rocketed. Tom's London sensors were tuning in to the signs as he walked up her road; looking through large, clean bay windows at walls painted in either bold matt shades or subtle natural finishes and clocking the clutter of traditional toys strewn amongst hi-spec hi-fi, he smelled money and media and a faint whiff of Humanities. Despite Cressida's northern upbringing and state education it was inexplicably important to Tom that he could categorise her as being in the higher echelons of society, certainly higher than he was, and her house gave his categorisation some justification. It was all linked to his long-held but utterly false assumption that his working-class accent and demeanour (whatever the latter might mean) were constantly being used against him, whereas in fact they had opened doors to him throughout his life; it pleased him to feel victimised and then to conquer his tormentors by proving his superior intelligence. Perhaps too it pleased him to believe that the dozens of middle-class women he had seduced had fallen helplessly for his rough charms rather than understand that wit, warmth and erudition are attractive to a great many women however they are packaged.

It was this familiar but almost inexpressible feature of Tom's psyche that Cressida was pondering when the doorbell rang, imagining, with great accuracy, what his swiftly drawn opinion of her home environs would be. She started at the bell and grabbed Harry's hand as he turned towards the hall.

'Harry, before you answer that, listen to me. Are you sure you want to meet him now?' Harry was pacing the room, as he had been for the past half hour, in a state of extreme agitation.

'Yes, yes, I'm sure. It'll take my mind off this afternoon.'

'You can't be more nervous about that bloody speech than you are about meeting Tom!'

'As it happens, I am. Meeting Tom isn't going to change my life – he's managed to do that from remote – but this "bloody speech" is infinitely more terrifying. My audience here will be you and Grace, both of whom I feel more than able to cope with, but later today I'll be facing five hundred of my peers and . . .'

'OK, OK. Listen, he's ringing again, if you don't answer the door he'll think we've done a runner.'

'I'm going, I'm going . . .'

'Hello, Tom. Harry Shepherd.' Tom shook the proffered hand firmly. He had known that Harry would be at some advantage over him having seen publicity shots on his books and therefore knowing what he looked like, but standing on the bottom step and looking up at Harry's handsome, open face, the gap between them seemed much more than five inches. Tom didn't know that the last thing Harry was interested in was his physique, and began, with automatic defensiveness, to keep a mental score. One nil to Shepherd at this stage. Maybe two-nil on account of Harry's apparent ease and grace with a more than sticky situation. The tally continued to mount in Harry's favour as they walked through the tasteful family home filled with books and *objets* of which Tom could only approve and into the kitchen whose gleaming fittings would have graced the most stylish contemporary TV cookery programme. Somewhere between looking up at the suspended pan-rack hung with spotless steel and down at the genuine Welsh slate tiles, Tom screwed up and binned the scorecard because it was just getting silly. Cressida sat at the table holding Grace. She didn't speak, but held the bundle out to Tom, who accepted it and sat beside her. Grace was sleeping, and the relaxed weight of her body, dressed in soft jersey, felt perfect in the crook of his arm, her warmth was just right for his skin, her shape exactly fitted the space he had made for her. All Tom could do was stare at his daughter's beauty, notice how her long lashes and the shape of her brow were Cressida's and feel her naked feet against his skin like cool water. Tom's eyes filled with tears. Harry left the room.

Viewing him with an unfeigned indifference which verged on, but was not, coldness, Cressida asked him simply, 'Why are you crying?' at which it became obvious to Tom that the woman he loved was on the warpath to truth and justice and his heart sank.

'She's so – beautiful.'

'Yes.'

'And she's *ours*. We made her.'

'Yes.'

'Well, isn't that enough?'

'Enough for tears? I don't think so. She's beautiful and we made her and – what?'

'For Christ's sake, Cressida, what are you getting at? Isn't it obvious that I'm finding this moment somewhat moving?' Tom tried to tone it down. 'I mean – I'm just overcome, that's all. Cress, pet, why are you looking at me like that?'

Cressida's face was calm and enquiring and her heart was steady but she still felt the internal damage caused by loving this man with a passion that could not be blocked or diverted. By now, in any case, she knew that she was going to do The Right Thing, but that didn't stop her clutching at one residual straw, one tiny dream that Tom might swoop his lover and baby up in his arms and swear to adore and protect them for eternity. Tom saw the impatient frown pass over her face as she dismissed the intrusive, hopeless dream, and thought it was directed at him.

'Cress, honey, what have I done wrong now?'

'How's your son?'

'He's fine.'

'And Nita?'

'Yes, fine, they're all fine. The girls are up with them now, helping with Katie and everything. And Justin's wife has had her baby too, the day after Jack was born. Everything's fine.'

'Good.'

'Cress, please speak to me normally. Please stop being polite to me.'

'Those are normal things, Tom. Asking about your new baby and his mother. Your family. What did you expect me to talk about?'

'Us. Love. Our baby.'

'Those words don't really mean anything, do they? We've had so many conversations about the first two but to what end? And very few, recently, about the third. Our baby, yes – but really, my baby. Part of my family. Nothing to do with yours.'

'Pet, I do love you, you know. I still –'

'No more of that. I don't need it.' Cressida became animated. 'I really don't need it, Tom. I've done without it for several months and – look! – I'm still alive. Still able to love my children and find happiness in them and do my job and find satisfaction in that – still almost a fully functioning human being. So your love isn't part of my life any more. And before you ask, yes – I still love you. Although those words sound odd now, don't they? I realised that I wanted the impossible – you coming to rescue me on the white charger – and that there's a measurable difference in the way we use That word. You see, in a daft old-fashioned romantic way, I'd do anything for love. Whereas you – well, you would do love for anything. Use the word to get what you want. Change its meaning, its significance, its – essence.'

Tom was shaking his head vehemently, 'That's not true. Not about what I feel for you. You'd do anything for love and I – I wouldn't. You're right on that count. Cressida, I spent so long thinking that I'd never truly find it and when I did – well. By the time I did, I'd already filled all the gaps, with Katie mostly. I was set on doing the right thing, couldn't trust that I'd actually found my – fuck knows what to call it – my *soulmate*. That's what you are, isn't it? Whatever we believe or suspect we believe? And I kept telling myself it was the right thing to do, keep the family together, don't rock the boat at Katie's expense – so when Nita dumped me it felt like such a huge shock firstly because I was scared about losing Katie and then because I just didn't know what to do about you. I obviously couldn't rush down here and spirit you away, couldn't break up your family too. But being stuck on my own, away from Katie, without my baby and without you or any prospect of you has been sheer misery. I've missed you every goddamned day.'

'You never thought about the fact that you were free?'

'No, of course not. As if you – with this house and that husband and your kids and everything – would throw your lot in with me, when I'd only asked you after being kicked out of my girlfriend's house. As if I'd suggest that. Cress, I have too much respect for you, I know what you'd have said if I'd come down here with a dozen red roses and told you I was free at last. I mean, you can imagine, can't you?'

'Yes,' said Cressida, feeling sickness rise in her throat, an acrid burning behind her eyes. 'Yes, I suppose I can. So you're still not jealous?' Two years ago and more Tom had told her he rarely got jealous, certainly never fiercely so, and wondered if it was because he couldn't care sufficiently for someone else to feel that way. The conversation was in the context of The Artist and His Ego and Cressida had dismissed it optimistically. But now, she thought, perhaps it was true all along. Perhaps the gut-wrenching, trembling pain she used to feel every time she imagined Tom kissing Nita really was alien to Tom, who could shut off his mind at the requisite points and avoid the pain.

'Not jealous? I'm jealous all the time, pet.'

'Not enough, though.'

'Pet, I've always been jealous.'

'No, the only thing that really got to you was when I told you I'd had an erotic dream about Martin Amis. You were enraged with jealousy. Even the fact that it was a dream, not even a daydream, wasn't enough to convince you I hadn't been unfaithful in my mind! And I've never even vaguely had the hots for Martin Amis, it was just because he's the only kind of rival you rate. Husbands aren't important enough, but another writer – the mere prospect of it almost *killed* you with jealousy. But the things which should have really made you jealous didn't. Not enough.'

'You used to say I didn't love you enough.'

'It's probably the same thing.'

'I loved you – love you – as much and more than I've loved any woman, I swear it.'

'I believe you. I know. Big deal.'

Tom stayed for an hour during which time he held on to Grace determinedly except for handing her back to Cressida for a twenty-minute feed halfway through. He was disappointed that Cressida just pulled up her shirt and put Grace underneath it, as he had been looking forward to seeing her breasts feeding his baby, for all sorts of very obvious reasons, not least of which was the great yearning he had to latch on to one of them himself. Despite having fed both Ben and Jemima for eighteen months, Cressida's breasts had escaped serious loss of elasticity and Tom remembered too well their firm liquidity in his hands or his mouth or against his chest. His desire for her was as strong as ever and he wanted to convey that, he wanted to feel he had made one satisfactory remark, one comment of which Cressida didn't disapprove, that wasn't a disappointment. He leaned towards her, looked her in the eye and whispered, 'I want you as much as ever. I'll always want you,' then kissed her mouth gently. The kiss sent a bolt of electricity through her entire body, made her shudder with longing and despair, and the tears which had kept their distance until now suddenly made their presence known. The spasm made her milk spurt into Grace's mouth and the baby protested with an over-flowing gurgle while Cressida's eyes streamed. 'Baby, I'm sorry, I didn't mean to make you cry.'

'You didn't. I'm making me cry. It doesn't matter.' Cressida was aware that the 'baby blues' were beginning to kick in, as they had done four or five days after both her previous births. She wanted to scratch Tom's eyes out. But at least she knew she wanted to, and that she wasn't going to give in to the urge, hard though that was.

'But, can I –'

'It doesn't matter.' Cressida shook Tom's hand off her arm and turned her face until it was under control. 'There. I'm fine now. Please don't do that again. It's not fair.'

When Tom stood to leave he could hardly bear to let go of Grace. He wanted to stay with her and Cressida, make lunch, chat, put on some music, take them for a walk, bath his baby, snuggle up in bed with this little family, make gentle love to this woman. But he was unable even to touch Cressida and decided against any further attempts to tell her what he wanted. Harry, having heard the noises of departure from his office, came down to open the door. At the bottom of the stairs Cressida handed Grace to him and turned to Tom. 'I'm dying for the loo. Safe journey, Tom,' she said and dashed upstairs. It was only then that he remembered the gift he had brought with him; a porcelain cup emblazoned with *Tuesday's child is full of grace* in heavily curlicued calligraphy. 'Thank you.' said Harry, 'bye, now.' Tom's final glance back up the path showed him the husband of the woman he loved, holding his own baby daughter in his arms, leaning to kiss her head while he closed the door. As Tom turned to walk away his eyes were misted over and his fists clenched. Finally, he understood what Cressida meant by jealousy.

Harry had one more duty to perform before giving his lecture. He made his way to the hospital where Sophie was preparing to come home and where he had promised to meet her mother. On arriving, he saw two figures sitting by her bed where she sat feeding Marlon, clothed and ready to leave.

Sophie looked up, smiling. 'Hello, Harry. This is my mother, Vivienne. And this is Josh Diamond – my father.' Vivienne had visited her daughter and new grandson earlier in the week. She had swept into Sophie's room with a large bouquet and a bright unblinking smile, unprepared for the tearful tenderness which enveloped her on finding the pair asleep. Sophie's face had looked so vulnerable, so tired and proud, that her mother suffered a crisis of conscience and decided to tell her the true story of her conception. Amidst the ensuing confusion, Sophie had felt great relief at the news: it explained so much about her mother's behaviour and, as she told Harry afterwards, Josh had always been her favourite uncle. Even so, Harry was surprised to find that things had moved so quickly. The man who now stood up and offered his hand was stocky and strong-featured with thick white hair; he so clearly filled in the gaps – Sophie's short, voluptuous physique was obviously from this side of the family while her fair hair and colouring were like Vivienne's – and was so evidently delighted to be there that Harry couldn't help but mirror his broad grin.

'Very pleased to meet you, young man,' he boomed in a strong East London accent. Harry turned and shook hands with Vivienne as well, 'Pleased to meet both of these young men, eh, Vivi?' he added.

Sophie's mother smiled her agreement and said, 'Yes, I'm pleased to meet you, Harry. Sophie has said so much about you.'

'And don't worry,' added Josh jovially, verging on, but just resisting, a wink, 'we know how all this came about, so to speak, and we're too old to be shocked, so no need to be anxious you know.'

'Josh. I mean, Dad,' chided Sophie, and blushed, which made Josh blush too and even Vivienne lost some of her composure.

'Look at the pair of you,' she laughed, but only Harry saw what she meant; with heightened colour and the same expression in their eyes Sophie and Josh were the image of each other. After having confessed all to Sophie, Vivienne had been terribly nervous at her meeting with Josh when she broke the news, but so determined to make amends for her behaviour that she just blurted out the truth and was already well into the explanatory and apologetic phase before she realised that Josh was smiling and hugging her. She wasn't the only one who had felt guilty about their tryst, although his shame was for the way he had left her afterwards, the callousness of callow youth. It seemed right to him that their one night together had resulted in something and the something being Sophie seemed like only the best kind of news. And now that Vivienne was in her early seventies and he a decade younger, his wife dead five years and his two boys in America, now was the perfect time for a new family to enter his life and make some inroads into the loneliness which no number of nostalgic evenings with old buddies and trips to the dogs could ever assuage. Marlon was guaranteed, in a way that Sophie could never have imagined happening, a granny and grandpa who viewed the prospect of a child in their lives as their final chance to get it right. Harry saw the group off to their car; Josh huffing and puffing under all the suitcases and bags of nappies, Vivienne carrying three enormous floral arrangements with great care, and Sophie hugging Marlon, wrapped in a hand-crocheted shawl – all home together for Christmas.

Kyria and Justin were preparing for the arrival of several members of her large family. The proud father was still euphoric and, between putting up decorations and filling the freezer, he constantly rushed to his wife and baby to smother them both with kisses and tell them how beautiful they were. Kyria was luxuriating in new motherhood and the joy of doing nothing except feed her baby and sleep, but she also felt inspired to action. As Justin sat by her feet gazing at Patrick in wonderment, she prodded his shoulder and said, 'Listen, love, I need to get working again soon. All those lazy months – no regrets and all that, but I've got so many ideas and my fingers are itching to get working.'

Justin, torn from his reverie, laughed. 'OK, OK. Tell you what. How about I set up a website for you to sell what you do and get new commissions? I could do it for you in a week.'

'Fantastic! In a month or two, OK? And let's buy somewhere to live. Near Fliss and Harm. Near here. I like it here.'

'Are you sure?'

'Positive. Let's get it all sorted soon.'

Margaret's nipples were sore and raw and she couldn't help sniffling a little as she took a deep breath and tried once more to get Ama to take one of them into her mouth and feed. Kwame had been suckling almost non-stop throughout the night, but every attempt was a struggle for his sister. Their mother and Mary were only just beginning to be tired in a way they hadn't been tired before but were, sensibly, beginning to get used to. As she brought in a tray of tea and cereal, Mary remembered what day it was.

'Oh damn. It's Sunday. Looks like I'll be missing Mass.' Margaret was not too tired to comment on her partner's odd relationship with her cradle Catholicism.

'You are funny, Mary. You've been kicked out of the convent, you're living in the very worst kind of sin, and yet you still want to be a member of the club.'

'No, not the club. I want to go to Mass. That's entirely different.'

'Do you still *believe* in it all?'

'Of course.'

'What, transubstantiation and the sacraments and all that?'

'Those are what I believe in. The magic. Not the incense and poetry and gold and lace. Not the Latin or the singing or the coffee mornings. The water and wine becoming body and blood, the everyday becoming transformed into the divine. I've always thought that the great thing about Catholicism is the way in which the fantastical things are at the centre, rather than the sensible po-faced stuff about love thy neighbour or whatever.'

'But surely being kind to other people is more important than believing in miracles?' Margaret was amused, and both babies were beginning to cry, but Mary was not to be deterred.

'Wrong. If you really believe in the miracle, then all the rest follows. I mean, if you think that really is Christ's body and blood, how could you do anything other than obey his teachings? And the sacraments mark great moments in our lives, they're important rituals, they're *natural*.'

'Oh my love, you're so entirely *good*. You miss it, don't you?'

'Not the convent. Not at all. Living with you and these babies is *glorious*. But I don't want to turn my back on the Church, even if she's turned hers on me. I can't, Peggy. Do you think I'm silly?'

'No. I wish I had your convictions. I plod along with my earthly stuff and have to make do. Between us, our babies will be able to swoop from the sublime to the –'

'Corblimey,' Mary intervened, by which point both Kwame and Ama were yelling noisily and Margaret was once again trying to feed them simultaneously.

'Oh shit,' she muttered, almost in tears, 'I don't want to give up so soon, but it really feels like this isn't going to work. Maybe you'll have to get some bottles after all.'

'Just try one at a time. Give Kwame to me and maybe Ama will be relaxed enough to have a go.'

'OK. One more time. But if it doesn't work . . .' While Margaret concentrated on her daughter, Mary tried to quell the tiny boy's screams, which were becoming more and more piercing. She put him over her shoulder, patted his back as he lay, struggling, across her knees, bounced him around the room, walked up and down-stairs in an attempt to give Margaret at least a little respite, and finally sat down at the end of the bed, tired and hopeless while his cries soared above the traffic noise.

'What can I do for you, baby love, what can I do?' she asked desperately, her heart aching to help him, to stop the noise. Kwame lay cradled in her arms, his arms and legs working violently, and she hugged him against her soft velour-clad chest, rocking determinedly and praying for the insistent, painfully pitched noise to stop. When she realised it had, she had a moment of pure fear, thinking she had smothered the child, whose head was buried deep in the fabric of her dressing gown. Her realisation a moment afterwards that he had burrowed through the gap and was clamped firmly onto her right nipple was no less terrifying. The sensation she had felt a moment before was not heartache, but lactation. As the baby sucked greedily, milk dripped on to her lap.

'Jesus,' she whispered, 'Holy Mother of God.' Margaret heard the unearthly tone of her voice and stared at what she saw. Mary was suddenly frightened and guilty, and pulled the child away from her, milk spurting ridiculously, hilariously, in an arc over his face as he began to cry in rage.

'Peggy, I'm sorry, I didn't mean to, he just –'

'Mary, put the little bastard back on there right now. This is fantastic. A miracle. Hairy Mary Mother of God and baby bloody Jesus, I do believe in you after all. Thank. You. God. Mary, sweetheart, it's OK. I've heard of it happening in droughts and famines and you must have wanted it so much that you got it. It's wonderful. Don't you think?' Mary could only nod mutely as she replaced her nipple in Kwame's enraged mouth and his crying stopped with a pop. The tears streamed down her cheeks, her nose began to run in sympathy and her left breast leaked a slow trickle of milk as the child sucked vigorously on her right. All that flowing was a blessed release, she felt near to ecstasy and full of gratitude.

'That's right, honey,' Margaret said as Ama finally, mercifully settled to a steady suck, 'there's a good girl. Now then, aren't we going to have a wonderful Christmas?'

'Mum, you're not still trying to call that flippin' doctor, are you?' Fliss was becoming impatient, her mother seemed to be obsessed with complaining about her medical treatment but wouldn't go via the usual channels, was insisting upon speaking to Dr Krishna himself and refused to give up despite being quite obviously prevented from speaking to him.

'I know he's there and I've just left another message. I know his rota now, and he's definitely on call. And fair enough, he might be at a birth or whatever, but he could certainly get back to me. I need to talk it through with him, I know you think I'm crazy, Fliss, even Louise is starting to lose patience and she was all for it at first.'

'Well, it does seem a bit negative. When Jack's such an angel and we're all having such a lovely time, and just before Christmas and everything.'

'Oh I'm sorry, love, I hope you and Harm aren't worried about it. Look, I'll not call again until after Christmas, OK? But I want to get him while he remembers who I am and what happened, I want to make sure the facts are all right. Sorry, sorry, I'll shut up about it. And give me that baby boy now, he's agitating for a feed.' Just as Felicity had handed Jack over the telephone rang and Nita grabbed it. She hardly spoke, but scribbled down a date and time and then said, 'Thank you. I appreciate it,' before putting the phone down.

'There,' she said to her daughter with satisfaction. 'I'm going to see him between Christmas and New Year. So no more need to worry about that, OK?' Harmony and Katie came in from the kitchen with the paper chains they had been making to decorate the fireplace and Felicity remembered the cake she had in the oven and rushed off to put it to cool.

'My, what a hive of domestic activity,' commented Nita happily. 'Now, are you sure you don't want to spend Christmas with your dad? I know you're dying to see Patrick too.'

Harmony was adamant. 'Mum, will you just stop it? We'll see him in a few days' time. Dad and Kyria will be glad of the peace before her folks arrive. And we want to be here, with you and Katie and Jack. Don't we, Fliss?' Felicity, who had just returned, offered further reassurances.

'My lovely girls,' said Nita fondly. 'And our little man here. The only man I need. It's all perfect.' And, for the time being, that's exactly what she meant.

Five hundred delegates filled the lecture hall and rustled their papers as they waited for Dr Harry Shepherd to take the podium. Early leaks of his work had already become the subject of impassioned debate in a number of key professional journals and, unusually for this kind of conference, almost everyone present was genuinely keen to be there. Harry walked to the microphone with the full weight of expectation on his shoulders, which were squared to take it. Looking steadily at the mass of fellow psychologists and psychotherapists before him, he waited for complete silence to fall upon the room before he spoke – quietly, assuredly, gravely.

'Ladies and gentlemen. You are waiting for me to outline my theories on the relevance of the Seven Deadly Sins today. You expect me to develop a number of controversial ideas about Sin and Virtue which explode age-old myths and replace them with sound, contemporary psychological truths. You hope that I will present a hard-hitting and, preferably, titillating series of case studies focusing on Anger, Sloth, Pride, Gluttony, Avarice, Envy and of course Lust. I am afraid that you are going to be bitterly disappointed.'

As a murmur buzzed along the rows of surprised men and women, Harry allowed himself one small sigh of satisfaction before continuing.

'For the past week I have known that my artfully-constructed arguments, my insightful analyses, my impressive prose, all of which you have, thankfully, been denied this afternoon, were nothing more than my puny attempt to eclipse the cool moon of received wisdom with the brilliant sun of the new order, which I evidently believed shone out of my own arse.' More buzzing. 'At first, I assumed that my sin was arrogance – Pride – and that in constructing my elegant theory I had been blind to the sin which defined my prime motivations. Not so. Today I had a revelation. *The blindness itself was the sin.* When I wrote my fine paper I was an ignorant man. Educated, knowledgeable, analytical, I knew *nothing*. At this moment, I know very little more than nothing, but the few things I have begun to know are the only things that matter.

'On Monday, a woman who conceived our child without my knowledge gave birth to my son. On Tuesday my wife gave birth to another man's daughter. On Wednesday a woman whose pregnancy had only been known to me for a month gave birth to my son. On Thursday the ex-girlfriend of my wife's lover gave birth to his son. And on Friday the wife of the ex-husband of my wife's lover's ex-girlfriend gave birth to *his* son. Have you ever heard anything more sordid, more uncivilised, more *absurd*?

'One of the things I now know is that it is none of the above. It is a series of circles overlapping one another in an unexpected manner. It is a Venn Diagram of extreme complexity. There is no room for one circle to obstruct another, they are entwined, co-dependent, equal. They each contain love and pain, fear and comfort, passion and calm. The people within each circle are not saints or sinners; their acts are not explained by simple theories of motivation, or nature, or nurture, or *humour*.

'I don't mean that we exist in a moral vacuum, nor that finding and adhering to an ethical framework for our lives is a worthless quest; far from it. But I've been attempting to judge from afar, something in which I'm not alone, however we all subscribe to the neutrality of the consulting room, even, ridiculously, when I have been one of the confused protagonists of an extraordinary situation. Yes, that's Pride, *hubris*, arrogance, vanity, call it what you will. But it's not as though I've been a stranger to the other six Sins, not as though my misbehaviour was limited, or even dominated, by just the one. And, having believed that the Seven covered every conceivable human misdemeanour I've discovered that they simply don't. Where is Deceit? Where is Faint-heartedness? Where is Cruelty? Where is the deadliest sin of all, which doesn't even make the Seven – Despair?

'Trying to define – to pin down – what happened when, and why, and how, takes us further and further from the heart of the matter, which is that last week five new lives entered the world in a variety of circumstances and what they each brought with them was a clean slate. Like their parents, they already tread the line between beast and angel. Our mistake is to believe that aspiring to the angelic is desirable while sinking towards the beastly is reprehensible. Both convictions are simply further proof of ignorance. Our middle path, our human condition, gives us plenty of both the higher and the lower facets of existence but also, if we walk it with ease, it gives us the wisdom to see the beauty of its ordinariness, the perfection of its many flaws. We can accept the mess of life without the martyrdom of stoicism. We can rejoice in its riches without the burden of faith. We can reach some understanding without the proof of science.

'I apologise, ladies and gentlemen, for failing to give you what you wanted. I have longed for the validation of my esteemed colleagues more than I can say, and in my oft-imagined leaving of this room it was always with a particular image in my mind's eye – the expression of stunned admiration upon the faces of everyone on the front row. Well. The stunned bit is right, it appears. And, mostly, I apologise for insulting the intelligence of everyone in this profession by wasting three years of my life chasing my tail and only now, in this week of arrivals, finally coming to the right conclusions too late. The Seven Deadly Sins. I mean, really. I'm sorry.

'And now, if you'll excuse me, I'm going home to my family.'

Harry left the stage to a round of tumultuous heartbeats as his audience emptied their lungs and relaxed their spines. His professor was waiting in the wings, distraught, and as he opened his hands into a question Harry filled them with his letter of resignation.

BOOK FOUR: Chaos Theory

A butterfly flies through the forest rain
And turns the wind into a hurricane.
I know that it will happen
'Cause I believe in
The certainty of chance

from 'The Certainty of Chance',
The Divine Comedy

One year later, New Year's Eve

Cressida took a box off a shelf and put it on the kitchen table. It had once contained a Wedgwood cup and saucer but was now so light as to feel empty save for a faint rattle when it was moved. She repositioned Grace, who was sleeping, from her lap to her shoulder and took off the lid with her free hand, shaking the box's contents on to the table.

'I told you about these, do you remember?' she asked Harry, who was rifling through drawers, wearing only a shirt and socks. He had come straight from three appointments with severely disturbed patients at the clinical psychology unit where he now worked, and was already feeling guilty at having rushed their sessions to get home on time.

'What's that?' he responded distractedly. 'Cress, have you seen my cufflinks?'

'They're in a little drawstring bag at the bottom of my jewellery box so stop panicking and look at these.' Harry glanced at the table.

'Ah, the infamous Shell Project. A gift from Mother?'

'Yes, she found them in the shed at the new house. The box is a bit soggy but they're in pretty good shape considering they've been in there for twenty-odd years.'

'Cress, I'm fascinated, you know I am, but is now the time?'

'Calm down. We've got loads of time. Look at them.' Harry looked. Fragile and translucent, like husks of husks, lay a pile of snail shells, some of them marked with one or more tiny dots of pink or red. 'And here's the Project Report, and the chart. And here are me and Polly on the job.' Cressida took a much-folded piece of light cardboard from an envelope along with a notepad and two photographs. In the first, two blonde girls – one on the verge of adolescence, the other still clearly a child – smiled, in faded colour, at the camera. They each shaded their eyes against the sun with one hand and held out the other to display an object which couldn't be identified at that distance. The second photograph zoomed in on their upturned hands and showed, on each palm, a snail, its shell marked with a splash of colour.

'What on earth possessed your mother to send you mapping snails?'

'No idea. It was much more Dad's style to come up with crazy scientific schemes to keep us usefully occupied in the holidays, and we always hated them. Mind you, they never involved the liberal use of nail varnish . . .' Cressida unfolded the cardboard and smoothed it out. It featured a 'chart'; a complex web of crossing lines in different colours, each representing the journey of one nail varnish-adorned snail across the grid-marked garden plan of her childhood home. On the reverse was the logbook of sightings, which were taken at morning, noon and dusk, and the key of markings by which each snail could be recognised. The first half dozen were simply spots of nail varnish in different shades; as the project expanded a more sophisticated series of patterns involving two or even three colours had been created after experimentation confirmed that writing letters or numbers of identification was impossible on so small a surface area. Cressida began to read the Project Report and laughed at the officious prose of her twelve-year-old self. She scanned to the final paragraph.

'Listen to this, Harry – *Thereby, we can conclude the following: 1. Snails do not congregate together very frequently. 2. Snails do not have favourite places in the garden that they visit more frequently than other places. 3. Snails tend to remain within a thirty-foot area although within that they can travel twice that distance in a day. 4. Snails may not be aware of where they are going.* That's classic.' She held the cardboard up for him to see. 'The chart's rather beautiful, don't you think? If you squint a bit and look at it from a distance. It's completely random but looks like a pattern, like an old tapestry.' Harry looked doubtful. 'Although, you know, I did sometimes wonder if they really *were* moving around as entirely randomly as our great experiment proved. I used to imagine them being engaged in a very, very slow dance which lasted days and days but had absolutely strict rules and parameters.'

'You would,' Harry muttered ungraciously, then added, 'hardly surprising when your mother was so obsessive she actually saved the bloody things.'

'I know, when I was at uni she'd sometimes call to say she'd found one with a bit of pearly pink and a bit of crimson by the compost bin and did I remember it? Did I remember a snail shell which I'd painted six years before? That's weird, I suppose.'

'What are you going to do with them?'

'Put them back in the box and stick them in our shed. Maybe I'll put the chart on the wall – in a clipframe or something. You can tell visitors it's a unique unconscious commentary on free will and determinism.'

'Very amusing. Look, Cress, I've been in such a rush this morning, luckily none of my clients noticed that the fifty-minute hour got even shorter, but now we *really must* get ready. We need to be there in an hour and this snow is settling so we'll need to leave plenty of time because the roads are going to be hell. You're not even dressed yet!'

'Harry, relax. Your suit's all ready, the kids are dressed and stuck in front of a video, all we need to do is wait for Josh and Vivienne to drop by with Marlon, then pick up the buttonholes from the florist and bingo. It'll take me ten minutes to get Grace and me ready. Go on!'

'It's all right for you to be cool – you're not the best man.'

'Neither are you – well, not exactly.'

'Since I have to do the speech and the toasts and whatever, to all intents and purposes I *am*. Now *come on*!' Cressida slowly moved into action and followed her husband upstairs.

Vivienne picked the photograph off the floor where it had fallen and turned it over. She could see the impact made by its glancing off the corner of her coffee table, an intense matt circle in the glass from which lines of fracture radiated unevenly. She began to cry, at which noise Marlon, sitting on the floor amongst gobbets of chewed banana, looked up, puzzled.

'It's all right, my precious. Granny's just a bit upset. Don't worry, little sausage, I know you didn't mean to knock it over. Silly Granny shouldn't have left it there, should she? Look, it's a lovely picture of you and Mummy. Aren't you tiny? Isn't Mummy lovely?'

Josh came into the sitting room carrying a changing bag and outdoor clothing for the baby.

'Vivi, what's the matter?' He saw the broken frame, 'Hey, don't worry about that, we can get a new frame, honey, don't worry.'

'That's not why I'm crying. The frame doesn't matter. Look at her! So beautiful. And so happy. And now . . .'

'I know, sugar, I know. But don't cry now – she'll be calling from the hospice soon to see if we've set off, we need to be brave and make sure she can't see how worried we are.'

'But it shouldn't happen so quickly! The doctor said she could have been fine for years, no reason to believe otherwise, and she was feeling so strong and positive. Then – whoomph! Down she went. And she won't get the sight back in her right eye, you know? Whatever happens she'll always be blind in that eye. Her beautiful eyes. My baby.' Josh finished dressing Marlon in his outdoor clothes and put him, swaddled in a snowsuit, on his grand-mother's lap.

'And this is her baby. Our lovely baby boy. Sophie's not dumb; she knows how badly things are going. But she's keeping cheerful for Marlon, keeping upbeat for him. And we have to try to do the same, whatever happens.'

'I know.' Vivienne blew her nose. 'And I'm sorry. It was just seeing this photo, and the broken glass like crazy paving so you can hardly see her face, and remembering how she looked last time – so thin and with all those tubes and those machines around her – and feeling so completely helpless.'

'We can help, sugar. We are helping. For Sophie and for Marlon. Come on now, it's time to drop him at Harry's.'

'Are you sure Sophie doesn't want him to come this time?'

'Positive. She's in a pretty bad way, thinks it would confuse him too much. Better by far that he's with his –' Josh faltered.

'His family! You were going to say his family!'

Josh blushed. 'You know what I mean. They will be his family. Once . . .'

'Once my baby is dead! That's what you mean.'

'Vivi, stop this. Listen to me, we've gone through this before. You and I are too old to look after Marlon all the time. Having him when Sophie is in for treatment wears us both out. Now, that's fine, that's OK, we'll do anything for him, look after him till it kills us, and enjoy it. Until the time we can't. And then what happens to him? This is what Sophie has always said she wanted – even before he was born she made sure he could be with his father if she – if she didn't make it. And Cressida and Harry agreed, agree that it's the right thing to do.'

'I know, I know. And it makes sense. But what if we don't get to see him?'

'Are you kidding me? Do you really think Harry would stop us? Do you honestly see that happening? You've said he's the best son-in-law you never had.'

'It's true. I'm being paranoid and foolish. Of course you're right. It's just something to worry about which takes my mind off what I'm really worried about.'

'Which there's no point worrying about for now because no-body knows what's going to happen. I mean, sometimes life throws up unexpected joy, doesn't it? Like it threw you up.'

'Josh, what a way of putting it!'

'That's a good attempt at a smile. Not there yet, but an excellent try.'

'Oh, Josh Diamond, you're so good for me.'

'Not good to you?'

'No, good for me. Like medicine.'

'Well, thank you, madam, for that glowing compliment. Now, let's get all those magazines and fruit and the contents of the florist shop you've emptied and go. It's an hour's drive once we've dropped Marlon off and Sophie's expecting us before noon.'

Kyria took one final glance at her first commissioned wall-hanging, wondering, and not for the first time, if it wasn't all a bit too *busy*. Too many colours and patterns, too complicated a structure of strands and textures. But her clients had approved the original designs, and the photographs she had sent them, and the customer would have to be right if she was going to make any kind of living out of her craft. She rolled the weaving carefully then put it in a box and held out her arms for Patrick. Harmony handed him over. 'There you go, one clean, changed, sweet-smelling baby.'

'Oh, thanks for seeing to him, Harm, I really needed to get this nicely wrapped up for the journey down, can't risk any creases. Now, are you sure you're going to be OK?'

Harmony raised her eyes heavenwards. 'Kyria, you're as bad as Mum. Of course I'll be OK. A couple of girls from school are coming to stay for the night so I'll stay at Mum's and then you'll be back tomorrow so I'll come back here. It's cool. No worries.'

'Which friends?'

'Erm – Sue and Kate.'

'Have I met either of them?'

'Don't think so.'

'Well, if you want to have them round here any time when your mum's away, you know that's fine, don't you?'

'Yeah, thanks, Kyria, I probably will. But don't worry about me, OK? Has Fliss decided whether she's going down with you and Dad yet?'

'We're picking her up from your mum's. She said she'd rather get a lift with an old married couple plus baby than love's young dream plus two kids. No room for her in the back of the car with all their stuff and the things for Katie and Jack, anyway.'

'Yeah, I can imagine. *He* seems OK, don't you think? Ravi?'

'I guess so. I've only met him a couple of times but he seemed – nice. A nice bloke.'

'He's a damn sight better than Tom, that's for sure. At least you can tell he's besotted with Mum. Which is exactly how she likes it.'

'Well, who wouldn't?'

'Well, before you met Dad – after your divorce – did you find someone else straight away?'

Kyria looked at the girl closely. 'What's up, Harm? What are you getting at?'

'I bet you didn't *need* to have a bloke around all the time, you didn't sink into a depression just because you were single.'

Kyria responded with sympathy and a little impatience, 'Harm, everyone's different. Some women can't operate properly, can't be happy, unless they're with a man. Some men are the same about women. That's just how they're made.'

'Yeah, but if they've got kids they should think about them first. Mum hooked up with Tom really soon after Dad left, she was desperate to get a replacement in quickly. And then she was stupid enough to start breeding again. And I've read about all that now, it was a really bad stage of our development – mine and Fliss's – for her to be bringing a new man into the house and pushing us out by having Katie.'

'Is that really how it felt?'

'Yes. That's exactly how it felt. I remember when I heard about how much Tom had put it about – you know, all those women he was seeing behind her back – and feeling really glad. Feeling really superior to Mum. Isn't that disgusting? I felt that about my own mum.'

'It was a tricky time, love. And now it's over. Nita seems happy now, and you wouldn't want her to be miserable, would you?'

'No, of course not. All the things I want her to be – well, it's too late. Like – someone with some time for me. And someone who understood how much I missed my dad. And someone who thought, just for a second, before she got so mad about a man who didn't love her. And someone who could just have looked after me and Fliss for another couple of years before moving some bloke in. Just a bit more time and I think we'd have been much better about it all.'

'Better about what?' asked Justin, on his way to the car with a suitcase and a bag of baby equipment. Harmony smiled quickly at Kyria, who looked anxious, and gave her no chance to reply.

'Nothing, Dad. Just talking to Kyria. Now listen, you two have a great time, OK? And *don't worry about me*! I'll be fine.'

'I can see it!' shouted Katie excitedly, her face screwed up with the effort of squinting through one eye. 'I can see the colour thing.'

'Hey, good girl!' said Felicity. 'And can you remember what the colour thing's real name is?' The child shook her head. 'It's a *kaleidoscope*. Can you say that?'

'Kaleiscodope.'

'Not bad. Look at this, look at this end. It's all just little beads that fall around when you turn it. See, they're making that scattering noise, aren't they? But there are some tiny mirrors inside here, so when you look through the hole you see a lovely pattern. Don't you? Katie!' Katie had given up listening halfway through her half-sister's patient explanation and was picking her nose.

'I know,' she said, indignant. 'I knowed that already.'

Nita came downstairs with a fat backpack which appeared to be half her size and weight.

'Mum, you'll never manage to carry that!'

'I'll be fine. You should see Ravi's, it's even bigger.' Struggling downstairs behind her was Dr Krishna, hidden behind his over-stuffed rucksack.

'This is crazy,' he was grumbling, 'I live a sedentary lifestyle, I can afford hotels. In India, I can afford the best hotels in the country. So why I am letting this woman talk me into bumming around the subcontinent like a bloody student?'

Nita cuffed him adoringly. 'I've told you before, you talk like that and I'll sue you.'

The doctor looked pained. 'Nita, can we drop the subject? After you came to see me the first time I caved in straight away. Didn't even put up a fight. Admitted that I'd probably made a hasty judgement. Promised to change my ways. Now please, give me a break.'

Felicity enjoyed seeing the couple fight in this way. When it became obvious that Nita's initial complaints to the consultant had initiated yet another hastily passionate relationship she had felt some of the old insecurity, but Ravi was such a jovial man, and so clearly in love with Nita, that she felt almost patronisingly tolerant of the pair of them. He had to care, didn't he, if he was allowing her mother to drag him around India so that she could find her lost family, and hopefully herself into the bargain. And he had been patient in the face of Nita's ritual mockery of all his formal training, accepting her faith in evening primrose oil and meditation (all of which had returned to her life, although not quite so dizzily as before) without question. He also had two grown-up sons from his first marriage which had ended a decade ago, and had made it clear that he had no plans to have any more.

'Are you sure it's a good idea to leave the babies with Tom,

Mum? You know Dad would be happy to have them and he and Kyria are probably more reliable.'

'Don't be such a fusspot, Fliss. Tom can damn well take some care of them; it's about time. After all the "we must stay together for the sake of the kids" stuff, he's the one who moved back to London six months ago and has only been up here half a dozen times since. Katie misses him and Jack doesn't know him well enough. It'll do them all good to have three weeks together. And you'll be down there too; you can always pay a visit from time to time, can't you? Or take them out for the day or whatever?'

'I suppose so. I mean, I will if I can, but I don't know how heavy the schedule's going to be. And even though I'm not getting paid for it, I'll need to be around all the time if I'm going to be a good runner. People kill to get gap-year jobs like this, I don't want to blow it.'

'I know, love, I didn't mean you have to see them when you should be working. Just that maybe you could pop by on a weekend or something.'

'I'm sure I can. Of course, Mum. I'll miss them too, anyway. Three weeks is ages when you're that little, I hope they'll be OK.'

'Fliss! Will you stop making me feel guilty? This is going to be the trip of a lifetime and I have to do it now before I'm too old.'

'I'm already too old,' Ravi butted in. 'So can we get a move on so that I can get a good night's kip? Driving in snow always exhausts me. Take me away from this damned country!'

'Too old indeed. You're not much older than me.'

'Precisely. Now come on, stop glaring at me, start acting your age and get in the car.'

'Nearly done. Just leaving a note for Harmony about food in the fridge. She's having a couple of friends over tonight. Fliss, you do think she'll be all right, don't you?'

'She's sixteen years old!'

'I know, but she's not been left alone before, you've always been there.'

'Mum, will you stop fussing? We're going to be late. And it was really kind of Steve to let you come at all.'

'Charming!'

'You know what I mean. As soon as I explained about you

needing to hand the kids over to their dad and Tom not getting back from Newcastle until really late and everything he instantly suggested you come in to wait with me rather than rush about all over London. He's just nice like that. I'm really looking forward to working with him, I think he's great.'

'You just watch yourself, my girl.'

'Erm, not necessary in the circumstances, Mother, as you know.'

'You never can tell. Anyway. Just be careful. Generally. OK?'

'Yeah right, Mum. You set a good example there.' Nita didn't answer; she was trying to catch Ravi's eye while he strapped the babies into their car seats.

'Look, here's your dad's car, kiss me goodbye and we'll see you down there.'

'Have you got the address?'

'Yes, we'll be fine. Bye for now, love, have a good journey.'

'See you later, Mum. Bye, Ravi.'

The occupants of the cars waved at one another as they began their southward journeys.

'Shit shit shit. This isn't working. Nothing is fucking working. What's *wrong* with me?' Tom was hunched over the plan for his latest novel. These days, as soon as he had the first inkling of story ideas he began to chart the course of the book on paper, a method he had learned from a playwright friend. In the case of drama the plan showed which characters were onstage when, and for how long. It had clear practical uses for thinking ahead to casting and rehearsing the production. Tom's version was far more baroque and, while it certainly worked on the axis of character over time, it was also designed to differentiate between narrative, dialogue and description and enable its creator to adjust the ratios of each in order to produce the perfect book. The older Tom got, the more formulaic his approach to writing became, although he was convinced that his graphic interpretation was merely a short cut to perfection of form. Perhaps he was right. At any rate, six perfect prototype novel plans graced his desktop, none of which seemed capable of fulfilling its potential.

He picked up the cup of tea which his mother had silently left on the cupboard by the door. He put it down again. He longed to leave Newcastle and get back to his new flat in London. Or more precisely, get back to his new girlfriend. Since the births of his two youngest children, Tom had mustered all his powers of deception against himself and attempted to have sex with one of the women on whom he had regularly dropped in during the pre-Cressida days. Sharon was surprised but not unpleasantly so; her fondness for Tom was such that she asked no questions just as he asked none of her. But the moment he felt her flesh touch his, the erection he had been nursing all the way to her house had simply vanished and could not be persuaded to reappear despite Sharon's best, and they were verging on the expert, efforts. Impotence was the greatest shame Tom could imagine, and even he could tell that Sharon's sympathy was not entirely heartfelt, particularly when his erectile dysfunction heralded total sexual shut-down. He could not even be prevailed upon to use other methods at his disposal for her satisfaction which would have been, she thought, the gentlemanly thing to do in the circumstances. Instead, he muttered apologies and left, cursing Cressida for the spell she had cast upon him.

That, along with occasional, desultory masturbation fuelled by memories whose very vividness mocked any hopes Tom had for escaping their grip, had been the extent of his sexual activity for many months. But then his luck changed; he had left a television studio where he was recording an interview for an arts review programme and met, in the green room, a woman so stunning that he found himself staring as they were introduced. She was working on a documentary with an independent producer and as they shook hands and she smiled vaguely Tom realised, with a thrill, that she didn't have a clue who he was, and he felt for a moment the old predatory stirrings which had held sway over so many years of his life and which he had hardly believed would return. Determined not to quell them, or rather not to allow them to be swamped, he managed to track the beautiful woman down, take her for dinner, woo her in his most polished style and finally to make love to her, which he had done with success and aplomb. If Cressida, with her knowledge and her flaws, her flailing about in the fertile garden of womanhood, was Eve, then this new woman was Lilith. She seemed otherworldly to Tom, not just because of her extraordinary beauty but because she was unlike all other women he had met. She never asked him a question that he felt might trap him, never queried his arrangements or acted with suspicion. After Cressida's open desire to know every detail of every aspect of his life and Nita's studious avoidance of expressing the same, this seemingly genuine lack of concern was liberating. He was able to lavish attention and gifts upon her, which took up much of the space and time in his life previously occupied with grief for his lost love, and to make love to her without sensing she had any hold over him, or wished to. It wasn't the dissolving experience of making love with Cressida; at no point in the proceedings did he forget who he was or where he was or why, or feel that their flesh was made one, but the vivid awareness of her stunning body and his own skilful one, conjoined in a variety of pleasing patterns, offered him much relief. Looking into her eyes he saw only her looking back, never himself reflected. Inside her body, he did not feel for one moment that he might never bring himself to leave. At orgasm, he never wanted to sob and hold on to her for dear life. She was intelligent, concise, reserved and unprobing, though sufficiently good-humoured to be pleasant company as well as unsurpassably decorative. Her life was a mystery which he had no desire to unravel and she seemed quite disinterested in his past. So, enviably, they had nothing at all to be jealous of, or about.

Still, Tom was a little anxious that the next three weeks – when he would be prime carer for Katie and Jack – might prove somewhat offputting for such a new girlfriend. He had already arranged for his parents to come down from Newcastle and stay for the middle week to give him and his paramour plenty of time alone together. And she hadn't flinched when he explained the situation, although he had been a little sparing with the precise facts surrounding his relationship with the children's mother. He hadn't mentioned Cressida to her, or Grace, although she had, once, asked him if he had ever been 'truly' in love and he had said no, he wasn't sure what that meant, which seemed to satisfy her. He had not asked the question in return.

Despite feeling a new spring in his step, Tom was concerned that his relationships with all of his children were not going according to plan. Since moving to London he had lost some motivation in making the trip to Manchester and it had dwindled in regularity to once a month which even he thought of as shoddy. Every time he thought of little Katie he shed some tears, but Jack, fine boy that he was, could not tug at his daddy's heartstrings in the same way. He was beginning to understand that his insistence on living with Katie had been a desperate clinging to some notion of the life he should have led. In reality, without going through the motions of family life as he had for the past three years, that proximity was less significant, and once he had been forced to admit that it was all fake – not his love for Katie, or his broad concern for Nita and her daughters, but everything else in the equation – the question of closeness seemed more vague. As for Grace, she eluded him, kept him out, with his own green eyes gazing at him in question once a fortnight, and turning away from his kisses, the cool skin of her cheek so like Cressida's to the touch. Going to fetch her from the house in Queen's Park was torturous. It was so chaotic and lively, so full of babies and noise, so full of Harry and his new-found love of human life in all its peculiar chaos, and it felt odd for Tom to smuggle Grace out to the park in her buggy, away from her family. He talked to her as though she were her mother, told her the things he wanted to tell Cressida, and then felt guilty and angry when no reply came, no hand was offered. He and Cressida never spent any time with her together, or indeed any time talking to each other about anything except Grace. Seeing each other, once so vital, was now painful enough to make them both blink and move away quickly. They both knew that the love they had felt was still between them, it didn't even have the decency to sleep for a moment, but she also saw how he had let her down and he saw her seeing. For everyone's sake they must spend no time together either with their daughter or alone, so they policed themselves and each other wearily. Now that Grace was a year old and beginning to stand up, holding on to furniture and stepping tentatively around it, she would demand to get out of the buggy and stagger about for a few minutes, holding on to him tightly. Last week she had looked up while he helped her balance and said, clearly, 'Tom,' and his heart had almost burst with the pain of it. She called him Tom. She had been saying Dada for over a month. Still, at least he wasn't lonely any more.

'Look at the ice in this cobweb, children. Isn't that beautiful? No, no, Kwame, be careful, you mustn't break it. It's a spider's pantry and he made it all by himself. Just think, this tiny spider can weave something so much bigger than he is.' Abena watched the two tiny boys stare in uncomprehending wonder at the snowflakes resting on their fleece jackets. She felt Ama shiver against her and hugged the child to her side. 'Let's come inside now, babies. Come and tell Mama and Mary about the clever spider.' She scooped up George, who as yet showed no signs of taking any steps unaided, in her other arm and walked behind Kwame who tottered towards the door unsteadily, and was met by a pale and fidgety Mary. 'You look nervous!'

'I am terribly nervous. This is my first one. I've been longing to do it but now the moment's here – I'm terrified.'

'You will enjoy it. They sound like nice people. Margaret will be with you, and we'll all be there afterwards.'

'I know, I'm sure it will be a lovely day, I just so much want to get it right.'

'Mary, relax and be happy. You have found a way to work for the glory of God, be glad.'

'Abena, you always know how to say everything so . . .'

'So simply. English works well as a second language; the less fluent you are the wiser you sound. Each word has more – import.'

'I think there's more to it than that but I take your point.' Mary and Margaret often congratulated themselves on their perfect childcare solution – having Abena live in as a nanny meant that she could foster and hopefully eventually adopt little George, while Margaret worked part-time at the surgery and Mary trained as a registrar. They had a long-term plan – to be marriage counsellors. With Margaret's medical background and Mary's community-based religious experience they felt they could ask the questions – and provide some of the answers – which were never put these days before a couple made a commitment to each other. Their aims were slightly different – Margaret wishing to prevent a great many ill-gotten relationships being formalised and Mary hoping to instil a sense of seriousness and care amidst the talk of seating plans and menus – but they both wanted to find a way to work together. Mary's qualification as a registrar was a step on this path, as well as a way of helping her feel constructively linked to the rest of humanity, one element of convent life she had missed since leaving. Her original concerns about the secular nature of her new vocation were laid to rest when Margaret pointed out that 'He' would be unlikely to insist on a name-check, unless He was a disappointingly human deity. Meanwhile, the continual presence of Abena and George meant that Kwame would have a playmate whose development would take place at a similar speed to his own while Ama could have the extra attention her Down's syndrome required. At one year old it was still difficult to say how severe her condition was, but there was no sign of heart problems, which had been Margaret's main worry, and Ama had smiled before her brother did and continued to be a happy, gentle little being. Despite her initial calm at having given birth to a disabled child, Margaret's deep-rooted distaste of physical and mental imperfection took months to shake off, and there had been times when she had shrunk from touching her slower, quieter baby, ashamed at having produced something so clearly substandard. Then came a further shame, at her own unnatural callousness. Unsurprisingly, it was Mary who helped her accept her daughter's shortcomings until they became, most of the time, irrelevant. She even managed to accept her own sometimes difficult feelings about them. Fortunately, the child's ability to delight in her world was never in question, and while all three women loved her dearly, Margaret found her chubby limbs and beatific face eternally irresistible and could not pass by Ama without picking her up and burying her nose in the child's neck. She adored Kwame too, and loved little George as though he were her nephew, but secretly she thought of Ama as a message especially for her, a perfectly chosen gift which both humbled her and gave her great joy.

'I've got lines on my face. Look. Millions of them. My eyes are wrecked and all around my mouth you can see them.' Nicola was pouting disappointedly in her magnifying mirror, as Christine braided her hair. She could see the craquelure of her skin, the minuscule system of lines which criss-crossed her complexion, invisible to the unaided human eye.

'That's such rubbish, honey. You're finally starting to look somewhere near your age, that's all. You'll be thirty next year, you can't expect to look like a sixteen-year-old. And you're beautiful, you know you are, could pass for twenty-five if you want to, but who wants to?'

Nicola put the hand mirror down and looked at her sister in the dressing-table mirror instead. Her pout disappeared and was replaced by an earnest expression as she said, 'I know everything you've done for me, Chris. This past year, I do know, and I do appreciate it –'

'There's no need to –'

'Hush, there is a need to. Everyone's been great, but you've held it all together, you were there from the beginning, and I know all the things you've done and truly, I appreciate it.'

'There's no need. You're my little sis. You'd do the same for me.'

'I don't know if I would, or could. And you've been kind and patient when I know I've behaved in a way which would – I don't know, annoy you or worry you. I know all the – all the baby stuff – was difficult for you.'

'Not as difficult as it was for you, honey.'

'I'm not sure about that. Listen, I wish I could explain it to you, but it's hard. I didn't want to be pregnant. Then I was, and it came at a time I was questioning lots of things I was doing, and I was staying with Mum who got all excited and somehow it seemed like the best thing to do was just relax into it, go with the flow, use it as some kind of *healing* almost. Does that sound weird?'

'Not yet.'

'And then Mum was so thrilled and supportive and I could see this great future and me being stronger and better, and having this lovely baby and a new career and everything – and suddenly I was able to think, yeah, I'm the seventh child of a seventh child and look! I really *can* see the future, I finally have second sight, I really do. I can see it all spread out in front of me and it's going to be just fine. Before, I always thought I should be able to predict world events and whether all your marriages would work and what "A"

272

level results I'd get. But then – those months when I was here with Mum – I scaled it down to the essentials, started trying to see only those things which affected me directly, reduced the scope of my "powers". It was a revelation; it made me so relaxed. I know it's stupid, I know it's not real, but that's how it felt. And then the morning Mum died she'd told me I was her eighth child. You knew that, didn't you?'

'The miscarriage? Yes, I was old enough to know, of course. And old enough to realise it should never be mentioned again.'

'Right. Everyone seems to know about that. Well, it was shocking. I had to suddenly rethink. Far from finding and grounding myself, I'd been deluding myself for years – and it was nobody's fault, just a really bad coincidence of facts and assumptions. So that morning, when we went shopping, I was already unsettled, suddenly not sure things were going the way I wanted them to. I'd seen the baby's father a few weeks before and he really wanted to talk to me but I wouldn't speak, I drove away without talking to him because I wanted to get back to Mum and my dream life. If I'd known I wasn't the seventh child I think everything would have been different, don't even know if I'd have stayed pregnant.'

'Nicola!'

'Don't be so shocked. They were hardly ideal circumstances, were they? I just seemed to feel really complacent and content and as though everything was going to be OK. But it was all false, all based on a lie. When I look back on that day I remember every second of what happened with Mum and I've tried to piece together all the other bits, but it feels too far away from me now. I don't see the point. And now – well, I really love this new work I'm doing, don't want to finish my PhD after all, don't want to have a baby. I know you think it's shocking, but I'd like his foster mother to adopt him, I don't feel he's mine or that I have any rights. Or want any.'

'You know you can keep the status quo, you don't need to fix anything yet.'

'But I want to fix it. Besides, it's not fair on Abena or –' She paused, unable to speak the word.

'George.'

'George. Right. It's an old-fashioned name for a little baby, don't you think?'

'You could always change it.'

'No, Chris, get this into your head, I Do Not Want Him. You say she's nice and she loves him and he has a good home. And I'm glad I could give him to someone who was there at the start. So that's fine.'

'You could always visit – meet her, see how he's doing, you know.' The family had tried to keep links with their nephew but as all hope in Nicola deciding to take up motherhood died, the visits dwindled and now, although all six older Mackenzie children contributed to George's upkeep, only Christine still kept in touch personally. But every time she picked the baby up, kissed his soft brown cheek and smiled into his big hazel eyes, she had to resist the urge to cry, because she could feel the distance between them widening every week.

'No. I don't want to. Have no wish to see her or him. I almost forgot it was his first birthday the other week, the only thing I associate that date with is Mum's death. I don't want him to be unhappy or uncared for, but – and I know you don't get this – I have no wish to make him happy or to care for him. Ouch! That hurt – how long will this take?'

'Nearly there.' Christine caught the braids together in a jewelled clasp at the back of her sister's head. 'There. Will that do, madam?'

'That's great. Thanks, Chris. Look, I need to leave in half an hour for this party thing at Stephen's house, have you got time for a coffee before I go?'

'Sure. When are you going to actually start filming this documentary? Seems like you've been working on it for months now.'

'These things take a long time to get together. But the whole team should be at this do so I'll get to meet everyone. I'm really looking forward to it. Chrissie, are you angry with me?'

'Not angry. I don't understand, but I do see how much happier you are. Although I don't think that's just because of this new job.'

'Yeah, well. Don't wait up.'

'Mystery man again?'

'He's not a mystery man. It's just early days, that's all.' Christine heard the excitement in her little sister's voice and felt both glad and scared. Nicola was certainly cheerier than she had been for the past year, but it seemed like she was almost too bright, too loud, too brittle. Her new work seemed to settle her for a while but since she had been seeing a new man she was often at the far reaches of her nerves and her best attempts at composure didn't come near to fooling the people who knew her best.

'When are you going to introduce us then?'

'Pretty soon. Listen, Chris, he's so sweet to me, so thoughtful. And he's a family man, loves his kids – I'm going to meet them later. And he loves me so much, maybe one day I'll want to have a child with him.'

'You're that serious about him?'

'Oh yes. He's just – he's just the most loving person I've met. He persevered for quite a while, you know. Not just in it for the short run. He's not really good looking or anything, but he's cute, and he just,' Nicola lowered her eyes shyly, 'he just takes my breath away sometimes.'

'I'm pleased for you, honey. Really pleased.' Christine kissed her sister's cheek and felt the heat of her besottedness, and the fragility of her heart. 'But you be careful, hey? And will you call me tonight? After the party?' Nicola promised.

The Party

Adam's mother was viewing the cards on the mantelpiece. Every now and then she picked one up to read the message, and more often than not she replaced it hurriedly with a blush. Harry was watching her with much amusement and some sympathy when a voice in his ear whispered, 'She's thinking it should have been you.'

'Steve. Congratulations.' The men hugged. 'Somehow, I don't think that would have made her any happier though.'

'Oh, I don't know. She always thought you were such a nice friend for Adam. And at least you're not a Paki.'

'Has she said anything?'

'No, she's far too polite to say anything. And she did cheer up when I said my mum was Sri Lankan. Sounds a bit classy, you know. But basically, once she'd accepted her son was a poof she'd rather he marry a nice Jewish boy. Or just any white boy, even a goy like you.'

Harry smiled. 'Nice ceremony. I liked the registrar and her surprising extended family. Good speech from her.'

'Mary. Yeah, she's great. Adam and I specified a gay registrar if at all possible but we didn't think it would be a lesbian ex-nun.'

'Did you realise that her partner, the one with the twins, is our GP?'

'No! As they say, small world.'

'I thought they were triplets for a moment – their nanny's got one about the same age.'

'Yeah, he's so cute. Actually, I don't think he's hers – she's fostering him or something. Anyway, look, I've got some more people to say hi to, and when we have open house later this afternoon I've got the entire crew coming to meet for the first time, so I'd better see the caterers.'

'Sure, I need to find Adam. Catch you later.'

'Yeah. And Harry – thanks for your speech. Just perfect.'

'Cheers. My pleasure.'

Harry looked around for Cressida and found her in a corner of the room that had been colonised by the babies. Grace and Marlon were clinging to the coffee table, which was strewn with toys brought by Margaret and which Kwame and George were systematically moving on to the floor, while Ama sat by Margaret's feet. Ben and Jemima were roaming the three-storey house looking for the collection of carved wooden figures they always played with at Uncle Adam and Uncle Steve's house but which seemed to have disappeared entirely. Cressida was deep in conversation with the doctor and just as Harry joined the group she was looking discomfited.

'So,' Margaret was saying, 'the family were only too pleased to have someone so experienced and obviously loving to look after the poor little thing. And it does look as though she's going to be able to adopt him; the mother shows no sign at all of wanting him.'

Harry smiled a hello at Margaret and asked, 'Not wanting who?'

'Harry,' Cressida's voice was faint.

'What's the matter, darling?'

'Abena's foster son is called George. He was born the day after Grace. At St Mary's Hospital. His mother's name was Nicola.'

Harry sat down heavily, looking at his baby. Margaret, always open to the realities of unusual family circumstances these days, drew accurate conclusions swiftly.

'My goodness. You two *were* busy that month. Didn't you know . . . ?'

'Nicola didn't want me to have anything to do with it. I only found out she was pregnant by accident. Then her family just blocked any attempt I made to find out what had happened, and I soon found out I had no rights if Nicola wouldn't even name me as the father. Apart from which, Grace and Marlon had both been born that week and I didn't exactly have time on my hands. To find out more, I'd have had to become her stalker. Cress and I discussed it and decided that we'd have to leave it for a while and maybe re-approach Nicola sometime in the future. I knew she wasn't looking after the baby and her family assured us he was safe and well, but all I knew was his name. This is – quite a shock.'

Abena, carrying a tray of drinks back to the table, saw the man who looked like her foster-child talking to Margaret. Handing the doctor a gin and tonic, she turned to Harry.

'Are you trying to take him away?' she asked quietly.

Harry looked surprised. 'No. No, I'm not – although – you must be Abena?'

'Yes, I am Abena. George's foster mother. And I want to be his mother.'

'Abena, he didn't know,' Margaret said quickly. 'This is sheer coincidence. This is Harry Shepherd, by the way. Now, why don't you introduce him to George and then the two of you can have a chat? And Harry, I'm sure Abena would love to say hello to Grace and Marlon too.'

'Marlon?' Abena smiled in spite of herself, and the baby turned around at the sound of his name and grinned widely at his father.

'Yes, well, he's more *Godfather II* than *On the Waterfront* at present – those cheeks – but we have high hopes.'

'Just keep that boy away from butter,' interjected Adam, which met with a frown from Harry and a blank stare from Abena. '*Last Tango* . . . you know . . . Anyway, more peanuts?' He put a bowl on the table and hurried off with a hint of a mince, an affectation that only emerged in the presence of his parents.

'Have you known Adam and Steve long?' Abena asked politely.

'Adam for years, since I was eleven. But Steve, only since they've been together – seven years or so. Believe it or not, Steve's a very good influence on him. Cuts him down to size after a hard day's work listening to the sound of his own voice and prancing about in a wig.'

'Sorry?'

'He's a lawyer. Barrister. And he was always pompous, even as a child, so you can imagine how bad it gets when he's on an important case. But Steve's much more serious-minded, much less prone to queeny fits. He's a good stabilising influence.'

'But Steve works in television, doesn't he? I thought television people were always – wild and unstable.'

'Not documentary film makers. Well, not Steve, I don't know any others.' Abena saw someone over Harry's shoulder and drew her breath in sharply. 'What's the matter? Who have you seen?' Harry turned around to see a slim, muscular man in his late thirties approaching them with a faintly worried expression.

He smiled at Abena. 'Hi. What are you doing here?'

She began to stammer a reply. 'You remember who I am, don't you? And I've seen young George already, recognised him at once; that's why I came looking for you.'

'Yes, of course I remember you. You're one of George's uncles.'

'Listen, I'm sorry we don't see him any more. It got so difficult, Nicola not wanting to see him and everything. It seemed easier on everyone if we didn't insist on family rights like that. But look, I'm really sorry about this; I don't know why you're here but I don't think it's a good idea, you see . . .' The man realised he had butted in to a conversation and turned to Harry. 'Sorry mate, bit of a complicated situation here. You're Harry, aren't you? Great best man's speech. My name's Anthony Mackenzie, I play squash with Steve.' They shook hands.

'Good to meet you, Anthony. Yes, I'm Harry Shepherd, went to school with Adam.'

Anthony was nodding and turning again to Abena but Harry carried on, 'I was also Nicola's PhD tutor. And I'm George's father.' Anthony let his hand drop limply.

'Oh shit.' He turned to Abena angrily but Harry stopped him.

'It's not her fault. She had no idea I'd be here. It's just a weird coincidence and not planned at all. There's nothing going on, no funny business. We're all a bit shell-shocked actually.' Anthony believed him and relaxed as Harry went on, 'How is Nicola? I didn't know anything about what went on except what – it's Christine, isn't it, your older sister? – except what Christine told me at the time and that wasn't much.'

'She's doing OK I guess. Stopped studying, got a job she really likes. In fact . . .' He looked anxious again. 'She'll be here. Later, I mean. She's working with Steve on this film, that's what I was coming to tell Abena. To say she can't see her. Shit. Oh shit. Man, she can't see you here, or the baby. She'll freak completely. I mean,

I say she's doing OK, but she's not really back to normal. She's still a bit fragile. You see what I'm saying?'

Harry considered for a moment before saying, 'Yes, I see what you're saying and I understand. But I'm the best man; I'm here with my wife and children, and Abena is here as nanny to the registrar and her kids – so for us all just to up and leave would be crazy. Can you not call Nicola and forewarn her or dissuade her from coming or something?'

'I don't see how I could. Maybe I could postpone her though. Hold on, I'm going to phone her now, I'll get back to you if I manage to get hold of her.'

Cressida was enjoying a conversation with Margaret who had hit the gin just after lunch and was at a benign, unguarded stage of drunkenness. She had already relived the twins' conception in vivid detail and was now listing all the benefits of not having a man around.

'But surely, especially if you have boy children, it's important for them to have male role models? And Jemmy and Grace both love Harry just as much as they love me. I think you're being unfair.'

'The role model point may be true,' conceded the doctor. 'And Mary and I have discussed what we might do about that. We don't have many male friends but we did wonder about getting in touch with a gay couple who wanted to get involved in parenting somehow – that might be a way of having close contact with a man. Men, even.'

Cressida looked dubious. 'What, you mean you could make some kind of deal with Adam and Steve?'

'Not a deal, exactly, more of an arrangement. And I didn't necessarily mean this gay couple, although actually they'd do very well. Lovely boys, aren't they?'

'I guess so. I don't think either of them is that interested in fatherhood though – Adam's always said he's far too selfish to let anyone smaller and cuter steal the scene and it sounds as though Steve's relationship with his father was abysmal. He blames him for the death of his mother.'

'My, we are getting Freudian.'

'Don't start, I get enough of that at home.'

'Sorry, sorry. But do tell, did his father drive her to suicide?'

'Kind of. It sounds as though after having Steve she'd had post-natal depression, which was never diagnosed and never really went away. His father was a bully, always mocking Steve for being a mummy's boy and telling her she was spoiling him, and then when Steve was nineteen and just about to go to college he came out and his father kicked him out, wouldn't support him through college, so he had to work through the whole four years, and wouldn't let him see his mother. By this time she was inconsolable and used to wake the neighbours with all this screaming and wailing, so he had her sectioned and put away. She was only forty-eight when she died. And her husband never came to visit her all the time she was there.'

'The bastard. What an utter bastard. Jesus, no wonder Stephen's not keen on fatherhood if that's what it gave him. I hardly remember my father, which must be better than having such awful memories. Why was he like that?'

'No idea. It was his second marriage – he had a child from his first, a girl, and he never saw her again either, never discussed it. Stephen only knew about that from his mother. She was a nurse at the hospital his father worked at – they had an affair and she got pregnant, he left his wife, though she never asked him to and it sounds as though she always felt guilty about that, but he was a consultant and she'd just arrived from Sri Lanka; he must have seemed very powerful.'

'But he's Stephen Sameresinghe, isn't he? I thought his father wasn't English . . .'

'No, he took his mother's name after she died. And besides, it's better to have a more unusual name in his business – in the last two years he reckons he's met at least three Stephen Greenes.'

'Greene? Where was Stephen born? Where did his father practise?' Cressida did not understand the urgency in Margaret's voice but she did recognise it.

'Guildford. His father still lives there, though obviously they're not in touch. Margaret, are you all right?'

Margaret's face was white. 'Where is he? Where is Stephen now?'

'I don't know. In the kitchen maybe. Or they could be in the garden with Mary; they were doing photos a minute ago. Margaret, what's the matter, do you want me to –' But Margaret had already gone to find her brother.

Harry and Abena were deep in conversation in the baby corner so Cressida went for a wander around the house, whose many spacious rooms she had often coveted. A buffet was being laid out in the dining room and she opened the door to see how the caterers were getting on. As neat rows of cutlery and glasses were being set out on the white linen by women wearing cotton gloves, a procession of waiters set dozens of silver serving dishes on the table and three men carried in an immense confection, a mountainous swirl of madeira cake draped in folds of thick white chocolate sprinkled with dark chocolate curls. Cressida almost began to drool.

'Looks fantastic, doesn't it? Do you mind if I get by you, I need to get to that wall.' A short buxom woman with wiry dark hair stood at the door holding a large cardboard roll under her arm.

'Sorry.' Cressida stepped back and watched the woman walk to the far end of the room and begin unrolling her parcel. Just as she was about to uncover it from the protective layers around it she looked up.

'Hey, I should really kick you out until the official unveiling!'

'Is this the surprise Adam's being going on about? The work of art to commemorate their love?'

The woman laughed. 'Sounds about right. I guess the caterers will see it anyway, and to be honest I could really do with someone playing lookout – my husband was supposed to but he's looking after baby – do you think you could do that? I'm Kyria, by the way.'

'Cressida. Pleased to meet you. You're Australian?'

Kyria made a spitting noise. 'Kiwi, thanks very much.'

'Oops. I'm always doing that with Canadians. You know, calling them American. Sorry.'

'No worries, I was only joking. Here, can you leave the door a minute and hold this end for me?'

As the women worked together Cressida tried to work out why the name Kyria seemed familiar, but couldn't recall where from.

They chatted about their babies, who were born within a few days of each other, and about their families.

'In fact, it's thanks to my stepdaughter that I got this commission,' Kyria confided. 'She'd written to dozens of people asking about working as a runner during her gap year – she's got a place at a Film and Media course down here starting next year and wanted to get some work experience – and Steve met her and gave her the job. They were just chatting about this and that and he mentioned the wedding and wanting to commission something really special to commemorate it but not wanting a painting and not knowing where to start and she suggested he check out my website. So he did, and I got the job too!'

'That's lucky. Funny how things work out, isn't it?'

'You bet. Anyway, my stepdaughter's down here too; sounds like Steve has invited the whole team to come for the evening do. He and Adam are only having a weekend's holiday – honeymoon I mean – before he starts filming, so she's going to get settled in. And to make matters even more complicated, her mum's going away for three weeks and she's coming here to hand over her two youngest kids to their dad who's going to be looking after them. So practically the whole family will be here!'

'That sounds a bit complicated. Do you all get on?'

'Oh yeah. Well, not bad, you know. Life's like that.'

'Yes.' As Kyria held up the weaving to check it was smooth Cressida walked back a few steps to view it. 'Oh Kyria, that's absolutely gorgeous. What lovely colours. And it's so – rich.'

Kyria blushed. 'You really like it?'

'It's – stupendous. Truly. I like all the – interweaving. It's sort of snaky.'

Kyria looked worried. 'Oh. Now you say it, I think you're right. Oh dear, snakes are bad luck, aren't they? It's not supposed to be a snake but if you're doing that kind of patterning I suppose it's difficult to avoid . . .'

'Damn, have I put my foot in it? I didn't mean it looked like a snake, just that it's all sinewy and lithe. It's beautiful. Truly.' Cressida and Kyria placed iron battens in the channels at the top and bottom of the weaving and then hung it on the waiting hooks.

'You see?' said Cressida. 'It looks stunning. Perfect. Congratulations.'

'Thanks. And thanks for helping. Guess we should both be getting back to our babies now.'

'Yes, I'll go through now. See you later.'

'Yeah, see you when I've cleared up and covered this up before the grand unveiling.'

The room was filling up with guests and the guests were filling up with drink. Adam, envying his new spouse's thoroughly integrated social circle, sallied forth between his sharp-suited colleagues from chambers, and his moustachioed friends from the gym, checking in on his bewildered family from time to time. As well as his parents, both his older sisters were there with husbands in tow but, he noted, they'd left the kids at home, ostensibly to avoid fractiousness and late bedtimes but actually, obviously, to avoid potential corruption by his unsatisfactory friends. He was glad that the latter were on their best behaviour, more stylishly dressed than the lawyers, and infinitely better at smalltalk. He was just about to risk introducing two of his most straight-acting friends to his parents when Ben and Jemima skipped into the group shouting, 'We found them, Uncle Adam, we found where you were hiding them.' Each was clutching a handful of carved figures featuring a host of what Adam referred to as 'holes and poles' which fitted together in all sorts of interesting ways.

'Look, I can put all these four together!' said Ben happily as Adam's mother started from her chair and his friends fell about laughing.

'Cressida! Harry!' Adam shouted. 'Control your children, will you?' He scooped the carvings from the children's hands and dropped them in a drawer, saying, 'Now, Mum, come on, that's just African art,' while scanning the room for Steve who should, any moment now, signal that the time had come for the grand unveiling. He finally caught sight of him in the baby corner, sitting with a twin on each knee, apparently crying. Adam made his way through the crowd, accepting pats on the back and kisses as he passed.

'Don't you know a lot of breeders!' commented an ex-lover

with mock distaste, seeing where Adam's eyes were focused. 'And doesn't Steve look at home in Poo Corner?'

Adam ignored the joke and headed for that part of the room, bursting on to the tearful scene with a bewildered, 'What on earth is going on here?'

By this time Nita and Ravi had arrived and Nita was already gravitating towards the comfortable corner of the room, where she could see Kyria and Justin amongst numerous children, to settle Katie and Jack, both of whom were exhausted and grumpy after the long drive.

Cressida saw them approach and asked, 'Is this your husband's ex coming now?' Kyria turned around.

'Oh yes, thank goodness they got here OK. Let me introduce you.' She waved the couple over. 'Ravi, this is Cressida, her husband's the best man, and Cressida, meet Ravi Krishna, or should I say *Dr* Ravi Krishna.' The two smiled and nodded at each other over the heads of Grace and Jack, then just as Kyria was about to continue her introductions, there was a sound of silver hitting lead crystal and Adam called for silence.

'That's my cue,' said Kyria and made her way over to him while Cressida and Nita smiled at each other wordlessly in their innocence and two waiters drew back the hinged wooden screens which separated the downstairs rooms. There was an appreciative gasp as the table, laden with food piled into glass and silver, appeared in view. Behind it, Adam and Steve stood by the covered wallhanging.

'Friends, family,' began Adam, 'thank you for joining us on a day we never thought would happen.' He raised his hand in anticipation of heckles and continued, '*Not* because we'd be arguing over who would wear the dress, thank you. Simply because when we got together seven years ago there was no publicly acknowledged way of celebrating gay relationships.'

Harry, watching his friend with a fond smile, felt someone touch his arm. Anthony was gesturing him towards the hall where they spoke in whispers.

'Did you get hold of her?'

'Yes, and it's really strange but when I told her who was here she said it was fine. I mean, she didn't say anything for a while but then she just shrugged – she's my sister, I know if she's shrugging on the phone – and said it was fine. She said she didn't want to chat but she'd say hello and it's just as well if she sees you – and George – in a kind of unpressured environment. You know, where you and she aren't the centre of attention. She's going straight on from here to her boyfriend's flat so won't be staying long anyway.'

Anthony looked slightly incredulous at the news he was imparting but he had attempted to dissuade his sister several times and she had not moved an inch, so all he could do was pass on the message.

'OK,' said Harry. 'I won't make it difficult for her, of course, and if you can let Abena know, there'll be no problem, I'm sure. When is she due?'

'Well, any moment now, since she's already an hour late.'

'Right, I'd better tell my wife. Let's go back in.'

Ten minutes later, Adam was still talking and the throng was becoming restless. Cressida, standing near the door to the hall, heard a knocking at the front door and tiptoed out to answer it, relieved that Harry had prepared her for the moment. She opened the door, smiled mechanically at the tall, beautiful woman who stood there and spoke in hushed tones.

'Hello. Come in. We've met once before, I'm Cressida.'

'Yes. Hello. I'm Nicola.'

'I know. It's OK. Come in, Adam's still blathering on so you haven't missed the main event.' They entered the sitting room and Cressida led the way to baby corner, catching Harry's eye to share a frozen moment of bemusement. Nicola scanned the crowd discreetly, nodded at Harry and then saw the babies behind him. She was surprised and confused to see so many and then ashamed of herself for the second her heart had stopped at the sight of Kwame, before it began to thump when her eyes rested on George. He was standing, supported by his hands on the coffee table and giggling while Abena nuzzled the back of his neck. She stopped abruptly when she felt eyes upon her and returned Nicola's gaze steadily until they each cracked a tiny smile and turned their attention to Adam, who was just, finally, handing over to Steve who had clearly been crying.

'Thanks, Adam. Don't worry, folks, I'll be brief. But before anything else happens, you'll probably want to know why I look such a wreck. Well, I've just had a shock, I mean a surprise, a great surprise but it's all a bit – amazing really. In fact, instead of trying to explain, why don't I just introduce you to my long-lost sister?' He held out his arms to Margaret who was flushed with gin and emotion and beaming idiotically.

There was a moment of stunned silence and then the room began to fill with delighted laughter and congratulations. Cressida noticed that one small cluster of guests, standing just to her left, did not react to the news and she guessed, correctly, that they must comprise the crew of the film Steve was about to start making and which Nicola, by some remarkable coincidence, was also working on. The significance of Steve's announcement would be lost on them. She noticed one pretty girl in her late teens whispering something to a young man next to her. He opened his mouth in mock horror and whispered, 'Fliss!' Idly, Cressida remembered that Nita's oldest daughter was called Felicity. For a moment she thought the girl was looking straight at her but then saw she was trying to attract the attention of the woman who had arrived with Dr Krishna and the two children. 'Mum!' Fliss stage-whispered, 'Watch out for Katie!'

Nita swooped down upon her three-year-old daughter who was quietly downing a glass of champagne and Cressida's mouth went dry as she remembered why the name Kyria was so familiar. She clutched the back of the sofa and saw Steve's mouth moving and his hand reaching for the cord which would unveil the weaving she had helped Kyria position, but his words and the applause which followed the unveiling were drowned out by the tidal sound in her head.

Before the clapping died down everyone near the baby corner heard a loud tapping at the bay window and Ravi, who was nearest, pulled back the curtain and gestured towards the front door.

'Sorry, mate, didn't hear the door, good job you caught a lull,' he was saying as he showed the latecomer to the corner where all seven of our babies, plus a selection of their older siblings and most of their parents, were gathered. 'They're just over here.'

Cressida's shock was superseded by an even greater one; while her conversation with Kyria had forewarned her, her brain hadn't quite finished making the complex series of connections which would prepare her for this arrival. Still, at least she had some, even semi-conscious, preparation. At least she had enough knowledge to keep her upright. Three voices spoke at once:

'Tom,' said Cressida, unable to stop the precious syllable escaping her lips in a breath that verged on sighing.

'Tom!' said Nicola, who had sat down heavily in an armchair, eyes wide and flitting back and forth between her charming new boyfriend and the women and children who seemed to know him.

'Dada,' said Grace, clear as a bell, which should have warmed her father's heart but seemed instead, to him, to be almost malicious.

Nicola's exit, brushing past a seriously confused Tom, and elbowing a concerned Anthony out of her way towards the front door, was otherwise discreet. She had glimpsed the present more vividly than she cared to when she saw the look which passed between Cressida and Tom, a look of which even they could not be entirely aware. Tom was at once cast in a new light, one which no longer illuminated her path forward in time but which blinded her in all its glorious faithlessness. Nita too had seen that flash and saw that the blonde girl sitting next to Jack shared his profile; the curve of his cheek and the colour and shape of his eyes. Of Tom's eyes. Bustle and strife overtook the group; years from now all that Cressida would remember of those moments clearly was Harry's voice saying, 'How does he know Nicola? What's going on?' to whoever would listen, and the sight of Kyria touching Nita's arm in puzzlement while Felicity, who had come over when she saw Tom arrive, stared at Jack and Grace. Making the rounds of his guests and ushering them towards the buffet, Adam stood before a group of happy babies, engaged in various acts of mild destruction, and their parents, whose faces were variously clouded by confusion, shock, anger and tears. Deciding the best course of action might be to leave them to it, he moved silently along.

By accidentally providing the missing link within Nita's and Nicola's story of him, Tom had simultaneously made any attempt at pretence useless. For a second, he toyed with the idea of staging a chaotic introduction between the Manchester contingent and Cressida's family. She did, after all, work at his publishers and if she and Harry would back him up on it . . . The next second he saw the babies who had given the game away and understood that it would take more than fast thinking and several assured performances to convince anyone that they weren't related. It was equally impossible for him to say a word to Cressida, who was in any case hurriedly collecting offspring and coats in order to leave while Harry rushed off to make some baby-linked excuse to Adam and Steve for their premature departure. For the second time in her life, Nita had the upper hand. It wasn't so much that she suddenly *knew* more than Cressida or Nicola, but that she was so much less emotionally involved in Tom's life and it enabled her to feel sorry for the women who were still so evidently hung up on him. She also enjoyed a brief return of some of the mental astuteness which had helped her become free of him and made her own guesses at the order of events and the pressures upon both Tom and Cressida which rested on the unfortunate double pregnancy coincidence. She felt only the very faintest pang of jealousy towards the woman who must have captured her lover's heart while he was ostensibly with her, largely because that was clearly all she had captured and, as she sank back comfortably further and further into her forties, Nita was becoming aware that there were more important things in life. As for Nicola, Nita didn't give her a second thought. She looked at Ravi, politely trying to help with the gathering of coats and toys amidst the whirlwind of Cressida's shock, with considerable satisfaction. He drank a little too much, was stuck irretrievably into certain middle-aged habits and tried far too hard in bed. But he was well-meaning, self-deprecating and what her mother would have called 'steady'. Plus, his eyes would never wander further than his mind, which even Nita felt was less than probing, and showed every sign of staying put. It seemed that Ravi offered her contentment and she was pleased to accept.

The handover of Katie and Jack to their father happened directly in the wake of Cressida's departure and was understandably subdued. Nita had done her best with the packing but her attempt at talking Tom through the contents of the suitcases she handed him served only to irritate him and he eventually hushed her with a bad-tempered, 'Look, I'm sure I can work out how to dress and feed my children, OK, and I'm sure I'll find my way around these beautifully organised cases.' Ravi opened his mouth to appeal to Tom's sense of reason but Nita silenced him with a shake of her head.

'OK. But Tom, I'm warning you, don't let your complicated love life interfere with how you care for my children. Do you hear me?' Nita's calm determination was a surprise to Tom; even more surprising was his equally calm assurance that she had nothing to worry about. Not a hint of bitterness or self-defence. Even so, when Nita and Felicity waved goodbye to Tom and the children, having helped strap them in their seats in the back of his car, Felicity needed to hug her mother and offer her similar reassurances.

'Little Jack doesn't know what's happening.' Nita wiped a tear from her cheek. 'I mean, our Katie's all right but Jack hardly knows him.'

'They'll be fine. He loves them, Mum, I know he's got a funny way of showing it, but he does, and he will look after them.'

'It's not him I'm worried about. It's that new woman he's got. Didn't look like a baby person to me.'

'Didn't look like he's got her to me. Not any more. Nor – the other one. You looked so calm, Mum. Were you not even a bit surprised?'

'I'm just disappointed that your extensive research into the subject missed out the Big One.' Nita smiled to show she was joking. 'It's OK, love. Just proves how little I knew him. And what a fool he's been, in every possible way. And how he can always pull them – I mean, her husband was gorgeous. But she only had eyes for Tom. How does he do it?' Nita's memory was conveniently blurred; she had convinced herself that there was really no point dwelling on what had gone before, and was finding the self-imposed suppression of all unpleasant features of her past immensely relaxing.

Felicity was relieved to say her goodbyes to Nita and Ravi as they left for their hotel, and to go back to join the party and enjoy her first night in her London digs. Before going to bed,

Nita tried to phone Harmony since their flight was too early in the morning to fit in a call, but the answerphone was on every time.

'Don't worry, love,' said Ravi. 'You know what those girls are like. They're probably screaming at horror films or listening to loud music and can't hear the phone. Call her from India as soon as you can.'

Harmony was indeed listening to loud music, or at least, loud music was playing, but if you'd asked her the next morning what tracks had accompanied the gentle but nevertheless relentless progress of Matthew Hardwick, who one minute was next to her, the next on top of her and the next inside her, she wouldn't have been able to tell you. Nor would she quite recall why the box of condoms she had felt in his jeans pocket half an hour earlier never saw the light of day. But she remembered very clearly, and always would, the moment when he screwed up his face, rolled his eyes heavenwards and almost pushed her off the sofa as he hissed, ecstatically, 'Flissssssss!'

Little sisters don't always learn from the mistakes of their elders; poor Harmony's copycat misdemeanour was over-shadowed by her sister's presence even at its moment of truth. Matthew's ejaculation was not discussed but he exited soon afterwards and Harmony cried at her mother's answerphone message, '. . . and Fliss says, don't do anything she wouldn't do, which leaves the field wide open. OK, love, I'll call you when we get there. Take care, sweetheart, bye for now.' But those tears were only a rehearsal for the ones she would shed in a fortnight or so.

It took Tom nearly two hours to settle Katie, who was excited, and Jack, who was distressed, during which his attempts to call Nicola were also unanswered. Deciding to give up until later, he used the unexpected spare time more wisely than he had used any time in his entire existence. He sat at his table and wrote. What he wrote was no fiction, nor even a plan for a fiction, it was an exercise in automatic writing in its purest sense. It was as though his hand was connected to his heart not just by muscles and veins and arteries but via his soul. It still felt like his heart was the source of the words; there was a rhythm and power to it which remained recognisably physical, but it seemed to him that he was unlocking a great storehouse of energy, emotion, pain and love which he had believed lost to him for ever. He wrote hard and fast for an hour, after which his black scrawl covered thirteen pages. He read them and marvelled at their coherence, their uniformity and their clarity. His stream of consciousness had flowed with both more sympathy and more impatience than he usually reserved for himself: sympathy for the great sorrows of his life which had been put away, still raw, to haunt his future, and impatience at his refusal ever to look at them again, a refusal which had held back his capacity to love and enjoy being loved to the extent that he genuinely believed that it was something he didn't need. His mother and father and brothers were written into the stream, his lost sister appeared several times, and there were a few names which surfaced too – cuckolded friends, unloved conquests, Katie, Grace, Jack, Bronwen, and, everywhere, Cressida. In the good and bad of each page, came Cressida.

The shock of discovery left Tom's pulse beating fast enough to start bothering him. He gulped in air and breathed out slowly until it subsided enough for him to hear himself think. The adrenaline of anticipation took its place as he resolved to do the things which would, finally, help him find his own integrity, live life as it should be lived and even regain happiness – more than regain, actually experience happiness, truly, for the first time. First, he would go to Nicola and apologise. For not telling the whole truth and for giving her such a shock. And, mostly, for not loving her. A bright, beautiful woman with a promising TV career beckoning, it was unlikely, he believed, that the news would be too upsetting for her. The fact that she was the woman who had borne Harry's child struck him as the most bizarre coincidence and one which made him uncomfortable, but no more. Then he would go to Cressida – no, no impositions; then he would arrange to meet Cressida – with Grace and with his children, in the park maybe, and tell her that he loved her and wanted to be with her. That he realised that might not be what she wanted now, and that he understood all the difficulties it would pose for her and Harry and Sophie and Marlon and so on, but that whatever arrangements she cared to make and whenever she cared to make them he would be there, waiting to love her again. He would be contrite about his blindness, his dumbness, his crass stupidity. He would tell her everything, terrible and shameful and hilarious, about himself. And he would show her this writing, the product of this most extraordinary hour. Finally, whatever happened with Cressida, whether or not she agreed to return this love he would always have for her, he would be the best kind of father to all of his children.

Tom was not in the least mad when he made these resolutions, and the process he went through was neither supernatural nor eccentric. Years of pulling a protective cloak around himself which would let nothing or no one through had almost cocooned him entirely. Cressida's ability to simply pull it away, whenever she felt like it, had terrified him. Now he understood that he needed her, had always needed her, but had long ago rejected the truth of his needing anybody. He had just found that truth for himself and could scarcely believe his luck.

Having dropped Marlon off at Vivienne's house, Cressida and Harry went home and put the children through the rituals of bath and bedtime. They said very little to each other. Harry knew that she was thinking about Tom. About how she loved Tom. Cressida knew that her love for this man was always hanging about her neck and she wished she could be free of it. She and Harry both knew that their strained, kindly, companionable love would never recover its former glory and looked ahead, sadly, to a life together which held no surprises and no passion, the only joy present being provided by the children and the only sex the dull, eyes-closed mutual clinging on for which they turned to each other every few weeks. Harry would pour his compassion into his job, into listening for the recognisable resonances amongst his patients and echoing them back to them. The success of empathy, the relief it gave these people, was his reward. In the early evenings, Cressida would feel the edges of each day crinkling a little, reminding her of a child's peeling collage, tissue paper drying up and falling away piece by piece. She longed to understand how Tom could *choose* to feel like this – she had no doubt, for some reason, that he did feel the same – when it was in his gift to change it all. She had given up all hope that he would ever do so.

The New Year's morning was bitterly cold and London's laughable attempt at hanging on to snowfall looked grubbier than ever. Tom could hardly fit the seat straps around Katie and Jack, who were wearing so many layers of clothing they couldn't bend their limbs, so sat in comically padded cruciform poses. It was early and the children were sleepy, having been woken gently and dressed by their father before fully gaining consciousness. Nicola was still not answering her land line or her mobile but Tom, energised by last night's resolutions, was determined to be brave. Once he had freed himself – and her – from their cold attempt at love he could think about what he could say to Cressida that wouldn't court her anger or increase her hurt. He was still framing the words when he turned into Nicola's road and saw the police cars and the ambulance outside her flat. He parked the car and walked quickly, slipping on the compacted ice, to the police cordon; a thin line of blue striped plastic tape fluttering in the wind. He crossed it but was stopped by a policeman before reaching the door.

Later, sitting in an interview room at the police station watching Katie and Jack play with the motley collection of toys provided, Tom's shaking hands held a mug of tea and he heard how Christine, worried that her sister hadn't called her, had left the family's New Year celebrations at one a.m. and driven to the flat. There was no answer to the doorbell so she used her spare keys. Nicola was sitting at her desk, her head on her folded arms, already dead. In front of her were a few of the sleeping tablets she had been prescribed six months before and which her sister had believed were finished, and a bag from the local pharmacy. The shop assistant remembered her – he'd already locked up, but she was knocking on the door so determinedly he served her just to make her go away – and its contents were in her grip: an empty bottle of paracetamol held loosely in her left hand; her right clenched around a pregnancy testing stick; the window showing a faint but undeniable blue line.

CODA: World Without End

And maybe there's a god above
But all I ever learnt from love
Was how to shoot somebody who outdrew you
And it's not a cry you hear at night,
It's not somebody who's seen the light
It's a cold and it's a broken Hallelujah
Hallelujah. Hallelujah
Hallelujah. Hallelujah

From 'Hallelujah,' Leonard Cohen

Critics were divided about the quality of the change in Tom Webster's style. But they were wholly in agreement about the year in which it began and, later, biographers' research would lead them back to Nicola's flat, to the chill of a new year seeing out its first death, to a traumatic discovery which shocked the celebrated writer into a change of gear, of pace, of focus, from which he never turned back. Fluent, precise, compelling, Webster's novels after this incident won him great acclaim, admiring reviews, numerous prizes and a more trendy literary readership than he had hitherto attracted. There were some old die-hards who occasionally posited the theory that the work had developed in a way which, though fine and crafted, was somehow less *human*, or even humane, that there was at its heart none of the breadth, chaos and breathless humour of his earlier writing, that his newer books were, in the final analysis, *cold*. But even they could not deny the brilliance of the mind that created and controlled the tight psychological dramas whose every sentence was a marvel of balance and grace. His series of books whose heroine was a police forensic scientist subverted the crime genre, avoided every kind of cliché and slammed the door on a creeping tendency towards magical realism in a thoroughly conclusive manner. And of the personal myths which grew up around Tom Webster, the theories pertaining to his lost love and the guilt he felt at her untimely death flourished most of all, so that in ten, fifteen, twenty years' time the story of Nicola, too beautiful and too betrayed to live in this world, would be linked to his name, would be Sylvia to his Ted. Nicola, more than anyone, could hardly have foreseen the connection, could not have predicted how posterity would place her firmly in the arms of the man whose deceit had provided her with a portal into oblivion. Nor how the connection would cut into the hearts of both Tom and Cressida with every casual mention of a story which had become public property.

A whole forest of myths sprang up around Tom's romantic life. When the Nicola story hit the tabloid headlines half a dozen women came forward, each swearing indignantly that she had been the love of Tom Webster's life, and each being cruelly, publicly ridiculed for her gullibility. Many more of his ex-lovers remained silent, dealing privately with their sense of betrayal and foolishness. Every time he opened a newspaper and read the latest revelations about his faithless past, Tom felt genuine self-disgust. He felt a disdain for many of the love affairs he had almost succeeded in forgetting and a terror at the pain Cressida would find in being reminded of them. He remembered a line in the email she had sent him after their first afternoon together: 'The last thing I want to be is a minor blip in some list of conquests at the back of your biography.' He had emailed her back straight away: 'You overestimate the length of the list; my vice is to overestimate the length of the biography.' Such light-hearted words, so well meant.

At the moment he crossed the police line Tom had seen his plans laid waste before him. He became aware that Nicola's psychological problems had been a well-kept secret and that the blame for her suicide could not rest wholly on his head. But he also knew that it was not something he could ever speak about, to anyone, but most particularly to his waiting public. And he felt it was the roughest sort of justice for all of his past misdemeanours, perfectly timed to ensure that his one chance of redemption – coming clean to Cressida and perhaps even making a future with her – could, obviously, never happen. Even now, even after his revelatory brush with truth, in all its brutality and beauty, Tom could not open the final door, the one closest to his heart, which might allow in a love which could sustain and support him through his most painful times. He could conceive of throwing himself upon Cressida's mercy to ask forgiveness and suggest a second chance, but the self he envisaged offering was a strong, successful man who had taken hard decisions and acted upon them. Not a needy, suffering, failed fool whose very efforts to right his life's wrongs were so ludicrously, tragically, mistimed. He would never know what Cressida might have said, how she might have welcomed him, how they might have lived and loved together. Nor would she. For all she knew, for all she would ever know, the stories about Tom and Nicola were true: distraught at the death of his one true love, Tom Webster changed beyond recognition, withdrew from social situations wherever possible, lost contact with his children, became fascinated with violent deaths and their aftermath, inhabited a lonely world occupied by thoughts of the slab and the scalpel, illuminated only by the stark white flash of the police photographer's camera.

Tom was acutely conscious that his mind had taken a sinister turn and played up to it, consciously at first and then instinctively. The walls of his flat were painted in matt colours several shades deeper than the fashionable burgundies, sages and midnight blues which were *de rigueur* in North London at the time: he chose oxblood red, the dark green of a surgeon's gown, the stormcloud grey of a sky in which the sun would never rise. He tracked down and hung on his walls seventeenth-century illustrations of surgical operations: trepannings and tracheotomies, in which the unanaesthetised patient, his skin folded back in flaps which opened like a curtain on the viscera within, grimaced in melodramatic agony. He became an expert on both the art and the science of surgery and could no longer view the pages of his antique medical textbooks without imagining the invisible expression on the face of each flayed victim. Eventually, even botanical line drawings seemed to hide some violent procedure visible only to him, and by the time he realised the extent of his psychosis, it was too late to change. It was all he deserved, he believed, and there were worse tortures.

Little by little, his dark moods became darker and it was a relief to both Cressida and Nita when he finally stopped visiting his children. His infrequent trips to Manchester were always chaperoned by Ravi, at Nita's insistence, which irritated him until he realised he wasn't the kind of man people would want to leave their children with and that Katie in particular was in constant distress during his visits. He only missed her once or twice a week, and then only for a second's pang. Sex with strangers – which even in his dog days had been rare – became an obsession and he was never again plagued by impotence, or by love. In this way Tom drew screens around himself and his fiction became the only message he was sending to the outside world. Anything to convince himself that the wind created by the wings of a butterfly at the other side of the globe would not blow over him. Would not blow him over.

Cressida felt heavy all the time. Her body, whose curves had previously given her pleasure and ease, seemed to have a weighty, wobbly life of its own and no amount of dieting could give her the slenderness she sought. Her attention returned to religion, or at least to churches, and family holidays became pilgrimages to the great cathedrals of European cities. They must be ever taller, grander, richer, more intricate, and yet Cressida was never even partially satisfied until, standing at the back of the Duomo in Milan, she looked up and along the avenue of arches from entrance to altar and swooned. Harry's arm reached her head before the floor did. But, while sacred architecture gave her the temporary relief of vanishing, it never gave her faith nor any kind of belief. Her search was transparent to Harry, who wished he could find the answers and present them to her in one of the gilt and crystal chalices she would gaze upon, dazzled, in cathedral crypts. He resolved, instead, always to be there to catch her the next time she fell. They both remained committed to their marriage and, after Sophie's death, to all four of their children, but Cressida missed even the occasional happiness of her life before Nicola's death. Their love was a sad, strong, low note underscoring their life together and Harry longed to offer his wife some of the comfort he had found in recent years.

Sophie died on the first day of spring, her fifteen-month-old son asleep on her breast and her hand gently loosening its hold on Vivienne's. Since her admission into the hospice just before Nicola's final New Year's Eve both her mother and Josh had been praying, independently, to take her place.

Now I've found her, pleaded Josh, now I've known my daughter and my new grandson, after all these years of not knowing, I want nothing more than to think of the years they have ahead of them. That they should have. That's all I want. Take an old happy man and leave this young woman to bring up her son. There's sense in it. Please. Please.

Vivienne was more demanding.

If you're there, if you want me to believe in you, you can't *possibly* let this happen. I'm an old woman and this would be the one useful thing I've done in my entire life. I'm not saying save her, I'm saying take me, give me a chance to do something for my daughter, whom I've neglected all her life. Let me do this one thing for her, damn you, or I'll not believe in anything again.

The thin March air was too cold for Sophie's lungs that morning; her painkillers were ineffective and she hadn't eaten for four days. She didn't want to die that day, wondered if she could hang on for another week, but the thought wearied her. When Vivienne and Josh came in with Marlon for their daily visit her heart ached with love for her baby and with despair that she was about to leave his life.

Unlike her parents, Sophie had never prayed. As her body began to let her down, she began an equally unfamiliar interior monologue – to herself. From the moment she understood the diagnosis she had taken up the challenge without a thought of where it came from, or a hope that she could ever send it back. Nor did she see the process as a fight or a game or a gamble, or any other metaphorical explanation of the neurological disease that had hit her. Once she began the decline, so much sooner than she thought she would, she spent her prone hours, of which there were hundreds, thousands even, going through the textbook of her life and marking it, making improvements, corrections, and bestowing praise where it was due. Then she thought her way through Marlon's life, wished herself forward with him to two, three, four, five years, and then throughout his school years, university, his experiences of love, sex, pain, happiness, failure and success and onwards, through work and travel and family life, towards contentment, optimism, calm. In Sophie's projection, Vivienne and Josh eventually left their grandson's life as they were bound to do but Harry and Cressida remained, being his parents, being with him as she would be with him if she could. Sophie wished all her hopes and dreams into Harry and Cressida, put all her trust in her baby's father and his wife, and when she dropped into the unconsciousness that would lead her to death the last picture in her head was of Marlon, held by Cressida, with Harry's arms around them both.

At that same moment, a weeping Vivienne gathered all she could of her dead daughter into her arms and wept yet more, not just for the fact of death itself but for the sudden jolt of realisation it brought her: this was the first time she had held this body with the sense of ownership and adoration which a mother feels for her baby, her beloved. Throughout Sophie's early years her mother had constantly turned her away, cut off the occasional feelings of tenderness she had for her tiny girl by thinking of her conception and cursing her existence. Sophie's forgiveness, which she had freely given, could barely atone for her mother's terrible guilt, crystallised and set for ever in this moment; that she had waited until her baby was grown-up and dead before holding her, *Pietà*-like, too late.

On the morning of Sophie's funeral, in response to Cressida's rant about the unfairness of it all, conducted over Marlon's unknowing head, Harry tried, through the dry coughs by which men try to hide tears, and then through freely-flowing weeping, to explain his views:

'Cress, the only meaning in it all that I can find is that everything which happens to us and which we do is always a combination of luck and judgement. A random combination but one which seems to have some element of balance. So Sophie made a "bad" judgement – stealing my sperm – but as luck would have it she gave birth to a baby who gave her the experience of love she had always longed for *and* brought her parents together and the truth into the open.'

'So what kind of a judgement does that make her death at thirty-four?'

'No, that wasn't judgement, that was bad luck. But she *had* judged Marlon's needs well and made arrangements to ensure his happiness – so it's not ideal, not without great sadness and sorrow but it's – liveable. Workable.'

'Oh,' said Cressida. 'I misunderstood.'

'What did you misunderstand?'

'I thought you meant luck – as in chance or whatever – and *judgement*. Not free will, not making your own judgements, but *being judged*.'

'But that takes any kind of human responsibility or power out of the equation. If you combine that kind of judgement – of the gods, I assume you mean – with luck, then you're being practically mediaeval!'

Cressida was impatient, 'You still don't understand. I don't mean the bloody gods judging you; I mean *other people*.'

'But that doesn't radically alter your life. The judgement of others isn't going to change the basic direction of your life!'

'Isn't it? Makes more sense to me than your Candidesque wallpapering over the cracks. Harry, the mothers of your two baby boys are dead. It's horrific. How can you try to – justify it? How can you find some pleasing theory to fit it?'

Cressida could no more take comfort in well-balanced secularity than she could hope that Tom's love for her still lived. Now that she no longer saw him she felt some small relief that this man for whom she had been prepared to give up so much and who repaid her by sanctifying, albeit unintentionally, the mother of her husband's misconceived son, was utterly unlike the man she loved so passionately. Occasionally a gruesome notion came to her: that the old Tom was trapped inside; she had the odd semi-eidetic flash of his beloved face, his eyes full of love for her, but they always disappeared to be replaced by the unfamiliar sight of his 'new' physiognomy which scowled out from his smartly designed book-jackets and was more handsome and chiselled than before, sporting a smart goatee on his previously clean-shaven chin, but also less expressive, more bland.

The continuing trickle of stories about women he'd kissed who were now telling sickened her. There were no surprises – Tom had given her every name years ago – but their becoming public knowledge was grotesque, and tainted her own attachment to him. She wondered how Tom felt about the list in the back of his biography now, and whether her erasure from his history, or worse, her name's demotion to the rank and file of his roll call of conquests, would matter to him.

She found it difficult to cope with Marlon, even harder to give him the love she knew she should. Occasionally she felt murderous towards him, and understood that he risked becoming the repository of her great, bottled mass of anger. So she left much of his care to Harry while she concentrated on Grace and her older children, and only trusted herself to spend longer spells of time with Sophie's child when he was more solid, verbal, almost able to take care of himself. She dreaded the day when Harry would try to talk her into giving a home to George as well, which she knew he wanted to do, and felt relief at each piece of news which suggested the boy was settling further and further into a new life away from them. Cressida managed not to hate herself for her lack of charity, so didn't hate the baby boys either. But she wished she could harness her maternal instincts more successfully and marvelled at Harry's expansive love for all of them.

Abena forgave herself the brief thrill she had experienced when news of Nicola's death broke. The private adoption of George was completed and when Christine picked up her nephew in her arms to say goodbye Abena was suddenly scared at the void which might appear in his life.

'You must keep in touch. Please,' she begged Christine.

'I don't think so. You need to make a fresh start. Especially if you're moving to Liverpool with the doctor.'

'But I want him to know his – family. I'm going to keep in touch with his father, but he needs a link to his mother's family too.'

'If Nicola had lived this would probably all be happening anyway. It's not your fault, or your responsibility.'

'That's not what I mean. I just want him to know everything from the beginning so that there are no nasty shocks when he's older.'

Christine thought for a while and said, 'Listen, tell him all about us and whenever – if ever – he wants to meet us we'll be waiting for him. OK? I can't think of a better way of doing it, and at least then he can make the choice. But I don't think we can be part of his life in the way you mean. Have some time with him and your family and see how it goes. How does that sound?'

Abena realised the wisdom of the suggestion and finally agreed.

'But I'll send you pictures and tell you news – is that OK?'

'Of course. I'd like that, thank you. When you want to though, all right? No pressure.'

'I understand. Thank you – thank you so much.'

Christine kissed George again and left before her tears began to fall.

Margaret's decision to move back to Liverpool to nurse her mother had been difficult for one reason alone: Steve. Once she recovered from the initial shock of meeting him on his wedding day, her fascination at discovering what kind of father her father had been in the years after he left her was the primary attraction in maintaining contact but she and her half-brother found themselves naturally at ease with each other, sharing the same dry humour and the same lack of confidence in what the world had to offer, a lack which the newfound, or newly renewed, loves in their lives were beginning to challenge. He admired his sister's noble profession and maternal resourcefulness; she was in awe of his creativity and kindness. Uncle Steve had become a regular visitor to the house in Kensal Rise; he and Mary were great friends and even Adam made the effort to accompany him from time to time, feigning indifference to the babies' beguiling charms but letting slip the odd smile in response to a four-toothed grin or bestowing a kiss on a plump cheek from time to time. Family life suited Margaret as never before. So the news of her mother's decline was doubly unwelcome; it made her anxious for her mother but it also threatened her happiness, or so she at first thought. But Mary's firm reminder of her daughterly responsibilities and Steve's instant understanding of what she had to do, plus his obvious regret that he had been denied the same duty of care for his own mother, reassured her that a couple of hundred miles could do no great harm, and that the move was, in any case, an acknowledgement of family life at its most basic. Her mother used to joke that Peggy would come back home once she had made her fortune – well, now she would return to her mother richer by the value of a lover, two children and a brother, not to mention Abena and her child, and that had to be worth something.

'We'll buy a huge house so that you can come and stay,' she told Steve the day before the move to a rented house near her mother's sheltered accommodation.

'I should think you could buy three streets in Liverpool.'

'It's not that grim up north, you know.'

'God, your vowels are flattening by the minute, you're turning into a scouser overnight.'

'I'll flatten you if you crack any more northern jokes. You will come, won't you?'

'Try stopping me. I mean it Peg. Just call, OK?'

'OK. And you'll tell me when the programme's on telly?'

'Of course, of course. The editing's nearly done so it's all going to schedule. To be honest, I'll be glad to see the back of it. It was always meant to be a kind of *in memoriam* for Mum but with all that business . . . with such a recent death looming over us – well, it was a hell of a start for the project. Even though the team hadn't begun working together it cast a shadow, you know?'

'Of course it did. It was terrible. But we're so glad that the adoption is all sorted out and that Abena and George will be with us. The kids would miss him so much and I don't know what we'd do without her.' The three toddlers were a happy unit; Kwame and George had been given the freedom to explore and discover their world while Ama was watched over by Margaret, Mary or Abena whose shared main concern was to ensure that she should never be treated as a burden. Consequently, the little boys developed their own sense of protection for their slower, less agile companion and their widening circle out into the world always kept Ama at its centre. They chatted to her constantly, occasionally lugged her around between them to show her their latest find in the garden, and showed no sign of resentment or irritation at her inability to keep up all the time. She, meanwhile, remained good-natured and in good health, and once Margaret had controlled her natural tendency to hothouse her daughter with flashcards and intensive physical training, to protect her from the wide world and its impatient cruelty, she began to develop gradually and with ease.

'What did Harry say?' asked Steve.

'Poor Harry. Not much. We'll keep in touch but there's not a lot he can do. Maybe when George is older – we'll tell him everything and just see what happens. What he wants to do. Meanwhile he and Cressida have got their hands full with their three and – Marlon.'

Brother and sister laughed uncontrollably as they hugged one another goodbye.

Kyria had another baby nine months after the wedding party. Years of infertility had rendered the practice of any birth control pointless and so she never even considered contraception after Patrick's arrival. When he was eleven months old and she was still breastfeeding him assiduously, she began to menstruate again; a month later she conceived a daughter. Lying next to Justin in the large bed in the comfortable South London hotel which Adam had booked for them that New Year's Eve, Kyria thought very little about the traumatic elements of the evening and a great deal about her artistic triumph; there was no mistaking the reaction of the crowd to the unveiling of her work, nor the heartfelt praise she received from the many guests who sought her out and took her card. Patrick lay asleep in a cot beside the bed and Justin had almost dropped off to sleep when he felt his wife's tongue, first on his lips and then moving slowly down his body. When she was sure she had his full attention, Kyria moved back up the bed and kissed his mouth while she lowered herself on to him, clutched the headboard and rode the bed repeatedly into the wall.

It's impossible to explain why Justin and Kyria's two babies were conceived at precisely the same hour as first Felicity's and then Harmony's. The first time it was a strange and sad coincidence, the second it verged on the bizarre, but it happened. Justin knew that if he and Kyria were childless, Harmony, whatever her decisions about the pregnancy, would live with them, but exchanging an uncomfortable life with her mother's new family (Ravi moved in shortly after the return from India) for an equally superfluous role in her father's was not an attractive option. Harmony missed Fliss and longed to be with her, but Fliss was eighteen and behaving accordingly; even after hearing about her sister's woes – especially after hearing about her sister's woes – she could not bring herself to give up her exciting London life to return to Manchester and babies and gloom. So Harmony, who was, in any case, sick of playing second fiddle, went her own sweet way, left Nita's house one afternoon and didn't come back. She would turn up, in two years' time, with her daughter whom she named Melody, but for now she was opting out, sorry for the anxiety she would cause her father and sad at the relief which her mother would, albeit for an instant, feel at the discovery of her empty room. She placated Justin with a reassuring postcard every fortnight – always with a different postmark – and punished her mother by sending nothing. It gave Nita only occasional moments of sadness; she was happy to be starting over with a new man and a new family – having failed yet again to find herself in India she had enjoyed the food immensely and was beginning to grow plump for the first time in her life, her physical state finally beginning to match her returning mental indolence.

Shortly after his youngest children's seventh birthdays, sitting at the desk near the window of his living room, Tom saw the reflection of a woman, wearing his dressing gown, his towel turban-style around her wet hair, approaching him. She set down a mug of coffee for him and looked with interest at the screen of his PC. 'I really admire your work, Tom. Especially the last novel, that was absolutely stunning. Tell me, where *do* you get your ideas from?' Tom turned to see her in the flesh and realised he didn't know her name. He was perturbed; he always knew their names. And last night had been remarkable; she had been extraordinarily supple and unfazed by even his most pressing demands.

'Thank you for the coffee,' he began, his eyes flicking away from her and becoming fixed to the opposite wall. 'But I'm afraid I'd like you to leave now. I have some ideas and I – need time with them.' He sensed the woman's instinctive flinch and imagined the mental grappling in which she had to engage in order to get her response out, which she managed to do with an understanding smile.

'Of course. No problem. I'll just get dressed and let myself out.'

'Thank you.'

'And I'll leave my number here, OK, so if you want to . . .' Tom interrupted her,

'No. Thank you. But no, I don't think so.' Again, she controlled her response of hurt or insult or outrage and simply nodded before leaving the room.

When he heard the front door shut quietly behind her, and watched her walk out of the gate without looking back, Tom sighed and sat back in his chair. He was thinking of his personal unholy trinity, which wouldn't release him from its grasp: his children. Cressida. Fate. And in particular why he was fated to dream forever of Cressida but be prevented from loving her, and to long for the touch of his children's skin but be denied contact with them. Since Nicola's death – or even before, just before he had made his useless avowal to change his life – everyone he cared about had been cast adrift in their own precarious rafts upon the sea which could only be Fate. Still cursing his bad fortune and ignoring the fame and wealth which Fate had also, apparently, bestowed on him, Tom turned back to his keyboard and began to write.

On his fortieth birthday, as the sandy shelf beneath his feet receded, Mark realised, to his shame, that he had forgotten how to swim.

'Shit.' said Tom aloud. 'I'm writing a fucking mid-life crisis novel. Just my luck.'

'It's like an enormous Venn diagram. Like I was going to say in that stupid speech, remember?' Harry tried another tack with Cressida, drawing as he spoke. 'All of us in our individual little circles and then the overlap with our partners and families and babies and then all of the ways in which *they* relate to us and to each other . . . there. Do you see?' Cressida peered at the mass of interrelated circles, each with an initial at its centre.

'Looks like *spawn*,' she muttered with disgust, 'or cells dividing.'

Harry looked excitedly at his artwork, 'You're right! It looks exactly like that! And of course, that's what it really is. I never realised before, those circles could easily represent our cellular physiognomy, and the interrelations do mirror the patterns of cell division. Frogspawn. How extraordinary.'

Cressida kissed the very slightly thinning crown of her husband's head. 'What a mess it all is. What a blobby scraggly mess.'

Harry looked up, concerned. 'Why do you need a pattern so much? A plan? Cress, I thought you were the great Unbeliever in Fate, the leading voice against determinism?'

'I am. I don't believe in Fate because it lets everyone off the hook. But the alternative is that it's all my fault, of course.'

'No middle way? No luck and judgement? No beasts and angels?'

'Doesn't make any difference. Still just us. Still my fault.'

'Oh, honey. Come here.'

'Remember your Seven Deadly Sins?' she asked, her head on his shoulder, 'Those Prime Motivators?'

She felt him shudder, 'Don't remind me. Oh Jesus, what was I going on about? I'm so glad I got that out of my system, it was unforgivable.'

'Maybe. I just think that it makes a bit more sense than being Pollyanna about everything.'

'Oh that's not fair! I'm not that relentlessly optimistic. Just a hell of a lot more than you are, which isn't saying much.' Cressida didn't answer; she was thinking about how her head used to feel on Tom's shoulder. 'We've been through some terrible times, my love, but we're coming out of the tunnel. Don't you think?'

'Maybe.'

'Of course we are. And we have our lovely children, don't we?'

'Yes,' said Cressida dully then, feeling guilty, 'yes, of course, and they are beautiful and the best thing . . .'

'Precisely.' Harry picked up his diagram and threw it in the bin. 'And let's not worry about this stuff so much, hey? What can we do about it anyway?'

'Nothing.'

'That's right. So let's do nothing. It will be – refreshing.' Harry put his arms around her. 'Cress, love, it's all going to be OK. Trust me.'

At that moment Cressida felt the most exquisite relief. She did trust him. She could always trust him. Not necessarily to do the best thing or the right thing or the thing she wanted, but always to tell her the truth. Tom's habitual lying, even the pettiest, most pointless fibs, had once amused her; her knowledge of it reduced its threat and made her feel relaxed and in control. But she had never been in control; for all she knew there could have been many more lies, a far more complex series of untruths in which she had lain tangled. Perhaps not infidelities, or at least not physical infidelities, but dozens of tiny decisions not to tell her the truth, for reasons ranging from fear at her reaction to a need to withhold knowledge and thus maintain some imaginary upper hand. Or for no reason at all.

A year into their affair, Cressida had sent Tom a parcel containing a silk shirt. It was a delicate *eau de nil*, a shade which went so perfectly with the green of his eyes that as soon as she saw the garment in a shop window she knew she had to buy it. They rarely bought each other gifts, were careful to give impersonal books or music if anything, but this was irresistible. Tom was reading at a festival that week so she sent the parcel, with a typed address label, care of the festival director who she knew would pass it on to him. Thoughtfully, she included no note so that if he opened it in front of anyone there would be no embarrassing fumblings. He didn't mention it that week but a fortnight later he was waiting for her at Euston station wearing the shirt. He still didn't thank her. At that point Cressida realised two things: firstly that he didn't know it was from her and secondly that he had no intention of telling her about his mystery gift. Then a third, more alarming fact occurred to her – that he still wore it, didn't put it in his wardrobe or throw it or give it away; he had deliberately chosen to wear the shirt, sent to him anonymously, while meeting his lover. She did countenance the possibility that this was Tom's way of finding out whether she had been the giver, that he expected her to berate him for his lack of manners and exclaim about how perfectly it complemented his eyes. But that wasn't fair, the onus to reveal all should still rest with him.

'Lovely shirt!' she said, wondering if he would now come clean.

'Nice, isn't it? Found it in a sale in Manchester and thought it was about time I owned a silk shirt. And this is my colour, you know,' he preened, with a camp flutter. 'Brings out my eyes.'

Cressida said nothing.

Thus his lie became her lie and lay between them, and nine years later Cressida saw how their life together would have been. Some moments of happiness, a great deal of laughter, maybe a continuation of the sexual fulfilment they had shared and possibly even fidelity, yes, that might all have worked out perfectly, but undercut, all the time, by untruth. By the undervaluing of truth. Tom was not a man in whom she could put any faith – even her own stumbling, peering version of faith. Whereas here was Harry, whom she liked to cuddle up to and who liked to lie on the rug with all his children in his arms, who spent his working days listening to people tell him about their terrible problems, their awful pains, but who found himself in each one of them and quietly gave them the means to find themselves in the world; Harry who was bright and funny and tender and who grappled constantly with his universe. Tom's passivity – a strange adjective for someone with such an active mind, but accurate nevertheless – was the mark of a man who had given up all hope of happiness or change, as a means of protection. Whether from disappointment or failure or the painful solitude of the surviving twin, no one could tell, but his reliance on Fate to come up with the eternally shoddy goods was anathema to her. Without some tiny spark of hope Cressida could not survive, and she was unable to strike the light for herself; needed to be cajoled or escorted or dragged into hopefulness. Tom couldn't, wouldn't ever do that for her. The knowledge was a cool hand on her hot brow. Her love for him was undiminished but would never make her burn again.

'What are you thinking about, Cress?' Harry asked, stroking her hair.

'What a good man you are.'

'Aw shucks.' The phrase, which Cressida bestowed upon him frequently, had come to mean only negatives for Harry, a synonym for dutiful or regular or predictable, and he was ever aware that it represented a comparison with one particular Bad Man whom, he knew, Cressida still loved. But now her tone was different, she sounded somehow less in need of convincing than usual. He clung to the hope of a sea change.

'My love.' Harry held his wife close and counted his blessings (one, two, three, four, perhaps even, one day, five) while Cressida, her face buried in his shirt, cried a little and counted on nothing more than her own ability to stop.

A NOTE ON THE AUTHOR

Clare Brown was born in Liverpool in 1966 and lived in Sheffield from the age of five. After studying English at Liverpool University she worked in theatre for seven years before becoming director of the Poetry Book Society. She now lives in Nottingham and this is her first novel.